RAINY NORTH WOODS

ST. MARTIN'S PRESS NEW YORK

RAINY NORTH WOODS

VINCE KOHLER

The quotation on page 66 from *Journey to the End of the Night* by Louis-Ferdinand Céline is from the translation by John H. P. Marks, published by New Directions Publishing Corp., New York, 1960.

Library of Congress Cataloging-in-Publication Data

Kohler, Vincent.
    Rainy north woods.
        p. cm.
    ISBN 0-312-03918-2
    I. Title.
PS3561.0358R35 1990   813'.54—dc20   89-24169

Book Design by Jaye Zimet.

10 9 8 7 6 5 4 3 2

For my parents
and in memory of
Morris and Marguerite Levy

"The natives of the rain are rainy men."
—Wallace Stevens,

The Comedian as the Letter C, IV, 1

"Everyone is more or less mad on one point."
—Rudyard Kipling,

Plain Tales from the Hills

ACKNOWLEDGMENTS

The following persons have my gratitude for their help in creating *Rainy North Woods*.

Mary Joan O'Connell, my wife, gave much encouragement and inspiration and skillfully edited the manuscript. Additional assistance came from Brian McCullough and Bridget Madill of Kanata, Ontario, Canada.

Jim Lane of Sacramento, California, offered much advice on plotting. Sharon Jarvis of New York, my agent, displayed great patience.

Robert Schumacher, director of the Oregon Intergovernmental Affairs Division, and Loletta Schmollinger of the Clackamas County Assessor's office advised me on Oregon property records and state land-use laws circa 1978. Marilyn Switzer, D.M.D., of McMinnville, Oregon, told me about Eldon's dentition.

Jerome P. Baron, publisher of the *World* in Coos Bay, Oregon; Douglas Lynch of The Design Source, Portland; and Paul Pintarich of the *Oregonian*, Portland, taught Eldon how to fish.

Special thanks are due Steve Perry of Beaverton, Oregon, who launched the spaceship, and Steven Hardesty of the U.S. Foreign Service, who strung up the elephant.

AUTHOR'S NOTE

Rainy North Woods is a work of fiction. There is no such place as Port Jerome, Oregon, and no Nekaemas County in that state. To the best of the author's knowledge, there never was an Oregon newspaper named the *South Coast Sun*.

The characters and events in this story are products of the imagination, as well. No resemblance to actual persons or events is intended or should be inferred. Any reference to actual persons, places, vessels, agencies, or creeds is fictitious.

RAINY NORTH WOODS

1 One moment Eldon Larkin was slurping chowder and daydreaming about meeting the newspaper's new female photographer, his elbow resting atop the dog-eared French paperback on the restaurant table beside his notebook and camera. The next moment he was lumbering through the rain toward his car, pulling his coat around his belly to shield his camera from the rain.

His world, Eldon realized later, turned over in the jangle of a telephone bell as the downpour drove across Port Jerome, Oregon. Rain drummed on the window of the café at the Nekaemas Bay boat basin where three-dimensional portraits of horses and cats, stamped from plastic, blighted the walls. The waitress clawed the telephone from its hook and bellowed Eldon's name. Fiske, his editor, was on the line: "Some kinda Chinaman's been stomped to death by an elephant at the circus—"

"I'm on my way," said Eldon, feeling adrenaline heat his face.

Elephant squashes Chinaman! It was the craziest thing since the belly dancer who could eat glass. The craziest thing since he had received the notice in the mail from Berkeley that his divorce was final, two years ago.

He wiped chowder from his walrus mustache, stuffed his things under his coat, and rushed across the gravel parking lot. The paint on his old wreck of a Citroën Deux Chevaux was faded to the color of weathered bone. Eldon threw the heavy paperback book—it was Louis-Ferdinand Céline's *Journey to the End of the Night* in French—into the humpbacked little car and climbed inside.

He glimpsed himself in the rearview mirror as he squeezed his girth behind the steering wheel. Tired blue eyes, sandy hair starting to recede, fair, fleshy cheeks framing an unkempt mustache and capped front teeth—"a face like a weary choirboy," as Bernice used to say. Eldon faced the dashboard. "Start, you bastard!" He pounded the car's gas pedal, twisted the key, and laughed in triumph as the ancient engine twitched to life.

The Citroën bounced past weather-beaten boats and shanties. Douglas fir and pine formed a gray scrim against the flat, white, rain-filled sky. He steered along the winding road into Port Jerome, wondering what the wire service would pay him for a photo. Eldon was a reporter, but on the small staff of the *South Coast Sun*, even reporters carried cameras. He could use the extra twenty-five bucks the wire service would pay. The Citroën gave a grinding clatter. Christ, don't blow now!

He reached the top of the hill. Below was the miserable heart of Port Jerome—a strip of hardware stores, service stations, and lumberjack bars skirting the steel-colored bay where mill stacks pushed into the sky. Weathered stucco cottages and peeling Victorian houses spread away from the bay, disappearing into hills where the mist hung in the trees.

The circus tent stood out like a dirty yellow stain against the gray country. Eldon headed for it. He fancied he could smell death.

The fire department was on the scene, red light blinking on the rescue truck in front of the big top. A crowd of barflies, obese salesclerks, pensioners, and other gawkers stood in the mud beneath a flapping banner that announced the Port Jerome Pioneer Days Festival. Eldon parked the car. He hadn't beaten the ambulance, but with any luck, the Chinaman was still stuck to the bottom of the elephant's foot.

Two sheriff's deputies guarded the tent's entrance. Eldon hustled to one side, dropped to his knees in the mud, and squirmed under the canvas.

Inside, he struggled to his feet, blinking in the gloom. He sneezed and brushed sawdust from his old coat and the threadbare knees of his gray corduroy pants. A group of firemen stood in the glare of an emergency lamp, their helmets casting mushroomlike shadows. On the far side of the tent, a woman with a riding crop was prodding a small elephant from the tent. Eldon glimpsed the woman's flashing red hair before the tent flap swung closed.

A fireman waved casually. "Hi, Eldon. Guess you won't be running a shot of *this*."

"I'll take one for history." Eldon swung up the camera and

sighted. The dead Oriental lay on his back. His chest looked like a collapsed piecrust. His arms and legs were flung wide in the sawdust. The cuffs of the man's jeans were full of sawdust and wood chips. Beside him lay a few shards of green glass, as if from a broken bottle.

Eldon felt a cool thrill as he checked the camera's light meter. He was about to press the shutter release when the view through the lens went black.

"No way."

Eldon looked up into a face, so close that for a moment he could not recognize it: Detective Art Nola of the Nekaemas County Sheriff's Department, lantern-jawed, long-nosed, with bushy russet hair going prematurely gray, like some aging fox. Nola's big hand covered the camera lens.

"You're not supposed to be in here, Eldon."

"It's my job," Eldon said. "Leggo my camera, Art."

"You're not going to take a picture of that. Not after the last time."

"Take it up with Fiske." Eldon tried to raise the camera, but Nola tightened his grip on the lens. Eldon tried to get around him; Nola swayed into his path. The detective had a somehow amiable expression on his face. They swayed silently, neither prepared to give ground and neither prepared to give the yank that might break the camera.

There was a blinding burst of light and an electronic whine. The two men jumped apart. Eldon blinked at floating blue spots as Nola turned, to be caught in the face by a second flash. The whining noise cut through the darkness as the strobe recharged. Eldon glimpsed a chubby female outline before it was erased in a third burst of light.

"Goddammit, how'd you get in here, young lady? Pardon my French," Nola said.

"The deputy at the door said to go right in. I'm Shelly Sherwood from the *Sun*."

"That's my new colleague," Eldon said. "I'm Eldon Larkin. Fire away, Shelly."

Stocky as a small bear, yet poised, the young woman carefully stepped around the ring of firemen. Eldon watched as she focused her camera and snapped another picture. She was no more than twenty-three, dressed in jeans and a bunchy maroon turtleneck sweater. Curly dark hair fell to her shoulders, framing a pleasant square face with steel-gray eyes, round and bright with excitement. Her buttocks were substantial, but that was not such a bad thing, Eldon thought.

He hadn't had a woman in months, not since the high school counselor had suddenly decided, in one of the twists of mood common around Port Jerome, to stop speaking to him. She had been only the fourth woman in five years, and sex was a subject that preyed on Eldon's mind in the rainy north woods. It was a nagging lack, like his lack of money. Actually, there was a solution—visit the bars. But seeking companionship there was too grisly to contemplate, impractical in the supreme sense, like mugging someone to get cash to repair his car. Going native was what Eldon feared most.

He wondered whether this Shelly Sherwood liked pornography. In Port Jerome, only skin magazines and lurid detective pulps were available. One made do.

Nola swung angrily toward the door of the tent. One of the guards called, "The sheriff said she was okay, Art."

"What about an I.D. on the victim?" Eldon asked.

"Get it when we file the report," Art said.

"Foul play?"

"No comment. Now git."

Eldon headed for the door of the tent as a fresh gust of rain rattled on the canvas. The crowd outside had dispersed in the downpour. A pair of stringy roustabouts in jeans and ragged T-shirts stood beneath the awning of a hot-dog cart. Eldon slogged over to them through the deepening mud and introduced himself. "He's stone-dead. It's really a mess in there."

One of the roustabouts had a star tattooed on his cheek. He said after a moment, "He got crushed while he was feedin' 'im. Horton was a mean bugger, I al'ays said. Now they'll hafta shoot that elephant."

"What was his name?"

"Horton."

"No, no—the victim."

The tattooed man shrugged.

The second roustabout had green teeth. "He was a Vietnamese. Only been with us a little while."

"Longer 'n that," the first man said.

"Naw, that was the other Vietnamese that joined up in Newport. Anyway, that other guy wasn't a Vietnamese at all, he was a Cambodian. He quit in Florence. This guy joined us here."

"They all look alike," the first man said slowly. "Looked the same way in Nam."

"But did you know his name?" Eldon asked.

"They all got the same names. Just like in Nam."

The man with green teeth said, "Nung, Nong, somethin' like that. Never did get it. His English wasn't any good. He lived up north of the bay. A lot of 'em live up around Muskrat. Lot of refugees."

The first man shrugged and began fishing in the cart for a hot dog. Thin steam came out of the spotted steel bin and swirled away in the rain. Eldon asked, "Can I get your names?"

"You don't need our names, mister."

"How about a hot dog? I didn't finish lunch."

"Hot dogs are a dollar."

"Thanks anyway." Eldon turned away, to see Shelly Sherwood emerge from the tent, beaming. She marched up to the hot-dog cart. "So you're Eldon Larkin. Mr. Fiske told me about you. I got a lot of great shots, Eldon. Hey, how about a hot dog, boys?"

The tattooed man fished out a hot dog with steel tongs and placed it expertly in a bun. "Compliments of the house, little lady."

"Let me take your picture, guys? It would be real cute, with the hot dogs." The roustabouts postured and beamed, striking suggestive poses with the wieners.

Shelly collected their names and ages and steered Eldon away.

"That one guy ought to get dentures," Eldon said.

"Nola says the victim was a sailor," Shelly said.

"He wouldn't tell me a thing."

"He really doesn't know anything yet. They're still fishing around for a wallet. A sailor working in a circus?"

"He must've meant he was a fisherman. Probably hard up for work. Times are bad around here, except for exporting wood chips."

"What's your problem with Nola? He seems okay."

Eldon sighed. "Oh, a while ago we ran one of my body shots of a real bad murder. Nola was in charge at the scene, and the victim's relatives gave him hell about letting me in. The sheriff didn't much care, but Art's sensitive."

"He has kindly eyes," Shelly said. "He even seems to like you."

"What Art likes is to mess with my head." Eldon smiled to mask his irritation. "I'm glad you got those pictures, anyway. I'll get the police report. Don't let 'em brush you off."

"Right. This might be big."

"Well, it's tomorrow's lead story. Weird, huh?"

"I mean, it could be *murder*."

Eldon suppressed a smirk. On Oregon's South Coast, murder was a straightforward thing—an act of rage or frustration or hatred, a solution to infidelity, a fight in a bar, a lumberjack snapping after a long winter of rain and no work. It had the clarity of news copy, and there was a Zen-like purity to it that Eldon found comforting.

"Suppose someone pushed him under that elephant?" Shelly asked.

Crazy idea—yet Eldon was impressed that she had thought of it. Murder by elephant had a sick attraction. *Good copy!* as Fiske always said, with that way he had of making the phrase unintentionally obscene. Eldon could not say whether it was the obscenity or the prospect of extra money from the wire service for a good murder story that excited him more. No, what excited him was Shelly.

"It would be a great story," he said. "And the sheriff would have this place completely cordoned off."

"I hadn't thought of that."

"No matter. It just wouldn't be the innocent norm of South Coast assassinations. Crimes of passion are the big thing here, and nothing ever changes."

"It's crazy, I suppose."

"Well, I'll check on it. You always check. But it's not likely."

"There still might be a good story in this," Shelly said. "A foreign sailor dying in a strange land and all."

"I was thinking that, too," Eldon said, annoyed that Shelly was thinking faster than he.

"What do they do with the wood chips?" Shelly asked.

Eldon smiled again. "The Japanese press 'em into little

wooden ice cream spoons and sell 'em back to us. There's a tall tale that there was a Sasquatch buried in one of the chip piles on the wharf."

Shelly returned a look that was half fascination and half contempt. It was the look of a churchgoer who had wandered into a fun house on the way to divine services and was beginning to enjoy herself immensely.

"I'd better get to the office and develop this film," Shelly said.

"Yes, I'll see you there."

Shelly hurried over to a big beige van with California plates, got in, and drove off.

Fortunately, the Citroën's engine was still warm and started promptly, but the grinding noise persisted. He wondered what it would cost to get it fixed. Citroën parts cost an incredible amount and had to be specially ordered. He could no more afford to repair the car than he could finance the Third Crusade. He knew he should sell it, but it was a relic of his life in Berkeley and he did not want to part with it. Gripping the wheel, Eldon backed out of the circus lot and rolled down Main Street toward the offices of the *South Coast Sun*.

The low orange and white newspaper plant jarred with the weather-beaten gray of the buildings around it. The plant had been built by the out-of-state corporation that had acquired the newspaper in 1970 and now guided it with an indifferent, absentee hand. The paper's name, however, was the work of a madman—the late Lyman Dunthorpe, manic-depressive visionary publisher until his death in 1968—who, one day, his imagination on the upswing and fueled to orbital velocity by alcohol, had changed the paper's name from the *Times-Chronicle*, which was redundant, to the *Sun*, which on Oregon's rainswept South Coast was ridiculous. Old-timers told of Dunthorpe's boozy vision of a chain of four daily newspapers, one in Buffalo, one in Brussels, one in Bombay, and the flagship in Port Jerome, all named the *Sun*.

Renaming the Port Jerome newspaper was the only part of the vision that became reality; there had not been booze or madness enough to realize the rest. Eldon knew he would have liked Brussels—he spoke good French—and whenever he reflected on

Dunthorpe's vision, he felt as if he were an attendant at a tomb erected in the aftermath of some bizarre spiritual defeat.

How long had he been here? It was September 1978. Five years. He had to stop to count. During these rainy fall days, it was difficult to keep going. He felt as if he were turning into concrete.

Eldon pulled into the newspaper's parking lot. Someone had parked in his reserved parking space—a rusty pickup in even worse shape than his Citroën. It was full of refuse decorously protected from the rain by dirty canvas. Eldon, outraged, parked to block the pickup's exit and trudged into the office by the side door, through the vestibule separating the news and advertising offices from the pressroom. The rich, acrid smell of printer's ink assailed his nostrils, mingling with the damp odor of rain-soaked coats.

In the office, up at the front counter, one of the ad salesmen was talking with a seedy, whiskered old man clad in grimy ill-fitting jeans and a tattered flannel plaid shirt. In any civilized community, he would have been thrown out as a wino, but here he was a customer. The discussion was animated, but Eldon could not make it out as he crossed the rough orange industrial carpet toward the huddle of cluttered desks that was the news department.

Eldon looked in vain for his colleagues—gawky young Frank Juliano from L.A., who worked the county courthouse beat; Marsha Cox, who wrote somnolently about school boards, planning commissions, and other rule-barnacled bureaucracies; Ambrose McFee, the amiable, trollish sports editor. . . . But here was Editor James O. "Jimbo" Fiske, hair slicked back and bright clip-on tie too wide, foul old pipe clenched between his stained, gold-backed teeth below a pencil-thin mustache, humming tunelessly and shuffling long, curling rolls of Teletype paper across his desk as the wire service printer buzzed nearby.

"What'd ya get me, Eldon? A dead Chinaman, huh?"

"A dead Vietnamese. Elephant stomped him flat, all right."

"*Good* copy." Fiske rolled the phrase across his tongue like a delectable morsel. "The new girl came in with the pix. She's in the darkroom now. Moves quick."

Eldon opened his mouth to speak but not quickly enough. Fiske took his pipe from his mouth and cupped its worn bowl lovingly in the palm of one hand. "Reminds me of the time I covered the last scalping in Oregon . . . Klamath Falls, 1954. This carpet salesman went into an Indian bar one cold winter night and like a damn fool started messin' around with the squaws . . ."

From the darkroom Shelly cried, "Do I see a body? *Do I see a body?*" The sliding door flew open and she burst out, rolls of negatives streaming from her upraised fists.

Fiske snatched the negatives. "Bloodthirsty little gal, ain't she?" He pressed a viewing lens to his eye and squinted toward the ceiling lights, running the black strips across the lens, frame by frame, and then tossing them at Eldon. "Print number three, print number nine, print number eleven on the second roll. This is pretty good stuff, Shelly."

Eldon clipped the edges of the designated negatives with a hole punch. Shelly grabbed the strips and dived back into the darkroom.

"What's the victim's name?" Fiske demanded of Eldon. "How'd it happen?"

"I . . . don't really have that yet."

"Well, get it and let's get outta here. Wet-nosed girl is way ahead of you. As long as we don't have an airplane crash, page one for tomorrow is dead."

Jimbo stuck the pipe back in his mouth and hummed for a moment as he reached for page dummy sheets on which to diagram the front-page layout. "Anyway, this damn fool in Kay-Falls was messin' around with this squaw and some of the braves didn't like that. Big, mean devils, see . . ."

There was a bang at the front counter. Eldon looked up to see the ad seller jump a foot as the old man slammed his palm down on the countertop. "I won't pay it! It's not . . . *constitutional!*" the old man screamed, staring out the big glass front doors. "You can't keep me here like a prisoner!"

"Nobody's keeping you here," the ad man said. "You owe fifteen dollars for the ad."

The old man drummed the counter with knobby fists. "Don't you lie to me! Look out there! Some federal agent's *blocked in my car!*"

"Did you do that again, Eldon?" Fiske said. "I asked you not to do that. Anyway, these Injuns were pretty sly. They kept buy-

ing that salesman drinks till he was pie-eyed drunk. It was a
mighty cold night . . ."

Eldon's attention focused on the screaming old man. He went
forward. "I'll move my car, old-timer. You're in my parking
space."

The old man clamped his toothless mouth shut and breathed
rhythmically through his nose, complexion gradually purpling as
his eyes, dingy malevolent marbles, swiveled to fix on Eldon. His
stubbled cheeks puffed like balloons, his breathing forcing the
dirty seams of his face smooth, as if a mangy boiler were about to
burst.

I've seen better damn circus acts, Eldon thought, and
hunched his shoulders and glared. The old man drew up his
skinny body. His arms stuck straight down at his sides and his
fists trembled. For a moment, there was only the sound of the
buzzing wire service machine and the old man's rhythmic snorts.
Then he released his breath with a teakettle wheeze that Eldon
realized was laughter.

"Had ya going there, boy, I surely did. Ya got spunk, though.
I like spunk. Now move yer car, sonny." The old man headed for
the door.

"I'm thirty-three years old," Eldon said, following him out
into the slackening rain. "What about your bill?"

"Not constitutional, I told ya. That debt's in paper, funny
money. Might as well use it for asswipe for all it's worth. Money
won't matter soon, anyway, and neither will asswipe. The Star
Days'll soon be on us."

"I see." Eldon slid behind the wheel of his car and attacked
the ignition and the pedals. There was a brutal sawing racket
beneath the hood. "Start, you bastard!" Eldon tried again. Nothing.

The old man hooted and wheezed. "Pitiful damn Frog-made
machine! But American know-how is in decline, too . . . it just
goes to show. Henry Ford was a communist. I was in Seattle for
the General Strike in '19, don't ya know. Later, there was that
bastard Roosevelt . . ." He sprang into the rear of his truck and
rooted under the tattered canvas, to emerge with pliers and a
hammer. "Bet I can fix 'er."

"Let's just roll it out of the way," Eldon said hastily. As he
climbed from the Citroën, he caught a glimpse of the truck's

cargo: tangled rusty wire, battered red Prince Albert tobacco cans, and yards of old tinfoil, crumpled and balled and wadded. The old man flipped the canvas back into place and glared.

Together, they rolled the Citroën out into the parking lot. The old man leaped spryly into his truck and backed out with a faint screech of tires. He leaned out the pickup's window. "You're a reporter, eh? Might have a story for ya sometime. Biggest one of your career."

"Yeah? Can you belly dance and eat glass . . . at the same time?"

The old man snorted and drove away.

The rain stopped. Clouds rushed through the sky on a rising breeze. Eldon trudged back into the office, thinking he might have to walk home that night.

The ad salesman had slipped away. Jimbo, using his eye-piece, was examining big, damp, black and white prints of the dead Vietnamese. Shelly fidgeted nearby.

". . . and after all this, they took him four or five miles out of town and dumped him in the snow and scalped him," Fiske said. "We found him the next day in a snowdrift, and by God, that hair was *lifted*. That's a great dot pattern, Shelly."

Eldon went up to the desk. The photos were good—crisp. "That old guy's crazier than a bedbug."

Shelly gave a huge grin. "Here's his ad." She handed Eldon a tear sheet of the previous day's classified ad page:

STAR DAYS BRING CHARIOTS OF FIRE
When Elisha saw the Chariots of Fire, and even the pilots thereof, he was ridiculed. Now we see chariots with horsepower unknown on this earth. The Star Days are upon us.

"He'll never pay us," Eldon said.

"Let the ad department worry about that," Fiske said. "What about this dead Vietcong?"

"Maybe he was pushed," Shelly said. "Maybe he had enemies."

"Haw, that's good! That would be as good as the Injuns!"

"Well, I'll call the cop-shop and find out about it," Eldon said.

Eldon telephoned the sheriff's department. A dispatcher read off a news release that said that the man, age thirty-four, had been killed while feeding the elephant. "The victim's identity is being withheld until next of kin are notified."

"Where did he live?"

"Up in Muskrat," the dispatcher said.

"Any indication of foul play?"

"The case remains under investigation."

Eldon told Fiske. The editor frowned. "Oh, just write a cutline for Shelly's body shot. A good accident photo with a meaty caption is lots better than a story that says nothin'. Do a follow-up story tomorrow, when you can get details. That way, we can milk it for a second day." He hummed and toyed with a blank page dummy.

Eldon watched Fiske, feeling thwarted. He had been gearing up to write, but for now the story seemed mostly a mirage. "My car's shot," he said. "Can somebody give me a ride home?"

"I will, Eldon," Shelly said. Eldon felt a stab of pleasure. He rushed to the old Royal 440 typewriter on his desk, knocked out the cutline, and handed it to Fiske.

"Behave now, kids," Jimbo said absently, peering at the photographs. "Nice job, Shelly. You'll do real well here." He hummed.

Eldon and Shelly went outside, where Eldon introduced her to the Citroën. "Poor old car," Shelly said, giving it a pat. "How will you get here in the morning?"

"Someone can pick me up. Sometimes it starts up if you leave it alone overnight." Eldon glowered at the Citroën and sank into gloom, an emotion so familiar that he could not say whether it had fallen upon him here or whether he had brought it with him from Berkeley long ago.

"I'll pick you up tomorrow," Shelly said.

"Thanks," Eldon said, brightening. The afternoon's excitement had fired him with horny enthusiasm. He essayed a grand thought: A few newspaper war stories and some sage analysis of the elephant incident might turn the trick for a seduction.

Eldon pulled open the van's passenger door, climbed inside, and gaped in astonishment. Jesus, he thought, it's like finding Scheherazade's boudoir inside a delivery truck. The van was lined throughout with voluptuous red velvet padding trimmed in soft gray. It even covered the dashboard and transmission hump. The twin seats were like red thrones. In the rear was a shelf bed made up with red satin sheets and piled with pillows. On either wall were paintings on black velvet of muscle men. The gearshift was topped with an ivory phallus.

"How do you like it?" Shelly asked.

"A bit . . . overwhelming," Eldon said—urbanely, he hoped.

"I bought it for a song from this gay guy who had to pay off some gambling debts real quick. It was really hot the day I looked at it, so I climbed inside and turned on the air conditioner. The more the air conditioner ran, the more I got to thinking how the shell was keeping the heat out, and the more I realized that this gay guy's tastes were a lot like mine . . . I mean, it's got a real up-to-the-hilt philosophy about it, you know?"

Eldon's throat went dry. The van started smoothly. As they rolled down Main Street, he thought, It's a goddamn Ship of Love, like the L.A. pachucos drive. And I'm sitting in it in Port Jerome, Oregon. Wouldn't these crackers just shit if they knew?

They turned south onto Bayside Drive on the way to his rented hilltop cottage in Regret, across Wapello Slough.

"I guess I let my imagination run away with me back there," Shelly said.

"How? Oh . . . the squashing," Eldon said, pulling his mind from his fantasies. "Rule Number One: Conspiracy theories are a function of having nothing better to do with your mind."

"Well, at least I made a good impression on Mr. Fiske."

"He answers to Jimbo," Eldon said as the rain began again. "His major mania is Bigfoot; don't get him started. And he hums that same tune all the time."

Fresh rain hit in sheets, spattering, then pouring, and finally gushing over the windshield, beating on the van as if it were a drum, splashing and forming new rivers in the streets and lakes in the yards.

"Those little kids are playing hopscotch in the rain," Shelly said with mild shock. "Does it always rain like this?"

"They play in the rain or they don't play. Less than forty-five inches of rain a year here is considered a drought. Sixty-five inches is better." Eldon relaxed. He liked to think of the rain as a heavy blanket on his chest, pressing him back into warm security until finally there would be only Eldon and the rain and his bed.

Mountains of cut logs marked the city's south end, stacked at the now-demolished Wapello Head Mill as if to make gateways into some cold tropical temple. Islands of logs roped together into angular clusters floated in the slough near the mill site, bumping against the pilings that supported Buster's, a ramshackle restaurant–bar wedged onto a scrap of pier—Eldon's favorite place for greasy bacon and eggs. It was a short stroll from the circus site. The van rolled across the bridge as they drove into Regret, named for a nineteenth-century French trapper.

A pitted road stretched north along the slough, where a view of the ruined mill was broken only by a stucco municipal utility shed and a weathered gas station at the foot of the great hill atop which Eldon lived. The ill-kept buildings seemed to crouch like sullen watchdogs in the rain.

Along the slope above were ranks of bungalows and a trailer park crowded with rusting mobile homes. "Turn here and go up the hill," Eldon said. "You'd better get a running start. This hill rises eight hundred feet in half a mile. It's bad when it's icy. Then you have to use the gravel road down the other side."

"Sounds like a nuisance."

"The only real nuisance here is the damn wind. And the people. And the isolation."

"I wondered about that," Shelly said as she swung the van around the corner and downshifted. "It took two and a half hours to get out here from the Interstate. What's there to do?"

"Admire the scenery. Or go to the bars and fight. Or perhaps you fancy lumberjacks."

A half-distasteful smile crossed Shelly's face. "Sometimes I get in a rough-and-tumble mood."

Eldon's nostrils quivered. "The main thing is the isolation."

Engine roaring, they reached the hilltop, a flat, grassy plateau with fir trees and a muddy gravel road. To the road's windward side were the Regret municipal tennis courts, flooded, tattered nets sagging in the rain. Nearby stood a stalklike scaffold holding weather instruments and a laser reflector, erected by a dredging company using lasers to guide its dredges in the choppy bay far below. To the road's leeward side, sheltered in a slight depression, was a green stucco cottage. A rural mailbox stood before it.

"My citadel," Eldon said. "Come in for coffee."

They parked and ran through the rain to the tiny porch. "We're out of the wind," Shelly said in surprise.

"It's so well placed that I can stand out here and not get a drop of rain on me." Eldon drew out his keys. "There's quite a view." He pointed north, across the sodden lawn. Birches framed a view of the bay. The mill stacks were not visible from this angle; there was only the wide gray plate of water and the forested shore beyond.

"Beautiful," said Shelly. "The end of the world."

"Just about." Eldon snapped on the light as they went inside and paused to allow Shelly to take in the neat front room. It was lined with books on brick and board shelves. Mounted photos of car accidents and timber festival queens hung on the pale green walls. A black Franklin stove, flanked by worn armchairs, stood by the entrance to the kitchen. Eldon's fly-tying table, covered with lures, hooks, and thread, was close by. The effect was rustic and artful. Eldon was thankful that he'd tidied the place this morning and put away the porno magazines before leaving for work.

"Very nice," Shelly said. "Your photographs?"

"For the past five years I've been to just about every murder and every fatal accident in Nekaemas County. Be good to have some assistance, now that you're around. Especially with the festival starting."

Shelly studied the pictures while Eldon built a fire and made coffee on the electric range in the kitchen. She behaved as if she were in an art museum, considering each picture with care, asking about the lenses he had used and the circumstances under which he had taken each shot, before issuing a compliment. Her seriousness surprised Eldon after her eagerness in the circus tent and the photo lab and the lurid promise of the van.

How should he time his move? Even at age thirty-three, it was a classic question, so he put on classical music, an album of Bach lute suites that he considered lucky. If memory served, he had played it the night he had first seduced his ex-wife, Bernice, years before in Berkeley. He had also served ice cream and cognac.

"Your pictures today were pretty good," Eldon said from the kitchen as he pulled a tub of French vanilla from the freezer.

"Thanks. I had to do well on my first day. That situation was so weird, I still have trouble believing it was just an accident."

"I can tell this is your first newspaper job. The trick is learning not to make more of something than it is."

"Actually, I had some summer internships here and there."

"So why'd you come up here?"

A pause. "It's where the job was. I was working as a flack in Sacramento and I had to get out of that."

"Sacramento? I'm from Berkeley."

"So Jimbo said. Why'd you come up here?"

"It's where the job was." Eldon brought in the coffee. "And it was a long way from where I was at the time."

Shelly gazed uneasily at a photo of a log-truck accident. "I was doing PR for a company that made stereo equipment and it was a real zoo environment. It was the toy business, really, but some people think stereos are a religion. I had to get out. The *Sun* advertised for a photog. Fiske said to send up my resumé and some samples of my work. When I flew up for the interview, he acted as if I already had the job."

"You were the only decent applicant. One guy was one-eyed and another one had just gotten out of jail. Your predecessor had a breakdown from too much weed and booze and ran off to Idaho to pick mushrooms. He couldn't hack the climate. You're an improvement . . . in more ways than one."

He returned to the kitchen and got the green bottle of cognac down from the shelf. He carefully laced two healthy servings of ice cream with cognac and returned to the front room, setting one of the dishes on the arm of Shelly's chair. "That's Courvoisier V.S.O.P."

Shelly only stared at the ice cream.

"I try to enjoy the good things," Eldon said, "because there's nothing to do here but work. You'll work night and day until you drop and then get up in the morning and throw water in your face and go out and do it again. You'll talk to anybody, photograph anything. Do or die." He paused. "What's the matter?"

"I don't think I want any ice cream, thank you. Not after today."

"Oh . . . sorry! I didn't think corpses bothered you. Today was the name of the game around here."

"It was awful. I can't believe how excited I was. I can't believe that I walked out of that tent and . . . asked for a hot dog."

"Are you going to be all right?"

"I . . . think so. Yeah."

"This is just a delayed reaction. You need a neck rub."

"Uh, I'd better go. Sorry."

"Not at all. Get some air. Thanks for the ride home."

"I'm okay. I'll come up and get you tomorrow." Car keys in hand, Shelly hurried out into the rain.

Being noble will pay off in the long run, Eldon told himself, watching her from the doorway as the fire crackled and the lute played. Then he thought bitterly, It's going to be business as usual. He tossed off a goodbye wave.

2 "You're writing fast this morning," Fiske said.

Eldon handed over his copy. "The elephant victim is Nguyen Xuan. His death is termed a 'bizarre accident.'"

"How'd it happen?"

"He was feeding the elephant and it grabbed him with its trunk and threw him down and stepped on him. I guess he pissed it off."

"It's what *I'd* do if I got pissed off," Fiske said. "Eyewitnesses?"

"No."

"Groovy quotes? No doubt your copy really sings, but there's got to be more to it than just this."

"He was a fisherman or something. I'd like to—"

"Where'd he live?"

"Muskrat. It's in the story."

"Good. Run up there and talk with the family, with his neighbors. The boat person's tragic end. Stomped to death by an elephant is pretty bizarre."

"I thought I should do a follow-up, yeah."

"Get a picture of him from his friends or something, from before he was stomped. Take Shelly along to shoot some pix. It was her idea, anyway." Fiske read the copy and hummed.

Eldon waved to Frank Juliano and Marsha Cox at their desks. Frank pushed his horn-rimmed glasses up his long square nose in a typically awkward gesture of greeting. His clothes hung on his gawky frame, giving him a scarecrow air that belied his abilities. Marsha looked primly at Eldon and sniffed. She always wore somber formal clothing, like an undertaker's assistant. Eldon went out into the parking lot past his inert Citroën. Shelly was revving her van in the bright morning.

Eldon flicked his tongue across his front teeth—a quick, halfconscious gesture behind closed lips. He did it when he wanted to think or when some great possibility portended.

Shelly had been ruddy-cheeked and smiling when she had picked him up for work, radiating cheer bright as the morning sun, betraying not a trace of nausea over yesterday's events. Eldon was still irritated by his failure to bed her the night before. Riding again in the Ship of Love only compounded his depression. Today, there was no rain to give emotional succor.

Eldon assumed that Shelly had sold Jimbo on the follow-up story while he, Eldon, had made the morning check of the incident log at the sheriff's office, collecting the identity of the dead Vietnamese. That was irritating, too. And what was wrong with his car? Would it ever start again, or would it simply rust in the parking lot? He climbed into the van's plush right-hand seat and muttered, "Drive north."

They sped along the western rim of the bay, past the abandoned dairy and the padlocked shipyard. A rust-streaked Asian freighter was moored at the dock behind three big golden mounds of wood chips.

"The chip piles," Eldon said. "Small ones, these days. There used to be a regular mountain range when all the mills were operating; this place was as big a chip port as Coos Bay. Ships like that one come from Asia to pick up the wood chips every few weeks."

They wound through the north end of town, with its nearly vacant shopping center, and across the high bridge spanning the broad entrance to Nekaemas Bay. The sunlight was brilliant as it scattered over the water, and Eldon found himself relaxing, breathing in the clean air. He gazed out to the Pacific's shining horizon, reveling in the feeling of vertigo that the vision always gave him. He enjoyed living on the edge of the continent. Berkeley had been no less precipitously sited, but he had never had this feeling there.

"Across the bridge starts the Dunes National Recreation Area," Eldon said. "Muskrat is nearby . . . a whole little wind-swept colony along the seashore and across the highway. Full of artists and lumberjacks and oddballs."

At the bridge's north end loomed the first of a long range of high pale sand dunes rising behind the trees. Eldon directed Shelly up a narrow side road dusted with blown white sand, hemmed with firs and beach plants.

"When I was a little girl," Shelly said, gazing down the vanishing track and shifting the van into a lower gear, "I had a fantasy that I would like to disappear. Drop out of sight altogether."

"Port Jerome is the right place for it," Eldon said. "How'd you get that idea?"

"I had a great-uncle who disappeared without a trace years ago. He was in silent films. Ever heard of Ogden O. Sherwood?"

Eldon snapped his fingers. "Sure. He played the murdering deaf-mute in *Secret Passages*. He disappeared in 1932 to protest the election of Franklin D. Roosevelt."

"You're a cinema buff!"

"One of the side effects of living in Berkeley. Not all of them were good."

"He was having trouble adapting to sound," Shelly said. "So he just vanished. When Mother told me the story, I was tremendously impressed."

"It would've been easier to do then . . . less paperwork," Eldon said. "Nowadays, there's always a paper trail. You pull one thread and if it's the right one, it all falls into place."

"Can you show me how to track down my great-uncle?" Shelly asked with determination.

"Seriously? The trail's pretty cold after nearly fifty years. How old was he when he vanished?"

"Forty, maybe. I don't know. I'm sure he's been dead for decades. It just would be . . . interesting to know. . . . Ah, maybe this guy knows something."

In the dusty road ahead, a huge man with a curly rust-colored beard confronted a snapping cur. The dog snarled and rushed in. The man jabbed the dog with a fishing rod sunk in one immense fist. The man's torso, encased in overalls and a filthy T-shirt, was running to fat but remained thick with power. His eyes peeped out like some immense squirrel's from beneath the visor of an old baseball cap.

Shelly halted the van. The big man glanced up at the sound and the dog sprang. The big man twirled the fishing rod like a quarterstaff and rapped the animal's skull with the pole's heavy butt. The dog scuttled off yelping, tail between its legs.

"It might not be my fishin' hole anymore, but it's still my road," the big man declared. "Sorry if I've delayed you folks, but there are times when you gotta play the human."

Eldon said, "Some people sure keep mean dogs."

"Oh, they can keep mean dogs or not, as they please," the big man said. "I just gotta have respect. Ladder of nature, y'know. Where'd the natural order be if dogs lorded it?"

"In the doghouse," Shelly said.

"That's good!" the big man said. "I don't believe that dog will be a problem much longer, what with Vietnamese around and them havin' no love for its master."

"Vietnamese are what brings us up here," Eldon said.

"Oh, they live up the way, mostly," the big man said, slightly surprised. "Sometimes they work on old Pugh's tower. Gosh, that's a nice van ya got there." He added jokingly, "Ya don't wanna sell it?"

"Then I'd have to walk," Shelly said.

"You can ride with me anytime, gorgeous." The big man considered the vehicle's lines. "I might hafta reinforce the suspension so's it'd hold me up."

"Where do you fish?" Eldon asked.

"Why, all around here. You a fisherman?"

"Freshwater fly, mostly. Any good spots around here?"

The big man's expression darkened. "There *was* a good spot on the Patterson place . . . but no more. Old man Patterson's sold out. He charged two dollars a head to let ya fish there. I didn't really mind that; it kept the riffraff out. He'd give ya a break when he knew the mill was down and there wasn't any work, too. But the new owner keeps the gate locked and runs people off with this dog. Ran a tenant off, too. One of the Vietnamese."

"Sounds no friendlier than his mutt," Eldon said.

"Probably from California." The big man glanced at the van's license plate. "No offense."

"I'm Eldon Larkin. We ought to talk about fishing sometime."

"Huey Bellows. I'm always around. Say, you write for the newspaper, don'cha?"

"Right."

"Well, pleased t'meetcha! A lot of people say the *Sun* is a piece of shit, but they're wrong. It's just long enough to read on the johnny when I have my sit-down—no more, no less. Keep up the good work. Up here to do a story?"

"Did you happen to know a Vietnamese named Nguyen Xuan?"

Bellows's eyes flickered. "As a matter of fact, he was the tenant that the new guy threw off the Patterson ranch. He worked for Pugh awhile."

"Where's Pugh's place?"

"Just follow the road," Bellows said. "You can't miss Pugh's tower. No way."

They drove on. The road grew rutted as it wound through the forest. They passed a metal gate secured by a new chain and padlock, bright and heavy against the gate's rust. There was a NO TRESPASSING—NO FISHING—NO HUNTING sign on the gate. As they slowed for a look, the cur vanquished by Huey Bellows rushed out snarling. Shelly scowled and steered straight ahead, forcing the dog to dodge.

Eldon studied her as the road narrowed and ferns brushed the van's sides. His stomach knotted slightly: Shelly's determined expression reminded him of Bernice. In Berkeley, she had woven intricate macrame mats, had created sculptures by welding iron rods into mazes, and had passionately collected butterflies. When she spiked butterflies or wielded her acetylene torch, Bernice had gotten the same expression as Shelly's, her eyes bright and hard behind round spectacles. Eldon one day had found that he was a butterfly.

"A penny for your thoughts," Shelly said self-consciously.

"Uh, I was thinking of my ex there for a minute. She went to Australia."

"So that's what brought you to Port Jerome."

"Here I am, anyhow."

"And here we are, from the looks of it." Shelly pointed ahead to where the flat top of what looked like a cinder-block blockhouse peeped through the trees. A scrawny figure moved about the roof.

"When that guy said *tower*, I thought he meant a radio tower or something like that," Eldon said.

"It's three stories high if it's an inch," Shelly said.

An Oriental man slogged around a bend in the road, a long black PVC conduit balanced on his left shoulder. The man went up a rutted driveway that led uphill into the trees in the direction of the blockhouse. Shelly steered after him and slowly passed the workman.

"Looks Vietnamese to me," Eldon said. "We'll talk with him."

Shelly drove to the top of the hill, slowing as the van bottomed out for a moment. The drive dropped down into a glade cradling a ramshackle house. The house was filthy and peeling, crudely patched and oddly jointed, a Frankenstein's monster of a dwelling. Between two high Victorian gables rose a shabby geodesic dome, a patchwork of stiffened canvas panels. The house was surrounded by junk sheltered beneath rude lean-tos. A familiar-looking junker pickup was parked nearby.

Behind the house, at the far end of a ditch presumably meant for the PVC pipe, was the blockhouse. Shelly steered around the debris and parked the van beside the ditch.

"I know that pickup," Eldon said. "It belongs to the old coot who raised the ruckus at the newspaper yesterday."

"This house would be a story of its own," Shelly said.

A rasping voice floated down from the tower as they climbed from the van. "Who the hell's there, hah? CIA spies?"

"It's him, all right," Shelly said.

"Eldon Larkin of the *South Coast Sun*," Eldon called, amused.

"Not spies?" The old man peered down at them. The blockhouse easily matched the height of the gables on the house. Nimbly, the old codger swung over the roof's edge and scrambled down a ladder fixed to the wall. "Yer blockin' the landin' zone, and they could come anytime. . . . Haw, it's you, after all; come for the biggest story of yer life, hah?"

"Actually, we came to talk to your workman," Eldon said.

"Ya gotta name?"

"Eldon Larkin, I said. You got one?"

"Pugh. Lessee yer press card."

Eldon produced it. "Pugh what?"

"Pugh's name enough. I think I remember ya from yesterday, but faces can be changed." Pugh squinted at them as the workman walked past with the pipe.

The Vietnamese was a thin-faced man with a sparse mustache and watchful eyes. Eldon said, "Got a minute?"

"Ah . . . no," the man muttered, shaking his head as he dumped the pipe into the ditch. He hurried away.

Pugh wheezed with amusement. "He don't wanta upstage me. *I've* got the best quotes."

"Did you know a man named Nguyen Xuan? He got killed by an elephant at the circus yesterday. We're doing a story on him."

"Yer up here on a damn thing like that? Man's too stupid to avoid gettin' stepped on by a elephant and you're interested in that? With the biggest story of the century starin' ya in the face?"

"The tower?" Shelly asked. Eldon sighed.

"You betcha, the tower!" Pugh said. "I'm ready when they come! You wanta come up and see?"

"Okay," Shelly said. "But I don't think Eldon will. He's, ah, afraid of heights. Can I go up and take some pictures?"

"Sure, sure, I'll take ya up myself!" Pugh said. "There's quite a view."

Shelly started up the ladder. Eldon realized he had been given a cue, and he hurried after the Vietnamese workman, giving his front teeth a lick as he did so.

The thin-faced man was drinking from a water jug. He was about Eldon's age but looked like a spindly, suspicious boy in a dirty denim shirt too big for him.

"Hey, no," the man said as Eldon sauntered up.

"Huey Bellows said you could maybe help me."

"Huey sen' you?" The man's accent was thick. "Wha' you want?"

"I write for the newspaper. I'm writing about Nguyen Xuan."

"Nguyen Xuan," the man said distinctly, pronouncing the name correctly. "Wha' you . . . write?"

"An obituary, sort of."

The man shook his head in puzzlement.

"I'm writing a story about him because he's dead. About his life." On impulse, Eldon added, *"une notice des morts."*

"Vous parlez français," the Vietnamese said in surprise.

"Oui," Eldon said. *"Assez bien, si j'ose dire."*

"Mais vous voulez dire la nécrologie, pas notice des morts."

"Ah. Voulez-vous parler en français?"

"Yes, I would prefer to, thank you," the man replied in French. "My French is much better than my English. You speak French very well. But *obituary* is *la nécrologie*, not *notice des morts.*"

The Vietnamese man's manner now seemed imperious, aristocratic. He pulled a package of cigarettes from his shirt pocket and regarded Eldon alertly.

"I learned French in school," Eldon replied. "I traveled in France as a student."

"Are you a policeman, sir?"

"A reporter. Eldon Larkin of the *Sun*."

"I am Tran Minh. How is it you know Huey Bellows?"

"From fishing."

"Ah, that ancient brotherhood," Tran said, lighting a cigarette. He did not offer one to Eldon. "And Nguyen Xuan?"

"I didn't know him. Yesterday I covered his death."

Tran Minh blew smoke. "A sad accident."

"Sad enough that my editor felt that we should write about his life," Eldon said. "How he came to this country and died so strangely."

"Strangely? I would have thought it merely very bad luck. Xuan was an unlucky man. There is news in that?"

"Does he have a family?"

Tran shrugged.

"Did you know him well?" Eldon asked. "How did he come here?"

"Did you serve in the Vietnam War, monsieur?"

Eldon had been subjected to four pre-induction physicals and had gotten two draft notices. He had declared pacifism, but it was "substandard dentition" that had at last turned the trick. "I did not have the honor," he said.

Tran Minh smiled coldly. His front teeth were gold. "Then you were lucky! Or perhaps very wise. Nguyen Xuan was neither. He hated communists. He had a small business in Saigon, a tailor shop. After the fall of the city, there was no place for small entrepreneurs who hated communists. He left the country, as did so many of us."

"I am told he was a sailor."

"Oh, yes! He learned to be a sailor the hard way . . . in a tiny boat jammed with people," Tran said. "They finally landed in Thailand, their belongings gone, their women raped. They had met Thai pirates along the way. They had no money to give them; that had all gone to bribe the communist officials to let them leave Vietnam. So the pirates took other things and in a fine gesture left them their lives. Most pirates kill all witnesses. Is that story enough for you?"

"That is quite a story, yes."

"Is it quite strange enough?"

"What is the matter, Monsieur Minh? Perhaps I have expressed myself badly."

"*Captain* Minh. Of the Army of the Republic of Vietnam," Tran said with pride.

"Were you with him on the boat, Captain?"

"No. I have told you Nguyen Xuan's story, not mine. Not all Vietnamese are ragamuffin boat people. You should not treat us as freaks." Tran Minh smoked his cigarette slowly, with calculation. "That is the entire story."

"Did Nguyen Xuan have family or other friends?"

"I do not think they will talk to you, monsieur. They like their privacy."

"Did you know him well?"

"It does not matter. The interview is finished, monsieur."

"Thank you for your trouble," Eldon said. "We must speak French again sometime."

"I am studying English," Tran said coldly.

"Keep studying. You still speak it like a laborer. Au revoir."

Well, that's one source shot, Eldon thought ruefully as he walked back up toward the house. He should have held his tongue—probably a proud man like Tran simply was sick of being deferential to Oregon red-necks. His story sounded like bull, anyway. The little anticommunist tailor. Crap.

Eldon hoped he hadn't blushed at the snap of Tran's voice. Speaking French had helped; he could be very cool in French. It had put the little bastard off balance. People were so damned hostile here. Like in the Céline novel. He should be used to it after five years, but his stomach still flip-flopped whenever the hostility erupted.

Shelly and Pugh were atop the blockhouse. Shelly called for Eldon to come up. The tower had a wide unglassed window in each wall but no door. Within, a carefully built cinder-block stairway led upward. Eldon climbed through a window and started up the stairs.

The walls were easily two feet thick. There were windows at each level. The tower looked strong enough to withstand any storm and support the weight of an army in the bargain.

On the second floor, a foil-lined alcove in the wall held a battered Prince Albert tobacco can as if it were an icon. The third floor was strewn with crumpled tinfoil. The stairway led up through a hole to the roof. Shelly and Pugh stared down through it.

"Took the wimp's route, eh?" Pugh said with a cackle.

"Prince Albert watched over me," Eldon said.

Pugh's jaw clamped shut. "Climb up."

The view from the tower's broad roof was splendid. They could see across the woods, over the dunes, and far out to the shining rim of the sea.

"The Patterson ranch is over there," Shelly said, and gestured toward a dark red frame farmhouse and a weathered barn among the trees. Sunshine gleamed on a squat radio tower.

"A ham radio," Eldon said. "Did the old owner put up the antenna?"

"It's new and I don't like it," Pugh said. "Interference."

Eldon nodded. "TV reception stinks around here as it is."

"I don't mean TV!" said Pugh with a snarl. "Who watches TV? I mean for when they come!"

"When who comes?" Eldon asked, abruptly regretting that he stood on an open rooftop with an aged eccentric.

"Pugh has been telling me all about the Space Brothers," Shelly said.

She was clearly delighted and fighting to keep a straight face. Eldon glared at her. The kid had to learn that you played these South Coast zanies fast and loose—otherwise, you never shook them.

"This is my UFO observation platform," Pugh said grandly. "Officially certified; I've got a county building permit. This is the biggest story of your career."

"It's not a story just because you've built a blockhouse," Eldon said with irritation. "The UFOs have to show up."

"They're around. I've seen 'em. Lights. Out in the ocean at night. Skimmin' low on the water, like nothin' manmade."

"Sounds to me like helicopters from the coast guard station."

"No way these were choppers. These were *lights*."

"You think one of 'em's going to land up here, don't you?"

"Didn't say that," Pugh said hastily.

"How's he coming in? Antigravity? Retro-rockets? If it's rockets, you'll have a forest fire and the Space Brothers'll have hell to pay."

"No fires from *these* chariots." Pugh added bitterly, "The right UFO story in the newspapers would cause people to put more faith in God, in the Bible. Criminal minds would start looking up."

"We have to return to earth now, if you don't mind," Eldon said. "We've got a story to do on a dead Vietnamese."

"More to *that* than meets the eye," said Pugh.

"You figure the Vietnamese are Space Brothers?"

"Xuan was no Space Brother. But he did some work for me on this tower." Pugh went down the roof hole.

Eldon followed him down the stairs to the third floor. "What about him, then?"

Pugh was balling tinfoil under one arm. "Now that I got somethin' you want, I get respect! Xuan jumped ship at the port sometime back. He got along on two-bit jobs. Then the new guy kicked him outta the little house he rented from Patterson, an' that was the end of his luck."

"So he wasn't a fisherman," Shelly said.

"He came in on a chip ship," Pugh said.

"He must've jumped ship here because he'd gotten to know the town a little and decided to stay in America," Eldon said. "It happens from time to time. The paper never really has done anything on it—"

"But this might be a way into that story," Shelly said.

"I keep tabs on everybody around here," Pugh said. "Like t'know who's workin' for me. Too many pot smokers and other undesirables in this parta the country."

"Did Xuan have a wife?" Shelly asked. "Or relatives?"

"I don't think he'd've jumped ship with a wife," Eldon said.

"I meant an American wife," Shelly said. "It's one way to stay in the country legally."

"Xuan di'n't have no wife, though he had somethin' sorta like one. If you take m' meanin'."

Shelly shrugged. "A live-in girl friend? I was one myself."

Pugh started down the stairs with the foil. "Naw, nothing like that, even."

"Then what?" Eldon asked, following, filled with a new optimism at Shelly's revelation. He would catch her on the rebound and this time she would eat his ice cream, all right. He would chase this story all over the county if that was what it took.

Pugh descended the stairs rapidly, crunching the tinfoil in his hands as if mauling prey. "Don't wanta say. I could have troubles if talk got around. UFOs are a touchy subject."

I've been in the woods too long, Eldon thought. I'm so self-pitying and horny that I can't tell a good story when I see one anymore.

But when they reached the tower's ground floor, Pugh turned. "Ask Huey Bellows. He can tell you what's what. After all, he ran off with Xuan's woman."

3 "Ran off with Xuan's wife?" Shelly asked.

"I ain't saying I said. I don't need trouble," Pugh said.

"We protect our sources," Shelly said.

The idea nudged Eldon: murder. "When did Bellows run away with Xuan's woman?"

"She left Xuan, more properly," Pugh said. "Not that it *was* proper. Moved out on Xuan and in with Huey. Musta been afore last Christmas. Or was it Thanksgiving? Naw, it was two summers ago. The UFOs had just started showin' their lights—"

"Last Christmas?" Eldon said. "That's pretty stale stuff."

"Stale as ya wanta make it," Pugh said. "Now I wanta show ya something *important*."

Pugh headed for the moldering house. Eldon and Shelly followed. Pugh led them up the creaking back porch steps and shoved the warped back door.

Eldon paused inside the door to let his eyes adjust to the gloom. Dark shapes stood around him. He realized they were heaps of rubbish. He followed Pugh and Shelly down narrow rabbit trails that wound among the mounds.

In the living room was a gutted television set covered with fishnet. Glass Japanese fishing floats—blue and green baseball-size globes—dangled from the net. A Prince Albert tobacco can stood atop the TV set.

Fascination stole over Eldon as he surveyed the sea of trash: newspapers, plastic fruit, automobile parts, manila folders stuffed with decaying papers, buckled furniture and rusty tools, a tire, X rays of teeth stapled to a dental chart, barbells, heaps of musty clothing, a Hollywood phone book. . . .

Pugh shuffled up a flight of stairs. There was a sudden sharp spatter of rain outside as Eldon and Shelly followed him up to the landing and stopped, amazed.

Upstairs, the center of the house had been torn out—much of

the third floor sawn away, the roof removed. The geodesic dome roofed the gap, forming a huge loft or hangar. Sunlight suffused the yellow canvas despite the rain shower and glinted on a crazy upright cylinder three yards across and made of wooden struts, metal tubing, and chicken wire half-covered with crinkled tinfoil. Wire-mesh fins held the tube upright. Wheels were mounted on either side of the tapering nose, where a wagon tongue stuck out at an awkward angle.

It was like something out of a 1930s science-fiction magazine, a mad scientist's attic project. Only this time, thought Eldon with dismay, the mad scientist was a crazy tuned to the mental frequency that psyched the whole weird South Coast, patiently smoothing tinfoil and wrapping it around chicken wire as rain beat on his geodesic dome. "You're building a spaceship," Eldon said.

Pugh held the tinfoil in his hands like a holy offering. "The Star Days are nearly upon us."

"How's it fly?"

"The chariots of the Space Brothers will hitch on and pull."

"I'd prefer a Chevy-eight engine, but your way saves gas. How long have you been working on it?"

Pugh molded tinfoil around the mesh of a skeletal tail fin. "Sometimes I think I been workin' on it my whole life. I usta be like you . . . things never made much sense t'me, 'til after I got hit in the head with a log settin' a choker chain in these very woods. It was all clear enough after that. Funny how things come t'ya. I woke up after the accident, lookin' in the bottom of a Prince Albert can . . . *an' God was in there!* In the bottom. So help me."

"So God told you to build this."

"It was after I saw the lights and studied the Bible, then I knew. I've seen the lights over the sea," Pugh said. "I'm about the only person in all southwest Oregon taking an active stand on UFOs. Xuan and Tran and some others helped me build this loft. Huey smokes Prince Albert tobacco. Once Xuan's woman went over to Huey, the connection was obvious." Pugh cocked his head back and gave a crazy grin. "But now you're gettin' inta somethin' that might be a little too big for ya."

Nguyen Xuan's obituary was still unwritten, Eldon thought.

"Anytime you want to get more off your chest, Pop, you let me know."

"Ya aren't gonna do a story?" Pugh asked in surprise.

Eldon turned away. Shelly stood in the shadows in a corner of the room, staring at a big tattered black and white movie poster with the antique image of an imperious man in the baggy trousers and high stiff collar of the silent-film era. "It's Great-Uncle Ogden," Shelly said softly.

Ogden O. Sherwood was posed before a backdrop of heavy dark stage drapes, the twin masks of Comedy and Tragedy woven into the fabric above his head. The design's position in relation to the floor of the studio suggested how short Sherwood really was, and Sherwood seemed to know it. His hands gripped his coat lapels firmly, his shoulders were thrown back, his jaw was angled high. Sherwood seemed to be attempting to gaze regally down on the onlooker, but his stature sabotaged his effort. He looked as if something was wrong with his neck.

"Mr. Pugh, can I buy this?" Shelly asked.

"I'm no 'mister,' I'm a man of the people. Like he was. I'm kinda sentimental about him," Pugh said. "Al'ays admired Sherwood. I worked in movies once myself, a long time ago."

"After the Seattle strike," Eldon said with deadpan maliciousness.

Pugh nodded obliviously. "Movies never were worth a damn after they put in sound because of that bastard Roosevelt—"

"Ogden O. Sherwood was my great-uncle," Shelly said. "This poster really would mean a lot to me."

Pugh's eyes rolled around the dark loft, and Eldon heard again that astonishing compressorlike breathing. "Blood's blood," Pugh said. "Blood's a tight thing. . . . Tell ya what . . . swap ya a picture of my spaceship for the poster."

"You're on," Shelly said, attaching the strobe unit to her camera. "We can use this, can't we, Eldon?"

"Maybe as a filler photo, no story. But only maybe," Eldon said. "And we haven't got all day."

Shelly locked a 28mm lens onto her camera and began shooting as Pugh posed stiffly but with an eager smile beside his tinfoil creation. The bond of Ogden O. Sherwood seemed to transform Pugh and Shelly. Fierce, crazy Pugh was an old man grateful for attention. Shelly, hard-driving in the presence of violent death, was soft-eyed and full of warmth.

It was her warmth that made Eldon determined to follow through with the story as well as the seduction. One or the other had to be worth something. Seduction was a fancy name for it, he thought as he rolled up the absurd poster. The South Coast was a wet and chilly region. Mushrooms grew on your bones and your soul. He didn't give a damn about means and ends. Beneath the predatory impulse to drag home the kill was the need to find something worth dragging home. He enjoyed the thought's coarse irony, hoping it would lead him to a miracle after five years of prayer in this cold temple.

"Let's go see Huey Bellows," Eldon said.

"Not a word about me!" said Pugh. "I dunno why I tole ya anything."

"Because you want ink," Eldon said with pleasure.

They made their way downstairs through the mess and out into the light intermittent rain.

"I thought you were mean to him," Shelly said as she started the van.

"You can't let the crazies get all over you or you never shake them. They'll hound you day and night."

Shelly peered intently through the windshield at Pugh climbing the rickety ladder to the top of his UFO tower. "I sort of like him. He's about the same age as Great-Uncle Ogden would be."

"Oh, come on. Your uncle's dead."

"The family never knew for sure." Shelly turned the van and headed it down the driveway.

"He doesn't look like Ogden O. Sherwood to me," Eldon said. "He's the wrong height."

"There is a way to tell for certain," Shelly said seriously. "Great-Uncle Ogden had tattoos."

"Don't be silly," said Eldon, surprised at her persistence. "Pugh's no more Ogden O. Sherwood than I am. Want to know Rule Number Two? Keep some distance from the people on your beat. You can't screw 'em one night and catch 'em with their hand in the cash register the next morning. It doesn't work."

"So why do you want to go fishing with Huey Bellows? Do you believe what Pugh said?"

Fishing was something different, and Eldon didn't want to argue about that. "We can go check out the part about Xuan's woman right now. If it's true, why was Tran Minh so hostile?"

"Well, *I* believe Pugh," Shelly said as the rain died away and sunlight gleamed again on the foliage flanking the muddy driveway. "He's got no reason to lie."

They bumped down the lane and onto the road, picking their way, reading mailboxes canted by the ceaseless ocean wind. Eldon directed Shelly up an unmarked turnoff.

"What's here?" she demanded. "Not Bellows."

"The dunes. Park the van and I'll show you something."

The rutted path halted at an immense wall of sand that gleamed white-gold in the sun, ribbed with wind ridges regular as logic. They traversed the long and slippery sand ridge to its crest.

"I feel tiny," Shelly said, gazing over the creamy expanse of sand that stretched as far as the eye could see. "It's like an unmoving ocean with trees."

"It runs up the coast for miles. Come on."

Eldon led her across the sand and in among a cluster of pine trees at the edge of the dunes. The trees bordered a sharp cliff, from where they looked down into a cove with white sand and dark sea-rounded rocks and tidal pools.

Shelly marveled at the cove's beauty.

"I'm irrationally annoyed when I find other people here," Eldon said, leading the way down to the beach. "Sometimes I fish off the rocks, but mostly I just come here to sit. This is part of your education, and possibly a story." Eldon led her onto a slick rock outcropping where the ocean beat and tiny black mussels grew in pools worn in the rock by wave action. The tide was out, and they could walk on the stone a score of yards into the ocean. In a few hours, Eldon knew, the outcropping would be submerged.

"It looks gentle," Shelly said. "The California coast is rougher."

"Yeah, more crags. But Oregon's got the treachery. Never turn your back on the ocean here. Wish I had a spyglass." Eldon pointed north, up the long strip of beach bordering the dunes. "Just as I thought . . . from here you can see the Patterson place."

Shelly squinted at the distant buildings. "You already saw it from the tower."

"Not the beach approach. All beaches in Oregon are publicly owned. It's easy enough to stroll right onto the place, or at least up to the fence. So now I know there's a clear approach along the shoreline."

"So what?"

"So just to know. One summer we had a rock star who called attention to himself the same way, by renting a beach place and locking himself away. It made a pretty good feature. He was annoyed, but finally he talked to me."

"You're really into reporting, Eldon."

"I'm not up here in the rainy north woods playing newspaper, no, ma'am."

"There's nothing you do for fun?"

"All too little." Eldon thought of advancing on Shelly and kissing her among the rocks and the pounding surf, but he told himself to be reasonable. Gad.

"Who's that walking along the beach up there?" Shelly said.

Eldon saw a distant figure in a red woolen shirt, hiking stolidly along the beach north of them, toward the cove. "It's a woman. Maybe she's studying sea urchins. It would seem that you definitely can make your way up to the Patterson place, and to Pugh's."

"You think this new guy's another California rock star?"

"More likely just an unfriendly California son of a bitch."

The distant woman began pulling at a tangled pile of white driftwood that lay on the beach. "A lot of people collect driftwood and burn it," Eldon said. "It makes a pretty fire because of the salt." The woman stopped and stood looking toward them. Eldon slowly raised a hand and waved. After a moment, the figure slowly returned the wave and then went back to her work.

The mailbox marked BELLOWS was down the road from the turnoff into the dunes.

A short path led to a weather-beaten cottage decorated with gnarled whitewashed driftwood and seashells and wind chimes that whirled in the breeze. On an enclosed porch, Huey Bellows worked with a small power grinder. Eldon banged on the porch door.

Bellows looked up, eyes cold for a moment before they decided to be friendly.

"Got a few minutes, Huey?"

"Guess so," Bellows said, snapping off the grinder.

Eldon saw that he was grinding stained glass. An intricate glass lamp shade, big dragonflies in its design, stood on a wooden mount, half-assembled.

"I'm copyin' a Tiffany design," Bellows said with pride, seeing Eldon's interest. "The original's got five thousand pieces. I'm improvin' it a bit. Find Pugh?"

"He showed us the spaceship. I found, ah, Captain Minh, too. He wasn't very friendly."

"Pugh's nutty as a bedbug. Tran misses being a captain."

"Want to tell me about Xuan's wife?"

"She never was married to Xuan, but she's my wife now," Bellows said after a moment. "You got quite a lot out of Tran, from the sound of it; his English ain't too good."

"Knowing French helped."

Bellows paused again. "Xuan used to beat shit outta her. You want to put that in his obituary? He was a bastard, but puttin' that in the paper is like pissin' into the wind at the ocean. Who's gettin' wet?"

"Xuan's obit isn't all that important," Eldon said. "There's a story up here about the Vietnamese. I'm after it."

Bellows fitted a chunk of green glass into the lamp shade's channeled lead framework. The daggerlike fragment made Eldon think of the glass that had glittered in the sawdust of the circus tent, around Nguyen Xuan.

"Just leave me and my wife out of it," Bellows said. "This is off the record." He pronounced the phrase in layman's fashion, as if the words were an incantation. Shelly came in with her camera, and he added, "No pictures." "Hey, Theresa," Bellows called. "Company."

An Oriental woman appeared. She had a trim build and a broad face with slightly pocked cheeks. Her black hair was gathered in a bun. She wore threadbare jeans and a man's large red woolen shirt. Eldon realized that it was the woman they had seen on the beach.

"Fix us some coffee, will ya, hon?" Bellows said. "How do reporters like it?"

"Black," Shelly said. "Hello."

"*Noir*," Eldon said. "*Bonjour, Madame. Parlez-vous français?*"

The woman regarded them silently and was gone.

"No, she don't," Bellows said. "She's not educated, like Tran. Good try, though."

"Job," Eldon said.

"So what'd Tran Minh have to say?"

"Some stuff about boat people. Nguyen Xuan the little tailor who escaped to Thailand in a boat. It was too good to be true."

Huey snickered. "That happened to Tran, not Nguyen Xuan. Tran doesn't like to admit he deserted the army. Of course, we all deserted, if you think about it."

"You were in Vietnam?" Shelly said.

"Fourteen months at An Khe," Bellows said. "I was a forward observer in the artillery. Lieutenant Huey Bellows. Wouldn't think it, t'look at me now, eh? Were you over there, Larkin?"

"I never had the honor."

"You didn't miss a fucking thing," Bellows said.

Theresa brought the coffee. They each took a cup and Theresa departed. Bellows, looking after her, continued. "After nine months humping through the jungle, I'd had enough. You have to hump that jungle yourself to know what I mean. And that was how I met Tran Minh."

"You knew Tran in Vietnam?" Shelly asked.

"Small world, ain't it?" Bellows raised his cup with a delicate gesture, blew on the coffee, and sipped it like a ragged epicurean king. "Small enough that it's curious, and when you get t'understandin' just how curious, you don't mind tellin' people how you come to see it that way, because you think they should know. Never have understood why people don't like talking about that war. For me, talkin' helps. One day, humpin' through the countryside with an infantry platoon, I walked about six paces into the jungle to take a piss . . . *and the platoon wasn't there anymore!* Thirty guys just disappeared. The growth was that thick. The piss shut off like a faucet.

"I fought my way back through the undergrowth, like in one of those bad dreams where something's after you and you can't run. The damn vines had claws, I swear. The platoon was right where I'd left 'em, but it musta been a hundred and ten in the shade and I was wringing wet like somebody'd turned a hose on me. I started shivering. I couldn't stop. I humped all right but I kept shivering. Everyone knew it was the FO's last walk. Finally I couldn't walk; they had to call a chopper. That helicopter was

like an angel descending. I was still shivering when we got back
to base. Since then, I haven't had a hell of a lot to hide."

"And Tran?" Eldon asked.

"I went to see the Old Man and told him I'd had enough,"
Bellows said. "I was too shit-scared to hump anymore. Combat
fatigue. Thought I'd be court-martialed, but the Old Man told me
it was okay. He assigned me as liaison to a South Vietnamese
supply company . . . commanded by Tran. His English was even
worse then, of course.

"Tran and I became buddies. A funny match. I was pretty
rustic, even in those days, while he always wore starched khakis
and spit-shined boots, peaked hat just so, and those aviator sun-
glasses. A real playboy–soldier. Tran believed in life and
money."

"He doesn't look much like a playboy now," Eldon said.

"Yeah, well, the war changed a lot of things. We died when
South Vietnam died."

"Who? America?" asked Eldon, confused.

"Don't be stupid," Bellows said. "Countries don't have souls;
that's why they do the things they do. I died, me and Tran. But I
also lived. Thanks to Tran. He taught me about Vietnamese
women." Huey's eyes rested on Shelly. "Best women there are."

"Did Xuan think so, too?" Shelly asked.

"I imagine Xuan did," Huey said. "But I didn't meet him and
Theresa until he jumped ship here in Port Jerome. He deserted
the *Orient Star;* it's in port now, at the chip pile, matter of fact.
He made money in Nam same way Tran Minh did, on the black
market. They both liked good living, and the way to live well over
there was dealing black."

Eldon said, "Some of that black-market dough must've gotten
them out of Vietnam when the time came."

"You got it," Bellows said.

"Did you get a share?"

"Not a dime. I don't need money. What difference would it
make now, if I had?"

"None, I guess," Eldon said, "if you're a happy man."

"Damn straight," Bellows said. "Listen, this whole thing's not
got squat to do with money or Oriental poontang. It's got to do
with the Lord."

"Let's stick to Xuan."

"It leads up to Xuan," Bellows said. "I can see what you're thinkin', Eldon, but it's not true. I don't preach and I don't care what other people believe, or if they believe me. Because I know what I saw: *the hand of God in a Vietnamese cathouse*. Sounds crazy enough, I know."

"I don't doubt you saw it," said Eldon, thinking of battlefield hallucinations.

"It's what I owe to Tran," Bellows said.

"God's hand?" Shelly said.

"He brought me to a place where God could reach me. That jungle is *deep*."

"God reached you in the whorehouse," Eldon said.

"While I was fully at the gallop, y'might say. It was a noisy, hazy place . . . maybe from all the pot smoke, with lights flashing through it. Maybe 'cause everything seemed hazy once I'd stopped shivering. I wasn't in touch anymore. The Rolling Stones were playing full bore, and I was humpin' away, staring straight into the strobe lights, walking on my tiptoes somewhere off the world, the way they do on the moon.

"I was going but going nowhere. I was still lost in the jungle. But then I was going *somewhere*. I was picking up speed. This wasn't what you're thinking! It was better, greater. The strength I'd lost in combat was surgin' back inta me. . . . All the time I had my eyes fixed on those lights flashing through the smoke."

"And then?"

"The smoke parted!" Huey's little eyes glowed. "There was the hand of God reachin' down to help me out. Suddenly, I felt warm and relaxed; warmth was all around me, all through me. I wasn't afraid anymore. The smoke cleared."

Somebody probably turned on a fan, Eldon thought.

"And how does what you owe Tran connect with Xuan?" Shelly asked.

Gravel crunched outside. They looked up to see a plain sedan pull into the driveway, whip antennae swaying on its roof and trunk. A familiar lanky figure climbed out.

"Detective Nola!" Bellows said. "Looks like the rest of the story'll have to wait for later. Maybe when we go fishin'."

"Huey, I can't wait that long," Eldon said.

"Just remember to check out the *Orient Star*."

"Why's Nola here?"

"Might be because I had a little trouble with The Man some years ago. Nothin' too bad."

"Just what was that?"

"Let's not say. After all, you *are* reporters," Bellows said. Nola banged on the screen door, and Bellows called, "It's open!"

Nola entered. "What the hell're *you* doin' here, Eldon? Pardon my French, miss."

"Just passing by," Eldon said.

"Art's like you, he just dropped in for a chat," Bellows said. "Coffee, Art?"

"Don't mind if I do."

"Are you busting him, Art?"

"No, this is not a bust." Nola forced a smile; he looked at Shelly and the smile became genuine. "You'd better get back into town. It's time for one of Eldon's famous photographs. They're going to impound—and destroy—that killer elephant."

4 The circus had pitched its tents close to the railroad switchyard on the edge of the bay, where the smell of sawdust mingled with the odors of diesel oil and the salt water of the sea. The rusty camper belonging to the ringmaster of the circus stood close to the gray water. With its peaked shingled roof, the camper looked like a motorized doghouse, and the ringmaster like a gloomy, agitated dog.

As he and Shelly picked their way through the mud, Eldon thought of the magic of the circus midways of his childhood. This circus was not magic, never had been—its tents were patched and filthy, its clowns ruffians, its ringmaster a scowling seedy man whom Eldon could imagine constantly wringing his big flat hands over the prospect of dwindling proceeds.

A sheriff's deputy, wide-hipped but tapering upward to rail-thin, like a human bowling pin, shirt neck too big for him, huge impassive horse's face topped by a brush cut, stood at the door of the ringmaster's camper, holding up a writ.

"Impound Horton?" the ringmaster whined, shifting his feet in his floppy rubber boots and squinting at the paper with watery blue eyes. "We're going to Coos Bay."

"That elephant's killed a man," the deputy said.

"Ya wanna try it for murder?"

"Maybe we ought to. The animal stays."

The ringmaster threw up his hands, brought them down again, wrung bony fingers over knuckles big and knobby as hex bolts. "Times are bad. Every day's delay costs money. You can't have a circus without an elephant."

"Wish we could supply a replacement," the deputy said, "but we don't breed 'em around here."

The ringmaster turned to Eldon. "You hear what he says? How he talks to me? Take a picture of this! Write all this down! Put it in your paper!"

Shelly clicked off a photo as the deputy examined the ring-master like a weary cook deciding how best to knead a stubborn mound of dough. "The animal's transport van and a supply of food is impounded as well," the deputy said. "You'll have to give a deposition."

"Deposition?"

"For the investigation. Man's been killed."

"I'll give it now!"

"Not my baby. District attorney'll contact you tomorrow."

"I have to go to Coos Bay!"

The deputy shrugged. "Maybe you can give your deposition there. But you go without the elephant."

"When do I get him back? Horton's valuable."

"If it was up to me, I'd shoot it. It's a man-killer."

"Right, it's a man-killer!" The ringmaster ran through the mud to the front of his camper, pointing angrily into the dented, muck-spattered cab. "I'll shoot it myself, I'll shoot it myself! Right now! Got my .30-30 on the rack right in there!"

"Let's not talk like that," the deputy remarked, eyes sliding to the rifle and back to the ringmaster. "It's illegal to shoot a firearm in the city limits. That weapon loaded? No? Good. It's probably too light to do much to an elephant, anyway, don't'cha think? When d'you roll?"

"Tomorrow dawn."

"I'll tell the DA. Maybe he can work something out." The deputy nodded to Eldon and Shelly and headed back to his car.

The ringmaster clenched and unclenched his hands as the deputy turned away. He flexed them faster and harder with every step the deputy took. The ringmaster's blue eyes grew larger, rounder. His face grew red. "D'ja hear him? Talks to me like that! Takes my elephant away!"

"Well, it's a dangerous beast," Eldon said, watching the ring-master for his reaction.

"That elephant cost me two thousand dollars! Came all the way from India! Raised 'im from a pup! People pay lots more for a car, and cars kill people . . . lots more people than elephants do! They don't shoot cars."

"They impound them, though."

"They're not gonna take my elephant away! I'm gonna defend Horton to . . . to . . . the death . . ." The ringmaster trailed off.

"Death," he repeated, gasping for air. "A man shoots his own dog. No way *they're* gonna put *my* elephant down."

The ringmaster's voice rose to a shout: "Bring me Horton! Marie! Bring the damned elephant out! I'll try 'im for murder right now . . . judge, jury, and executioner. I find Horton *guilty!*"

Eldon scribbled in his notebook. The ringmaster charged through the mud to a moving van parked nearby and jumped into its rear. There were crashes, thumps; tools were thrown from the van and splashed into the mud.

Eldon inched over to the van. "What're you gonna do?"

"Dynamite! Where's the goddamn dynamite! What kinda circus don't have dynamite?"

"*Dynamite?*" Eldon asked.

"Black powder, then! We had black powder for the human cannonball act—"

"That act walked eighteen months ago," a woman said.

The voice was peremptory, distinct as a rare bell. Eldon turned to look into the ice-blue eyes of a woman leading an elephant. It was the red-haired mahout he had briefly glimpsed in the big top the day before. She led the muddy elephant by its bridle, guiding it with light flicks of a worn leather riding crop.

The woman's features transfixed Eldon—high cheekbones, long nose, pointed chin, pearly skin, those eyes like cold jewels. Her body was lean, long-legged, full-breasted, and hard as the look in her eyes. She was nothing like Shelly or the dolorous mountains of Port Jerome female fat Eldon confronted every day when he emerged from his hilltop den. The scent of perfume reached his nostrils.

"Horton the elephant at your service, sir," the woman said in a mocking tone, saluting the ringmaster with the crop. Tone and gesture were practiced, as if she had goaded the ringmaster in this way many times before.

"Marie, this is the end of the line for Horton."

"You sound as if you're introducing an act."

"That elephant has got to be killed."

Marie laughed. "So Horton's trampled his last roustabout. Shall we string him up?"

"That's an idea!" The ringmaster dived into the van's gloom.

The woman chuckled as the elephant stood placidly chewing, flicking the mud with its trunk. Shelly began shooting pictures.

The redhead postured carefully, as though she were a model in an ad.

Chains crashed in the van. Shelly fired off a series of frames as the ringmaster jumped down into the mud, his arms full of chains, heavy black links draped over his shoulders. "String 'im up!" he cried.

Marie used her crop to flick a piece of mud from her pants. "That will take a big tree."

"Bring the bastard to the switchyard. We'll deal with 'im there! Goddamn! Everybody turn out for the hanging of the elephant! The greatest act on earth!" The ringmaster pulled a long brass whistle from his shirt pocket and blew it.

A clown emerged from one of the trucks, hitching up his pants. He was joined by a prancing curly-tailed little dog and a tattooed fat lady with disheveled clothes, who alighted from the truck as gently as a grounding blimp. Roustabouts, dwarfs, and a cowgirl ballerina hurried from a cook tent, chewing hamburgers and slurping steaming coffee from Styrofoam cups. A drizzle began.

"He can't mean this," Shelly said.

Marie gave her a cool patronizing smile and used her crop to guide Horton toward the unfenced switchyard—unattended rusty alleys of track where a few sooty freight cars stood. On a spur was a huge wrecker with a crane used for hoisting derailed freight cars back onto their tracks.

"Here! Bring 'im here!" the ringmaster cried, capering to the wrecker like an agitated monkey. He threw himself up the ladder into the wrecker's cab, and the monstrous apparatus came to life and swiveled, a huge hook on a chain cranking down from the crane winch.

Horton lumbered forward, guided by Marie's crop. Marie brought the elephant to a halt beneath the swinging hook. With his trunk, Horton grubbed between the railroad ties. The ringmaster shouted from the cab to the crowd, "Get that chain around his neck! Make a noose and get it over that hook!"

A roustabout spat coffee into the mud. "Not me. You do that yourself."

Marie merely smiled and waited.

The ringmaster hurried down from the cab and made fast the heavy chain around Horton's neck. The elephant snorted. "Hold him there!" the ringmaster ordered. Marie calmed the elephant as the ringmaster leaped back into the wrecker cab and the clanking winch slowly twisted the luckless elephant off its feet. Horton lunged and trumpeted; the carnies began shouting.

"Let 'im go, for Chrissake!"

"You sonofabitch!"

"That chain's gotta break!"

"Shoot this," Eldon told Shelly. His gut started to turn over, then braked to a halt as the powerful, detached awareness of being the observer enveloped him.

His instruction to Shelly was unnecessary. She moved in, crouching to shoot upward in order to use the 28mm lens to best effect.

The chain held fast. Horton's front feet were well off the ground. A dwarf sprang up the ladder of the wrecker, pounded angrily on the cab door, shouting. The ringmaster snarled and bore back on the winch's gearshift, hauling the elephant heavenward.

Horton rotated like a huge gray top, trunk lashing, legs thrashing, tail spinning furiously as if it could propel him upward and put slack in the chain. The fat lady's little dog pranced and yapped. Shelly dodged the elephant's flailing limbs and shot off a series of frames. Marie stood poised, riding crop to her shoulder, watching. Horton's waving trunk abruptly wilted. The whirling gray body went slack as a sack. Turds plopped out of the sack's bottom, past the still-twitching tail.

As the smell of urine and new manure filled his nostrils, Eldon thought, Marie is more interested in how she looks in the photographs than in what happens to Horton. He nerved himself and spoke to the redhead. "This is pretty horrible," said Eldon, testing her by forcing a little distress into his voice. Truthfully, he was not upset after the first shock. He felt only the airy, clean sense of focus and distance that had been his ally for five years, ever since the day he had covered his first fatal traffic accident.

"Come off it," Marie said clinically. "You're a hard man. I saw you with that notebook. You were taking it all in."

"Comes with the territory."

"Well, I like it," Marie said. "You're really hard. You get so many marshmallows out here pretending to be men." Her eyes glittered. "I've never seen a really big animal die before. Do you hunt?"

"I do traffic accidents and murders."

Marie smiled broadly, a smile as perfectly engineered as the capped teeth it revealed. "That must be exciting."

Pure theater, Eldon decided. But his glands were stirring. They liked the act. "You took care of the animal?"

"I'm an animal trainer," Marie said regally. "Dogs, sometimes elephants, but mostly small stuff."

Shelly sniffed. "Trained dogs? Where's that at?"

"You'd be surprised," Marie said dryly. "Who is your little friend?"

"Shelly Sherwood, photographer for the *Sun*," Shelly said.

"I can tell you're no animal lover," Marie said.

Eldon took pleasure in the angry flash in Shelly's eyes. The voyeur in him was in full flower. He hadn't been around such female electricity in months. He imagined himself bounding around the exotic cushioned depths of Shelly's van, pursued by Shelly with a camera as he rode Marie, all of them sweatily naked. The riding crop. Eldon was about to add dogs when sirens cut the air.

A fire truck and two sheriff's cars plowed into the switchyard, throwing up breakers of mud. A fresh assault wave of dwarfs, clowns, roustabouts, and policemen stormed the wrecking crane and dragged out the hysterical ringmaster. A fireman worked the crane, dropping Horton to the muddy earth. Other firemen rushed in with resuscitation equipment, then halted and stood foolishly in their muddy turnouts, holding the human-size plastic breathing mask and puny oxygen tank.

"Dead," said one fireman, pointing at Horton's blue lolling tongue.

"Who's got an oxygen tent?" another asked.

"We could use the big top," said a third, deadpan, "pump it up with a fire hose."

Marie strolled behind the ringmaster's camper.

Eldon went after her. "Can we talk?"

"You might invite a girl to have a drink." There was a flash of something lupine in the set of the capped teeth. Here's a bad one, Eldon thought with sudden clarity. I could wind up just like the elephant.

On the metabolic level, however, the caveman warred with the reporter. Well, he could always put his notebook aside for a club. "Down there, then," Eldon said, pointing to Buster's, an easy stroll from the switchyard.

"It's as good a place as any other," Marie said.

Eldon thought that going to Buster's would get Marie clear of the switchyard, which plainly she was anxious to leave. And Buster's, of course, was directly on the route to Eldon's mountaintop retreat. Perhaps he could lure her up there. If his car would start. If nothing else, it might make Shelly jealous.

The tavern was nearly deserted. Its few afternoon customers were outside marveling at Horton's sordid demise. The stuffy little place smelled of spilled beer. Beams of sunlight passed through the filthy windowpanes, sabering drifting ridges of cigarette smoke. Cap'n Jasper, the cashiered alcoholic tugboat master, snored in the corner booth, his grubby tam-o'-shanter askew. Buster, the pinch-faced, slow-moving proprietor, stood absently wiping the burned and chipped red linoleum of the bar. Buster's gaze was fixed out the window, on the switchyard. A cigarette butt smoldered close to his fat ·undershot lip. Jimbo Fiske said that Buster moved the slowest he'd ever seen for a non-Mexican, theorizing that the bartender's vitals were sapped by a tapeworm.

Eldon and Marie took a table by a window overlooking the bay, Eldon admiring the swing of Marie's trim hips as she sat down. Eldon called to Buster, "A Henry's dark for me, Buster, and—"

The bartender's lips jerked; ash spilled onto the bar. "An' wha' f'r th' lady."

Marie said, "Wild Turkey. Neat."

Eldon flinched inwardly at the thought of the cost of a shot but told himself this was no time to turn back. Maybe Fiske would let him charge the drinks to the paper.

"Been with the circus long?" Eldon asked.

"I go off with one or another most seasons."

"There's a living in it?"

"It keeps my hand in. I live up in Newport. I have a dog-obedience school." Marie's eyes rested on Eldon. Had she placed a faint suggestive accent on the word *obedience*? On the word *dog*? Marie laid her crop on the table and flexed it. "I know my business."

Eldon pulled his imagination up sharply. "How'd the elephant stomp that fellow, then?"

"I wasn't there, is how. He must've angered it."

"Didn't he know any better? I thought they had elephants over there in Vietnam."

"You would as likely see an elephant in downtown An Khe as you would see one walking along the Port Jerome wharf."

An Khe. Reporter's instinct reared within Eldon at the unexpected detail. "I'm writing about the man who was killed."

"I can't help you. I didn't know him. These roustabouts come and go."

Eldon opened his notebook on the table. "Lots of Vietnamese?"

"I never paid attention. I guess not."

"He helped you with the elephant."

"Oh, the little shrimp fed all the animals and cleaned their cages. He did all that slopwork. It pays next to nothing." The drinks arrived. Marie plucked the shot glass of whiskey from Buster's tray, drained it, and put it back onto the tray. "I'll have another."

Eldon's eyes widened. People drank like that in Western movies. The sight filled him with abandon. "One for me, too, Buster." Whiskey on beer, never fear. "This is a good human-interest story."

"Love that blood and guts, eh?"

"This one has all sorts of interesting byways," Eldon said. "Xuan was from An Khe, as a matter of fact."

"Fancy that." Marie's expression didn't change; Eldon knew he had hit home. He said, "Tell me about Xuan's last day on the job."

"There's not much to tell. He carried the feed buckets and hosed down the cages."

"Nice guy? Dumb guy?"

"I don't care for Asian men. Too small. His English was pretty bad."

"So there wasn't much to talk about."

"He used to tease Horton," Marie said. "You shouldn't tease animals and you shouldn't tease people. You're teasing me now."

"I think you know more about him than you're telling me," Eldon said.

The second round of drinks arrived; Buster always acceler-ated at the promise of money. This time, Marie merely set her drink before her. Eldon asked, "No feelings about him at all?"

"He was just like the other pigs you meet in a circus, and I don't want to see that in the paper," Marie said. "He was always grinning at me with his gold teeth like I was an appetizing piece of food."

"Um. He worked unsupervised?"

"What's to supervise? The animals are caged, except for the late elephant."

"You usually watched when he fed Horton?"

"Not always," Marie said. "An elephant won't hurt you if you're decent to it. It was just a matter of throwing it some hay." Eldon sipped his Wild Turkey. The action seemed to galvanize Marie. Her cold eyes flashed and she said, "He used to drink. Are you a drinking man?"

"Only in the proper company, Marie."

"Violence and drinking go together, don't they?"

"Frequently. So you think Xuan was drunk when he was feed-ing Horton and started teasing him?"

"You don't have to have it particularly together in order to toss hay and hose out cages," Marie said. "You'd be surprised at the things that go on. Those Asians and their Thai stick."

"Thai stick?"

"I didn't say that. I'd better not say that." Marie wriggled on the chair and neatly downed half her drink.

Eldon swallowed half his whiskey in one gulp, something he never did with expensive booze, and gasped as the liquor burned. "Well, call on me anytime you feel like you want to get it off your chest."

"You don't believe me."

"That's too harsh. I don't want to argue in such pleasant com-pany. Tell me about your dogs."

"Xuan reminded me of a dog. He had a dog's way of panting. Disgusting. But you could mold him. Do you mind if I smoke?"

Eldon lied: "No."

Marie slid a hand into her jacket, extracted a match box, rolling papers, and a flat red tin of Prince Albert tobacco, which made Eldon think with amusement of Pugh's odd tobacco-tin horde. She carefully licked the papers after tapping the tobacco across them in a tidy brown line. The can now was empty, but Marie returned it to her jacket.

"I always roll my own. It makes a more rugged smoke. Half the men in this town are lousy at rolling. Jerks." Her eyes rested on Eldon. "I'll bet you roll pretty well."

"Under the right circumstances," Eldon said with a smile. "But I don't smoke, myself. Never have."

"A strong will. That's good."

"Was Xuan a smoker?"

"Back to Xuan? You're slippery. He smoked like a stove. All the Viets do. He used to roll his own."

"Tobacco? Or. . . ?"

"I showed him how to do a neater job of it one day. He read a lot into that."

"Lonely in a strange land, I guess."

"He had a wife."

"Oh," Eldon said. "What was her name?"

"She ran off," Marie said indifferently. "Are you married?"

"Not anymore. Do you want another whiskey?"

"Sure." Marie leaned in and smiled intimately. Someone had done beautiful work on her crowns. The warmth of the Wild Turkey and the pleasure of this unfolding adventure with a woman dimmed the alarm bells already fading in Eldon's head. He thought of himself with a white angel on one shoulder and a dark angel on the other. Both were dressed as lumberjacks and carried chain saws. They had the usual advice, the pros and cons of the rules he had laid down for Shelly about not messing around on the beat. The angels were insistent. Eldon spitefully gave them big South Coast potbellies, grew them right on the angels while the little spirits nagged. That shut them up for a while so he could draw out Marie. He had never seduced anyone for information before.

". . . I had my first affair at sixteen, my high school biology teacher," Marie was saying. "It went on for several years. At first I just baby-sat for him and his wife, but after she left him and took the kids, he and I went on to better things. He'd had his eye on me for years. I've always liked older men . . ."

The tale spilled out with practiced cruelty, emphasized with subtle body shifts, arch looks, and smiles. Everything calculated to raise male blood pressure. Eldon's groin stirred deliciously.

The curious part was that Eldon sensed Marie was happy. She really was interested in him, orbiting closer and closer. Certainly he was interested in her.

"I like directing things." Marie leaned toward Eldon, and he toward her; their lips brushed, all too briefly, all too lightly: a morsel deliberately dropped into his lap, bait to a starving beast.

Encouraged, Eldon reached for Marie. He connected; after a moment, she slipped smoothly away. She continued the history of her love life, yarning about college days as more and more whiskey arrived. The Wild Turkey tasted good to Eldon and the story was fascinating. It was a new experience to sit here drinking whiskey while a good-looking woman talked dirty to him. Buster's down-and-out patrons had more or less drifted back into place, and Eldon knew that every man's eye paused upon Marie. He was on a roll. He kept drinking, kept smooching, one up on these macho clowns at last.

It was Cap'n Jasper who broke the spell. Jump-started from a stupor by his body's need for ethyl-alcohol fuel, Jasper rose from his corner and weaved to the table where Eldon sat with Marie. As he walked, the puny, muttonchopped salt moved his hands around a big arc, as if steering a tug among log floats. Jasper insistently mooched spare change when not unconscious, which made him the success at his second, land-bound career that he had not been at his first. Thirty seconds of Jasper's nonstop keening was enough to make the most hardhearted mill worker bid silver to shut off the noise. Eldon had seen groups of men go in together to buy Jasper enough booze to quickly knock him out for the night.

"Mister ya got anny spare change I left m' wallet in m'othe' pan's y'know an' i's gonna rain anny time 's Oregon y'know—"

"Shove off, Jasper," Eldon said.

". . . an' in Oregon anny man's a rea' man buy anothe' man a drink 'cause 'at's th' kin' o' place in which we live, na like th' ou'si' world where there's killer gooks an' 'bominable snowm'n an' mean dawgs . . ."

Eldon took out his wallet and shook it out to show that it was empty. *Empty?* How many rounds had they consumed? How would he purchase another?

". . . na li' this boo'ful lady who prob'bly got a l'il spare change f'r an' ol' man gave 'is life f'r 'is country so long ago y'r boo'ful red ha'ar ya spare annythin' f'r ol' times' sake—"

"Beat it, Jasper," Eldon repeated.

But Marie could not resist flirting with a male, even a sodden one. "Here, old-timer, have one on me." She reached into her jacket pocket, movements now a shade unsteady, and carefully removed the Prince Albert tobacco can and a sheaf of miscellaneous folded papers to get at her flat wallet. Eldon examined them absently as she placed them on the table by the riding crop and began to tempt Jasper with one-dollar bills: handwritten notes, a napkin, gasoline-purchase receipts, half a pack of sugarless gum. . . . A newspaper clipping stuck out of the pile: The *Sun*'s regular listing of ship arrivals and sailings. Eldon had proofread it himself. The name *Orient Star* was circled in red. He recognized it upside down, half-smashed though he was.

"They've charged the ringmaster with murder," said an impatient voice.

Eldon looked up, surprised. Shelly stood before them, camera hanging between her ample breasts. Just behind her was Frank Juliano. Marie gave a frosty smile, but Eldon sensed a new ease in her, as if Shelly's words magically had made the rigid structure of a crystal relax.

"Shelly! Join us!" Eldon said.

"You've got a story to write," Shelly said. Her eyes were like flat steel disks. "I've got photos to develop."

Marie slipped away from the table, smoothly gathering up her possessions. "Wait," Eldon said. "I've got to talk to you."

"Another time. Thanks for the drinks." Marie sauntered out the door. Eldon stared blearily after her.

Shelly hauled at his collar. "Fiske is waiting for you. It's just lucky I saw you in here . . . you *drunk*."

"I've never done this before," Eldon said.

"Help me get him to my van," Shelly said to Frank.

They wrestled Eldon out the door and threw him onto the bed in the Ship of Love.

"The ringmaster was charged with *murder*?" Eldon asked as Shelly started the van.

"I just said that to get rid of Ms. Tightjeans," Shelly replied as they sped downtown. Eldon squirmed with shame. Shelly continued: "Actually, it was disturbing the peace, cruelty to animals and trespassing. That jackass ought to be charged with destroying evidence, too."

"Evidence?"

"I overheard a deputy saying it looks like foul play," Frank said. "They think the guy was hit on the head. Pushed under the elephant to be crunched. Have to have an autopsy to be sure, but—"

"And who is the elephant trainer?" Shelly demanded. "That red-haired trollop!"

"Christ." Eldon thought of the *Orient Star* timetable. He had to sober up and track that down. He lusted for Shelly; clearly, getting the story was the way to get the girl.

The white angel and the dark angel reappeared, carrying their chain saws. Neither had a potbelly. The white angel declared that a year ago, Eldon wouldn't have blinked at a come-on from a tramp like Marie because he had professional integrity.

The dark angel said nothing at all. He merely started his chain saw. The white angel started up his saw, too. Eldon groaned and pressed his hands to his temples. After they sawed through his skull, he would visit the *Orient Star*.

5 "Jimbo, they've lynched the elephant!" Eldon yelled as they reeled into the newsroom.

Fiske dropped his pipe. "Pull back page one."

Frank Juliano leaped toward the composing area, glasses flying off his nose. He caught the glasses on the fly, but Jimbo's pipe banged into a tall wastebasket; people looked up all around the office as Eldon jumped to his typewriter. Advertising salesmen in polyester suits, pudgy secretaries with ratted hair, back-shop typesetters with beer guts pushed up against their keyboards—all looked Eldon's way. Eldon's heart beat faster.

He rolled a sheet of newsprint into the typewriter as Shelly ran into the darkroom. The headache faded; he felt light and wiry and clean. This was what he lived for. He ascended from the stews of Port Jerome into a storyteller's heaven of clear thought and exquisite motion. He pounded the Royal's keys.

PORT JEROME—An elephant that trampled a circus roustabout to death was lynched today by its owner, the ringmaster of the circus. The ringmaster, Cyrus Peake, became enraged by an order impounding the elephant.

Peake hanged Horton, an 800-pound Indian elephant, from a wrecking crane in the Oregon Pacific Railroad's bayside switchyard. A shrieking crowd of circus performers vainly fought to save the small pachyderm from death.

Peake, 47, of Cathlamet, Wash., was charged with first-degree cruelty to animals, trespassing, and impeding an investigation. The ringmaster, who was hysterical when taken away by Nekaemas County sheriff's deputies, was being held in lieu of $XXXX bail in the county jail.

Fire fighters were unable to revive the elephant.

"Bring the damned elephant out!" Peake shouted to Marie Payne of Newport, an animal trainer for the circus. "Try it for

murder, he says! I'll try it right now . . . judge, jury, and
executioner. I find Horton guilty!"

"I've got to move the quote up higher," Eldon said. "Why
can't we buy word processors?"

"It's okay where it is," said Fiske, reading over Eldon's
shoulder. "This could beat the scalping. Go ahead and put your
by-line on it. And take out *damned*. You get photos?"

"Shelly did. I need some background; where's yesterday's paper?" Eldon cribbed three paragraphs from his story about
Nguyen Xuan's death and rifled his notes for fresh information.
Marie had given him precious little, but he worked in what she
had told him about Xuan's duties. "An elephant won't hurt you if
you're decent to it." The notes, buttressed with the older material
and dressed up with the scramble to drag the ringmaster from the
crane, made *good copy*. The story went together like a snap—
after five years at the grind, he could write even half-crocked. It
was just a matter of stacking up the bricks until you had the
edifice. Journalism was exciting work, like scaling the Tower of
Babel to meet Jehovah at the top. There might be other profes-
sions, but they weren't going to heaven.

"Dee-de-dee," Jimbo sang as he drew a new page-one
dummy. "Did Shelly shoot a horizontal or a vertical?"

Frank beat on the darkroom door and shouted Fiske's question. "She says vertical."

"Vertical it is," Fiske said. "We'll run the story double col-
umn. I want sixteen inches of copy, Eldon. Your story on one
side, young Frank's down the other. Dee-de-dee!"

Eldon typed on. Frank grabbed the sheets as they dropped
from the typewriter and corrected them with a soft copy pencil
before passing them to Fiske. Shelly came out of the darkroom
with the photo—Horton aloft, trunk straight up, dancing Danny
Deever with tree-trunk feet, while Marie stood poised nearby with
her riding crop, sneering at the carnie mob.

Shelly's good, Eldon thought. She'll be off to a bigger paper
in a year.

"That one's gonna fill the whole center of the page," Fiske
said.

"We'll get some calls about 'bad taste,'" Frank said with relish. "Oh, we'll give the bastards their twenty cents' worth tomorrow!"

"This issue's a keeper, all right," Fiske said. "What's the I.D. on this honey with the riding crop?"

Eldon said, "That's Marie—"

"Payne," Shelly finished snappishly, looking straight at Eldon.

"Not bad lookin'," Jimbo remarked. "Reminds me of the time out in Pendleton when the mayor and the Presbyterian minister's red-haired wife used to go huntin' mushrooms together by moonlight. See, she was a kootch dancer in a previous life . . ."

Jimbo's drone seemed to fade into the background as Eldon typed. The next step with Shelly is seduction over burgers, Eldon thought, feeling as eager as a fifteen-year-old certain he would score after the big football game. This story's got her adrenaline pumping.

Shelly glared at Eldon and marched out the front door.

". . . hacked to pieces," Jimbo said. "The heck of it was, she never had learned to read!"

Frank looked at the swinging front door. "What was that all about?"

"Shelly reminds me of that minister's wife," Jimbo said. "Y'see, she used to get wound up for action just drinking coffee in the morning. Three, four cups o' caffeine and she'd be ready to go—"

"Something's burning," said Frank.

"I don't smell anything," Fiske said.

Smoke and crackling flame belched from the tall wastebasket that had received the contents from Jimbo's pipe. Eldon ducked away from his typewriter. Frank sprang away with a leap that launched his spectacles into the fire. Jimbo circled the blazing can twice, flapping his hands like some grounded bird, before Frank slapped a desk blotter across the wastebasket's top, smothering the flames.

"Jimbo, you're an idiot!" Eldon said.

Fiske crowed with delight. "She sure blazed up there, didn't she? That was some jump, Frank. You play basketball in school?"

"My glasses! That was my only pair!" Frank desperately poked through the charred paper with a metal pica ruler, loosing a fierce billow of trapped heat and black smoke. The sprinkler in the ceiling above the desk spurted into action.

Amid the yells, Eldon ducked out the front door.

It was twilight. Rain clouds moved through the sky. The Ship of Love had vanished. Frank could give him a ride home, but Eldon did not like to think of Frank driving without glasses. He would walk home—after he had gotten something to eat. The booze was clearing from his head, leaving him hungry. The Citroën lay in its coma in the parking lot. Eldon slid behind the wheel and inserted the key.

"All right, you bastard"—he switched the key, thumped the gas pedal—"*start!*" The motor belched awake.

Should he drive after Shelly? If so, which way? Where was her apartment? Eldon did not want to ask Fiske; years from now, Fiske would say, "Dee-de-dee! Reminds me of the time the elephant was lynched. This fat reporter was chasin' this fat little girl photographer. . . ."

Eldon slipped the car into gear and drove slowly across the parking lot. The grinding noise was no worse; maybe slightly better. Some troublesome nonessential part was being ground off. Shelly would keep. Food would keep. Now, he would visit the *Orient Star*.

Paper lanterns like glowing rotten fruit swung from the rail of the *Orient Star*, gilding the dark, wet gangplank in the drizzle. Eldon paused by the chip pile, listening to the sounds of tipsy revelry coming from the ship as evening fell.

"A party," he said aloud. More paper lanterns festooned the vessel's afterdeck, where a crowd celebrated beneath a canvas awning. Rock music blared from a stereo. An empty champagne magnum flashed off the poop and into the bay's dark water. Not only was there a story here, there was a good chance of getting something to eat.

Eldon advanced to the gangplank. "Permission to come aboard!" The music drowned his voice. No one was on duty. Eldon pulled his camera from beneath his coat and trudged up the ribbed plank into another world.

The revel was in high gear. Couples gyrated to the music beneath flashing strobe lights and ship's signal flags. American landlubbers—obese women and sallow, ponytailed men—

mingled with tough-looking Asian crewmen. There were low-riders, greasers, madmen, and Indians. The deck was slick with spilled beer, and the sharp scent of marijuana cut the wet air. In the corner, a pig-eyed young drunk with chipped teeth and a nose like a lumpy vertical tube banged a fork against a saw. He had spiderwebs tattooed on his elbows. The tune he played was inaudible in the blast of electronic riffs that churned an undercurrent of violence.

A long table was lavish with booze and food, and Eldon went straight for it. He chewed up bits of paper napkin and stuffed them in his ears against the deafening music.

"You so hungry you eat napkins, huh?" said a big, gold-toothed Malay. "Have some food. You like it? I am cook."

Eldon plucked a chicken wing from a bowl of spicy dark sauce. "This is the best. Sorry I'm late."

"Friend of bride?"

"I'm from the newspaper. I'm the wedding writer."

"Newspaper? Hey, grand!" The cook shoved a big paper cup of beer into Eldon's hand.

"This is a great story." Eldon peered around, recognizing no one. "A shipboard wedding. Who's getting married?"

"Assistant cook has married local girl. The captain has married them."

"Aw, isn't that nice. I love to cover weddings."

"You take lot of pictures for them. Good public relations."

"You bet." Eldon gobbled food as he surveyed the chaotic scene. The best thing was just to start asking about Nguyen Xuan.

Now, the gold-toothed cook wheeled forth a wedding cake shaped like the *Orient Star*, lavish with confectionery flowers. A miniature plastic bride and groom stood on the bridge. The music stopped and the real bridal couple separated themselves from the crowd and prepared to sink the knife into the cake. The groom was a tall, rancid-looking young Indonesian with a spotty mustache. Hair fell to his shoulders in oily black ringlets. The bride was a dark, plump-faced Caucasian teenager whose lush body was stuffed into a white dress crazy with ruffles. Their eyes were shrewd above their smiles.

Eldon had seen that look a million times on Port Jerome's hardscrabble streets; it was an appetite to seize whatever meager thing came to hand, coupled with a refusal to admit there could be anything better. Too many failed dreams. They were such a perfect pair. It made a great photo, and Eldon got the strobe out of his coat pocket and flashed away.

"He's from the newspaper," called the cook as Eldon photographed the bride and groom greedily eating from one another's hands.

"Isn't this beautiful?" gasped the bride, her flushed face heavy with makeup and smeared icing. "I always wanted a write-up in the paper!"

"What's your name?"

"Stephanie Hosfelder. I'm seventeen. This is Ahmed."

Eldon said, "Howdy, Ahmed. How'd you two meet?" The sailor glowered.

"Some of us local girls visit the ships when they're in port," Stephanie said eagerly. "These are real nice guys. They buy things here they can't get overseas. Dougie over there—he's the dude playing the saw—he helped them get a TV set one time. A bargain. You know."

Cheap girls, so why not cheap TV's? Eldon thought.

Dougie looked no more skilled in business than he did in music. You didn't need an M.B.A. to get cheap TV sets through means other than retail.

"Where's home?" Eldon asked Ahmed.

"Jakarta. We carry chips back to Japan, sometimes Hong Kong."

"Get in to port here often?"

"Once a month, man."

Eldon turned to the girl. "You're going to sail with him, Stephanie?"

"Oh, no! I'll wait for him!"

"What about your honeymoon?"

"Ahmed doesn't sail for three days. It's hard to wait for a guy, but if you love him, you're gonna do it."

It might not have to come to that, Eldon thought. Now that Ahmed had married a United States citizen, the tall sailor might quickly embrace a new career ashore, possibly in stolen TV sets. The story possibilities glowed. Here was a buzzard subculture that serviced the carnal needs of the ships when they came into port—sluts, dope dealers, petty smugglers, odd-jobber down-

and-outers who replenished their numbers from among their customers. How to tie Nguyen Xuan into it?

This ship could be a ticket to the big time, Eldon thought
with sudden hope. I'll get myself an award for a big series and get
a job on a metro newspaper, maybe even on the *Oregonian* in
Portland.

He seized a champagne bottle and splashed full the nuptial
couple's glasses. "You must handle a lot of exotic goods."

"I make good money a lot of ways," Ahmed said.

"Can you latch on to a TV set for me?"

Ahmed swirled his champagne. "I don't think so."

"Nguyen Xuan thought you could get me one." Eldon was
betting that none of these illiterates had read the *Sun*.

Ahmed smiled. "I don't know this man."

"No? He used to sail on the *Star*. A Vietnamese. How about
my friend Tran Minh? You know him?"

"So . . . you know Tran?"

"I know a lot of people around here," Eldon said. He began
to sweat. These were cutthroats, not members of a church choir.
But the chaos around them excited Eldon as the sight of food
excited his appetite. He felt exhilarated, invincible.

"So maybe I do know Xuan," said Ahmed. "He runs his own
deals."

"I just want a TV."

"You are a reporter, man. You snoop."

"This is off the record. Honest. I'm just writing about your
wedding. A little favor in return, is all."

The crude hint of bribery struck a receptive chord in Stephanie. "Show him what you can do, Ahmed honey. For me." It was
almost a taunt. Ahmed smiled greedily at his bride as she swayed
against him, their eyes shining.

"What kind of set you want?" Ahmed asked.

"A color portable."

"I can get you any kind of set. Two hundred."

"For a used portable? What d'you take me for?"

"Okay. One hundred bucks."

"Fifty, tops," Eldon said.

"Okay, fifty. It's a real good set."

"Done," Eldon said.

"Okay, give me the money."

"When I get the set."

"We talk about that later."

"We'll talk about the money later, too," Eldon said.

Stephanie giggled. "You're just like Xuan."

"Flattered," Eldon said, winking. "Known him long?"

"A couple of years, I guess."

Eldon nodded. "Xuan's had a hard time lately."

"Well"—music reached a blaring crescendo as she spoke a name—"ran him off, and I thought they had an arrangement," Stephanie said.

"I hear he's a mean bastard," Eldon said. "What did you say his name was? Ever met him?"

"Only a few people have met him," Stephanie said. "Xuan. And Dougie. And what's-her-name, that red-haired chick."

Ahmed hissed. "Shut up."

The bride shrugged, drank champagne. "When will my story be in the paper?"

"In the near future," Eldon said. "Every time I promise someone a specific date, I get screwed."

"After the story, the TV set," Stephanie said. "I never expected to grow up and marry a cook on an Indonesian merchant ship. My shoes . . . do you know where my shoes are?"

"I'll look for them," Eldon said. He moved away through the crowd and got another big cup of beer, then strolled forward.

Once away from the music, Eldon threw away his makeshift earplugs and heard the dull rumble of compressors in the forward holds. The rest of the ship was dark. Wood chips were being loaded even as the celebration progressed. The air smelled of salt water, machine oil, and pulverized wood. Long, pleated canvas conduits, shining with rain, swung over the side, slowly sucking up a ridge of chips by the pier.

Eldon took a swig of beer and stepped through an open hatchway. The clean white corridor within was silent and empty. He descended a metal stairway to the next deck, saw no one. Eldon climbed down the next stairway and the next. Down near the waterline, he found the crew quarters, illuminated two-man cabins along a corridor surprisingly wide and high. The vessel was becoming larger as Eldon descended. A hidden capaciousness was folded into the hull.

The cabin doors were open, the tidy cabins deserted. Over

the muted rumble of the pumps, a radio chattered like a distant monkey. A red-haired woman clad in a bathrobe stood in one of the doorways, looking absently into the corridor as she smoked a cigarette: Marie.

Eldon strolled down the corridor and said over the pounding of his heart, "Gotcha."

Color drained from Marie's face. Eldon had never seen that before. Marie actually turned two shades lighter, as if pale paint had surfaced beneath her skin.

"What're *you* doing here?" she said.

"Covering the wedding. You and I didn't get to finish our conversation."

"You got called away on business," Marie said with a taunting smile.

"What brings you aboard tonight? Taming the beasts of Asia?"

"I'm a friend of the bride," Marie said.

"You also were a friend of Nguyen Xuan's."

"Who told you that?"

"You knew his hometown."

"All right, so I knew him."

"Why'd you try to make me think otherwise?"

"Who wants something like that in the paper? It could hurt my animal business. That's all it was."

"That's not all it was. Xuan was clobbered and pushed under the elephant."

"Peake had it in for him from the first," Marie said nervously. "You saw how Peake is. A maniac."

"So Peake threw Xuan to the elephant?"

"Peake was capable of anything; you saw him hang the elephant, for God's sake."

"Why was he after Xuan?"

"Xuan stole some money. Some petty cash."

"Peake killed him over that?"

"That's what I think."

"Have you told the cops?"

Marie smiled slowly, her stare completely opaque. "No comment."

Goose pimples pranced across Eldon's skin. You're teasing a cobra, he thought. But he enjoyed getting people on the ropes—

no doubt about that. "Don't you know the guy who bought the Patterson place up in Muskrat?"

A shudder ran through Marie's features. "You're sniffing where you shouldn't, you fat fool."

"Fat, maybe, but not such a fool . . . even if I did buy the drinks. There'll be too many questions for comfort if some elephant steps on *me*."

"You're strong," Marie said as if by rote. She looked off over Eldon's shoulder. "I don't know anything about it. It was Peake."

"How I figure it, Xuan stiffed somebody on some stolen goods he was fencing and got stiffed in return. Am I right?"

"Things got out of hand," Marie said.

A heavy hand fell on Eldon's shoulder. He whirled around, backing into Marie. She shoved him into the arms of two men in rubber gorilla masks.

"You bother the lady, huh?" the bigger one said.

Gold teeth glinted behind the air slit in the mask's grinning rubber mouth. The cook. The smaller man was Dougie; Eldon saw the spiderwebbed elbows. He squawked and lurched to escape, but the smaller man drove his fist into Eldon's stomach. He struck again as Eldon doubled over gasping. Another blow, this one glancing off Eldon's camera. Eldon punched back as he gasped for wind. He broke for the stairs, swinging wildly in a haze of pain. The bigger man punched Eldon in the mouth, a glancing blow that split his lip. Spitting blood, Eldon scrabbled up the ladder, camera slamming against the rungs. The big man grabbed Eldon's ankle. Eldon freed himself with a kick to the masked face, and the man crashed down the ladder.

Eldon ran, yelling in panic, through hatchways, down corridors, up ladders. His body and mind were disconnected, the body working like some engine in a dream. He burst out into the cold air on deck and ran for the gangplank. He tumbled down the wet ramp, screaming for help and clumsily shielding his camera as he rolled.

He hit the wet dock and sat up, dazed. Figures ran toward him out of the darkness. There was a burst of sirens and red and blue lights. Weakly, Eldon raised his fists, saw the glint of a badge on a peaked hat. Cops.

"It's Eldon Larkin," one of them said. "What the hell?"

Sheriff's deputies in brown and blue-clad state troopers in

Smokey the Bear hats hurried past him and up the gangplank. The party music shut off abruptly.

A face shoved itself into Eldon's field of vision: Art Nola. "Hi, Art," Eldon said painfully.

"Just take it easy. Sit still," Nola said with professional calm. "We'll get an ambulance."

"Don't need one."

"Just sit still. Who jumped you?"

"I know who, but they had masks on. I won't be able to identify them in court." He began to cry. "Art, these guys are fencing stolen stuff, TV sets and like that."

"I know."

"You know?"

"I'm at least as good a cop as you are a reporter," Nola said gently.

"Marie, the red-haired woman. I think she killed Nguyen Xuan. Pushed him under the elephant."

"We'll pick her up in just a minute. Here's a clean handkerchief."

"Thank you." Eldon blotted his lip. He tasted blood and, abruptly, bile but swallowed them. "You know about her? Why didn't you arrest her before?"

"Two birds with one stone. And we had to wait for a warrant to go aboard ship. Extraterritorial."

"My mouth really hurts."

"Do you think you can stand up?" Nola asked. "Can you make it up the gangplank and try to identify the people who hit you?"

"I'll try. I want to testify on those bastards." Eldon tried to show bravado as Nola helped him up. "This is a great story, Art."

"You deserve to get it," Nola said to Eldon's surprise. "I guess I tempted you into it when I told you about the elephant at Huey's. I should've known you wouldn't let it rest there, though."

They climbed the gangplank, Eldon wobbling on Nola's arm. The party guests milled unhappily on the afterdeck as deputies questioned them and allowed a few to leave the ship. Eldon scanned the crowd for Dougie and the Malay cook. A state trooper came up from below decks and spoke quietly to Nola.

Nola whistled. "I'll have Larkin here take a look, just to be sure. Eldon, come with me."

He steered Eldon through the hatchway. They descended to the crew's quarters, where policemen crowded the corridor. Instinctively, Eldon checked his camera.

"Just hold off on that for a minute," Nola said quietly. "I want you to look in that room and tell me if that's Marie Payne."

"What—?" Eldon stepped to the hatch. A state trooper was shooting flash photos, and the strobe dazzled Eldon. His startled eyes could not analyze the scene, although he had seen its like many times. He picked out objects and identified them singly in the glare of the overhead light: a chair knocked askew, an overturned reading lamp, clothes on the floor and on the rumpled bunk. On the wall, all the way around the wall, were bloody handprints. Someone terribly wounded had groped for escape. Handprints decorated the cabin like prehistoric art.

The bloody images led down the wall to a bright splash of blood, and so Eldon could not avoid studying the final object in the cabin. He felt his mouth go dry and his throat constrict. His battered stomach contracted and his bowels almost squirted. He was not supposed to react like this—but he could not help it. He had not known any of the other corpses he had seen. The object on the cabin floor was Marie Payne, staring at the ceiling, with her bathrobe askew and fists clenched, staring past the bastard file shoved deep into her right eye.

6 Eldon passed his tongue over his bruised lips, winced, and whipped the fly rod. He imagined hitting Dougie with a hammer as the fishing line, hand-tied fly at its tip, unfurled across his sunny lawn toward the red plastic cup. He had never cast truer, but the line overshot into the tangled salmonberry bushes at the lawn's edge.

"Damn." Eldon rearranged his floppy fishing hat and limped forward, slowly reeling up the snagged line. He was pretty stiff today, but the cast had been perfect. Had the cup been Dougie, he'd have put the hook right into the ugly bastard's eye.

He had tried to relax that morning by resuming *Journey to the End of the Night*. He had closed the book with a shudder:

> . . . They were in each other's arms and would continue the
> embrace for ever, but the cavalryman hadn't his head anymore,
> only his neck open at the top with blood bubbling in it like stew
> in a pot. . . .

Reading the French had made Eldon think of Tran Minh, and Tran Minh had made him think of Nguyen Xuan and the dangling elephant, and that had made him think of last night and Marie Payne with the file rammed through her eye.

Eldon thrust out a hand, palm down. Steady as a rock. He freed the line from the brush, trudged back to his place, and cast again. Right through the old keyhole! And right into the bushes.

Fretfully, he touched his hat for luck. It was a floppy army jungle hat, studded with fishing flies. He wished he'd been wearing it last night on the ship.

Maybe his breathing was off.

I'm lucky to be breathing at all, Eldon thought, freeing the line to cast once more. This time, he was very careful to keep his back cast and fore cast aligned. Straight line for the power stroke—textbook stuff.

The cast shot off at an angle as Eldon imagined kicking the gold-toothed cook in the teeth. Just the way Eldon had been punched in the teeth. One of his front teeth was loose. What if he had to get a denture? He felt a twinge of fear. He hated dentists.

Dougie and the cook had been gone when the cops stormed through the ship. Apparently, they'd jumped overboard. A search of the waterfront had turned up nothing. Probably, the killers were well out of the state by now—but suppose they lurked in the woods, sweating in their rubber masks, waiting to finish him off?

He looked around uneasily. The masks had been a nice touch, really—*good copy* for the lead of the story he had painfully dictated to Fiske over the phone from the emergency ward.

> PORT JEROME—Two thugs in gorilla masks killed a Newport woman suspected of murder and beat up a *South Coast Sun* reporter Wednesday night during a wild nuptial party aboard a ship docked in Nekaemas Bay. . . .

Fiske, roused at home, was delighted. "This is the busiest week since lightning hit Lyman Dunthorpe's car with him and the topless librarian inside. Both of 'em drunk as skunks in the backseat. We ran it front page. Lyman insisted. He was all newsman."

"Jimbo . . . there's more."

"So give. We'll follow up in the morning. That librarian had quite a top. Dunthorpe's wife divorced him, and we ran every word of the divorce proceedings, too."

"You've told me. New 'graph: 'Slain was Marie Payne, an animal trainer who was a guest at the wedding aboard the freighter *Orient Star*. She was stabbed through the eye with a metal file—'"

"The looker who strung up the elephant? *Good copy!*"

"'Police said that Payne was about to be arrested in connection with the murder of Nguyen Xuan of Muskrat, a 34-year-old roustabout who was trampled to death by an elephant at the circus where he and Payne worked. Xuan's death previously was thought to be accidental, but Nekaemas County sheriff's deputies said that—'"

"Hang on, hang on, lemme get to my typewriter. The wife's at church. I'm sittin' home with five-fingered Rosie. You're beat up, you say?"

"Yeah."

"You don't have to come in tomorrow. The carpet around your desk is still kind of wet."

Afterward, Eldon had thrown up. His injuries were limited to cuts, bruises, and lumps. "You've escaped a concussion," the doctor had said, awarding him an ice bag like a shapeless cold prize.

Now he realized why the mill workers slugged it out so tirelessly every night in the bars. They fought to recoup every low blow they'd suffered, overlooking those they'd happily dealt, except that flesh and bone caved in, and spirit with it. If you're smart, you realize that early, Eldon thought, and run like hell.

So he had run like hell, right off the ship. Now what? How could he face Shelly? Nola had seen him cry. I didn't do so good, Eldon thought, casting. The line fell short.

Eldon squinted at the red cup. His eyes ached from the beating and from uneasy sleep. Once, he had met an old fisherman on the Rogue River who had shown off his "Zen cast." Insanity: The old man broke the cardinal rule of keeping one's eye on the target; the point was, he told Eldon, not to try too hard. Trying made the target *something else*, and everything was one thing. Therefore, the fly was connected to the target. You gave a fast unerring glance and made your cast.

The old fisherman had thrown both arms wide, whipping his rod back as if to hack off a head with a saber. The old man had rolled his gooseberry eyes across heaven and pivoted gracefully into classic casting position to complete the forward motion. His wrist had snapped with precision, and the fly had traveled thirty yards, landing lightly in water rich with trout for an instant strike.

Eldon shut off the memory. He glanced at the red cup, rolled his head back fiercely enough to feel neck vertebrae crack, and let fly. His back cast went wild like a tyro's. He turned to see the fly snagged on his Citroën, the line looped through the grass.

That goddamn car. A sympathetic deputy had driven it here while Fiske had picked up Eldon at the hospital. At least he could flee if the killers came—if the car started.

Whatever the wire service pays, no story is worth your life, Eldon thought. Except that you're not up here playing newspaper. You told Shelly that yourself. The only thing to do is get out there and start making noises like a reporter.

Running away wouldn't make such *good copy:* Reporter flees into the rainy north woods. . . . There was nowhere to go. The threads were tangled like his fishing line—Nguyen Xuan, Marie, Tran Minh, Dougie, and maybe even the Muskrat refugees were all connected in some evil network, tantalizingly unglimpsed, like Pugh's flying saucers.

He'd pull the court file on the *Orient Star* search warrant. It would list everything and everyone the cops were looking for. Eldon put the rod in the house, got his notebook, and paused to gulp a big spoonful of ice cream.

When he went out and tried to start the car, however, the Citroën was inert. Naturally. If the killers do come, my only defense is to ask for an interview, he thought bitterly.

Eldon climbed out and slowly pushed the car backward into the street. With awkward twists of the steering wheel, he got the ancient wreck aimed downhill on the graveled back road that dropped to the flats. The car began to roll. Eldon jumped inside, puffing as stones rattled like bullets against the floor pan. He thumped the gas pedal, twisted the key. No luck. The Citroën picked up speed, the door flapping like a wing. Eldon grabbed after it; a gust of wind lifted his lucky hat from his head.

The hat cartwheeled along beside the car. He tromped the brake, cursing, but dared not stop. Slowing the Citroën's roll, Eldon leaned down and snatched the hat from the road. A fishhook drove into his palm. He yelped and steered as he worked the fishhook free. The engine snarled awake. The Citroën hit a vast mud puddle. Eldon slammed the door as the car hydroplaned through the brown water. He stopped smoothly at the foot of the hill, the car streaming water, its engine running steadily.

Eldon grinned. He was bruised, out of breath, and covered with mud. Last night, he nearly had been murdered. But his car was running and his hat was safe. He was after a great story.

He felt pretty good.

"Been fishin', Eldon?" Fiske asked when Eldon tramped through the front door of the *Sun*. "You fall in the water?"

Eldon surveyed the office, squishing his feet on the still-soggy carpet. All around the room, people were whispering about him. In the news department, Marsha Cox sniffed and goggled at him over her typewriter like an appalled bird.

"I was practicing my fly casting," Eldon said.

Fiske reached for his pipe. "You've got on your lucky fishing hat, all right."

"I'm going to wear it from now on."

"Good," said Fiske. "How d'you feel?"

"Lucky. And kind of old, I guess."

"Don't you want to take another day?"

"I'm all right. This is one hell of a story."

"You're a good man, Eldon. We've been getting all kinds of calls for you; but I told them I didn't think you'd be in."

"Calls? About my murder story?"

"No, about you 'hanging the elephant' the other day," Fiske said.

"'Bad taste,'" Marsha said with a sneer. She was one woman Eldon had never desired.

"I didn't do it, I only reported it," Eldon said. "Can't they read? I didn't even take the picture."

"Reminds me of when I was a reporter," Fiske said. "I took a picture once of a big old hog that was hit by a truck. It must've been in '62—"

"I've got some ideas about this murder story," Eldon said.

"I was going to talk to you about that. Give 'em to Frank," Fiske said.

"I have to make some calls. But I'll get with him."

"No, just fill him in and forget it. You're off the story."

"But I'm okay. I'll take it easy, work at my desk."

Fiske nodded affably and lit his pipe. "Young Frank can get what we need through the police and courts. Think it through: For one thing, the grand jury will probably subpoena you, once they catch those studs. How're you gonna cover that? And you'll have to testify in court."

"This is big stuff. I think there's ties to—"

"You nearly got killed last night," Fiske said. "How're you going to be objective now? Answer me that. You can't."

Eldon was silent. His enthusiasm for the story flowered as much from an appetite for revenge as for achievement. Few reporters were above such feelings, though few admitted to them; but, of course, Jimbo knew.

"As long as you've come in today, I've got a good story for you," Fiske said. "You and Shelly go out to the boat basin and cover the Pioneer Days crab-eating contest."

"The crab-eating contest? Goddamn, Jimbo, do you want my resignation here and now?"

"Gee, you're pissy," Fiske said with mild wonder. "Pioneer Days is a big story around here. People eat it up."

"This is a community newspaper," Marsha said, "in case you've forgotten."

"We don't just hang pachyderms," Fiske said. "A fun feature is perfect recuperation for someone on the injured list . . . which you are on, Eldon."

"No, I'm not! This is a lot of crap."

"A lot of crab, you mean," said Fiske, smacking his lips and flashing ugly teeth. "Bring me back some. Jimbo needs vitamins."

"What about the follow-up on Nguyen Xuan's life? Does Frank get that story, too? There's a whole series just crying to be done on Vietnamese refugees in Muskrat. That's what I'm trying to tell you."

"Tell you what . . . keep the boat people as a long-term project. Take a month, do it right. But no more night visits to the wharf."

"All right." Eldon didn't want to argue anymore. "Where's Shelly?"

"Already at the boat basin. You'll find her. Have a good time." Fiske's pipe went out. As Eldon watched in horror, he knocked its smoking contents into the wastebasket next to his desk.

"This hog was the prize pet of a little eight-year-old 4-H girl," the editor said, "and the picture I took was of the hog busted open all over the road with the little girl mourning it. Had her 4-H hat on. This was as good as the elephant picture. The hog weighed eight hundred pounds, so that was about a hundred pounds for each year on the girl. It wrecked the truck—"

"*I'd* never take a picture like that," Marsha said.

"That's because you don't know good copy," Eldon said.

"I was a stringer for *Cosmopolitan*," Marsha said.

"So a couple weeks later—they always wait a couple of weeks—I get a call from an irate old lady," Fiske continued. "Wouldn't tell me her name, they never do. She says, 'You're the man who killed that poor pig. I hate you.' It was like you and the elephant, Eldon. Couldn't make her see the difference between the accident and the newspaper."

"It was in bad taste," Marsha said. "We shouldn't run pictures of corpses."

"We shouldn't run so many meeting stories," Eldon said.

"Eye of the beholder," Fiske said. "She mixed up the message and the messenger. The moral is, never mix up the messenger and the message." The wastebasket smoked faintly. Fiske edged it toward Marsha's desk with his foot. "Dee-de-dee. Now, Eldon, get down to the boat basin and see if you really think Dungeness crab is in bad taste."

"Be sure and remind Frank to pull the search-warrant file on the ship," Eldon said, smelling the smoke, and got out.

The crab-eating contest had yet to begin when Eldon reached the boat basin. It seemed as if half the population of Port Jerome, richly irrigated with beer, milled beneath a sky that again threatened rain. Eldon scanned the crowd. In the shallows, Cap'n Jasper, clutching a rubber duck, was trying to walk on water with barrel staves roped to his feet. Finalists in the log-rolling contest staggered on spinning logs, trying to remain upright. One by one, they pitched into the cold water. The last ruffian to fall was awarded a deep-sea fishing rod.

Shelly knelt on the pier, shooting the action through a zoom lens. Eldon's heart skipped when he saw her. Shelly had a fiery quality when she was at work, an absorption fierce and total. Those large solid buttocks packed into those jeans—a sexy combination, Eldon thought. Was she still angry with him? Well, the warrior had returned; he would shoot the moon.

Shelly looked up as Eldon strode down the pier. "My God, your mouth! They knocked out your teeth!"

Eldon brought a hand to his battered mouth. "Not quite, but they came close."

"Take your hand away and let me see," Shelly said. "You really got a beating—" Eldon forced a brave smile.

Shelly burst out laughing. "I'm . . . sorry . . . it's just that you—" she doubled over "—look . . . look . . . look like such . . . a *rube!*" She shrieked with laughter. "Grinning with all those bruises! And in that *hat!*"

"That's my lucky fishing hat."

Shelly's knees almost buckled. "I'm sorry, but you look so *funny!* Grinning at me like a *clown* who's been through *a washing machine!*" She clutched her sides, gasping, and at last gained composure.

"My mouth hurts," Eldon said.

"I'm sure it does. I read your story. Good story. I didn't like her—but how awful." Shelly leaned forward intently. "That guy Dougie really had tattoos on his elbows?"

"Surely they don't match your great-uncle Ogden's?"

"I was right, wasn't I? About Nguyen Xuan's death being more than an accident."

"You were right."

"Then we have a lot of work to do," Shelly said with satisfaction. "You're basically okay?"

"Basically. Fiske says we cover the crab-eating contest."

"I guess that's not exactly . . . your . . . *kind of contest today!* Oh . . . oh . . . God . . . I'm sorry. . . ."

"My front teeth are a really expensive root canal job," Eldon said as Shelly wiped her eyes. "Caps, too. Billy Vogel punched my lights out in third grade. My teeth went downhill from there." Eldon thought how he still would like to get Billy Vogel. "They did root canals. It hurt a lot. But later it kept me out of the army, oddly enough."

"Really? I can't imagine you . . . *in the army!*"

"People are staring."

Shelly took a deep breath. "I'm okay. Really."

"I'm glad you're okay. I could still lose my teeth."

"Don't be so sour, Eldon. This is the first crack I've seen in your damned tough-guy facade and I like it."

A chuck-wagon triangle clanged in the damp air, announcing the crab-eating competition. Spectators jostled toward the contest ring.

It was marked off with strings of soiled, drooping pennants. A score of contestants in the ring sat at picnic tables piled high with the South Coast's gourmet pride—fresh-cooked Dungeness crab, red-shelled, each crab the size of a small pie plate. The contestants included loggers, fishermen, an Indian, fat barmaids and hardware salesmen with wide Western sideburns. Eldon noted with interest that there was even a wiry little Vietnamese. The contestants donned paper bibs and fondled hammers, ready to smash the crab shells and gobble the succulent white meat. The goal was to outgorge one another. The prize was a new chain saw.

"Hey, there's Huey Bellows getting into the ring," Shelly said. "Small world."

Eldon pushed through the crowd to the ring's edge. "Huey! We've got to talk!"

Huey waved a hammer, expression bright as a clown's. "Eldon! Saw your story in the paper! It made a great read on the johnny, hee, hee! You're sure a good writer. But you took a pounding? You look pretty good; you're one tough sumbitch. I gave ya a good tip, huh?"

"You nearly got me killed."

Bellows' expression fell. "I just wanted t'give ya a chance to expose some petty crooks."

"You owe me one, Huey."

"Stick around, we'll talk. After I win this chain saw, that is. Wish me luck!"

Bellows grinned so eagerly that Eldon whipped off his hat and pulled a fishing fly from the olive green cloth. "Here's my luckiest one. Give 'em hell." He leaned across the rope and snagged the fly in Huey's baseball cap as the starting triangle clanged.

Twenty hammers slammed down. Crab shell and meat splashed. Huey and his rivals tore away shattered carapaces and stuffed handfuls of meat into their mouths. Their jaws worked, their cheeks swelled as the onlookers screamed, "Eat! Eat! Eat!" Fresh crab was dumped across the tables. Hammers kept slamming. The air was filled with flying bits of shell and meat.

"This is *gross*," said Shelly, rapidly shooting pictures. "How do they keep track of who eats the most?"

"They don't," Eldon said. "They eat until they drop."

"Disgusting! I'm getting great shots."

"I warned you about Nekaemas County."

"You can't dampen my enthusiasm," Shelly said. "I won't let you."

"Fiske took me off the murder story," Eldon said.

Shelly lowered her camera. "What? Why?"

"He doesn't want me to get killed," said Eldon, giving a hard-eyed squint.

"You're in danger? I hadn't thought of that."

"All part of the reporter's trade."

"They wouldn't really come after you?"

"We'll cross that bridge when we come to it," Eldon said. "Meanwhile, you're missing some good shots." I'm playing this just right, he thought. A few more tugs at her heartstrings and this sick man will enjoy a great convalescence.

"How're we going to cover the story, then?" Shelly asked.

"Fiske has turned it over to Frank Juliano."

"Oh, okay." To Eldon's dismay, Shelly immediately turned back to the ring, where contestants staggered from the tables, one after another. "Bellows is holding his own," Shelly said.

Huey hammered open crabs with his right hand and crunched the broken shells with his left, squeezing out crab meat and ramming it into his mouth. Shell and meat hung in his beard. Only Bellows and four other eaters remained. The triangle rang a breather.

Shelly clicked off zoom close-ups of the survivors.

Eldon did not know who would carry the day: Huey, flexing his wet hands and gasping like a landed fish? The Indian, wobbling slightly like a bronze statue on a faulty base? The round-faced cretin, grinning with vacant excitement, who smeared his hands over his pasty cheeks? The fat, red-faced barmaid, huge breasts wobbling beneath her stained pink T-shirt as she gulped air? Or the Vietnamese, sitting grimly erect, hammer clenched as if for some no-quarter assault?

The finalists tottered uncomfortably to a single table. Their pale faces were flecked with bits of crab, drool, and broken shell. Their eyes were like corks holding back enormous pressure. Crab was piled on. Pitilessly, the triangle clanged—sudden-death eat-off!

The Indian thumped a single shellfish with his hammer and worked his jaws, then toppled over, clutching his belly.

The cretin sputtered like a flooded lawn mower as his fat hands shoveled meat. A big claw wedged into his mouth sideways and his round cheeks distended as if wrapped around a two-by-four. The cretin choked and went out for the count.

The barmaid couldn't breathe. She wept as she packed her mascara-smeared face with crab. There was crab in her lank bleached hair. Her eyes bulged with panic when the cretin choked.

The crowd chanted, "Eat, eat, eat."

"It's like a Roman circus," Shelly said.

"Don't worry, nobody dies," Eldon said.

"I bet you watch this every year."

"This year it pays off. I'm going to get a story out of Huey. And talk to that Vietnamese."

The barmaid spewed down the front of her T-shirt and staggered from the ring toward the ladies' toilet.

Huey and the Vietnamese faced each other across the littered table. The sun broke through the clouds, casting Huey's shadow long across the picnic table.

The Vietnamese no longer seemed elfin, but muscular. He adjusted his ragged bib and smiled at Huey: *"Máy bay. Whop-whop."*

Huey laughed as the triangle clanged and he swooped at the crab. As he ate, Huey fixed his eyes on the glittering chain saw displayed across the ring. The Vietnamese sat filmed with sweat, snapping his hammer and whirling meat into his smoothly working jaws. He looked only at his food.

The men ate carefully now, one crab at a time. Huey broke open a Dungeness, flourished and devoured it. The Vietnamese kept chewing. Huey battered open another crab, nearly dropping his hammer, and shoved the meat into his open mouth. His hat, decorated with Eldon's hand-tied fly, fell to the ground. Huey's eyes glazed over with pain. "Dropped my lucky charm. I am done."

With a roar, the crowd broke through the ropes and hoisted the Vietnamese to their shoulders. The prize chain saw was pushed up into his lap. The saw seemed as big as the man, who gripped it in triumph.

Eldon picked his way over to Bellows as Shelly rushed into the melee to shoot the winner's picture.

"Another victory for the Southeast Asians, who've come to this country and will do well," Huey said with a belch. "It comes from years of being hungry. I'd have licked him, though, if I hadn't dropped your lucky fishing fly. When you gave me that pretty little thing, I knew it was a good omen. A sign."

"Keep it," Eldon said. He found two whole crabs among the debris and thrust them in his coat pockets. "Do you know the guy who won? I want to talk to him."

"Know him? He's a friend of mine. I'll introduce you. I really am sorry about what happened on that ship . . . I never thought you'd get hurt."

"Thanks. Did you know Marie Payne?"

"The woman who got it through the eye? The one who hung the elephant? No."

"I went to the ship and tried to buy a hot television set. I told them Nguyen Xuan sent me. I went poking around below decks and got jumped. After that, Marie—"

Bellows whistled ruefully. "And did you get yourself a TV?"

"They referred me to Tran Minh. Tran's still dealing black . . . isn't he?"

"It don't take you long to count up the eggs, does it? It's true. People who do it usually like it and stick with it. Tough habit to break."

"Xuan was dealing in smuggled and stolen goods, too. Or didn't you think I'd figure that out?"

"Sure, I did," Huey said. "Whatever you write, Tran has coming. But you gotta keep me out of it. I'm walking kind of a fine line with Art."

"Art Nola?"

"I'm a police contact . . . aw, the hell with that noise. I'm Art's stoolie."

7

"Don't lie to me," Eldon said. "I'll check everything you say."

"You'll find that it's only the truth," Bellows said. "Hand me my hat? It's hard to bend over."

Eldon tossed him the cap. He was fascinated by this new connection. He also felt a liking for the eccentric veteran, and he thought, You'd better put the kabosh on that. "Forget the fishing trip, Huey."

"Aw, don't be so pissed off."

"You nearly get me killed and I'm not supposed to be pissed off? Ever seen a woman with a file through her eye?"

"I saw worse than that in Nam, y'know. Art and I had a chuckle about him sendin' you off after the elephant, but that was as far as it went, honest. Art didn't know I told ya to go to the ship. He'd have my ass for that."

"He'd cut off your beer money, you mean. How much do you get for being a snitch?"

"Not a cent," Bellows said resentfully. "Art's my friend. This is service to my community. You think that just because you've got the power to write how things are, it makes you better. Well, it doesn't. Just because you *say* how things are, it doesn't mean you *know* how things are. That's a fact."

"So what are the facts?"

Bellows let go a colossal fart. "It's a matter of religion. Let's get a brew. Beer will settle my stomach."

They made their way slowly from the ring. Huey set course for the Dead Man's Hand, a tavern on the sheltered cove where the shrimp and salmon boats put in. The Dead Man's Hand was named for a corpse that had floated into the cove clutching a beer can. Eldon would have preferred the nameless café where he had taken Fiske's call about Nguyen Xuan—it was not as rough, and he wanted chowder.

"When I got back from Nam, I had what you might call a bad

attitude," Bellows said. "I couldn't hold a job. No woman in my life. I took to the road and for a time found comfort in the wonderful weed."

"Um." Marijuana was a vice Eldon had left behind in Berkeley with so much else. His predecessor on the staff of the *Sun* had missed out on good police stories because he had hung out with dopers too openly. So Eldon had never replenished the single lid he had brought with him from California.

"I drifted here and supported myself with a little growing and dealing . . . there wasn't much work, even then," Bellows said. "One of my customers was the reporter you replaced. Matter of fact, that's how I became a loyal *Sun* reader. I swapped him some joints for a trial subscription. As you can tell, I was strictly small-time."

"Where did you grow it?"

"I had a few plants back in the trees. Easy to hide . . . the woods are thick, and there were fewer people around here then. Nola was the Muskrat patrol deputy. He tracked me down."

"Good old Br'er Fox."

"He's as good as some of the trackers we had in Nam. Keeps his nose to the ground till he finds." Huey added, "He got me off with probation."

"Art did that?"

"He's not as hard a man as he might seem," Huey said. "You see, he had a vision once himself. God told him in a dream when he was a boy that he would grow up to be a cop. Art's church thumps and spouts a little more than I'm into, but he appreciated my holy whorehouse visitation."

Eldon nodded. Evangelical sects infected the South Coast. Weird shouter creeds won ready purchase and mutated wildly in the isolation. Pugh's one-man tobacco-can cult was only an extreme example. Nola's sect sounded as if it lay in the middle of the Nekaemas County spectrum.

"What's your persuasion?" Huey asked as they reached the Dead Man's Hand.

"I'm Catholic," Eldon said. "I haven't been to Mass in years."

"Art's not strict in his brand of observance, either. But when I told him about God's hand, he helped me get back on solid ground. We became friends like Providence wanted. When the

Vietnamese came, I started helping Art out with information . . . there are a few bad apples like Tran among 'em, like with anyone else, and I hate to see bad things happen to the good people."

They entered the Dead Man's Hand. The air of dissatisfaction in the tavern was as thick as the cigarette smoke—fishing was poor this season. Fishermen and unemployed mill workers lined the bar, where an enormous, hatchet-nosed Finn was bellowing a joke about cutting off a dick with a chain saw.

They got two beers and found a table by a window.

"I thought Tran Minh was your friend," Eldon said.

"Maybe he was, in another country. But he's too damn arrogant for me now. Tran's building a business fencing stolen goods. He gets a little money, a little biz, and lords it over the other refugees like a little god, like the U.S.A. did in Vietnam."

"Why hasn't Tran been busted?"

"It's like discovering a spy. You eliminate him, you got nothin'."

"Better to leave him in place."

"Right. Tran leads us to a lot of other guys . . . thieves, dopers, and the like. Sometimes, Tran even throws Art a fish himself. Someone who's doin' too many burglaries or sellin' dope to grade-school kids. Tran knows what Art likes."

"This is a mighty small area to support a crime lord," Eldon said. "But then . . . Marie said something about dope."

"You *do* get a lot out of people, don't you?" Huey marveled. Eldon smiled. Huey said, "Your mouth looks like hell. Just a few kilos comes in at a time, on the ships. From here it goes overland to Eugene and Portland. Tran's just a local jobber. It's small-time but big enough for him. His ticket to the big time, he thinks."

"So why do I see Tran carrying PVC pipe for a living?"

"To make ends meet, hee, hee," Huey said. "There's never enough work around here, even in crime. How Tran hates that, with his aristocratic airs!"

"I'd think opium would be a growth industry."

"That's just it. Port Jerome is too isolated a place to bring opium in, to any profit. Soon it won't come in here at all. Not enough ships call here anymore."

"Where's the opium hidden on the ships?"

"In the interhull. You can get in between the hulls below decks. That's probably what those two goons who jumped you thought you were snooping after."

"But why did they kill Marie Payne?" Eldon asked. "She knew those two; she shoved me right into their arms. And why did she kill Xuan in the first place?"

"That beats me, Eldon. I've been tryin' to figure that out since I read your story. Listen. Tran Minh and Xuan recently had a beef of some sort. I don't know about what—"

"Do you think Xuan chiseled drug money somehow?"

"Might be, might be. But having someone killed is a little stiff, even for Tran. Somehow, I don't think he had a hand in it. The two that killed the woman must've done her to cover their own tracks."

"Well, they've only attracted unseemly attention. Where's that leave Tran?"

"Tran's scared. He's going to have to fall back on fencing those ugly lamps you find in mobile homes . . . a big cut in income. Eventually, he'll outlast his usefulness." Bellows shrugged. "Maybe Art'll tell him to leave town, let him move on as a payoff for holding up his end."

"Maybe so." Raindrops spattered the window. Eldon looked through the glass to see Shelly approaching with the Vietnamese who had won the crab-eating contest. They lugged the prize chain saw between them.

"That's my friend Truong Van Vinh," Huey said. "He's clean as they come . . . nothing like Tran Minh. His English is lots better, too."

"What was that he called you out there?"

"*Máy bay?* That's just Vietnamese for airplane. We used to add on "whop-whop" in the army to mean a helicopter. A Huey's a kind of helicopter. It's a joke on my name, see? I told you his English was pretty good."

Shelly and Truong Van Vinh struggled through the door. The drinkers at the bar hooted and wolf-whistled, egged on by the huge Finn.

"Take your boyfriend back out in the rain!" the Finn called as Truong clunked the chain saw onto the table.

"Ignore that," Huey said.

"How are you, Huey?" Truong asked in English crisp as fresh paper. "One more bite of crab and I think I'd have dropped."

"I'm kind of full myself," Huey said with a grin. "Here's a friend of mine wants to talk to you, Eldon Larkin from the newspaper."

"Ah. Shelly Sherwood has taken my picture."

"How'd you manage to eat all that crab?" Eldon asked.

"Easily. I skipped two meals. You should have thought of that, Huey."

"Well, you need the saw more than I do."

"It will help support my family," said Truong. "I can sell firewood. I have a wife and three children. I work in the mills and on the fishing boats when I can. There is not much work now, though. Do you know a source of jute, by the way?"

"Jute?" said Eldon.

"No? My wife ties macrame for sale in Eugene. But there's not much work for her, either. The bottom has fallen out of the macramé market. This chain saw is a boon."

"I want to write about the Vietnamese here, tell their story," Eldon said. "Your winning the crab-eating contest is a good angle to lead off the series . . . your fitting into South Coast life."

"Fitting in is not so easy," said Truong, glancing toward the bar. "I read about the murders. And about the hanging elephant." Truong shook his head. "This is not a good thing for us."

"Was Nguyen Xuan a friend of yours?" Eldon asked.

"Once, I thought that any countryman is a friend, this far from home," Truong said. "But we must accept that *you* are our countrymen now. There is no going back to Vietnam."

"You talk like an educated man," Eldon said. "Why do you stay in this backwater port?"

"I am an architect but not yet certified in this country. I like living by the sea and . . . I feel responsible."

"For the refugees?"

"Yes. Not all are as well equipped for America as I." Truong smiled as Eldon jotted notes. "I *have* had a little architectural work, actually. I helped an old gentleman raise a geodesic dome."

"That's Pugh!" Shelly said. "We know him. Have you seen his chest?"

"Pardon?" asked Truong.

"Does he have tattoos?"

"I don't know," Truong said, bemused. "He never took off his shirt . . . wait, I did glimpse one, near the collar. A flower, perhaps. Quite faded."

"How did you come to this country?" Eldon asked as Shelly's eyes widened.

"I was stationed in Saigon," Truong said. "I managed to get my family on a plane to Guam just as the communists came." Truong looked out the window at something far beyond the misty scrim of trees. "That was . . . like being rolled around in a hot oil drum in hell. I could not find two of my five children that day. I left them behind in Vietnam."

"And from Guam you came here?"

"A church sponsored us. Would you like to see pictures of my family?" Truong got out his wallet. "Here is my wife, My, with our children."

"Only three," Shelly said.

"I have only these old pictures of the other two, taken in Vietnam. They must be getting big! One day . . ."

Eldon wondered how his ex, Bernice, looked now—whether she had gained or lost weight or still wore that gray sweater or had cut her hair. Eldon had gained thirty pounds since leaving Berkeley.

Eldon questioned Truong: who, what, when, where, why, and how. Names and ages of the kids, spell the names please. What did you think when you first saw America? When did you get to Oregon? It went like clockwork. Eldon found that his handwriting was jagged; writing with the ball-point pen was like holding a live wire. Excitement at following the story, delayed reaction to Marie Payne's death, and an irrational fear of meeting up with her killers, all were mounting up inside.

"What surprised you most about Port Jerome?" Eldon asked.

"That it is so familiar," Truong said after a moment. "People have jobs, homes, families. They hope to achieve things. They work all day and relax in the evenings, as in Vietnam or anywhere. . . . Yet it has the brightness of a strange place."

"I know that brightness," Eldon said.

"Then you know what having a friend in a strange place means," Truong said. "Huey here has been a true friend."

"If only I hadn't dropped Eldon's lucky fishing fly!" Huey said.

"You Americans are superstitious," Truong said with a laugh.

"Yeah?" Huey said. "What's that religion in Vietnam, worships Mickey Mantle? *Cao dai?* And what about that lucky charm I made for My? She was happy to have it."

"As a matter of fact, it's right here around my neck," Truong said, pulling an amulet from his shirt. "She insisted I wear it. I think it's why I won the contest, but I didn't want to tell you."

"See?" Huey said with glee. "You're an American, too!"

Eldon stared at the amulet, a metal ring enclosing a green glass butterfly. Green glass. "Where do you get your materials, Huey?"

"For this? I don't remember. I use a lot of scrap."

"Ever make one for Nguyen Xuan?"

"Hell, no. My only regret is that I don't get to make that bastard's coffin. Why?"

"There was glass like this around Xuan's body."

"Beats me."

We'll assume you're telling the truth—for now, Eldon thought, while at the bar the drinkers sought after a sweatier truth. The Finn and another man arm-wrestled, biceps bulging, faces red, knuckles blue. For long seconds, neither gave an inch. Suddenly, the Finn slammed his rival's hand to the bartop and ground the knuckles in. The loser's scream was lost in the onlookers' cheers. The Finn swilled a toast to himself from a beer pitcher and poured the rest over his rival's bowed head.

"The people around here must've come in flying saucers," Shelly said.

"What is the term, please?" Truong asked.

"Ships from other planets," Shelly said. "Pugh believes in flying saucers."

"Oh, that old man is always talking to himself while he digs in his rubbish piles," Truong said.

"Has he ever said anything about his past?" Shelly said. "Anything about being in the movies?"

"Pugh in the movies?" Huey said. "Haw, that's good!"

"It was strange, the way I met him," Truong said. "I was walking down to the highway one day to hitchhike into Port Jerome and look for work. Suddenly, he was there beside me, wearing a very odd hat. 'You want a job?' he asked. I was startled; it was as if he had come out of thin air."

"He knows the woods like the back of his hand," Huey said. "He has rabbit trails all over the place."

"He asked me if I wanted work," Truong said. "And that's how I helped him build that dome."

"Strange project," Eldon said.

"The strangest thing was his cap. It's hard to describe. It was a fur cap with a . . . an animal's tail hanging down behind, very bushy. And a sort of badge on the front made of tinfoil."

"A coonskin cap!" Huey said. "He was playin' Daniel Boone."

"He said he was 'scouting,'" Truong said. "Something about getting ready for the 'Star Days.' Crazy."

"If you worked for Pugh, you must've worked with Tran Minh," Eldon said. "Tran Minh and Nguyen Xuan had a quarrel—"

Truong's jaw closed tight. "These things are not well to speak of."

"*Không xâu*, Truong. Don't sweat it."

"I have three children here in Oregon," Truong said to Eldon. "I left two others behind in Vietnam. Do you know what that taught me? It taught me to protect what I have." He rose and lugged the chain saw off the table.

Truong turned to go, but the Finn blocked his way.

"My name's Paavo," the Finn said, sneering like a great white shark. "What's yours?"

"Excuse me. Please," Truong said, not flinching. He tried to step around the big man but staggered under the chain saw's weight.

"You scratched the table with your saw," Paavo said, playing to the house. "You take our work and take our women."

"I'm nobody's woman, asshole," Shelly said, to Eldon's horror.

That got a laugh from the whole bar. Paavo charged the table, eyes hard as marbles. Huey Bellows rose and threw a tremendous left-handed punch that broke Paavo's hatchet nose across his cheek at a right angle, like a gate. It sounded like a piece of kindling snapping. Vermilion blood shot from the Finn's skewed nostrils. The light in his eyes went out. "Did you see *that*?" Shelly said in amazement as Paavo toppled.

"Out!" the bartender shouted, waving a baseball bat.

"It's okay, Glenn," an awed drinker said, "Paavo messed with 'im."

"Yeah, just 'cause the little dink won the chain saw out there eatin' crabs," his companion said.

"They're tough little bastards," cried a third man. "Hung on like pit bulls at the A Shau Valley . . ."

The men along the bar nodded and murmured with satisfaction, like women at a church tea party discovering that the minister's wife smelled of gin. They were impressed. Life was a shit sandwich, but here was thick bread—the Finn himself, gurgling in a pool of blood.

Huey led Truong, Shelly, and Eldon from the tavern as the patrons of the Dead Man's Hand fell into a collective Vietnam flashback: Pleiku . . . An Khe . . . Con Thien . . . Tet. . . . The names were stitched in a vast mental tapestry. It was as if Truong, not Huey, had laid out Paavo.

Eldon's teeth chattered as he stepped across the Finn's twitching form. The emotional stops that had kept him calm since last night had broken with Paavo's nose. He felt chilled to the bone.

"That was exciting!" Shelly said breathlessly when they stood in the rain. "I never saw anything like it before. What a punch!"

"I thought we better get out of there while the rest of 'em were still on our side," Huey said, rubbing his knuckles. "Let's get out of the rain."

"I am going home," said Truong.

"The hell you are," Huey said. "I nearly broke my hand in there."

"I could've handled him."

"You want to do some good? Talk to Eldon here."

"I have talked."

"You want to see Tran Minh gone, don't you?"

Truong Van Vinh inclined his head by way of answer. They went across the graveled parking lot to the nameless café as Eldon tried to regain control of his jaws. Inside, Huey called for coffee and slid a big white mug across the table to Eldon. "Drink up. I've been cold that way, too."

"You really laid that big bastard out," Shelly said.

"Might not've had to do it if you'd kept your lip buttoned."

Shelly was unabashed. "What about Pugh's secret trails?"

"Who knows where all of them go?" Truong said. "But one of them leads down onto the Patterson place. That's where I saw Nguyen Xuan one day, fleeing."

The coffee had stopped Eldon's chattering teeth. "Fleeing?"

"From a large dog. This was when he was thrown off the ranch. I am telling you this as a favor to Huey. You did not hear this from me."

"That dog's likely the same nasty booger I clobbered," Huey said.

"There was a red-haired woman," Truong said. "The dog was snapping at Xuan's heels. The woman laughed as Xuan ran."

"That's the woman who murdered Nguyen Xuan," Eldon said. "And who was murdered herself last night aboard the *Orient Star*. Where did Xuan go?"

The Vietnamese hesitated. Huey said, "It's okay, Truong. I want to hear this, too. You can trust Eldon."

"Tran Minh met Xuan at the head of the path and took him to his house. I know nothing more. You do not ask questions of a man such as Tran Minh. But, yes, I would like to see him gone."

"Maybe Eldon can help us with that," Huey said.

"Don't get your hopes up," said Eldon. "I want to talk with other Vietnamese."

"To get them to denounce Tran Minh?" Truong shook his head. "They won't."

"I want them to tell their own stories. Tran's story will take care of itself."

"You'll get your chance," Huey said. "Tran's about played out his string. . . . Hee, hee . . . lookit! They're at it again in the Dead Man's Hand."

Through the café window, they could see that there was a commotion in the tavern. The reminiscences of war had bloomed into a battle of their own.

"I have talked enough," Truong said. He rose, got the chain saw onto his shoulder, and started for the door.

"I'll give you a lift home," Huey said.

"I hope this discussion was not a mistake," Truong said.

"We protect our sources," Shelly said.

"Your sources can take care of themselves," Huey said. "Tran doesn't mess with me because I told him *not to*. He won't mess with you, either, Truong, if you tell him the same."

"I prefer not to do things that way," Truong said.

"I'll make a couple of extra prints of you two stuffing yourselves at the crab feed," Shelly said.

Huey's face lit. "Wouldja? That'd be nice!"

The childlike gape unnerved Eldon. Bellows was like the South Coast's weather—somber one moment, sunny the next, with a streak of violence as potent as the breakers on the shore.

Huey and Truong left the café and started across the parking lot. The door of the Dead Man's Hand banged open and out staggered Paavo the Finn. His broken nose was packed with toilet paper; bloody white streamers hung down his chest like wilted pennants. He saw Huey and Truong and they him. Slowly, the Finn straightened his shoulders and saluted. Huey and Truong halted, returned the salute, walked on.

"Xuan and Marie together on the Patterson place," Eldon said, watching Huey and Truong trudge off into the rain.

"Running along a secret trail," Shelly said. "I say we go up and poke around. I've got to talk to Pugh."

"Stay away from there. There's groundwork I've got to do first. Leave Pugh be or the whole county'll know that the newspaper is getting interested."

"It's our job to be interested."

"You just better hope that Pugh's tattoo isn't in some outrageous location. Once I read a police report on a guy who had a rose tattooed on the tip of his—"

"Uncle Ogden had a rose tattooed on his chest."

"After that Tennessee Williams play, no doubt."

"Great-Uncle Ogden came a long time before Tennessee Williams. But he did play Daniel Boone in a silent movie. Or was it the Deerslayer?"

Eldon did not answer. A hollow sensation grew in the pit of his stomach as he turned the possibilities over in his mind. Vietnamese—drugs—murder. *Good copy.* If he survived to write it.

"I'm going back to the office and develop my film," Shelly said.

"Let's have some chowder."

"I can't."

Eldon thought of the crabs in his pockets. "Come on up to my place tonight. I'll make dinner."

"I've got plans."

"Oh? What?"

"Oh, plans." Shelly gave Eldon's shoulder a gentle push as she stood and grabbed her camera bag. "I'll take a rain check, though."

Sheriff's cars rumbled into the parking lot to suppress the ruckus in the Dead Man's Hand. Deputies emerged and matter-of-factly drew batons. Paavo wandered blindly away. Shelly stopped to shoot a photograph as Eldon looked miserably after her. Opium. Murder. Killers on the loose. Tonight above any other night he did not want to be alone.

I shouldn't have given that fishing fly to Huey, Eldon thought. It really *was* a lucky one, I just know it. I want it back. I need the luck.

The wall telephone rang. The waitress answered it and bayed Eldon's name. Fiske was on the line: "Eldon? Thought I'd find you there—"

"Yeah. Well, a Vietnamese won the crab-eating contest and there's a riot over at the Dead Man's Hand—"

"Chicken feed. We've got something *big*."

"I do, too."

"Not as big as this," said Fiske. "Bigfoot's been sighted in the woods!"

8 Fiske was in a frenzied state. Gone was the editor's usual calm out-to-lunch gaze. His eyes bugged and he paced about the newsroom. Beads of sweat stood out on his brow, and his hand clutched a garish-looking magazine. Fiske's mustache twitched as he talked around the pipe clenched in his teeth.

"A confirmed sighting, Eldon, or pretty near . . . up in the woods on the north side of the bay."

"Who saw it?"

"Ten-year-old kid comin' back from fishing. He saw a big thing like a man, covered with hair and ten feet tall."

"Sounds like a bear to me, Jimbo."

"No bears around here that are ten feet tall. Those are Kodiaks. All we've got here are leetle huckleberry bears . . . black bears, two hundred pounds, no more."

"That's right. They look like big dogs."

"That's why this has got to be a Sasquatch!" Fiske threw the magazine on Eldon's desk: *Sasquatch and UFO*. "The kid's description fits a recent Montana Bigfoot report to the letter."

"Maybe he reads *Sasquatch and UFO*. Where is this kid?"

"The report was phoned in from the Muskrat Store: possibly a Sasquatch . . . certainly tracks."

"The Muskrat Store? Someone's funnin' you, Jimbo! They're celebrating the festival up there and had a bunch to drink from Toby Wanker's still, is all."

Fiske's gaze grew shrewd. "Bigfoot discovered at the height of the Pioneer Days Festival . . . wouldn't that make *good copy*?"

"Oh, not me! I've got enough to do without chasing Bigfoot," Eldon said. "I'm wounded, remember?"

"Getting out in the country air will be good for you," Fiske said. "Young Frank can go along."

"I can do what?" Frank entered through the side door. His half-melted glasses, mended with tape, slid down his nose.

"Bigfoot hunt," Eldon said. "You're hired."

"No shit, bwana? You want interview?"

"If possible," Fiske said flatly.

Frank pushed up his glasses and stared at Fiske. "You're not kidding."

"No way. Bigfoot's been sighted above the bay," Fiske said. "Better take camping gear."

"Camping gear?" Eldon said.

"I know the chances of sighting Bigfoot are slim," Fiske said. "So I want you boys to spend the night in the woods, trolling for him—"

"It's *raining*!" Frank said.

"You won't melt. This way, you'll have a story whether you find Bigfoot or not."

"I've got calls to make about the murder," Frank said.

"It's Friday afternoon and the festival's on," said Fiske. "Everyone's closing up shop."

Eldon asked Frank, "Did you pull the search warrant on the ship? What were they after?"

"That's just it . . . the file is sealed."

Eldon whistled. "Hear that, Jimbo? That means an ongoing investigation, hot stuff!"

"Yeah, yeah," Fiske said. "Okay, Frank, call the sheriff and get some no-comment. Gimme a recap for Saturday; lead with the sealed file. Eldon, let's have your festival stuff. You boys are lucky we don't publish a Sunday paper, because you're still goin' out."

"Jimbo, c'mon!" Eldon said.

"You young guys have a lackadaisical attitude, not like in my day," Fiske said. "I remember my first Bigfoot. It was in '57, right after Sputnik. The whole country was hoppin' about UFOs, which are a bunch of nonsense, of course . . ."

Eldon pulled Frank aside and thrust his opened notebook at the younger reporter. "Just listen," Eldon said. "Look at my notes and nod. We're going camping, except that what we really do is spend the weekend at my place, laying low and drinking beer."

"And concocting a Sasquatch sighting. Gotcha."

"I want to brainstorm on this murder story. There's a drug angle now and it's tied in with the Vietnamese up in Muskrat. Did you pick up any rumors at the courthouse?"

"No. The lid's down tight."

"My story saying that Marie was thought to be Xuan's killer must have 'em hopping. Thanks for that tip."

"Don't get your hopes too high, Eldon. It might just be because those guys who jumped you are still at large."

Frank's glasses came apart and he scrambled after them, cursing.

". . . Bigfoot comes from the fourth dimension," Fiske was saying. "This woman told me how this accounts for his sudden appearances and disappearances as he pops in and out from the other dimension . . ."

Eldon nodded, ruffling through the pages of *Sasquatch and UFO*. A drawing of the purported Montana Bigfoot caught his eye. It appeared to have been executed by a dim child. Beside the drawing was a boxed ad.

UFO SIGNS & WONDERS
God sends signs and wonders for these times, like the Sasquatch
and the UFO. Why are they here? What have they come for?
When will they leave? It could jolt the criminal minds and
perhaps the whole world. The Star Days are upon us.

"Pugh!" Eldon said in disgust. The name made a good epithet. "I wonder if he paid for the ad." He glanced up and saw that the darkroom door was closed: Shelly was within.

"I want to take Shelly with me instead of Frank," Eldon said.

"I need Shelly here," Fiske said.

"Shelly's a better photographer than Frank. Suppose we find Bigfoot?"

"She's a better photographer than both of you. But you'll manage. I want her here for the Blessing of the Boats."

"That's not for a couple of days yet. What're you expecting us to do out there, build a cabin?"

"It wouldn't be proper sending a tender young gal out in the woods with you."

"I'm glad you still have faith in me, Jimbo," Eldon said with a smirk.

"Damn right. I know you'll get me something. So I'll send Shelly out to rendezvous with you and Frank and pick up your film."

Eldon banged on the darkroom door. At Shelly's muffled command, he entered and shut the door again. Shelly was readying the enlarger by the muted amber glow of the darkroom safety light. In the developing trays, prints drifted like harbor debris.

"I'm busy, Eldon," Shelly said. "I want to get these done so I can get out of here."

Quickly, Eldon sketched his plan to deceive Fiske. Shelly giggled. "He was waving that magazine when I came in," she said. "I see what you mean about Bigfoot."

"So you'll play along? The way I see it, our film just won't come out. You might as well drive over to my house on Saturday afternoon; we'll have beer and sandwiches." In the dim lighting, Eldon saw that misguided churchgoer's grin. "You'll save Frank and me from the mosquitoes. I'll owe you one."

"You bet you will." Shelly slipped a sheet of photographic paper under the enlarger's hinged frame. Eldon wanted to grab her in the darkness but instead drummed his itchy fingers on the countertop. The enlarger flashed on, connected to a ticking timer. On the framed paper appeared a scene of deputies and loggers struggling in front of the Dead Man's Hand.

"Good spot news," Eldon said.

"The composition could be better."

"So crop it. It's better than I could ever do. You shouldn't run yourself down. You've got a gift for photography. Me, I just try to snap the action."

"That's just it . . . I missed the moment," Shelly said. "It always disappears. Things always get past you." The timer buzzed and automatically shut off the enlarger. Shelly dropped the exposed paper into the developing tray. The amber safety light flicked on. Eldon watched as she sloshed the sheet around with tongs and finally flipped it into the stop bath.

"Let me show you something." Shelly fished another picture from the stop bath and placed it faceup in the rinsing tray. She switched on the overhead light. "Look."

"Pugh and his tinfoil rocket."

"Look at his neck, right by the shirt collar. I've studied it on the enlarger. It's a little bit of that rose tattoo."

"That's a shadow."

"You're always so damn cocksure."

"I know a wild-goose chase when I see one."

"Like Bigfoot?" Shelly asked. "I'll help you on one condition. You and I are going up to see Pugh again real soon."

"Okay," Eldon said with a sigh. "The old man does give work to the refugees. Maybe I can work him into my series."

"At least."

"Got your phone connected yet? I'll need your number in case I have to call you."

Shelly told him her number. "Now let me get back to work. I've got to leave soon."

"Have a nice time tonight," Eldon said, not too sourly, he hoped, and got out, holding the phone number in his mind like a squirrel clutching a nut.

". . . an old Injun left her near the cave," Fiske was telling Frank. "There are *lots* of caves in that area!"

Frank laughed, a little uncertainly.

"And this Injun didn't *have* a last name!" Fiske said, slapping his knee. "Dee-de-dee!" He saw Eldon. "D'ja get me some crab?"

Resignedly, Eldon dragged the Dungeness crabs from his coat and put them atop the Sasquatch magazine. Several legs had broken off in his pockets and Eldon dropped them on the desk.

"Yum, yum," Fiske said. "I can always tell when you've got somethin' in your pockets, Eldon. You and Frank finish up and roll. Photos of Bigfoot would put Port Jerome on the map. It's a chance for this town, don't you see?"

"How can you swallow this Bigfoot stuff?" Eldon asked.

"Maybe because anything's possible. I'm into the meta-physical."

There was nothing metaphysical about the takeout Chinese food that Eldon and Frank ate that night at Eldon's home. It had a clammy, all-too-concrete reality to it. A primitive sense of gratitude filled Eldon as he chewed the soggy egg roll. His house was intact. He would not have been surprised to find it ransacked, Marie Payne's killers waiting in the closet to finish him off.

"Too bad you had to give Fiske the crab; this food is really shit," Frank said as he devoured noodles from a carton. With his broken glasses, he looked like a shipwreck survivor hungrily chewing seaweed. "There are no good grits in Port Jerome. I'm going to show you how to cook in a wok. You ought to go to Eugene and buy a wok."

Eldon was annoyed by Frank's matter-of-factness. Frank could afford to chatter about woks; no one had tried to kill *him*. A trip to Eugene might be prudent, at that, Eldon thought. It would lower my profile around here. He tried to decide whether he could afford gasoline, let alone a motel.

"How long since you've taken a vacation?" Frank asked.

"I went fishing near Bend last spring."

"You always go fishing."

"I went to Berkeley last Thanksgiving. I should've gone fishing then, too. I looked up friends in Berkeley, from when I was married. They're still sitting around the coffeehouses. Maybe leaving Berkeley was good for me."

"You're doing a lot better than them," Frank said.

"I nearly got myself killed." Eldon couldn't fault Frank's optimism—he had worked for the *Sun* for just a year and was only twenty-four. Eldon enjoyed guiding him. Am I really nine years older? Eldon thought. Nine years was a long time. It made all the difference. He was filled with a fresh sense of helplessness, of going nowhere except toward death. He could go back to Berkeley and hide—but that would be another death.

Eldon pushed his worries aside and recounted his talks with Huey and Truong Van Vinh. "What was Xuan doing on the Patterson place? What was Marie doing there?"

"Good questions," Frank said. "Who bought the farm from old man Patterson, anyway?"

Eldon got his notebook and wrote, *Check county assessor's records re Patterson place. Who bought it?* "The county courthouse has deeds on new transactions. Damn, I hate waiting until Monday to find out about it."

"Is Patterson still around town?" Frank asked.

"Don't know."

"So let's call the ranch."

Having someone else suggest it made it easier to do. Eldon got the telephone directory. Among the Pattersons he found "Leslie Patterson," with a Muskrat-area exchange.

Eldon dialed the number. There were clicks, clangs, and hums as Port Jerome's Ma Bell telephone system punched through a connection to the antiquated equipment of the Greater Muskrat People's Rural Telephone Cooperative. "The number you have dialed has been disconnected," a twangy recorded voice chanted, "and there is no new number—"

Eldon hung up and dialed information. There was no new listing. Eldon wrote, *Les Patterson # disconnected*.

"I guess we ask around up there," Frank said.

"First, let's call another Patterson," Eldon said. "Likely it'll be a relative."

"Call Toby Wanker at the Muskrat Store," Frank said. "You'll have to, anyway, on account of Bigfoot. They know everything at the Muskrat Store. His wife's a Patterson, I think. I did that feature on Estelle's dahlias. Toby showed me his still."

"The still is the source of the Bigfoot sighting, I don't doubt." Eldon dialed the store. The telephone system roared and buzzed and clattered. It sounded as if there were cowbells on the line. The cacaphony kept up after Toby Wanker answered the phone, and Eldon realized that some sort of brawl was under way at the Muskrat Store.

"Buncha us celebratin' Pioneer Days with a few jars of mah best," Toby shouted. "It's Estelle an' me's am-niversary, too. Twenty-eight years! Pro wrasslin's on and it's sure good! 'Zat Eldon Larkin? Ya gotta speak up, Eldon, the telephones up this way sure are bad, haw, haw!" Toby was on the board of the telephone cooperative. "Bigfoot? Damned if I know . . . just a minute—" Toby's voice submerged in the general roar. Eldon heard laughter. "They say the tracks're up Allen Slope, on the way to the old cabin up there."

"Who saw them?"

"R. C. Getchell's boy, Garth. He got into some of mah best and called the paper, I guess. Then he passed out. R.C. hided him for it, but I doubt if Garth felt it. Lissen, Estelle sure liked that story you guys run 'bout her flowers. Anythin' we can do ta help ya, sing out."

"Is Estelle there?"

"Wanna say happy am-niversary? Jus' a minute. I'm savin' a jar of mah best for ya when ya get done huntin' Bigfoot, y'hear?"

Estelle Wanker had hiccups. It was like talking with a machine gun. Between bursts, Eldon learned that Les Patterson was Estelle's cousin and had sold the ranch to a man from Southern California.

"What's his name?" Eldon asked, straining to hear over the static and the howling of the wrestling fans. "Where was he from in California?"

"Hic-hic-hic . . . I don't know hic-hic!"

"Where can I get hold of your cousin?"

"Oh, you can't. Hic!"

"What?"

"Les got paid cash. Hic! I wouldn't know, hic! how much," Estelle said as the connection faded in and out, "but it was quite a lot . . . Les moved to Colom . . . hic! . . . bo."

"Do you have his number in Columbus?" Eldon yelled, wondering why anyone with a pile of cash would be fool enough to move to Ohio.

"Not Columbus! *Colombo!* Sri hic! Lanka! We got an anniversary card from him! Hic-hic-hic!"

Bingo, Eldon thought. He made Estelle recite her cousin's address, wished her a happy anniversary, and hung up. "Sri Lanka," he said with awe, rubbing his ringing ear. "Someone from Southern California bought the place with enough cash to let old man Patterson retire in Colombo, Sri Lanka."

"Let's call him!"

"Not on my phone. Fiske is too cheap to pay for the call. We could write, but we probably wouldn't get an answer for months."

"If ever. What's the buyer's name?"

"Didn't get it. But the deed records at the courthouse will have his name and address. It's just a matter of following the paper trail."

"Where's it going to lead?"

"Beats me. We've got two murders and a drug racket. And the victims were running around on that ranch. And there's that sealed file. And those secret trails."

"Maybe they have a Sasquatch imprisoned up there," Frank said. "Now, as long we're kicking back for the weekend, how about some of your famous ice cream and cognac?"

Eldon prepared the confection, at once elated and depressed. There was plenty to do. The conversation had taken his mind off the missing killers, but now the thought of them crept back again like ink seeping into the creases in his brain. Try as he might to persuade himself otherwise, Eldon felt—stalked.

Frank browsed the bookshelves. "Flaubert, Tolstoy, Huxley, William Burroughs, Durrell, medieval illuminations, the history of the Philadelphia yellow-fever outbreak. Kesey, Mailer. American Indian creation legends. George MacDonald Fraser. Suetonius. Hm! *Torture Instruments of the Middle Ages*, in English and French. Chandler, Cervantes, Dashiell Hammett . . . there are hundreds of books here. Have you read all these?"

"Most of 'em. I'm always behind," Eldon said, bringing in the dessert. "I started Céline so I wouldn't forget my French."

"We read Céline in school," Frank said. "In English, of course. Great stuff! Céline hates everything, the reading public, dogs, vegetables, doctors. . . . He trusts nobody. Céline should've lived in Port Jerome. He'd fit right in."

"I'm reading *Voyage au Bout de la Nuit*," Eldon said. "*Journey to the End of the Night*. It's about a Robinson Crusoe of the modern soul. Adrift in the modern age. He comes to no good."

"Sounds like you." Frank regarded Eldon seriously. "You ought to find a better job. You have five years' experience; plenty of papers would hire you."

"The fishing's too good here," Eldon said. "There's something about being out on the water. People and their problems are far away. It rejuvenates me."

"Maybe Shelly Sherwood will rejuvenate you. Clearly you lust for her. Good luck."

"So I like chunky girls. Any objections?"

"You like *any* girls, Eldon. Shelly's okay, but she seems kind of flaky."

That first part was slander. Eldon did not like just any girls. It had not yet come to that—no. Shelly was a bit eccentric, but so what? He described her fascination with Pugh.

"I wouldn't know about silent movies," Frank said, "but that old man might know more than he's telling about what's going on up around the ranch."

"Sifting through his chaff is a pain in the ass."

"You used to like to sift the chaff."

"It's gotten tougher lately," Eldon said. It was the first time he'd admitted it to anyone.

"Find a better job," Frank said. "You're getting burned out here."

"I can always go fishing." Eldon went to the fly bench and picked up a fluorescent red and green fly. "This is called a Zaddack. Great for sea-run cutthroat, or bluebacks, as they're called on the Coquille River. Good on the Rogue for summer steel-head." Eldon held up another fly, red and yellow and winged. "This one's a 'grasshopper.' Good for river cutthroat. I caught a bunch of cutthroat on the Elk River with one. The recipe was given to me by a very good fly-fisherman who got the pattern from his grandfather years ago in Minnesota. You need a long shank hook. You take some red impala yarn or calf hair and some yellow yarn . . ."

Frank nodded, eyes glazing over as if listening to one of Fiske's interminable stories.

"I've never told anyone the recipe for this fly until now," Eldon said, recognizing the expression, feeling a chill.

"It's pearls before swine, telling me," Frank admitted.

"I'm hitting the hay," Eldon said. "Stay up and read if you want. You've got your sleeping bag. Cot's in the closet."

Eldon took a snifter of cognac to bed with him. He pulled a porno magazine from under the bed but couldn't get interested. Finally, he switched off the light and lay in the dark bedroom, listening to the wind through the open window. The road out of town had seemed easy when he had boarded the *Orient Star*. Then the shadow of death had passed in front of his face and he had realized that the journey would be hard. He stared uneasily out the window at the darkness rubbing out the trees. He was afraid to leave Port Jerome. He had become a native.

Tears stung Eldon's eyes. He missed Bernice. She was the best woman he had ever known. He couldn't blame her for leaving him. He was an egotistical slob. It was the way she had gone about it—the "one-year art fellowship" in Australia that had suddenly become a permanent job. The departure. The letter. Eldon out of luck. It was as if there was a gap in his memory after that. Of course, he remembered everything quite clearly; but he felt as if he simply had surfaced one day in Port Jerome, shaking hands with Fiske in the rain.

He pulled the bedclothes protectively around him and listened to faint rustles and chirps in the trees beyond the window. Eldon started—what was that noise?

There it was again. Gravel crunching—someone walking close to the house! He rolled onto the floor. He found the flashlight he kept beside the bed and lay gripping it, listening, praying that the flashlight would somehow turn into a gun.

9 Call the sheriff—but the telephone was in the living room. He'd never reach it in time. Yell for Frank. The killers would charge in, shooting. Run for the back door—into an ambush.

It was quiet outside. The silence lengthened. The window seemed to beckon and the room seemed full of shapes. Eldon did not sense a human presence. Fighting panic, he crawled slowly toward the window. Finally, he was just beneath the sill. Silence.

He leaped up and flashed the light out the window—into the glowing eyes of a raccoon that reared back, hissing in surprise.

Eldon dropped gasping to the floor, his heart pounding so fiercely that he feared it would stop. His hands and feet felt numb. They'll come to kill me, he thought, and find that a raccoon already did the job.

There was a tap at the bedroom door. "Eldon? You all right?"

Eldon croaked.

Frank opened the door. "What're you doing on the floor? What's wrong?"

"I'm all right," said Eldon, getting up. "I'm getting my breath."

"I heard a thump."

"There's a raccoon outside, is all."

"Sure it isn't Bigfoot?"

"Oh, go to hell."

"What's this mag? *Lust Dolls #5*."

"Give me that—"

"I want to read it."

"I want to camp out tomorrow night," Eldon said.

"I thought the point was not to camp out."

"The point is to stay alive. I don't feel safe here."

"You're making too much of all this," said Frank.

"Nobody's tried to kill *you*!"

"Let's stay at my place, then. No one will look for you there."

"We might be followed there." Eldon gripped the doorsill. He did not actually want to forsake his citadel. He had leaped to the window for the same reason he had gone below decks aboard the *Orient Star*—because he had to see what was there. He remembered how the ship had seemed to fold out below decks. He had lived sparely for five years, and it had kindled in him an appetite for things complex.

"Nobody kills newspaper reporters, just like nobody kills cops," Frank said. "It attracts too much attention."

"Let's at least go out north of the bay tomorrow and look around," Eldon said. "I don't want to just sit around the house. We can take some pictures in the woods to please Fiske."

The rest of the night was endless. Eldon slept with the window locked and the light on—when he slept at all. He was eleven years old again, waiting for grizzly bears to invade camp. By morning, he was red-eyed and stiff. His head thumped, his bruises ached anew. Beyond the living room window, Nekaemas Bay gleamed blue with menace in the sun.

However, a mug of black coffee put hair on the day. Eldon scrambled eggs and prepared grapefruit. The mundane activity revived him, and each cold wedge of grapefruit tasted precious as a diamond.

He telephoned Shelly. No answer. Perhaps she was an early riser—or perhaps she had not gone home last night at all.

Eldon kept himself in motion. He put on old clothes and hiking boots while Frank sang in the shower. Shit, but the gawky bastard was cheerful. Eldon wrote a note for Shelly and stuck it on the front door: *Tried to call you. Back around 3*. He hoped the murderers would not drop by and see it. He put his hat on tight.

They started for the north side of the bay in Frank's green 1965 Chevelle. It was a venerable old tank but still in its prime compared to Eldon's Citroën.

Eldon relaxed as Frank's car rocketed down the hill and turned away from town on the road skirting the bay's lush eastern shore. Frank drove L.A. style, fast and with a loose hand; the Chevelle wallowed as it took the curves in the two-lane road. Frank's driving style often worried Eldon, but today he found it exhilarating. Frank's glasses, lumpy with tape, were holding their own.

They drove past dairy farms and ramshackle cottages huddled between the forest and the mud flats rimming the bay. The foliage was thick: bracken fern and Oregon grape, maple and alder. The road turned north and then ran west along the north shore. Here, the forest was more open and sunlit. Ranks of Douglas fir marched up steep hillsides where blackberry vines tangled over stumps of trees cut long ago. Log rafts lined the bay's shallows, half-submerged grids of timber awaiting the call of the somnolent mills.

"These logs have been there so long, there's bushes growing on 'em," Frank said. "They'll have a whole little forest out in the bay in a few more years, if they don't take it away to be cut."

"That's a lot likelier than the mills coming back," Eldon said, thinking that in the end the forest would reclaim all of Port Jerome. "Is that a siren?"

Frank glanced in the rearview mirror and then at his speedometer. "State trooper way behind us, coming up fast." He eased right, searching for a place to stop.

"He'll let you off if you say we're hunting Bigfoot."

"I'm not speeding, I tell ya."

The patrol car rushed up. Frank veered into a wide spot on the road's edge, bouncing the Chevelle over a huge rock and a fallen branch in his haste. The white car, crowned with flashing blue and red lights, passed them and disappeared around the next bend.

"Might be a good accident up the road," Eldon said. "Let's beat the ambulance."

Frank patched out, crashing over more rocks and spewing gravel. They laughed with excitement—this was what it was all about! Eldon checked and rechecked his camera.

They reached the scene a few minutes later, but it was not a traffic accident.

An ambulance was parked in a turnout on the shoreline. Its crew lugged a big stainless steel stretcher down toward the water's edge. State police and sheriff's cars lined both sides of the road. Parked among them was Shelly's Ship of Love.

"They're out on the logs," said Frank. "They must've found a floater."

"Shelly must be out there shooting. I bet this is why I couldn't get her on the phone," Eldon said. "I wonder who drowned?"

"Some fisherman, no doubt," Frank said. "It's better than Bigfoot."

They parked and climbed down the bank, waved on by a state trooper whom Frank knew slightly, and stepped onto the log float. The logs were lashed with rusting chains and moored to scattered pilings. A boardwalk crossed the bobbing, shrub-spotted raft, which spread for half an acre across the sun-splashed water. It was like walking on a trampoline.

Eldon led the way toward the float's far edge, where uniformed lawmen clustered. Eldon picked out Shelly moving among them. And Marsha Cox.

"I'll bet Marsha's pissed off," said Frank. "This is not a ladylike assignment."

"Marsha gets seasick swirling ice in a drink," Eldon said and snickered. Seasickness never bothered Eldon; he had spent too many hours fishing in boats. But Marsha had an arm wrapped around a piling as the log float rolled and jerked.

A rowboat with an outboard motor was moored to the logs. Two white-haired men sat in it, their fishing poles sticking straight up into the sky. Interviewing them was Art Nola, shoulders hunched and face thrust forward, reminding Eldon of a crouching fox.

The fishermen sat rigidly as they answered Nola's questions. One wore an orange baseball cap, the other a white baseball cap reading, RETIRED? HELL, YES! In younger days, they might have brawled in the Dead Man's Hand. The man with the white hat kept glancing over the rowboat's stern. There a body floated faceup, moored to the boat by one foot.

"Hi, Eldon!" Shelly called. "They found him while they were fishing. I got some gritty shots."

"Art let you take them? Better snap some stuff after they've got him in the body bag, in case Fiske decides on good taste. A floater really pushes the limits."

"He looks pretty fresh," said Frank. "Not bloated."

"And how are you, Marsha?" Eldon asked.

"I'm just fine," Marsha said stiffly.

"Glad you could come out," Eldon said. "The surroundings are a bit uncouth . . . but that's the biz."

"Fiske called me at home," Marsha said. "But now that you're here, Eldon—"

"Oh, no, Marsha, this one's yours," Eldon said. "Frank and I are on a special assignment. We're hunting Bigfoot. That's not a drowned Sasquatch, is it?"

"It's a man," Marsha said. "And his throat's been cut. It's one of *yours*. From the ship."

"For Chrissake, why didn't you say? Which one is it? And where's the other?"

"You can tell us which one," said Nola, stepping across the bobbing logs. "It's not pretty. The fisherman hit his head with the prop of their outboard, towing him in."

"How long's he been in the water?" Eldon asked.

"Just overnight," Nola said. "The crabs have barely been at him. I need you to take a look."

Marsha gave a malicious smile.

Eldon stepped from log to log over to the rowboat. "Out after bass, eh? Where'd you find him?"

"I snagged him yonder," the fisherman said in a guilty tone, pointing west. He looked at three large striped bass lying in the bottom of the boat. "I don't think I want these fish."

"He couldn't have floated all the way across the bay from the docks in one night," Eldon said to Art.

"No," Art said. "After they jumped ship, they hot-wired a pickup in town; we found it down the road, out of gas. Looks as if one did in the other. Probably got cold and desperate and killed his partner in a quarrel over where to run to. Now take a look; we need the I.D. for the all-points."

"I ought to go to work for the medical examiner." Eldon looked at the body out of the corner of his eye, hoping to glimpse as little of the face as possible. The throat had been opened with a great lateral gash, now deep purple. The mouth gaped. Eldon peeked closer, seeking a glimpse of gold teeth. "Don't know."

"You're going to have to look," Nola said quietly, stepping up beside him.

"Give me a second. Two in two days is kind of rough. Three this week, counting Nguyen Xuan."

"This is necessary. You did damn good on the boat, Eldon."

"I did not. I don't guess you expected me to admit that."

"Yes, you did do good. I don't guess you'd expect me to say *that*, either. Now please take a look."

"Just a minute. Roll him over. I want to see his elbows."

"What?"

"One of 'em had tattoos on his elbows. Spiderwebs."

Nola rolled the body with a log gaff while the old anglers grimaced. "The elbows are bare," Nola said.

"It's the cook," Eldon said. He stared at the floating corpse. It had been animated only a day before. It had wanted to kill him. Now it was dead meat, inconsequential, like an opossum squashed in the road. Burn in hell, Cookie, Eldon thought.

Marsha released the piling and tottered forward with her notebook, pen raised like a teacher about to give a student a black mark. She was not so queasy that she couldn't try to horn in on the action. Eldon put one foot on the end of a log supporting the boardwalk and pedaled gently. Marsha stopped short.

"Dougie's a maniac," Eldon said. "He helped kill Marie Payne. He tried to kill me. And he's on the loose."

"Funny thing . . . nothing to indicate it," Nola said, absently adjusting his balance. "He's got a rap sheet long as a crawlin' snake, but never anything like this before. Burglary, petty theft, car theft, and so forth. Receiving stolen property. Charlie Manson was the same way until—"

"What's his whole name?" Eldon asked. "If there's an APB we want to run something about it."

"Douglas J. Hartwig," Nola said. "D.O.B.: six–twenty-six–forty-eight. From Drain. The *J* doesn't stand for anything . . . the story of his life. A minor punk in way over his head."

"And the late cook?"

"Name of Tumpat. Malaysian national. U.S. Customs and the Drug Enforcement Administration have had their eye on him for some time."

"For smuggling drugs. Opium, specifically."

"Yes. I can see you've been busy."

"What about the rest of the *Star*'s crew?"

"We've questioned them and they aren't worth holding. The captain might've been in on the cut but there's no proof. He'll be expelled. Dougie and Tumpat decided to kill you on their own, near as we can tell."

"Marie, too?"

Nola shrugged. "She probably wanted a bigger share. They went down there to kill her and throw her body overboard. You got in the way."

This doesn't quite jibe with what Huey told me, Eldon thought. And what about Xuan? He stepped slowly from log to log. "We need to chat privately, Art. Let's you and me have some coffee."

"Monday. Off the record."

"Okay." Eldon was pleasantly surprised. Perhaps Nola had decided to forget their old feud. Perhaps he had acquitted himself well aboard the *Orient Star,* after all.

"So who's on the story here?" Nola asked. "You or Marsha?"

"Oh, Marsha, by all means," Eldon said. "First on the scene and all that."

"All right," Nola said. "You look a little green around the gills, Marsha."

"No, I'm not." Marsha stepped forward, missing her footing. She was wearing charcoal-colored wool slacks and one leg splashed into the water nearly up to the knee. "Shit!"

"Tsk-tsk. Good thing you wore slacks," Eldon said.

Frank extended a hand to help Marsha and nearly lost his glasses when she pulled him off balance. She sat down hard on the boardwalk with one hand clapped over her mouth, swallowing hard.

Shelly stepped off a short distance and began shooting. "Art, step in there, will you? I want to get one of you questioning the fishermen."

She's got the cops eating out of her hand, Eldon thought, as Art smiled and obliged. Eldon said jokingly, "I hope you're not seasick, too."

"I'm okay," Shelly said. "The excitement carries you along."

Eldon glanced back at the cook's floating body and suddenly thought, A little slower on my feet the other night and she'd have been taking pictures of *me.*

His flesh crawled as he imagined himself on the *Sun*'s front page, a gruesome display in grainy black and white with his throat cut like Tumpat's, or a file jammed through his eye. His death captured with a strobe, making the contrast extra harsh; Marsha crowing, pleased with the newspaper's standards at last. Eldon forced the image from his mind and beckoned to Frank. "We'd better be getting after Bigfoot."

"You're hunting Bigfoot?" Nola asked. "Three murders this week and *Bigfoot's* the big story?"

"You betcha," Eldon said. "Tracks up Allen Slope. Big scoop."

Nola shook his head, almost fondly. "You're in a damn weird business. Pardon my French, ladies."

He opened his detective's black pocket notebook, prepared to recite information to Marsha. Marsha nodded in a wobbly, grateful sort of way as she shook water out of her shoe. Nola offered her his handkerchief. What a couple those two would make! Eldon thought.

Eldon and Frank drove to the graveled turnoff for Allen Slope. The discovery of the cook's body had left them exhilarated. Adrenaline gave them shining armor—all they lacked was the cook's head on the end of a lance.

"I sure am glad they got one of 'em," said Eldon.

"I guess you are," said Frank.

"I always hated heroes that had something noble to say about their mortal enemies."

"Can Marsha handle the story?"

"It'll be the sleepiest murder story you ever read."

"I hate to see sleaze wasted," said Frank. "A good murder is a better lift than three cups of coffee. . . . Say, what's the news business do to your blood pressure after a few years?"

"You have a series of small strokes," Eldon said, "and after enough of them, you start to turn into Fiske." Frank laughed but Eldon was suddenly gloomy. Morbid high blood pressure ran in his family. Relatives on both sides of his family had blown out like cheap tires.

"Someday, I'm going to quit journalism," said Frank. "I think I'll be a teacher."

"The money couldn't be any worse."

"I like kids."

"Not me," Eldon said. Not since Berkeley, anyway. Kids had been an issue between him and Bernice, but Eldon had not realized it at the time. He had talked about having kids with an oblivious acceptance, and Bernice had nodded and muttered and burrowed deeper into her butterfly collection. She had never said no.

There were a lot of things she didn't say, Eldon thought. A lot of things I didn't realize. He chewed the old bitterness, like a dog mauling a well-worn rag. She deceived me, lay low and waited to get hers, he thought. Well, I won't be stupid again.

The gravel road dead-ended at a county picnic area. Two wooden picnic tables and a stone barbeque stood beneath the maples, among ferns that spread soft green fans over the forest floor. There was a trail through the ferns and up a mossy ravine, leading up to the open hillside and the Douglas fir.

They locked the car and began to climb. It was still sunny, but the air was cool and clouds gathered on the horizon. Eldon took a deep breath. No gasoline fumes, no oil, printer's ink, or ozone—acrid city smells that had filled his nose for so long that his brain had rendered them subtle. Here was the odor of damp humus and fir needles and the briny scent of the bay, like a bracing slap in the face.

"Too bad we have to go back to Port Jerome," Eldon said. "Sometimes out here I feel like I could just keep walking. Forever."

"That's what some people around here do, in their minds," Frank said. "Like the Bigfoot freaks."

"Or Pugh with his tinfoil spaceship."

Frank hummed a rock-and-roll tune as they followed the trail up the ravine. The incline was steep; Eldon puffed with the exertion of climbing, but Frank snapped his fingers and soon was exuberantly singing aloud: "Be-bop-a-lula, she's my baby. . . ." Eldon thought of Tumpat floating in the bay. One down, one to go! The thought straightened his back and put spring into his step. And Nola was developing as a source. Life was strange, but sometimes it wasn't so bad.

The trail climbed out of the ravine and up the hillside. A power line, strung between metal towers, ran along the crest. Frank hooted in amusement and rooted in the brush at the base of one of the towers. "Bigfoot club!" He held up a discarded power-pole insulator—a foot-long metal rod stacked with gray ceramic insulator disks perhaps five inches in diameter.

Eldon took it, hefted it. It weighed ten or twelve pounds. The metal rod was long enough to allow a good grip. "You could knock somebody's brains out with this."

"Strike down Bigfoot," Frank said, taking the insulator back and giving it a two-handed swing. He crouched apishly, jaw thrust out, glasses askew. "Unh. Hunt-um Bigfoot, catch-um, cut off glands for trophies. Take-um glands home to Fiske, throw-um on wire desk. Fiske say, 'Good copy!' Marsha bitch-um about 'bad taste.'" He capered around the tower, swinging the club. "I'm taking this along. We might meet Bigfoot."

"It's heavy," Eldon said.

"It's something to show Fiske," said Frank. "And insulators

have a sentimental attraction for me. They were a big factor in the first UFO story I ever covered, on that crummy weekly down in Placerville."

"Not you, too."

"Oh, Fiske wouldn't like this story; it makes too much sense," said Frank. "This drifty old couple in Coloma called us about a *blue flash* they'd seen at night near their place. The UFOs were coming, you see."

"You went out on something like that?"

"It was a slow day, like today. The old duffers were quivering as if the world was going to end . . . the press had arrived, which was me, and that made it real, you see." Frank smacked his lips with remembered gusto. "A transformer had blown out on a power pole up the hill. That caused the *blue flash*. Broken insulators were lying all around. I gave them one and took another one back to the office and used it as a paperweight. I wish I still had it. . . . You should've seen those two, Eldon, staring at that insulator. For them, it came from another planet."

"People really take reporters seriously," Eldon said.

"We're the tribal storytellers," Frank said. "We have magic powers. Why d'you think I'm in the business? You don't get respect if you're a damn shoe salesman . . . or a teacher. Maybe I won't quit, at that."

Frank slung the insulator on his shoulder and they continued up the path. The slope was shallower and the climbing easier.

They topped the slope. Now they had a view of the whole of Nekaemas Bay—a blue sweep of water glittering in the sun, the cottages of Regret on the nearer rim, the smoky town of Port Jerome on the far rim, toy ships scattered on the water and toy farms among the trees. Eldon could see the ridge where he lived but could not make out his house. He looked past the skeletal mill stacks toward town—there, very small, was the *Orient Star*. He swept his gaze north. Beyond the bridge was the sea.

Port Jerome was a complete little world, he thought, doing its secondhand-store dance around the ragged edges of the bay. He looked north toward Muskrat and the dunes. Shelly's remark about disappearing came to mind. Elephant lynchings, Bigfoot sightings. It was all here. In a place such as this, Pugh's tinfoil spaceship really might take off.

I disappeared when I moved to Nekaemas County, Eldon

thought. When I went back to Berkeley to visit, those clowns looked at me as if I'd come back from the dead. Breaking up with Bernice really changed me. But how? You keep walking all your life, through these terrains of the mind, and you constantly come to landmarks that you don't understand. Like a barbarian staring at giant ruined aqueducts and temples. All you can do is scratch your name on the stones and keep moving on.

"Listening for Bigfoot?" Frank asked.

"I wish it was that simple."

"This is the area the kid was talking about," said Frank. "Exactly what are we looking for?"

"Huge, clawed footprints with gobbets of bloody flesh sunk into the mud. The interview I'll leave to you."

Frank glanced at the sky. "Those clouds are getting dark."

"They're a ways off. We could sit it out in that old cabin if it rains."

The path veered into the woods, where the trees were thick and ferns once more overlaid the forest floor. Here it was cooler and wetter. The ground was spongy. Heavy drops of water hung from the ferns, and tree branches dripped constantly in the soft green light. A cool wind blew in behind them down the path, down the long tunnel formed by the trees, the wind a gentle continuo beneath the trickling sound of water from tiny streams and waterfalls created by the season's rain.

Frank tramped ahead, swinging the insulator from hand to hand, whistling. Abruptly, he halted, staring at something in the path. He remained stock-still until Eldon hurried up and then laughed.

"Here's your Bigfoot track, bwana."

Eldon stared. In the middle of the path was a comically big footprint. Footprints led down the path at intervals. "If Bigfoot made these, he was wearing a clown suit when he did it."

"The kid got the stride about right," Frank said.

"Guess so. Let's follow 'em a ways."

"Good thing I've got this killer club."

They followed the tracks. There were no human footprints. Presumably, the young prankster had walked in the ferns, pressing the cutout to the ground on the end of a stick. Cutouts, Eldon corrected himself—the kid had taken the trouble to create right and left feet.

"They go on and on," Frank said. "This is too much work for a kid."

"So somebody else did it. The kid only found 'em. A hoax will make a funny feature. At least we'll have the laugh on Fiske."

"But who'd put them up here?"

"Oh, some angler on his way to the creek," Eldon said. "He wanted to play a joke on another fisherman. The kid sees the tracks, drinks the hootch, throws in the ten-foot giant for color."

"No, it really is Bigfoot," said Frank playfully, foliage reflecting in his glasses. "Can't you smell him? Can't you sense his presence everywhere? In the clouds, in the green and gray trees, in the matted, rain-soaked earth?"

"We'll need art," Eldon said. "I'll take a picture."

Eldon got the camera out of his shoulder bag and clamped on the strobe. Then rain rattled among the trees. It began far away and rushed down upon them, hitting suddenly in sheets. The forest offered little shelter from the downpour; the path was like a wind tunnel, funneling the rain at them. Hastily, Eldon snapped the photo. "Make for the cabin! It isn't far."

They bounded over the slippery ground as the cold, drenching downpour picked up. "Where's the damn cabin?" Frank cried. Raindrops smeared his glasses, dripping from the crudely repaired frames. "Hey, dammit, the rain's falling upside down! It's hitting us from below!"

The rain blew down the forest path against a flat stone face that ran into another ravine and ricocheted up into their faces. They veered away from the blast of water and rain. Suddenly, it was peaceful, just the rain falling along the corridors formed by the trees.

Ahead was the cabin—dark and low and moss-covered, built of heavy logs and with a door black with age. A square chimney grew out of a mossy roof.

Frank reached the door first, seized the metal latch, and shoved the door open, flourishing the insulator. "Come outta there, Bigfoot! It's the *South Coast Sun!*"

There was a clatter and a scurry, as if a giant rodent had knocked over a can. Frank sucked air and backed into Eldon. Eldon's chin hooked over Frank's shoulder. In the greenish light streaming in the door, Eldon saw with terror that something *big* had taken refuge in the cabin.

It crouched in the corner, at bay—matted, ragged, piggy-eyed, the size of a man.

10

Eldon brought up the camera and fired—there would be one close-up of Bigfoot when they recovered his savaged corpse.

But it was no Sasquatch. In the strobe's flash, Eldon saw spiderwebbed elbows on raised arms—it was Dougie who cowered against the cabin's far wall, ragged and covered with mud, mouth open in a yell of terrified surprise.

The yell triggered a roar from Frank that came out of his lanky body like an explosion coming up a well. Eldon screamed, too. Dougie turned, jerked open a shutter, and was through the cabin window.

Frank rushed into the cabin, still yelling, and piled through the window after Dougie, charging through the rain after the fleeing killer, waving the insulator like a Maori braining club. Eldon rounded the cabin and followed. Surprise had given them the upper hand; he exulted in turning the tables on his erstwhile attacker. Long-legged Frank ran like a gazelle, insulator club gripped with both hands. Dougie looked back and poured on steam, dodging among the trees as Frank closed in.

Rain gusted in their faces. Frank hurled the insulator as his glasses fell in two. The insulator bounced off a tree, and Frank blindly tripped over it. Eldon saw Frank crash with a cry over the side of the ravine. Then Eldon collided with a tree and sat down with a grunt on the wet ground. Dougie was gone.

"Eldon! Help! Ow—shit!"

Eldon scrambled to the ravine's lip, gripping his camera. Frank sat below, clutching his right ankle and rocking in pain.

"I think I've busted it!" Frank yelled.

Eldon stood up, cocked the camera, and took Frank's photograph before dropping into the ravine.

"Bastard," Frank said through gritted teeth.

"Business. You can send a print to Mom."

"It hurts like hell," said Frank, trying vainly to rise. "Where are my glasses?"

"Straighten your leg," Eldon said. He manipulated the ankle, gently moving Frank's foot back and forth and from side to side.

Frank exhaled. "It must be broken."

"If it was, you'd be screaming now. I think it's just a bad sprain. Still, we'd better splint it."

"You're quite the Boy Scout."

"Star Scout, as a matter of fact. You'd be better off if I'd made Eagle." Eldon put the camera away and glanced around for sticks with which to make splints. Of course, none were handy, and the rain continued fiercely.

"My glasses," said Frank. "I can't see a thing."

"Sit still. I'll get them."

"They went every which way."

"Like Dougie. Did you bring a knife?"

"If I had, I'd have thrown it at the bastard."

"Well, if I can't cut something for a splint, you can sharpen a rock and cut your own throat."

Eldon climbed from the ravine and poked among the ferns. He found the right-hand side of the glasses immediately and tossed it down to Frank. He looked around for the left half of the glasses while he selected alder branches for a splint, but he could not find it. Eldon had to tug and twist limbs to break them by hand. At last, he had two that would do until they reached the car. Good thing Dougie ran into the woods and not down the slope, Eldon thought. I'd hate to get all the way down there and find out he'd stolen our wheels.

He peered into the forest. The rain gave it a soothing, primeval quality, and he felt like Robinson Crusoe stalking game. A very wet and battered castaway. The cold I'm going to catch will last a week, he thought. Two weeks.

Yet Eldon was not afraid. He had turned the tables on Dougie; they would stay turned. Eldon was the reporter, Dougie the story, the quarry. That was as it should be.

It's not that I feel so good, it's that I don't feel so bad anymore, Eldon realized. I've felt bad for so long that I've forgotten what it's like to be okay.

"Eldon? Did you find the other lens?"

"No. You've got yourself a monocle." Eldon slid down the

ravine with the tree limbs. It took them several more minutes of twisting to break the limbs to the correct length; by then, their teeth were chattering. They cinched the limbs to Frank's leg with their belts. Eldon helped Frank crawl painfully up the side of the ravine until Frank lay on his belly on the high ground.

"Maybe I can put some weight on it," Frank said.

"Don't try," Eldon said. "I'll leave you at the cabin and go for help."

"Like hell you will. I'm blind as a bat and the woods're full of Sasquatch."

"We've got to get to the car . . . get you to the doctor and call the sheriff. We'll make for the cabin, see how it goes."

They struggled erect, Frank leaning on Eldon's shoulder. Frank's pants started to fall down. Eldon felt grateful for once that he had some girth. They stumped forward like contestants in a three-legged race, Eldon huffing for breath and Frank clutching his trousers, gasping when his injured ankle inadvertently took weight. Footing was treacherous; the ground was turning mucky. Eldon slipped; Frank yowled. Eldon huffed for breath, half-dragging Frank through the rain. Finally, they reached the cabin and staggered inside.

The room had been a refuge for others before Dougie. There was a heavy homemade table, thick with dust, some broken chairs, and a fireplace full of old ash and paper scraps. Old beer cans littered the floor.

"We can wait until the rain lets up a little before we try for the car," Eldon said.

He helped Frank into the one sound chair. There was a yellowed stack of newspapers near the fireplace. Eldon twisted some pages into kindling and threw in a couple of hunks of scrap wood. Matches had remained dry in Frank's pocket; shortly, they had a fire.

"Look at that newspaper blaze," Eldon said. "Sure wish we had some beer." He picked up an old beer can from the dirt floor, crushed it one-handed, and threw it against the far wall.

"Every one of those cans could get us a nickel," said Frank, peering around the cabin through his impromptu monocle. He was more cheerful now that there was a fire.

"You sound like Marsha," Eldon said. "Live for today, I always say." Eldon crushed another can and pitched it after the first. He wanted a woman. Shelly. "Too bad you're not a beautiful girl. How's your ankle?"

"Hurts like a bandit. I'm going to loosen these belts. Looks like Dougie took a dump in the corner."

"Thanks for pointing that out, Frank; you've made my day." Eldon grimaced in disgust and watched the fire. But, of course, he had to peek at the turd. It lay long and mummylike in the corner in the light thrown by the fire, light that glinted off *green glass*.

"Shit," Eldon said, getting up.

"You do that outside," Frank said.

"No, look . . . green glass. Like I saw around Nguyen Xuan's body. Like in the glass butterfly that Huey made." Eldon plucked up a couple of the green shards. They lay close by the turd, as if they had fallen from the pocket of Dougie's dropped pants.

"Sure it's not just broken bottle?"

"I don't know where it's from," Eldon said. "But it keeps cropping up."

The fire snapped and sizzled over the sound of the rain. Eldon examined the shard; it was too thin to be bottle glass. It was a cheap grade, too, flecked with tiny air bubbles and flaws. Such stuff would not make a sturdy ornament.

Eldon stared at the flames, listening to the rain and trying to make sense of all of it: Nguyen Xuan and Tran Minh; Marie; Ahmed; Tumpat and Dougie; green glass and the sealed search-warrant file. . . . The rain was the real Oregon, all right, a steady pressure pushing him inside himself, giving everything outside soft edges. It helped him think. The cabin was full of the smell of wet clothes, of smoke and burning paper and wood.

"This is a hell of a story," Eldon said. "The opium runners are the same people as the fences. . . . This won't lead us just to a story about the Vietnamese and how they're trying to get along in the rainy north woods. And there won't be just another story about the underground economy. We can connect the two. And swing Tran Minh in the bargain. What a series! How the underground economy feeds itself and grows! There's an award in that, for sure."

"Maybe Dougie was up here waiting for help."

"Jeez, I hadn't thought of that."

"We won't be around to collect awards if Dougie's pals show up looking for him. We'd better move out."

They recinched the belts around Frank's swollen ankle, and Eldon helped Frank to his feet. The rain had slackened. They got through the cabin door and worked their way up the path, pausing frequently.

"By the way," Eldon said, "why'd you do it?"

"I fell when my glasses came apart. I couldn't help it."

"I mean go after Dougie like that. That was crazy."

"Oh. I couldn't think of anything else to do. I was so scared that all I could think was that if I yelled, I'd scare him away. And I did. I guess Frankie had his wits about him today."

The day was dying. They limped down the long forested tunnel in growing shadow. At last, they emerged on the hillside, looking out onto a bay choppy and gray as steel beneath an angry, cloud-filled sky.

"I want my insulator rod," Frank said.

"Shut up or I'll roll you down the mountain."

They picked their way down the hillside. It was windy, the rain frigid. Frank tried sitting down and sliding but the ground was too rocky. At last, as darkness fell, they stumbled into the picnic area, filled with relief at the sight of Frank's car.

Frank sat on the picnic bench and gratefully unlashed his leg.

Eldon flexed his aching shoulders and rubbed at his neck through the collar of his sodden jacket. His fishing hat was a sopping washrag on his head. His ears and nose were numb, his fingers ached, his body tingled with fatigue. He was seized with a sudden fearful thought: "Frank . . . you still have your keys?"

"They're right here."

"Thank God. I've had enough for today." Eldon took the keys and walked stiff-legged toward the car. Relief flooded through him. The Chevelle was a guaranteed starter, unlike another car he could name. Then Eldon saw that the car's front end was canted sharply to the right. "Aw, crap. We've got a flat."

"It must've happened when I ran over those rocks."

"I hope you've got a jack."

"In the trunk."

Eldon opened the trunk and fumbled in the darkness until he found the jack and tire iron. He imagined Dougie running endlessly through the woods, every passing minute carrying him farther from justice. Eldon dumped the equipment on the ground and released the tire from the floor of the trunk. He hated working on cars; the texture of grimy metal set his teeth on edge. Of course, his Citroën didn't have a spare at all. He got the spare loose, wearily balanced the tire on the trunk's lip, and pushed it off onto the ground.

The tire landed with a flaccid thud that told Eldon it had no more air in it than a fat man run over by a truck. Eldon stood silently, thinking about slamming the trunk on Frank's ankle, but no, he'd have to lift him. "Do you have a pump?"

"No pump."

"We'll have to drive it on the flat."

Eldon helped Frank into the car and climbed behind the wheel. The Chevelle started smoothly. Frank cheered and switched on the heater. Eldon put the car into drive and eased it forward. They bumped down the gravel road a few yards and bogged down in mud. Eldon tried to back up, to go forward. The Chevelle bottomed out. They could not get free on three wheels.

Frank rested his cheek against the foggy passenger window and began a sort of quiet keening, half to himself. Eldon shut off the motor and pressed his forehead to the steering wheel. It had turned into a day typical of his career in Nekaemas County.

Eldon left the car and picked his way down to the main road. He stood in the fog rolling in from the bay, waiting to flag down a vehicle. His feet were great cold balls of mud. A car passed him going the wrong way. A second blinded him with its lights and nearly ran him down. Both kept going; there was nothing else for more than an hour. Eldon spent the time thinking of Sasquatch in the fog. At last, he flung himself before an approaching farm truck, waving his arms, almost hoping that it would run him over.

The truck stopped. The driver's face looked as if it had often been worked over with a pop bottle. A younger man, presumably the driver's son—he had a similar face that had seen less modification—sat in the dark cab. The son's lower lip bulged with tobacco cud. He pulled something from the open glove compartment, probably his plug of chew. The truck had cattle in the back and stank of manure.

"I need help," Eldon said. "My friend's hurt up at the picnic area. Our car broke down."

"You look like hell. You mighta been the mad killer."

"We were chasing the mad killer. It's how my friend got hurt. We're reporters. For the *Sun*."

"For the *Sun*? Why, that's the most perverted newspaper I ever read"—the driver set the brake and shut off the truck's motor—"horrible; dead bodies and an elephant strung up right on the front page—"

"Shit, Dad, that's good readin'," the younger man said and closed the glove compartment with a snap.

"Disgusting, I call it."

Father and son debated journalistic standards afoot, all the way up the muddy road to the picnic area and all the way back down, Frank limping between the two cattlemen. Mercifully, they did not seek the views of either Eldon or Frank, implying that the two reporters were not officially present and therefore should not be insulted while the men aired their opinions of the *Sun*.

"Only room for three in the cab," the older man told Eldon. "You'll have to ride in back."

Eldon clambered into the truck's rear, pushing the cows aside, gripping the slats that formed the truck's sides as he skidded in the manure.

The younger cattleman paused before he got into the truck. "Sorry 'bout that."

"It's okay. Thank God for the ride." The passenger door was open, the younger man bleakly illuminated by the cab's dome light. Eldon saw a pistol butt sticking from his jeans pocket.

That's what was in the glove compartment, he thought.

"Good copy," said Jimbo Fiske, rolling his eyes at Eldon's stark flash photo of Dougie on page one. "Only thing that could possibly knock the floater story below the fold . . . and you bring it in."

It was Monday. Eldon had spent Sunday soaking in his bathtub, drinking cognac, while sheriff's patrols and coast guard helicopters fruitlessly combed the woods for Dougie.

"Good copy," Fiske repeated reverently. "And you brought me a Sasquatch picture, too. A footprint, at least. You're a good man, Eldon." Fiske's eyes glistened. "You're all so good to me."

"Too bad you had to send Marsha out to cover the search," Eldon said. "Her story's so dull, you can barely tell there's a search going on."

"You were in the bathtub and Frank is nursing his sprain," Fiske said. "I had to make do. We're stretched thin. With Marsha riding around in helicopters, you'll have to cover for Frank."

"Maybe Marsha will meet a handsome coastguardsman and marry him."

"Coasties are a little rude and crude for our Marsha."

"Maybe one of 'em's a chaplain."

"Frank was supposed to back up McFee on sports tonight," Fiske said, "laying out some pages and taking scores on the phone. I want you to take it. Easy stuff. There's never much to do Monday night, but you could use some boredom. Work a split shift. Go home for a while at lunch."

Eldon shook his head. "I'll work straight through. There are some calls we didn't get to make when you sent us out after the damn Sasquatch."

"Listen, the Sasquatch tip paid off."

"Circumstances have put me back on the murder story, Jimbo. I'm all you've got left."

"Dee-de-dee," Fiske said by way of acknowledgment. He raised a seven-by-twelve glossy of the bogus Bigfoot track and tapped it with his pipe. "I'm sending this to *Sasquatch and UFO*. It'll make the cover. You'll get credit, of course."

"Money?"

"No money. Glory."

"It's an obvious hoax. Who knows who made the tracks?"

"It's better with the mystery," Fiske said. "Reminds me of the time out in Lakeview, around 1963. I was doing a feature on this group of bird-watchers, see, and one of 'em had a dog that ate salad. Only it wasn't bird-watching that this group of swingers was up to . . ."

The Dougie story was worth twenty-five dollars from the wire service, Eldon decided, and the photo ten dollars more—no, he'd demand twenty-five for it, too. He'd take Shelly out to dinner with the money. In Eugene. "Shelly's with Marsha?"

"Aboard a chopper since before breakfast," Fiske said. "I put a bunch of her photos on the wire to Portland, the floater and stuff from the search on Sunday. They loved it." Fiske gave a gold-backed grin. "Say, maybe Shelly'll find herself a Coastie. It's a lot different than when I was your age, Eldon; nowadays, a young guy and gal fancy each other, they just grab on and roll. If I was your age, I'd sure cash in on some of that. It was a lot tougher to get any in 1963. Which brings me back to the salad-eating dog . . ."

Eldon flinched at the thought of Shelly with the hypothetical coastguardsman. How could he compete with a trim body, flight helmet, and dashing flying jacket with colorful badges? All he had was his fishing hat. He snatched it from his head; it was ridiculous. The lures made it look like the target in a game of pin-the-tail-on-the-donkey. His imagined military rival became almost palpable.

But I sure as hell know how to cover a story, he thought, and looked again at page one. She didn't get *that* shot—I got it. That one tops the elephant.

Determination filled Eldon's soul. He picked up the phone and dialed the Nekaemas County Courthouse in Preacher's Hole, fifteen miles down the road. The courthouse was Frank's turf, but Eldon had contacts there, too: "Gimme Loretta."

A woman came on the line with a hearty laugh. "Eldon Larkin? What have you been up to? Want your fortune told? That was some picture in the paper today, babes."

"What you see is what you get," said Eldon, visualizing County Assessor Loretta Starbuck, a jovial mound of a woman, with a crystal ball on her desk amid the property files, her eyes bright behind thick rimless glasses, a ringed hand with long carmine fingernails gripping the telephone. "It may get better next issue, if you're up to some snooping around."

"I'm always up for that, Eldon. What do you need to know?"

"Look into your crystal ball and tell me who bought some property in Muskrat from a man named Leslie Patterson?"

"How long ago?"

"This summer, I guess. Patterson got enough dough out of it to move to Sri Lanka."

"My, that pricks my interest. Hold on a minute." Eldon waited much longer than a minute. He knew that Loretta was rooting through property records, filed in dusty maroon ledgers, that dated back to Nekaemas County's founding in 1852. At last, the assessor came back on the line and read off a tax-lot number. "Patterson purchased the property in September 1958. Two hundred and fifty acres. My, my . . . in March of this year, he sold out to the Sherwood Forest Corporation for fifty thousand dollars 'plus other considerations.'"

"Fifty thousand for two hundred and fifty acres? That isn't enough to move to Sri Lanka."

"The secret lies in the 'other considerations,'" Loretta said. "A thousand dollars an acre is the assessed value of the property—"

"Patterson probably got two hundred and fifty grand, then."

"Maybe more. 'Other considerations' could hide a big cash payment. There's all kinds of sneaky ways to do things."

"Why would a legitimate buyer sneak?"

"A developer might well pay double the appraised value," Loretta said. "He wouldn't want me to reappraise the property to reflect true market value and thus raise the taxes, at least not until he developed it and sold it off."

"Do they do that a lot?"

"Durn tootin'. But I've got ways of finding out how much they paid and they know it. Point here is, somebody's willing to pay more than a grand an acre for seclusion."

"Maybe it's another rock star."

"Wouldn't I love it!" Loretta said.

"Is there an address for this Sherwood Forest Corporation?"

"Just a post-office box in Salem," Loretta said and read it off.

"Patterson sold to a guy from Southern California, not Salem."

"There might be a Salem agent. Ah, here's the register deed. The corporation agent is Walker J. Lane. Here's his address and, bless me, a phone number, too, in Santa Monica, California. This is the address that the deed was to be returned to—"

Eagerly, Eldon copied the information down. "California money, Loretta. They'll want their tarot read."

Loretta laughed. "I'll wear my gypsy dress. When do I read about this in the paper?"

"Keep an eye on your crystal ball. And thanks."

Eldon called the state Corporation Division at Salem. Incorporation records contained only standard information: The Sherwood Forest Corporation was an Oregon corporation in good standing, chartered the preceding January; its address was the Salem post-office box listed on the Nekaemas County register deed; its president was Walker J. Lane of the same post-office box.

Salem directory information listed no Walker J. Lane. Eldon called the Oregon Real Estate Board, also in Salem. No one named Walker J. Lane was licensed in Oregon as a real estate broker or salesperson.

Eldon drummed his fingers on the desk. He didn't want to call the California number yet. He tried the state Motor Vehicles Division—no record of a driver's license for Walker J. Lane. Last, he called the clerk of Marion County, in which Salem was located. No one named Walker J. Lane was registered to vote there. As an afterthought, he called the Nekaemas County clerk's office and checked local voter records: nothing.

Eldon double-checked Santa Monica's area code in the telephone directory and dialed the number. The phone line hummed. Eldon's heart speeded up. There was a click and two rings. The second ring was interrupted by a recorded voice: "—has been disconnected and there is no new number—"

". . . but the dog didn't eat the salad!" Fiske, flourishing wire copy, concluded in triumph as Eldon hung up.

"Jimbo, what do you make of this?" From his pocket, Eldon got one of the green glass shards he had found in the cabin and spun it across Fiske's desk.

"That's easy," said Fiske, picking the shard up. "Tektites."

"What?"

"Space glass, comes down on meteorites. It's always green. Glass from the moon!" Fiske hooted.

11

When the five-foot-tall troll with the paper bag over its head rushed into the newsroom, Eldon knew the night shift had begun. "Hi, Ambrose."

The troll rushed in circles, flailing its arms. FRIED CHICKEN, the bag read. The eyeholes poked through the upside-down slogan were askew. At last, the troll hit the pillar next to the sports desk and sat down on the floor.

"I did something like that myself, over the weekend," Eldon said.

"Gonna smother!" The troll clawed the bag off its head and looked around, blinking huge bloodshot blue eyes. "Am I safe?"

"You're in the newsroom, McFee. You're safe enough."

"I can see that. But I wouldn't bet on the safety of my immortal soul." Sports Editor Ambrose McFee wore jeans and a big shapeless coat that covered him like a turtle's shell. He spread his fingers and pulled them through his damp hair, making it stand out in bedraggled spikes. "I've sinned again, Eldon."

"So go to confession. What was this girl like?"

"Oh, God, I mighta been in Eden."

"At least you're on time for work."

"I have *him* to thank for that. He chased me here."

"Who? Old Nick?"

Ambrose shuddered. "Her husband."

Eldon glanced toward the front door. "I don't see anybody."

"Thanks to my disguise. I whipped this bag over my head before he could recognize me and ran outta the bar."

"Had a few, then, eh, Ambrose? If Fiske catches you—"

"Fiske's as good a drinkin' man as any," Ambrose said.

"Not at work." Eldon thought uncomfortably of his misadventure at Buster's and looked at Ambrose with pity. Ambrose's drinking had gotten worse, though the sports editor's love life retained a grotesque vigor. He pursued female barflies, the taller the better, and constantly was chased and pummeled by their murderous boyfriends and husbands. Ambrose had grit, Eldon reflected, though he doubted Ambrose ever actually scored. He could see himself, a few years further down the road, in that ravaged fat-cheeked little countenance.

"Where's Frank?" Ambrose demanded.

"Laid up. I'm covering."

"He's out from a little sprain? Why, I've seen 'em play two quarters in peewee football with worse." Ambrose grasped the edge of his desk and pulled himself erect, sat down in his swivel chair, and rotated slowly. "No one else is here."

"It's Monday night. There can't be much to do."

"There's some double-A stuff. And track tryouts at one of the high schools down the road. I sent the new girl photog down to get a picture. I need local art for tomorrow's page."

"Shelly will be in tonight?"

Ambrose nodded. "She was out on the killer search all day, but she was game to shoot the tryouts. She's a trouper."

"Amen," Eldon said. There would be something to look forward to tonight, after all.

The sports telephone rang and Ambrose grabbed it. "*Sun* Sports. Oh, Christ! Hold on a minute!"

"What the hell—?" Eldon felt a sudden terror that something had happened to Shelly.

Ambrose's eyes were huge. "Eldon . . . this is the first score of the evening *and I don't have on my cap*! My lucky baseball cap."

"So put it on. Where is it?"

"That's just it . . . I left it in the bar." Perspiration began to form on Ambrose's broad forehead. "I don't dare go back there."

"Put the bag back on your head."

"Will you go get it for me? Please?"

"Oh, all right. Where'd you leave it?"

"On the coatrack in the Timber Topper. Just a couple of blocks down the street."

"I know where it is."

Eldon left the office and trudged down the dark, wet street. Beer bottles from the Pioneer Days Festival rattled underfoot. Three teenaged drunks wandered down the middle of the street, screaming. Eldon screamed in reply. The young men screamed back.

"You look like a faggot in that hat," one said.

"You look like shit," Eldon said.

It was a typical Nekaemas County exchange. What am I doing here? Eldon asked himself for the thousandth time. What am I doing in Port Jerome?

You're recovering McFee's lucky hat, he thought as he reached the Timber Topper's door. The door handle was an ax embedded in wood. Eldon gripped the haft and pulled. The ghastly scene in the bar was just as he had known it would be—the smoke, the ugly people groping in the narrow booths, the screeching jukebox. Eldon headed for the coatrack.

Ambrose's hat was safe among the hard hats and feathered Stetsons—a purple baseball cap bearing a yellow Q, the livery of no local team or school. Ambrose had found the greasy thing deep in California and wore it as a badge of neutrality. School sports were viciously partisan on Oregon's South Coast, and the colors of Ambrose's cap had saved him more than once. Gradually, it had become a talisman.

Like my fishing hat, Eldon thought. Lucky things always look ridiculous. At least my hat has some fish dinners to its credit.

He turned to go, felt breasts against his arm. "Hey, Mr. Reporter. That's not your hat."

Eldon looked at a pink sweater filled with lush breasts and then into the eyes of Stephanie Hosfelder, the chippie who had gotten married aboard the *Orient Star*.

"It belongs to a friend of mine," Eldon said.

"He kind of left in a hurry," said the girl. "That was a real good write-up about my wedding. I want ten copies. I liked that picture of us on the society page."

"Your marriage got upstaged by the violence. I'm sorry."

"It was exciting. You got my gown in: 'The bride wore white.' I liked that. You really got writing skill."

"Thanks. How's Ahmed?"

"He had to go out of town on business."

"Right after the raid?"

"Yeah."

"What about my TV set?"

"I can help with that. After all, you came through for me. Got a pen?" Stephanie took a bar napkin and wrote on it. "This is Tran Minh's address in Muskrat. He always has things like TVs around."

"Why, thank you, Stephanie, this is very helpful."

"What about those copies?"

"Drop by the office in daylight. Circulation will fix you up."

"You know, that was slick, not telling us Xuan was dead while we were talking on the boat."

"Didn't I mention that?"

"No. But you had to get information. A reporter is always up to something. It taught me I should read the paper more." Stephanie's eyes misted. "I don't feel bad about Xuan. But that red-haired chick . . . I feel bad about her. You got to see what they did to her, right? You almost got nailed yourself."

"I'm okay."

"Then you went after that bastard Dougie and chased him through the forest. I saw that in the paper today. You reporters really have balls."

"All in a day's work," Eldon said.

"It must be great not to have to take crap from anybody," Stephanie said. "I hope you get the guys that did Marie."

"Since Dougie kindly took care of his assistant, there's just the one to go. Easy pickin's."

"I wouldn't say that," Stephanie said quietly. "Talk to Tran." Stephanie went on in a normal tone: "Gotta go. Tell your little friend I think he's cute."

She turned and waltzed up to a well-muscled young man who had just come out of the john. His blond hair was blow-dried, his pullover had a little alligator in the correct place, and his sun-lamp tan was sprayed over chiseled features. Not the Timber Topper's usual sort of patron. A Portland tourist slumming at the festival.

"It's okay," Stephanie told the young man as he frowned at Eldon. "He was at my wedding."

The man lifted a drink from a table. Eldon saw that it was a martini in a cocktail glass, complete with an olive—startling in a town where elegance was bottled beer. For an instant, it seemed as if the man was going to hurl the drink at him. Then the young man raised the lucent glass in a toast, so gracefully that the gesture seemed regal.

And condescending. Eldon knew that he had been dismissed. She would've been a conflict of interest, anyway, he thought. He nodded and left.

Eldon examined the napkin with Tran's address as he walked back to the office. He didn't recognize the name of the road but he could find it on a map. The address was information independent of Nola or Huey. He could stake out Tran's place, observe comings and goings. Bribe the trash collector to let him burrow through Tran's garbage. Or simply drive up to Muskrat, put his foot in the door, and holler questions in French. Even if Tran Minh remained uncooperative, where there was one Vietnamese, there would be others; and with a little aid from Huey Bellows, some of them would talk to the press.

Rain pattered on the sidewalk. Eldon stuffed the napkin into a pocket. He looked ahead and saw that the Ship of Love now nestled beside his Citroën in the *Sun*'s parking lot. He smiled at the heartwarming sight as he walked back to the office.

He began roughing out the series in his mind. First, a teaser recapping the week's violent events, leading up to Tran's illegal deeds. Then a look at the Vietnamese refugee community that Tran used for a front, with plenty of emphasis on the plight of the poor Asians. There could be a sidebar on Truong Van Vinh. Last, a story about the local underworld that Tran served.

Eldon reached the newspaper's side door and entered the office. Ambrose sat with telephones in both ears, fingers flying across his typewriter keyboard. A brawl had broken out at the track tryouts; it would be a busy night for sports, after all. Eldon dropped the baseball cap on McFee's head and tapped on the darkroom door.

"Dark!" Shelly yelled. Eldon smiled and strolled to his desk, still laying plans.

What about the drugs? That was for the story about the Patterson ranch and the Sherwood Forest Corporation. God knew where the stuff went once it left Port Jerome; the *Sun* lacked the resources to follow it further, anyway. A quote from the DEA flack in Seattle could tie off that loose end.

Eldon busied himself with sports page layouts and incoming calls. He could crank the series out quickly. Dougie soon would be in custody—Eldon's photo of the swine was all over the Pacific Northwest by now—and that would make a fine hard-news tie-in.

He made the night police checks, phoning dispatchers at the sheriff's office, the state police, and the few tiny municipal police departments in the county to see whether there was anything good other than the brawl. Maybe someone had bagged Dougie.

No one had. The festival had resulted in plenty of drunk-and-disorderly arrests—the Dead Man's Hand and the fracas at the school track helped push up the score. Drunken-driving busts were on the rise. Eldon wrote a statistical story Fiske could use as an excuse for an editorial. Copy generated copy; the news mill kept turning.

Eldon called the coast guard, too. No one was missing at sea, but a record number of vessels were coming into the harbor for the annual Blessing of the Boats. The ragtag regatta would be escorted past the reviewing stand at the festival's climax by the cutter *Veritable*. There was to be a helicopter flyover, as well. Eldon got a cheery quote from the watch officer and wrote an advance about the sacred occasion, fleshing it out with tidbits from the Pioneer Days press kit.

Fiske liked to come in each morning and find the copy basket primed. A glow of satisfaction stole over Eldon. He had helped fill the hole.

The darkroom door remained closed. Eldon decided to phone Frank. "Got your wits about you? How's your ankle?"

"My wits are sharp, but my ankle's stiff as a rusty hinge. Alternate cold packs and hot-water bottles. Aspirin for pain."

"I could loan you some porno books for company."

Frank chuckled. "I *have* company."

"Oh. I see. Don't let me keep you—"

"No need to hang up yet. Did you run down anything about the Patterson place?"

Eldon told what he had learned from the assessor. "The Santa Monica number is disconnected."

"I've got a friend on one of the L.A. papers. I'll get him to check out this Walter J. Lane."

"L.A.'s a mighty big city."

"It's worth a call." Frank giggled. Plainly he was being lasciviously tickled. Eldon hung up with a sinking feeling. Women always went for the cripples. Didn't *he* have honorable wounds?

Shelly emerged from the darkroom, sweater rumpled, looking tired. She took prints of the track event to Ambrose and conferred with him. Ambrose selected a photo and Shelly took it to Eldon so he could measure it for the sports page and write a caption.

"The fight started after I left," Shelly said. "I missed out again."

"How could you know to stick around? This is okay. It proves we were there."

"It proves we weren't there when it counted," Shelly said. "That was a hell of a picture you had today; I didn't get that one, either."

"That was just luck, if you want to call it that."

"I wish I had luck like yours."

"You got the hanging elephant, didn't you?"

"Thanks to you."

"You're tired," Eldon said. "I'm glad you were on the search story. Those were good photos; Fiske showed me. Meet any handsome Coasties?"

Shelly gave a tight smile. "I left those to Marsha. Has anything turned up on Dougie?"

"It's only a matter of time. Pretty weird case, huh?"

"I'll say. Had dinner yet, Eldon?"

"It's past that time, isn't it? Want to find some chili?"

"Care to smoke a joint first?" Shelly asked. "It'll put an edge on your appetite. And I need to unwind."

Eldon glanced toward Ambrose. The sports editor was riveted to the telephone. "Uh, sure," Eldon said. "You didn't score it around here, I hope?"

"Oh, no. I brought it with me from California. Sacramento Gold. It's in my van."

Eldon signaled Ambrose that they were going to eat and then followed Shelly outside to the Ship of Love.

They climbed through the van's side door and slid it shut behind them. Eldon reclined on the red velvet cushions, listening to the cozy rattle of rain on the roof. He looked up to see Ogden O. Sherwood glaring down, his antique poster now spread across the ceiling. Shelly switched on the interior lights and tape deck—some new rock singer. *I could teach her a lot about music,* Eldon thought.

The van was equipped with indirect lighting. It gave the satin sheets and the velvet paintings on the walls a rich, warm sheen. Eldon watched as Shelly slid a plastic Baggie and rolling papers from under a cushion and began rolling a joint.

"I enjoy watching a pretty girl roll a jay. You're a wicked woman, Shelly Sherwood."

"Smoke it while you've got it, I say." Shelly tapped brown marijuana into the paper, licked the paper's edge with delicate flicks of her tongue, and rolled the paper up.

"We can't make a habit of this," Eldon said.

"I've just got to get stoned tonight. It's been such a week." Shelly lit the joint, inhaled expertly, and passed it to Eldon.

"Yes, you've had quite a first week." Eldon took a long toke. Too long. The harsh smoke raked his lungs. He stifled a coughing fit with difficulty. It had been a long time. He looked around the van as he exhaled. Were the soft covers somewhat askew? Or had he done that when he climbed across them?

"Strong stuff," he said, feeling his temples pulse. "In Berkeley, we smoked it through a water pipe full of cheap red wine. Say, what's that?"

"What?"

"Is that a man's necktie crumpled in the corner?"

"An old souvenir," Shelly said with languid indifference. She took a second toke and lolled like a princess. She looked seductive—or like a woman with a secret. "Do you miss Berkeley?" she asked.

"Not really. The fishing's better here."

"Do you miss your wife? Think you'll ever get back together?"

"You know, I don't think I'd have her back." Eldon was surprised at his words. He felt as if he were a balloon suddenly cast free.

"Would you like to get married again?" Shelly asked.

"Are you proposing?"

"I'm offering you this joint."

Eldon took another toke. "Ahh . . . yes, that is fine weed, Shelly. Good for aches and pains. There are some things to be said for California."

"But you wouldn't go back. I wouldn't, either. I've disappeared from there."

"I gather you had a boyfriend there. Now ex-boyfriend?"

"Yes."

"Miss him?"

"I miss the sex. It was great sex."

"I miss sex, too."

"Men can be nice and fun to have around," Shelly said, "but they're not to be trusted."

"Some of us aren't so bad." Eldon passed the joint, taking the opportunity to move closer, and felt a thrill as their fingers touched.

"It was down the rabbit hole for me, coming here"—Shelly took a hit, held it, exhaled—"woo! To Uncle Ogden's place."

"You're being crazy, thinking Pugh is your great-uncle," Eldon said. "Why not just ask him? Ask him if he's your uncle."

Shelly looked at the poster on the ceiling for a long moment. He watched her eyes, enormously dilated, and thought of kissing the lids. He had started to lean forward when Shelly spoke: "If I ask him, he might deny it and disappear again. I have to trap him into it, somehow."

Shelly gave Eldon's shoulder a push. He rolled back and watched the ceiling, returning Ogden's imperious glare.

"This whole place has lost its way," Shelly said. "Unbelievable." Her eyelids fluttered. "Where was I? Oh, yeah . . . this murder thing sure is weird."

"It's sure good copy."

"Yeah. How do we *know* Marie killed Xuan? I mean, Dougie might've done that one, too. Or Huey Bellows. Or Pugh—"

Eldon thought of Stephanie's mumbled warning and then of Stephanie's breasts. He wondered how Shelly's breasts would compare and decided with pleasure that they would be okay.

He eased himself back up to watch her fit the smoldering roach into a paper clip and suck in smoke without touching the bright ember to her lips. Eldon moved in as he took the roach, feeling disembodied as he brought his face to hers. Their lips grazed. They did not quite kiss.

Shelly popped a sheaf of papers between them, peeking over the papers like a courtesan over a fan. "Better read these, Eldon."

"Later—"

"Art Nola said to give them to you."

That brought Eldon up short. "What are these?"

"Reports on the murders. Art gave them to me after we came back from recovering the cook's body." Shelly snapped on the dome light.

Eldon winced in the sudden harsh glare and squinted at the papers. "These are copies of toxicology reports."

"Art said to remember that he didn't give them to you."

Eldon grinned. "No, he didn't. You did. Art's in the clear. He can swear it under oath."

"Am *I* in the clear?"

"Sure. In Oregon, the burden of confidentiality is on the government. But these aren't things reporters usually get to see before a case goes to trial."

"What if they ask me where I got them?"

"Shield law, m'dear. They can't make us reveal our sources. This is a v-e-r-y progressive state."

"Just like *All the President's Men*."

"That's what makes this business fun." Eldon shook his head to clear it and studied the papers. "Here's the report on Nguyen Xuan. Yup, he was stoned to the gills. Very high levels of tetrahydrocannabinol in his blood when he died. That's THC and that means pot. The same for Marie Payne. I suspected as much . . . she was right out of Thomas De Quincey. Here's a report on Horton. Who the hell's Horton?"

"Who weighs hundreds of pounds and swings through the air with the greatest of ease?"

"This is a tox report on the elephant!"

"Do you realize how much dope it would take to get an elephant stoned?" Shelly said.

"They must've fed him their whole damn garden," said Eldon.

They laughed uproariously. A stoned elephant was the funniest thing in the world. Eldon fell upon Shelly and they rolled around on the cushions. She tickled him and Eldon had to roll away.

"How much grass *would* it take?" Shelly asked as Eldon gasped for breath. "Who'd waste good dope on an elephant?"

"Marie. It would be like her, I'll bet."

"Maybe Xuan and Marie got stoned and thought it would be funny if the elephant got high, too."

"No; it's how she got Horton to trample Nguyen Xuan," said Eldon. "Elephants won't normally step on human beings, you know."

"She got Horton loaded and then did the same with Xuan, with the aid of a few feminine wiles—"

"Right on."

"Then it's a mutual stroll into the tent, bop on the head with the riding crop—"

"And Xuan goes under the elephant's foot." Eldon studied the report on Horton. The words swam before him. "Blood analysis, fecal analysis—high concentrations of THC. . . . They really rushed these tests through. Tox reports usually take a couple of weeks."

"This case is *important*," Shelly said.

"I hope so . . . plenty of murders."

"Not just murder, Eldon . . . a *hell* of a lot of dope. Enough dope to stone an elephant. Enough dope to kill for."

Her words seeped into Eldon's pot-fuzzed brain. He imagined vast marijuana fields thriving in the rain, guarded by trumpeting elephants. It was no secret that marijuana plantations had sprung up inland, in other counties—why not here on the South Coast, so desperately in need of industry?

"South Coast pot growers versus opium smugglers," he said.

"The domestic growers must be pushing out the importers," Shelly said.

"It would explain a lot of things. Like the Patterson place. It's fenced off because it's a marijuana farm."

"No wonder they ran Xuan off."

"Didn't want their competitor hanging around," Eldon said. "He's an opium importer; he knows too much. Marie kills him later, and Dougie and Tumpat, who are importers themselves, kill her in revenge."

"Maybe Marie went aboard ship in the first place to tell them to quit or they'd get what Xuan got," Shelly said.

"She was arrogant enough." Eldon examined the reports. "There are autopsy summaries, here, too. Traces of human hair on Marie's riding crop match hair from Xuan's head." He read on. "This mentions the green glass I saw around Nguyen Xuan's body."

"What's it say about it?"

"Nothing. It was just broken green glass."

"Pieces of a pop bottle?"

"The lucky ornament that Huey made for Truong Van Vinh's wife was green glass, too. Huey works in glass. There was green glass in the cabin where Frank and I found Dougie. This glass business bothers the hell out of me."

"So you think Huey's involved."

"There was no love lost between Huey and Xuan. He had a motive to kill Xuan, or to arrange it."

"Because of Theresa?"

"Because of Theresa. And Huey told me himself that he used to grow dope."

"He helped you, though," said Shelly. "Why?"

"He's Nola's snitch . . . and that's not to be repeated. Art doesn't know I know. And maybe Art doesn't know some things about Huey."

"If Huey hated Xuan, how'd Xuan get green glass from Huey? What could green glass have to do with pot? How would Dougie get green glass? And what's the link, then, to the murder of Marie?"

"Damned if I know," Eldon said. "But it's going to make good copy when I figure it out."

"When *we* figure it out. It was my idea to start with."

Eldon frowned. Shelly was right. She was one jump ahead of him again by cozening the tox reports from Nola. Well, he could stand sharing the credit—but right now, the wench would have to be taught a lesson.

Eldon slid his arm around Shelly's waist. She slipped free, but in a promising sort of way.

"Pugh," she said.

"Forget Pugh for a minute."

"Pugh lives up there. You can see right onto the plantation from his place. He must know what's going on."

"He's too busy looking for UFOs."

"He has trails all over the place."

"And he's your great-uncle."

"I've been studying the poster. There's a definite resemblance."

"And there's the putative tattoo."

"All the more reason to make that visit. You promised."

"We have to do it discreetly. Let me run down a few more loose ends. Stay away from there. It's dangerous."

"I'm not afraid."

"You damn well ought to be. I don't want anything to happen to you."

Shelly gave him a soft look. "Eldon, that's sweet."

Eldon put a hand on Shelly's waist and slid it up her torso. She giggled and blocked him. "This is funny," she said.

"This is fun," Eldon said.

"It's funny. Ironic. I got this good leak from Art and now I'm stoned and so are you. Art'll never guess."

The hairs on the back of Eldon's neck prickled. "Listen, don't you fool with Br'er Fox. He's smarter than you think."

Shelly snapped at him playfully. They tussled on the velvet covers. Eldon got his hand onto the smooth, soft mound of a breast. Shelly cried, "God, look at the time! We've been gone over an hour."

"Impossible. Christ."

Shelly pushed herself upright. "I've got to do something with my hair."

I've been had, Eldon thought. Or have I? She gave me the tox reports. Marijuana fields whirled through his mind. And faces— Marie, Dougie, Xuan, Stephanie, Nola, Horton the elephant, Bigfoot.

Eldon clutched at Shelly's sweater but she slipped out the door. Cold air and rain blew into the van. Eldon's throat rasped. His groin ached; he would never get to sleep tonight. When he got home, he would comfort himself with *Lust Dolls* and Céline.

12

Eldon awoke.

Morning fog crawled across the windows. Eldon tried to tell himself that he was snug aboard the Ship of Love, but a rough seat cover, not a velvet pillow, pressed his cheek. He sat up with a start. He was sprawled in the front seat of his Citroën, still parked outside the *Sun*. He clutched a sheaf of papers. The tox reports.

His testicles ached. His head felt clear and empty as a jar. The morning light was cold, Shelly's van nowhere to be seen. The previous night was a haze. Eldon had sleepwalked through the rest of the shift like an elephant with its feet in buckets of concrete.

The keys hung from the Citroën's ignition. Eldon recalled stumbling from the office at midnight and trying to start the car. Which had failed—the engine or his metabolism? He checked his watch: 6:32 A.M. God, it was nearly time to make morning cop checks. No time to get home for a shower or change of clothes. Worse, no time to eat.

He decided to walk three blocks to the county jail rather than telephone. There would be coffee—thin, vile stuff but it would renew life. And Art Nola's office was there. He would wait for the detective to arrive; Art normally arrived for work early. Pumping Nola for information would give Eldon purpose after coffee had restored life. He got the car door open and climbed out into the clammy air.

The deserted street was littered with festival debris. It was as if Port Jerome had tried to destroy itself in revelry and failed even at that. The three-block walk to the jail seemed like three miles. At last, it loomed in the fog, a sprawled-out piece of California architecture like the *Sun* building, a prestige project constructed with a federal grant originally intended for renovation of the ancient county courthouse in Preacher's Hole.

At the dispatcher's desk, Eldon scanned the incident log. He noted a residential burglary and wondered whether the goods would find their way into the hands of Tran Minh. Eldon dropped a dime into the jar beside the coffee maker and poured himself a Styrofoam cup of brew. This barely even smells like coffee, he thought, blowing on the brown liquid as he stared through the bulletproof window that looked into the jail.

Jailers were hosing down the drunk tank. Big men with buzzcuts and enormous bellies, they shooed the night's catch of bleary rowdies into one corner of the fenced pen while they hosed down its concrete floor. The inmates shambled obediently, nursing wounds from brawls, their clothing foul. Among them was a large figure with a bandaged nose—Paavo the Finn, now in durance vile. Too broke to go bail, Eldon thought. At least they've bandaged his nose.

A smaller man shuffled in Paavo's wake—Cap'n Jasper. The drunken ex-tugboater no doubt had given the deputies ample reason to pull him in; but Jasper actually was a charity case, permitted the hard comfort of the drunk tank and a mug of bad coffee and a couple of slices of thick stale bread for breakfast, now that the weather was turning cold.

As Eldon watched, Jasper collided from behind with the Finn. Paavo whirled, swinging, but his haymaker passed well over Jasper's head. Jasper danced back; Paavo rushed after Jasper and they went down, rolling under the onslaught of the hose.

Eldon got the jail roster from the dispatcher and scanned for familiar names. With any luck, the fuzz had trolled in Dougie, or at least some prominent citizen, during the night's debauch. Nothing. Flipping the pages, Eldon came to the name *Peake, Cyrus*.

The hanging ringmaster. That was something to ask Art about.

He returned the clipboard and made his way up to the offices above the jail. Nola sat at his desk in a corner, still in his topcoat, examining telephone messages. The desk was bare. On the wall were a typed work schedule, a community-college diploma, and a small picture of Jesus Christ.

"Got time for that coffee, Art?"

"You're up early, Eldon."

"The early bird catches the fox," Eldon said, feeling as if the fact that he had smoked marijuana were written across his face.

"Not on the record," Nola said.

"Okay. But I could use a doughnut."

"I don't know about that," Nola said with a glance at Eldon's belly, "but we can talk."

They headed for Pop's coffee shop, known for its huge, sticky sweet rolls. Nola had a preoccupied little smile that seemed to conceal secrets.

Secrets are what I'm after, Eldon thought. "You're always up early yourself."

"No wife to keep me warm."

"We're alike in that respect. Were you ever married? If I may ask?"

"It didn't work out."

"Me, neither. She didn't like being married to a writer."

"Mine didn't like being married to a cop. But now I've met a lady who likes cops. Things are happening really fast for us. Something like that throws a whole new light on your life."

"Well, good for you." It's put you in a helpful mood, Eldon thought, meditating on his own sore balls.

At Pop's, they slid into a cramped booth with big sweet rolls and mugs of coffee. Nola frowned at his sticky roll as Eldon chomped. "Whoever said country boys eat good?" Nola wondered.

Eldon looked at his roll. Such rolls had been his breakfast many times in the past five years. He felt conscious of his paunch; Nola was lean and keen. He went on chewing, however—last night's high had left him ravenous.

"Anything on Dougie?" Eldon asked.

"Nope. The choppers won't go up again until this fog burns off."

Eldon wanted to ask about the tox reports but didn't dare. "Have they checked out the Patterson place?"

Nola looked surprised. "Why?"

"To look for Dougie."

"Yeah. He wasn't there. Obviously."

"Just wondered. There are a lot of trails up that way and some of 'em are supposed to run down onto the ranch."

"A patrol deputy talked with the owner."

"A deputy was on the ranch?"

"At the gate. There was a nasty watchdog."

"The owner's name is Lane?"

"No. I forget the name but it wasn't Lane."

"What about the *Orient Star*?"

"U.S. Customs let her sail."

"Even though opium was seized aboard?"

"Who told you about opium?" Nola said.

"I have my sources."

"We found nothing," Nola said. "We think Dougie and Tumpat took it with them. Dougie probably slit Tumpat's throat over how to divvy the treasure."

"Dougie didn't seem to have any opium at the cabin."

"We think he buried it."

"Maybe he's fenced it by now," Eldon said.

"He should've done that first, instead of hanging around."

"Why *was* Dougie at the cabin? Waiting for help from friends? Has he *got* friends?"

"Not anymore. He's too hot for them to handle. No loyalty among thieves."

"You'd think opium would buy loyalty. I keep thinking he was waiting for someone . . . or waiting to go somewhere. Like onto the Patterson ranch."

"What gives you that idea?"

"It's a fascinating place," Eldon said. "I'd like to try out the fishing hole there. I take a lot of interest in a story when it's almost cost me my skin."

"Let the law handle it, Eldon."

"You said you'd help me out, Art."

"I've helped you more than I should've."

"At least confirm some things for me."

"Maybe I will and maybe I won't," Nola said. "We're definitely off the record here."

"Okay, okay. I just don't want to be caught by surprise when it all comes down. Look, the *Orient Star* was allowed to sail because it was small change. Minor action. Am I right so far?"

"Okay, you're right."

"But three murders is too many over 'small change.'"

"You'd be surprised."

"Xuan and Marie Payne and Tumpat went down in a feud

between drug smugglers and local dope growers who're pushing them out. Am I right again?"

"That's not too bad."

"And the Patterson place is the main dope plantation."

Nola looked sharply at Eldon, as if the reporter had just played a fifth ace in a poker game. "I can't go into that."

"I can sit on the story. I won't blow the case. I just don't want to get scooped by the Portland papers. Come on, when does it pop? An exclusive on the bust would mean good ink for the sheriff's department."

"Ink's the last thing I care about, as you well know."

"It's the only thing I care about," Eldon said.

"I believe that's true," Nola said. "You're too good a reporter for your own good."

"Art, that's a compliment. We've had our differences in the past, but cops and reporters . . . they both pursue truth, in their own ways."

"Maybe so," Nola said. "But you've got an unlucky air about you. That's what I wanted to talk to you about."

"Don't I know it. I almost got laid last night, but no score."

"I mean it. You're unlucky."

"Damn right. It's been months. Did you have a dream or something?" Eldon immediately regretted the slip.

But Nola only nodded. "I had a dream about you. Say what you want . . . dreams count. I don't remember it clearly. There was a pistol. And you were talking in a strange language."

"I speak French."

"Just goes to show," Nola said.

"So, did I get shot?"

"That wasn't clear. It was a pretty crazy dream."

"What else do you remember?"

"This was all taking place on a fishing trip. Damned if I know why I was there; I've never been fishing in my life. You said, 'I've hooked him, I've hooked him, but he keeps slipping off.'"

"Did I say it in this strange language?"

"You were fishing for Bigfoot."

Eldon no longer wanted the rest of his sweet roll. An omen about fishing cut close to the bone. He pulled off his hat and touched the colorful flies. "You read the newspaper too much."

"I dreamed you're unlucky and you'd better heed it. Call it an old cop's hunch."

"I had a close shave on the boat, but I gave Dougie a close shave back."

"You're just lucky he ran."

"I won't run away from this story," Eldon said. "I'm not playing reporter."

Nola sighed. "I know you're not. I used to think you were a sadistic bastard. But after the other night on the ship, and then on the log float, I thought, no, you believe in what you do."

"I'm working on something about the Vietnamese living up in Muskrat," Eldon said, pleased. "Social awareness stuff . . . nothing to do with the Patterson place or the drug war. I'll be spending some time up there but I won't get in your way."

"Is that why you were visiting Huey?"

"He has Vietnamese contacts."

"And how did you happen to know to go aboard ship the night of the raid?"

Eldon's heart fluttered but he kept his voice even. "I got that out of Marie Payne. We talked after Cyrus Peake strung up the elephant. I put two and two together."

"You sure can charm the ladies."

"I also found out that Marie knew Nguyen Xuan. When Shelly—"

"Let's leave Shelly out of this."

"Ah, right. . . . Let me put it another way. When Frank and I were up in the cabin, I noticed that Dougie left some green glass behind."

"Green glass?"

"There were pieces of green glass around Xuan's body in the big top."

"I guess so. I wouldn't know about the cabin."

"Does it mean anything to you?"

"No," said Nola. "Dougie certainly wasn't at the big top. How do you know that the green glass in the cabin was Dougie's?"

"Well, gee, Art, it was right next to a fresh turd. Who else could've put it there?"

"The turd or the glass?"

"Both! Just remember that Dougie and Xuan are at least indirectly connected."

Nola took out a leather-backed notebook and jotted in it. "I'll look into that. Thanks."

"Since we're trading information—"

"We're having coffee."

"What about Peake, the ringmaster? You're still holding him. How's he fit in?"

"He doesn't. We're kicking him loose today. He's just a very excitable guy."

"He hung an elephant. He's crazy."

"Crazy must be an asset in the circus business. The jail's crowded. Stringing up an elephant may be cruelty to animals, but it's not exactly a capital offense."

"I want to get hold of him."

"Then step lively. He goes free this morning, and the circus has already left town. I'd go to the impound lot behind the annex if I were you, snag him when he goes to claim his vehicle."

"Maybe I can catch him—" Eldon stood up.

"I'll get the check," Nola said with his smile that refused to say whether its owner was foe or friend.

At the impound lot, a bony attendant with a shovel was scraping a freshly squashed cat off the street outside the gate. "Howdy. Lose your kitty?"

"Damn," Eldon said. There was no sign in the yard of a camper pickup. "Did a camper just pull out of here?"

"You betcha. Ran right over this cat. Wasn't your truck, was it? They had the receipt."

"I need to talk to them."

"Musta been the fattest woman on earth and her boyfriend." The attendant flipped the dead cat into an oil drum full of trash. "I don't guess you've got too far to look. She's 'round the corner with a busted axle."

The ringmaster's pickup was a few dozen yards away, canted sharply to one side. A pair of legs was sticking from beneath it. An immense blubber mountain of a woman sat on the curb, weeping. Eldon thought for a moment that the ringmaster lay crushed beneath the pickup, but then he saw that the vehicle was supported by a jack.

The fat lady had the biggest nose Eldon had ever seen. It jutted like a granite cliff from her shapeless pink face. She played solitaire as she wept, tossing the cards before her into the street. Every card landed unerringly faceup.

"Say, you're cute," the fat lady said hoarsely as Eldon came up. "Sit down with me and play some twenty-one."

"Is that Cyrus Peake under there?"

The fat lady squinted fearfully around her nose. "Oh, God, that wasn't your cat, was it?"

"I'm here about the elephant."

"Poor Horton! It was awful! Please, Mr. Humane Society, Cyrus didn't know what he was doin'. That red-haired woman made 'im crazy."

The legs beneath the truck retracted, were replaced after a moment by the ringmaster's oil-smeared face. "What do you want?"

"He's the humane society man," the fat lady said. "Isn't he cute?"

"He's a fat slob same as you," the ringmaster said. "I've got a busted axle and I don't need any noise about animal rights. Animals don't vote, they don't have rights. Anyway, where were you do-gooders when they tried to take away my elephant?"

"I'm not—"

Tears welled from the ringmaster's eyes and rolled across his stubbled cheeks. "I loved that elephant. In the jail, the cons showed me the newspaper, Horton a-swingin' on page one. Pushed it in my face and laughed like devils."

"I'm not from the humane society. I'm Eldon Larkin from the *South Coast Sun*."

"You took that picture. You were there!"

"I didn't take the picture. I want to ask some questions."

"Talk to 'im, Cyrus," the fat lady said, "set the record right. It was all the red-haired woman's fault, Mr. Newspaper, it was all her fault."

"Shuddup," the ringmaster said and rocked his head from side to side, squeezing his eyes and breathing like a bellows.

"The only way we can print the truth is if people tell us what we need to know," Eldon said.

The ringmaster groaned. "A hanging elephant, is that your truth?"

"How long did you know Marie Payne?"

The fat lady wailed. "Marie was with us a couple of seasons. She'd join up when we'd hit the coast. She was an evil woman, I knew it from the start. She had Cyrus in her thrall."

"Be quiet, you bloated sow," the ringmaster said in disgust.

"She only used you, Cyrus! I loved you truly."

"Marie's dead. I got nothin' left."

"You got me, Cyrus," the fat lady said. "I'll stand by you through thick an' thin."

"I loved her," the ringmaster said. "That how it was."

"You were angry at her when I first saw you," Eldon said.

"She had a way of touching the leather to a man, you know? It stung but it made you move."

"I think I know what you mean," Eldon said.

"It's like I can't move anymore. She was the source of my spirit."

"Was she the source of, ah, anything else?"

"Like what?"

"Like drugs."

"Drugs?" the fat lady asked. "Cyrus wouldn't have such stuff in his circus, Mr. Newspaper."

"Very commendable. But perhaps behind your back?"

The ringmaster smiled at the fat lady with malicious pleasure. "Me and Bobo the dwarf had a good toke the day Horton died. Marie always had good weed. And Thai stick." The fat lady gave an operatic gasp.

"Where'd she get the stuff?" Eldon asked.

"You think I was stupid enough to ask?" the ringmaster said. "The price was right."

"A circus is full of depravity," the fat lady said. "I was always having to look the other way."

"You're too fat to turn your own head," the ringmaster said. "I know you were doin' it with Bobo!"

The fat lady yowled and threw the cards at the ringmaster.

"Thai stick's an import," Eldon said as the cards fluttered down. "Did Marie ever talk about boats?"

The ringmaster shook his head sadly. "No. No. I always looked the other way for Marie. See what it's got me."

"There's other towns to play, Cyrus," the fat lady said.

"Not for me," the ringmaster said. "I can barely hold up my head, thinking of her getting it on with . . . with—"

"With Bobo?" Eldon asked politely.

"With that Viet we had doing scut work," the fat lady said.

Eldon stared. "Nguyen Xuan?"

"She flaunted it. She let me catch 'em at it," the ringmaster said suddenly, nearly gagging on the words. "They used to do it in the hay in the elephant tent. After Horton killed Xuan, I went crazy."

"He wasn't gonna be able to catch 'em at it anymore," the fat lady said with a cackle. "He *liked* to catch 'em!"

"I'll twist your fat neck!" the ringmaster cried.

"That was her way of twisting your nuts!" the fat lady screamed.

"Marie told me that she hardly knew Xuan," Eldon said.

"Marie said whatever she wanted," the fat lady said. "That's why Cyrus loved her. He loved her lies."

"She two-timed me for that little dink!" The ringmaster pounded the bottom of the truck chassis with his fists. "It was Marie's idea to put him on the payroll; she and him were old friends."

"They were *friends*?" Eldon asked.

"I should've seen what was coming," the ringmaster said.

"I'll never step out on you the way she did, Cyrus," the fat lady said. "I've got a lot more love to give." Unable to rise or bend over, she flailed vainly for the cards she had scattered in the street.

Eldon stared at the cards. They were like the pieces of his dope-war theory—bright bits, scattered, meaning nothing. Marie and Xuan were supposed to be on different sides.

Eldon scooped up some of the cards and held them out to the fat lady, but she was looking at the ringmaster with gleaming eyes. The ringmaster, prone in the street, looked back with the same expression—the greedy, serpentlike gaze that Stephanie Hosfelder and Ahmed had shared aboard the *Orient Star*.

Eldon dropped the cards and trudged off with a queasy shiver. Too much sugar and not enough sleep. Too much pot. I blew my chances with Shelly by getting too grabby—and now this.

The sun began to burn off the fog as he reached the newspaper office. Eldon went through the front door and into the newsroom.

Fiske, busy reading the morning wire copy, merely waved; Eldon thanked God for small mercies. Marsha stood at her desk, admiring a single red rosebud in a green glass vase. Eldon flinched at the sight of green glass and wondered whether the rose could possibly have come from Art Nola.

"It's from Lieutenant Beamish at the coast guard station,"

Marsha said. "He grows them by one corner of the helicopter hangar."

"Beamish isn't a chaplain, is he?" Eldon asked.

"Certainly not. He's a helicopter pilot. He's very busy with preparations for the flyover during the Blessing of the Boats. They're all busy polishing their guns."

Eldon went to his desk. Even Marsha had scored.

He made the rest of his routine morning telephone calls. Nothing added up. Three murders and a hanged elephant, connected with off-the-record material, hearsay, and supposition— pieces as scattered as the fat lady's cards.

Whatever Marie Payne's motive for killing Nguyen Xuan, it was not the motive that circumstances suggested, not the circumstances he had confirmed with Art Nola.

Or had he confirmed them? Just what had Nola told him? He was not sure that Nola had told him anything.

Eldon got the copied tox reports from his coat and studied them. High concentrations of THC—that would be from the Thai stick. No wonder it was easy to get the elephant stoned. Marie just fed him a wad of the stuff and let nature take its course.

But how did Marie get Thai stick if she was in with the local growers? Eldon wondered. If there are local growers. I haven't met any yet besides Huey, and he's retired.

Maybe he had the sides switched around. Marie was the smuggler and Xuan the grower. But then why would Dougie kill Marie?

He could write a story about the tox reports, but that would probably let a big fish off the hook in order to reel in a small one. This is big, like Shelly said, Eldon thought, or Art wouldn't have been so equivocal. I've got to bide my time, find out who has enough Thai stick to stone an elephant. I should have pressed Nola harder.

Fiske dropped a press release on Eldon's desk and wandered off humming. Nekaemas County had been awarded a large social-services grant. Dispirited, Eldon made some calls and fiddled with the routine story until lunch.

He was about to go out for a sandwich when Frank called.

"How's the foot?" Eldon asked.

"I'm getting lots of tender loving care," Frank said happily. "I'm getting it right now."

"Well, bingo for you. Anyone I know?"

"New girl who works at the library. But listen, I've got the word on Walker J. Lane and it's good."

"What? Your friend in L.A. does fast work."

"They've got the resources where he works. When I told him the circumstances, he got a hunch and it paid off. You're going to love this."

"So where can I find Lane?"

"Better get out your Ouija board. Lane's dead."

Eldon caught his breath. "Murdered?"

"Strictly natural causes. Convulsions." Frank added with deliberate gusto, "There's no indication of infant abuse."

"Infant abuse?"

"Walker J. Lane died three days after he was born, Eldon . . . in March 1948."

13

"A paper man!"

"You got it," said Frank. "Driver's license, Social Security number, even a California realtor's ticket, all fake. It all tracks back to the same birth certificate . . . Walker J. Lane, long dead."

"He probably has credit cards, too," Eldon said.

"We checked a reverse telephone directory on that Santa Monica address. The last listed occupant is Larry Chadwick. Or was. No Chadwick there long since."

"Someone's been a busy boy. I'd cover my tracks, too, if I was buying a dope plantation." Eldon explained his theory.

"You think that's really it? If pot's a burgeoning local industry, arrests for street sales and possession ought to be rising."

"There hasn't been anything like that on the police logs. Maybe they're just getting established."

"The way you tell it, Eldon, they're established enough to fight a war."

"Old man Patterson sold out in March," Eldon said. "Is that enough time for them to grow a crop?"

"Two crops. Pot matures in ten to fifteen weeks. They probably won't be planting another this year, though; the cold weather's coming."

"You seem to know a lot about it, Frank."

"We used to grow it behind the dorm in college. That ranch is how big?"

"Two hundred and fifty acres."

"Forty acres planted in good stuff would be worth a couple hundred thousand bucks."

"That's plenty enough to kill for," Eldon said.

"It isn't like they have vast fields of it, though. That would stick out like a sore thumb."

"Huey Bellows was a small-time grower here at one time. He used to hide his plants among the trees," Eldon said.

"Could he be back in business on a bigger scale?"

"It was years ago."

Eldon thought uneasily of the green glass charm Huey made for Truong Van Vinh's wife, of Huey's crazy talk of visions and of Huey striking down Paavo the Finn with a single ruthless blow. Eldon thought of Huey steering him toward the *Orient Star* on the correct night to be murdered. No—Huey had been too open. And Eldon could not imagine Truong Van Vinh consorting with a pot grower. Enough paranoia, he thought, and everything will be connected. "Frank, you have a romantic imagination."

"We're in a romantic business." Frank sounded somehow distracted. Then there was silence on the line except for the sound of rising breathing.

"Frank? What's your . . . ah . . . company up to?"

"I've . . . ah . . . ah . . . got to *go* now, Eldon!" Frank's voice rose to an ecstatic shout.

Eldon hung up the phone as Fiske returned from his orbit of the office. "Good story on the county grant," Fiske said.

"Damn it, Jimbo, I've got a real story here, but I can't make it fit together."

"You've done all right the past few days."

"I've got murders, I've got corpses full of THC, opium is being smuggled into the port and I've nearly gotten murdered—"

"All good copy."

"But I don't have the *story*."

"Which is?"

"The Patterson ranch is a dope plantation."

"We ought to get that into print."

"The name on the sale deed's a fake. Frank had a friend at one of the L.A. papers check it out. The man who bought the farm doesn't exist."

"Damn phone bills," Fiske said. "What makes you think it's a dope farm?"

Eldon explained what he had learned. "And Art Nola acted as if I was on the scent. But he wouldn't say yes or no."

"This reminds me of the time the mayor of Preacher's Hole feared he was an octoroon."

"Jimbo, please."

"Quite a story. The mayor finally wound up in the cork-lined hotel after outrageous deeds in public, but the proof of the pudding, the lack of proof, actually, was in the paperwork: the mayor's birth certificate."

"Yeah, the birth certificate is how we knew Walker J. Lane is a paper man—"

"So now you've got to connect Walker J. Lane with whoever really owns the ranch. Keep following the paper trail."

"I'm about out of paper to follow."

"Just like the mayor. The thing that sent him 'round the bend was that he turned out to be Greek."

"Huh?"

"The mayor was no octoroon; he found out he was Greek. His mother had lied to him after all, see? The mayor *was* pretty swarthy. You remind me of that mayor, Eldon. You've got all these strange thoughts but nothing you can put your finger on."

"Kind of like you and Bigfoot."

"Kind of the story of your life," Fiske said. His expression grew keen, as if he were a vulture sniffing ripe carrion. "Now think: Is there *anything else* that might have some official paper attached to it?" Without waiting for a reply, the editor wandered off to the wire desk, where his pipe lay smoldering in an old catfood can.

Eldon stared after him in annoyance. He's right, he decided, I'm all over the map.

It was lunchtime, anyway. Eldon went back to Pop's and treated himself to the Special Rueben Sandwich, which came with gooey yellow potato salad. He got a big Coke and ate packaged crackers one after another while his sandwich was prepared.

So how do I connect the owner of the ranch to what's going on? he wondered. Ask Huey? Unless Walker J. Lane *is* Huey.

That didn't sound right at all. The image of the affable, squirrel-eyed oaf laying a trail of forged paper all the way from California, lying in wait for years and finally cutting an expensive deal for ocean-front real estate made as much sense as the ringmaster's motives for stringing up Horton.

Besides, Huey had talked too freely. Eldon felt his earlier fear of the man ebb. And he couldn't imagine Truong Van Vinh consorting with a dope grower.

I'll have another talk with Truong, Eldon thought as his sandwich arrived, spiked together with toothpicks topped with colored cellophane tassels. He realized he had eaten all the packaged crackers on the table while he was waiting. The ashtray overflowed with torn wrappers. No wonder I've gained weight, Eldon thought. I've got to start running or swimming or something.

He took a big swig of Coke and gobbled the sandwich. In Berkeley, he had eaten more slowly because he had talked with Bernice during meals. Now, he sometimes lunched with Frank or McFee, but for five years there really had been no company at meals. I'll have to have Shelly up for dinner, fix my Cornish game hens, Eldon thought as he chewed. And really mind my manners.

He gazed, chewing, out the front window. Shelly's Ship of Love was pulling into the newspaper's parking lot! He'd extend the invitation right away.

Eldon hurried back to the office to find Shelly pacing nervously in front of the darkroom.

"Am I glad to see you," she said.

"I'm glad to see you, too. How'd you like to—"

"Listen, Eldon, something's afoot."

"That's right; I'm going to cook you dinner. And I've got something that'll make good dinner conversation. The guy who bought the Patterson ranch is a paper man."

"What's a paper man?"

"A fake identity."

"Aaah." Shelly led him into the darkroom and closed the door. "I think we're about to have a provocative exchange of ideas."

"The man who bought the ranch exists only on paper," Eldon said. "It's easy when you have a birth certificate but don't mention that you're dead."

"How?"

"I've always meant to try this myself," Eldon said. "Every state keeps birth and death records . . . but they don't usually correlate 'em. That's the key. Want a new identity?"

"Go on."

"You visit the place where they keep the death certificates . . . the county courthouse, or some states have a central registry. Anyway, it's public record. You find an infant of your sex and with about your birth date that died right after it was born. Now, there's no other paper on that human being except . . . what?"

"The birth certificate!"

"Bingo. You go to the registry of births and ask for a certified copy of that dead baby's birth certificate, which is also public record. Costs a couple of bucks. Now you've got an official birth certificate, with a name, birth date, place of birth, parents."

"I can guess what happens next," Shelly said. "You use the birth certificate to register to vote. To get a driver's license. To get a Social Security number and a checking account. Credit cards. To file a tax return. Even to get a passport."

"What if someone questions you?"

"Your wallet and papers were stolen in a burglary just before you moved in from another state," Shelly said with delight. "Or they got lost. But there are fewer and fewer questions because the paper keeps piling up, and it's all genuine. It's a disappearing act in reverse."

"It's even more or less legal, lots of places," Eldon said. "In Oregon, you can go by any name you want, as long as it's not for fraudulent purposes. California, too."

"That must be because of the film industry there . . . all those stars with stage names," Shelly said. A faraway look came into her eyes. "My family knew from records at the Screen Actors Guild that Uncle Ogden went north. That was one reason I took this job. Uncle Ogden could've—"

"I'm going to fix you my Cornish game hen special," Eldon said quickly.

"Not tonight," Shelly said. "Here's what *I've* found. It fits in with this. And with Pugh. I was up in Muskrat today, shooting scenics. So I stopped and talked with Theresa."

"Huey's wife? She doesn't speak English."

"Of course she speaks English. What else would she speak?"

"Just Vietnamese. She didn't speak . . ."

"She didn't speak *French*, Eldon. Huey spoke to her in English the day we were there, for God's sake."

"Christ, I really slipped on that one. What was I thinking about?"

"Anyway, Huey wasn't in. Theresa says he's really agitated and that it's got something to do with Great-Uncle Ogden . . . with Pugh. Theresa doesn't know what's going on. Pugh's ranting about the Space Brothers and Bigfoot and boats. Boats in the bay."

"The Blessing of the Boats?"

"That must be it.".

"That's festival lunacy."

"Maybe he's talking in code."

"So what else? We've got a big story cooking here and we can't afford to drop the ball."

Shelly looked subdued. "Theresa's worried about Tran Minh, too. Nothing very specific, but I think it's got something to do with the murders."

"What else did she say?"

"Just that Pugh's all wound up about Bigfoot, too."

"Nice to hear that he reads my stories."

"Maybe he thinks the activity at the ranch is Bigfoot."

"Any suspicious activity is secondary to his flying saucers."

Eldon visualized the Patterson ranch from the vantage point of Pugh's UFO observation tower. "I just thought of something. Where are your photo files?"

"Here are some of the week's discarded prints. Why?"

"Let me see them."

Eldon riffled through the pile of outtakes—Nguyen Xuan's body, Horton's amazing death, the fistfight in front of the Dead Man's Hand, Pugh's spaceship, the crab-eating contest. "Here . . . a shot of the Patterson ranch from Pugh's tower. I thought you might've taken one while you were up there."

"One thing about us shutterbugs, we never stop shootin'."

"Let's show this picture to Fiske."

Shelly pulled open the sliding door to find Fiske standing there with his hand cupped to his ear.

"Game hens sound pretty good," Fiske said cheerfully.

"Take a look at this shot of the Patterson ranch," Eldon said, examining the print through an eyepiece. "The barn door's open but you can't see inside. There are vehicle tracks."

"Never mind the spy—satellite stuff," Fiske said. "What about this radio tower on the farmhouse?"

"What about it?"

"You tell me—you're the investigative reporter. For instance, do you need a county building permit to put up a radio mast?"

"Why, I don't know," Eldon said.

"If you do, the permit file at the Planning Department will have the names you need," Fiske said.

"I'll call the Federal Communications Commission in Portland, too. A ham station would be licensed."

"Now you're thinking," Fiske said. "Dee-de-dee! I'll leave you now and tend to my pipe."

Eldon grinned and hurried to a telephone. A minute later, his grin faded. Nekaemas County required no permit to erect a radio tower. Well, there still were the feds. He assumed that the phrase *Now you're thinking* was a warrant to make a long-distance call to Portland, and he did so.

The FCC had issued no ham radio license to Walker J. Lane.

"Try Patterson," Eldon said. If the mast had belonged to the ranch's former owner, that was the end of the ball game.

"Nothing," said the unseen clerk.

"Could you please try Bellows?"

"First name?"

"Huey."

"Nothing," the clerk said. "Sorry."

"Do you have ham licenses listed by county?"

"No, by name. There are no amateur licenses in those names."

"I didn't think so. Thanks." Eldon hung up.

"Did you try Ogden O. Sherwood?" Shelly asked.

"Of course not."

"Nothing, huh?"

"Big damn zero. We'll just have to hope for a break."

"We could drive up there and try to buy some dope. . . . Sorry, Eldon, just kidding."

"There's one other possibility. What did Art tell you when he gave you those tox reports?"

"Just that you'd be able to figure 'em out."

"He must've expected I'd use them in a story."

"He didn't say not to."

"Art's got no say. Remember that."

"Sure."

"I'm going to write a story about the tox reports, saying that all the killings appear to be linked. I hate to tip our hand, but maybe it will break something loose."

"Maybe that's what Art wants, too."

"That's Art's lookout. If our purposes coincide, that's okay. But if he wants to jerk me around, he'll soon find out what he's got at the end of the chain."

Shelly's eyes flashed. "Macho."

The sound of the word on her lips made Eldon tingle. "Let's see; I'll call the state medical examiner in Portland. He'll probably say the tox reports are privileged information, refuse to discuss them. He'll answer general medical questions, though. And if I make it clear I've got copies of the reports, he might even confirm what they say."

"Can you get him to say that the killings are linked?"

"I don't think he'll speculate. But *I* can, in the story. I'll call the U.S. Customs district office in Portland and the Drug Enforcement Administration in Seattle. They won't even be polite. But it'll give the story a nice regionwide cast. The wire service ought to pick it up." Eldon thought how the extra money would buy the Cornish hens and a bottle of good wine.

"And the ranch?"

"We'll sit on that for now. We can't prove it."

"A few nights up on Pugh's UFO tower with binoculars might show us some things."

Eldon ran his tongue over his front teeth. "That could get dangerous; we can't trust Pugh to keep his mouth shut."

"Maybe if we told him we wanted to watch for UFOs—"

"He probably thinks a UFO will land at the Blessing of the Boats."

"Make a great photo, Eldon. It would top the elephant."

"You know, I'll bet that's it," Eldon said. "The old fool is planning some kind of religious demonstration at the Blessing of the Boats. That tinfoil spaceship . . . think it'll float?"

"It had a wooden skeleton," Shelly said.

"He'll enter it in the regatta," Eldon said.

"They'd allow that?"

"There's a comedy class, anything that'll float. It's notorious. I've seen the priest blessing make-believe pirates paddling a leaky wooden tub."

"A tinfoil spaceship would come apart. He'll sink."

"They'll fish him out. More's the fun."

"What about Huey?"

"You saw him in action at the crab feed; this nonsense is his kind of thing. Theresa's worried because Huey and Pugh have kept it under their hats and she thinks it's something worse."

"No," Shelly said. "Huey's a dip, but an old man with a tinfoil spaceship isn't going to wind him up like this. Huey knows something is up. Something to do with the killings and the dope. And he heard it from Pugh."

"Do you think Theresa's in danger?"

"There's Tran Minh."

"I think she's safe as long as Huey's around," Eldon said. "And if something ugly happens . . . well, it's a story."

"That's a nasty attitude."

"That's business," said Eldon, making the word distinct. He was struck by the essential passivity of his profession. A reporter was completely reactive, dependent almost entirely on the turnings of the dangerous wheels of events.

Eldon tugged at his lucky hat. "I'll look into it while I'm developing the refugee stories. I'd still like to pin Tran; I don't like him. But we still need paper. Official paper."

"Too bad that ham-license idea didn't pan out," Shelly said.

"Maybe their radio's a wildcat setup."

"You know, Eldon, there are other types of radio licenses. My ex-boyfriend was a CB'er. I couldn't stand him chattering into that thing. CB chatter is the most boring stuff I ever heard."

"What license did he have?"

"Just a CB permit," Shelly said. "But there are lots of others. He started studying for a ham license, to spite me. That's what really tore it between us."

"Let's check the library."

The Nekaemas County Public Library lay beyond the county annex, in a peeling green building that antedated the Depression. They climbed the worn concrete stairs and crossed the creaking wooden floors, Eldon on the lookout for Frank's "new girl" as they headed for the file cabinets storing government pamphlets.

There were no new faces among the library staff—no doubt the new girl was still ministering to Frank's needs—but in a bulky manila folder marked *Federal Communications Commission*, they found a brochure listing radio license classes and requirements.

"There are scads of them," Shelly said.

"Let's use our heads," said Eldon. "We've struck out on ham radio and CB, but we're down here on the coast . . . so what about, let's see, a marine radio? Or a ship-station operating license?"

"What are the requirements? How do you qualify?"

"There's no test for either one. You just have to be eighteen and a U.S. citizen. Perfect for a paper man."

"We still might have to work through all the classes."

"The FCC might cross-reference the names of applicants with license type."

"Then why didn't they tell you so?"

"You have to ask the right questions. Always."

Eldon checked out the brochure and they hurried back to the newsroom. There he called the FCC in Portland once more.

"Can I help you?" It was a different clerk.

"I need to know if you have any communications licenses listed in the name of Walker J. Lane. Any license, any class."

A pause. "No."

"Try Huey Bellows. Any license, any class." Eldon ruffled the pages of his notebook while he waited. At last the clerk said, "No."

"Just a minute," Eldon said. On a page of the pad he had scrawled *Larry Chadwick* while talking with the happily crippled Frank. "Try Chadwick. Larry. Any license, any class."

It was a long chance, but it was the last name he had— probably that of a law-abiding apartment renter in Santa Monica.

The wait stretched out. Then the clerk said, "I have a marine radio license issued in March to Lawrence R. Chadwick." The clerk read off the license number.

Eldon wrote it down. "What's his address?"

The clerk read off the Salem post-office-box number of the Sherwood Forest Corporation.

Eldon felt as if a logjam had broken and he were riding down a wild river on one of the logs. "Where's the transmitter located? Do you have a ship's name?" He was thinking of the *Orient Star*.

"It's a land-based station in Muskrat, Oregon."

"Bingo," Eldon said.

14

By Eldon Larkin
Sun Staff Writer

PORT JEROME—Police toxicology reports suggest that three murders in Nekaemas County in recent days are drug-related and interconnected.

The reports said the bodies of all three victims—and that of a circus elephant killed in a bizarre public hanging—contained unusually high amounts of THC, the mind-altering chemical found in marijuana.

Local, state, and federal law-enforcement agencies refused to comment on the reports. The documents, obtained by the *Sun*, are used in case investigations and normally are not made public.

The state medical examiner's office in Portland, which performed autopsies on the humans and which supervised the elephant's dissection by a meat packer, also would not comment.

But a source close to the investigation speculated that the drugs may all have come from the same source.

The concentrations in each case were so unusually high that they suggest quantities of a new, more potent form of marijuana than has been seen before on the South Coast, the source said.

That form could be "Thai stick." It is an extremely potent form of the weed cut into short stalks and packaged.

The employer of Marie Payne, one of the three murder victims, said Payne was a frequent user of Thai stick.

Cyrus Peak alleged that Payne, who was a Newport animal trainer, supplied the drug to members of his circus—including roustabout Nguyen Xuan of Muskrat, whose murder last week was the first of the three slayings. . . .

"Good copy," said Fiske, laying aside the day's edition. "I like how you worked in the ringmaster. Too bad the meat packer's not local . . . I'd have you do a feature."

"He's in Portland," said Eldon, not hiding his relief.

"We slipped up, missing when they shipped the elephant out of town," Fiske said. "Cutting up an elephant would make good art. I need page-one art."

"The Blessing of the Boats is coming up," Eldon said.

"This is the daily newspaper business," Fiske said. "Tomorrow's not today. Who'd you say your source was? Not the meat packer?"

"A deputy state medical examiner I know happened to be buying some steaks when I called the meat packer."

"Elephant steaks?"

"He wouldn't talk for attribution, but he's helped me out before and he was willing to speculate a little."

"Just speculate?"

"I couldn't get any more out of him," Eldon said. "I doubt he knows more. He wouldn't be privy to the local investigation."

"This Thai stick," Fiske said. "Is it a hippie thing?"

"A Southeast Asian preparation method, as my story said. They dry very potent pot plants and cut 'em into short lengths, say about as long as your hand. Then they tie 'em up in little packets, for convenience."

Fiske took his pipe from his mouth and peered into the bowl. "Like cee-gars, except illegal. The THC's what gets you stoned, huh? Is it like liquor?"

"You're asking me?"

"You went to Berkeley."

"THC is a generic compound; you can't trace it the way you can tar heroin," Eldon said. "If it was a particular compound, made in a laboratory, we could identify a specific substance, and a specific lab. But THC is one hundred percent natural. The only thing that ties these three stiffs together is quantitative."

"Too bad." Fiske sucked his pipe. It was dead. "Well, tying Chadwick to the ranch was nice work, even if you couldn't use it in this story. Keep up the research."

"How about we rent a radio, monitor the shortwave frequencies?"

"I'm not buying you a radio. We need more documents. Track down that Robin Hood company's history." Fiske picked up a ballpoint pen and began digging cinders from the pipe bowl. "What if that Thai stick's being smuggled in?"

"Here? Jimbo, that's outlandish."

"It's an Asian invention, you said. Maybe that little bit of opium on the *Orient Star* was just a dodge to occupy the cops." Fiske shook the loosened ashes from his pipe into the wastebasket. "Maybe the Thai stick comes in somewhere else on the coast. Typical Oriental subtlety, I call it."

"But where?"

Fiske shrugged. "It's a big coast. I pay you to figure that out. You're my hardest hitter, Eldon. Especially now that Frank is laid up, dee-de-dee." Fiske blew through his pipe, inspected the bowl, then sat at the news desk and began filling the pipe with tobacco. "Here's something you can do for me today." He handed Eldon a thick press release. Attached to it was a studio portrait of a Boy Scout.

Eldon stared at the photo. The Scout looked like a nasty pixie, big brown eyes too clever, lips pursed in a supercilious smirk. The kind of kid who nitpicked in class and ran around with a screwdriver hidden in the waistband of his plaid boxer undershorts, just in case. There actually was an American flag in the background.

He looks like a fruitcake, Eldon thought. "This is a damn Eagle Scout. A waste of time."

"This is not just any Eagle Scout," Fiske said. "This is Conrad DeVere. He's won every merit badge possible. There are more than a hundred."

"I only earned six, myself."

"So you see why it's good copy. This story'll take you an hour. You can blow it out your nose. This is a community newspaper. People—"

". . . love to read about Eagle Scouts, yeah, yeah."

"Help me out, will you? I need a feature," Fiske said. "His mother's after me to do a story."

"When are people going to stop wasting money on these soft-focus portraits?" Eldon said. "We can't use this. It won't reproduce."

"She's going to have him come in for a picture," Fiske said. "Shoot it yourself. Get in all the badges."

"A seven-page press release?"

"He wrote it himself. Part of his journalism merit badge."

The telephone rang. Eldon stretched over to his own desk to

answer it as Fiske strolled off. Sure enough, it was the Eagle
Scout's mother. Conrad was on his way to the *Sun* via bicycle, in
full uniform. He had taken time from school to be photographed.
She hoped that the photo and the accompanying story would be of
professional quality. The clipping would be useful in the scrap-
book Conrad was putting together to apply for a Scout scholarship. Eldon let his mind wander as the woman jabbered.

He needed a good follow-on to this morning's story. The
"Sherwood Forest Corporation" had covered its tracks pretty
well—but Lawrence R. Chadwick's putting the radio license in
his own name was a blunder.

Who and where was Chadwick? How had he come into conflict with Tran? How to get a handle on his pot plantation? Any
two-hundred-thousand-dollar operation was sure to have records,
even if its business was illegal. They would name names, record
the size of the crop, track sales. They would flush Chadwick.

Mrs. DeVere apparently intended to fill the time until her
son's arrival by recounting his entire scouting career. She did not
pause for breath. Eldon got the morning's newspaper and put up
his feet, telephone still in his ear, and reread his story with pleasure. It really was good. Writing stories like this made him feel
less like a tragic figure.

Chadwick's radio license has to lead to other paper, Eldon
thought. The FCC file in Portland might include a photocopy of a
check with which Chadwick had paid his license fee. A check
would give the name of the bank where he kept his money and
might have a real address and working telephone number printed
on it.

Maybe Fiske will spring for a jaunt to the big city, Eldon
thought. Maybe I could take Shelly along, and on the company's
dime.

Closer to home, assessor's records would show who was paying property taxes on the ranch. Taxes were not due until Novem-
ber, however—too long to wait. Corporate status reports filed
with the state? The Sherwood Forest Corporation had been formed
too recently for that.

Eldon frowned. He wanted names, not paper; he wanted faces
and deeds. He'd have to keep working on Art.

And what about Dougie? What about that green glass?

"Does your son by any chance have a merit badge in glass-blowing?" he asked, interrupting Mrs. DeVere. "Just curious. I guess they don't give one for that. I think they ought to. Don't you?"

He might learn something when he started looking into Vietnamese enterprises in the area. He'd call churches and social-services agencies that might have helped the refugees out. His inquiries might lead to Tran Minh and the opium and then the Thai stick and finally to Chadwick and the ranch.

But what was being done with the pot crop? A town the size of Port Jerome could not possibly consume so much marijuana, no matter what its hunger for oblivion. Obviously, the harvest was being shipped somewhere else. It would take trucks to carry it away, other trucks to carry the competing Thai stick shipments out of Nekaemas County. Maybe Chadwick was dispatching his trucks by radio. Eldon imagined a fleet of toy trucks speeding busily about, over the dunes and back and forth from the wharf, like the Lionel trains he'd had when he was a kid. He snickered. "What? Sorry, just clearing my throat—"

Maybe if he hung around Muskrat, he could spot some suspicious vehicles and check license numbers through the state Motor Vehicles Division. He could take along his fishing gear as cover. If they gave a merit badge in wiretapping, I'd put this fruitcake Eagle Scout to work, he thought—and then there was the sound of a car's horn outside, a howl of tires, and a crash like a giant soup can bursting.

"Excuse me. I have to go to an automobile accident." Eldon hung up the phone and grabbed his camera as other employees flocked to the front doors to gawk.

Eldon pushed his way through the doors and stared in horror.

Pugh's corroded pickup truck was piled into the rear of Eldon's Citroën. Water gushed from the pickup's shattered radiator. Pugh squatted on the truck's hood, like a genie in the rising steam, strangling Conrad DeVere with the boy's merit-badge sash. The Scout's feet thrashed in the spokes of his toppled bicycle as he struggled to escape.

"Give me the finger, little pissant?" Pugh shouted, twisting the wide sash tighter. "The world ends sooner fer you than fer me!"

Eldon tottered between rage and the cool, airy wonder that protected him at traffic accidents. He raised the camera with numb hands and snapped off three shots at different exposures, then rushed up to the wreck.

Pugh cackled. Eyes protruding and tongue popping, the desperate Boy Scout grabbed at Eldon. His feet were still tangled in the bicycle's spokes. Eldon skidded on something metallic—a Prince Albert tobacco can. The last steam hissed out of the radiator as the bike's wheels turned, the boy's legs twisted, and the three of them crashed down in a heap in the scattered garbage.

"Momma! Momma!" Conrad wrestled the sash free of his throat.

"Look at my car!" Eldon said in disgust.

"You're worried about that junker?" asked Pugh, astonished.

"You've wrecked my wheels!" Eldon said. "I'll sue you—"

"Sue away! Don't matter a damn! Want m' pickup? Take 'er! Nothin' matters now! The Star Days 're upon us! Signs and wonders! Lights in the sky and Bigfoot in the forest! The Space Brothers are coming! Commit yer way unto th' Lord! Trust also in him and he shall bring *it* to pass!"

The Boy Scout rolled over and looked down his sharp nose at Eldon in a practiced way, even though he lay on the ground. "Never mind *him*. I'm *Conrad DeVere*."

Eldon composed himself. He might need the kid's testimony to collect from Pugh in small-claims court—if there was anything worth collecting. "How'd this happen?"

"He tried to run me down," Conrad said.

"He gave me the finger!" Pugh screamed. "This little pissant cut in fronta me on his bike—"

"I was going to be late for my interview!" Conrad said.

"Well, you've arrived," Eldon said. "Let's get your feet out of these spokes."

"My mother will sue this newspaper," Conrad said.

"Get up." Eldon grabbed Conrad's arm and merit-badge sash and pulled him to his feet. One bright badge jogged Eldon's own Boy Scout memories—light blue with red lightning bolts and white flashes of Morse code. "What's this one for?"

"Radio, of course." Conrad straightened his regalia. "I have them all."

"You can answer some questions I have, then." A fantastic plan to eavesdrop on the Patterson ranch using Boy Scout ham operators began to form in Eldon's mind.

"Maybe I won't," Conrad said. "I'm not very satisfied with the treatment I've received here."

Eldon raised his camera. "You have the photography merit badge, so you know how this works. Inside this box are pictures of you and Pugh at play. I'm going to mail them to the Scout scholarship people. And to your mother."

"Perhaps I can be of assistance to you," Conrad said.

"Boy Scouts!" Pugh said. "They went to hell with Roosevelt."

"And just what brings *you* to town?" Eldon asked him.

"Tinfoil run. And I've gotta place an ad." Pugh waved a sheet of paper.

"You didn't pay for the first one."

"This is the biggest story of this or any other century! You can't keep it outta the paper!"

"You're gonna pay for my car, old man."

"What's one chariot when the chariots of God are twenty thousand?" Pugh asked. "It's obvious that there are wolves in sheep's clothing, hoping that the UFOs are satanic and not the chariots of God."

Conrad sniggered.

"Criminal minds always seek to confuse," Pugh said, glaring at the boy. "But they can't confuse me. Not this close to takeoff time."

Pugh climbed onto the hood of his truck. His back straightened and his bearing became commanding as he solemnly read out his ad:

"'Why do UFOs seek to draw me into a web of no return? What do they have to do with Bigfoot? These are signs and wonders in the heavens and on the seas. Because Jesus could take any earthly form he wished, he appeared as a pillar of fire. *So*—which body will he return in? When the flying roll is brought forth, it will stay until every cover-up falls apart. The Star Days are upon us.'"

"I believe he's had formal training in speech," Conrad said.

"Maybe he earned the merit badge once," Eldon said.

"Public speaking," Conrad said. "I have that one."

Eldon saw that Fiske had come outside and stood with the other onlookers, smoking his pipe. "Come down off there, Pugh."

"Not until I've delivered my message."

"The editor'll have you arrested for trespassing," Eldon said. "He's right over there."

Remarkably, the appeal worked. Pugh climbed down from the hood. "I can't afford to get on the wrong side of the law just now. I've got to deliver my message. The watchman must declare what he seeth. And I've got to finish my ship."

"What about my car?"

"If money's what it takes, here's money," Pugh said. He thrust a wad of bills at Eldon.

Eldon grabbed the money. It looked wrong—old. "This is play money. Stage money."

"Doesn't matter what it is anymore, I keep tellin' ya."

Eldon let the worthless stuff flutter to the asphalt.

"I have to get back to school," Conrad said with a whine.

"I'll interview you now," Eldon said.

Pugh's eyes bulged. His face reddened. The teakettle wheezing began. Conrad whined and tried to back away. Eldon grabbed the Scout's arm and was about to remonstrate when the Ship of Love swung into the parking lot.

Shelly stopped the motor and climbed out. "What's going on?"

Pugh threw up his hands. "The one lady on the whole South Coast who respects the truth!"

Shelly looked at the Citroën's fender, concealing a smile behind her hand. "It's drivable. That wheel will still turn."

"That fender's crushed!"

"It's not as if cosmetic damage is a big issue."

Pugh wheezed with glee and scurried about the parking lot, grabbing after stage money and tinfoil.

"He's crackers . . . crackers!" Conrad DeVere said dramatically, attempting to reclaim attention.

"Shelly, will you please shoot a picture of Conrad here?" Eldon asked.

But Shelly was staring after Pugh. She turned and slid open the side door of the Ship of Love, peered up at the poster on the ceiling, then at the old man, then back at the poster.

Eldon pulled Conrad into the newsroom.

"Someone's going to pay for my bicycle," the boy said.

"It looks just as drivable as my car," Eldon said, sitting at his desk. "If not, sell some Boy Scout cookies and earn yourself a new one. I'll shoot your picture myself in a minute. Your press release is pretty thorough."

"I have the journalism merit badge."

"But what do you know about ham radio?"

"I said I have the radio merit badge. Why?"

"I need information."

"Are you doing an investigative story?"

"What do you make of this?" Eldon displayed Shelly's photo of the Patterson barn.

"Is this someplace around here?" Conrad asked.

"What can you tell me about that antenna?"

"A radio antenna, clearly. Not TV."

"Yes, but for what?"

"You mean, what sort of communication is it used for? Hard to say. It looks like an amateur setup."

"Citizens' band?"

"Not with that antenna. It's not very big. Hmm . . . VHF wouldn't need a large antenna. It'd have to be up high, but it wouldn't have to be big. A roof mount like that would do."

"Go on."

"He could be talking to ships. VHF is used for ship-to-shore."

"What's so good about VHF?" Eldon asked.

"Well, you can make telephone calls on VHF, which you can't do with ham radio. And you don't have to pass a test for a license." Conrad studied the photograph. "I think he's talking to ships beyond the three-mile limit. That's what the antenna height's for. He'd need power, too . . . maybe twenty-five watts and an amplifier."

"I guess you can't tell anything about the transmitter from the photo?" Eldon said.

"No, you'd have to check the transmitter's license for that." Conrad licked his lips. "Unless this is a wildcat setup."

"Can you monitor VHF with citizens' band?" Eldon thought of springing for a cheap CB scanner.

"No, you'd have to have a VHF receiver."

"Thanks. Let's take your picture."

"I've got the fingerprinting merit badge, you know. Maybe we can be partners."

"I've got a partner."

"I hope nothing compromises your investigation," Conrad said. "It could happen. Rumors get around."

"Don't threaten me, you little maggot. Or those pictures I took outside could haunt you for a long time."

"Ahem! Indeed. When can I . . . obtain the negatives?"

"Keep reading the *Sun*. You'll know when to come in."

Conrad posed for his photograph sullenly, standing so as to hide a grease spot on his uniform that he'd picked up in the parking lot. Then they went outside. Conrad righted his bike and began pedaling in unsteady circles. Its spokes sounded like a broken fan.

Pugh's crippled truck had been pushed aside. The old man stood in its rear, bunching tinfoil into a huge ball and tossing Prince Albert tobacco cans into a sack. Shelly stood nearby, examining one of the fake bank notes that blew about the parking lot.

She looked up with wonder in her eyes as Eldon approached. "Look at this bill."

"Play money," Eldon said. "Some of the junk the old bozo keeps."

"That's just it," Shelly said. "Look at the design. What period would you say?"

"The teens or twenties . . . *no!*"

"Yes! This must be Silent Era stage money. Ogden O. Sherwood uses a wad of money just like it to start the fire that burns down the mansion in *Secret Passages!*" Shelly's gray eyes were hard as stone. "You must remember that scene."

"I do remember," Eldon said, raising his voice a little over the racket of Conrad's spokes. "This can't be the same money."

"How can you tell?"

"You can't see it that clearly in the movie."

"So how can you say that it isn't?" Shelly asked. "A long-lost silent-film star would be a good story, you have to admit."

"Pugh will claim anything to get attention for his flying saucers."

"My great-uncle is *lost*," Shelly said. "I want to find him. He went down the rabbit hole and disappeared, and I want to see where the rabbit hole comes out."

"God help us if it comes out in this town."

"I'll bet you dinner."

"We've already agreed to have dinner. Let's bet something else."

"Afraid you'll lose? If I'm wrong, I'll go up to your place and cook." Shelly accented the final word slightly, and Eldon thought she gave a slight wink.

"Okay," he said swiftly. "I know this means a lot to you."

"If I'm wrong, I'll need company, believe me."

"Well, it would be a story. If. But how can we find out?"

"The tattoo." Shelly took a deep breath and marched up to Pugh like a little girl about to confront a fierce older child. "Take off your shirt!"

Pugh's eyes started in their sockets. "Hee? What?"

"We want a look at your tattoo."

Pugh's cheeks and nose reddened with embarrassment as he kneaded the tinfoil he held. "My tattoo? Who told ya about that? It's nothin'—got it when I was a longshoreman in Seattle."

"I can see a little bit of it at your collar," Shelly said. "It looks like a flower, like a rose."

"Don't recall what flower it is." Pugh dropped his eyes. "It . . . it ain't reputable. After I saw God in the forest, I tried to have it fixed up."

"You didn't eradicate it?"

Pugh tugged his shirt collar together, shaking his head. "I can't let ya see it!"

A Prince Albert tobacco can sailed through the air from behind Eldon and bounced off Pugh's head. Eldon turned; the can had been hurled by Conrad DeVere, now speeding from the parking lot, middle finger aloft.

"I'm the only committed UFO researcher on the whole Oregon coast!" Pugh screamed. "The Space Brothers are comin' and I'm near t'liftin' off! Give me the finger, will you? I'll fly like a bird!" He tore open his shirt like Superman. Shelly's thrilled gasp instantly became a wail of despair.

Someone had drawn on the old man's scrawny chest, all right—and kept on drawing. Pugh's skin was a forest of blurred tattooing, navel to neck. Birds and foliage, clouds and anchors, angels and flying saucers battled for prominence in an inky tangle.

Near Pugh's neck was a blotted clump that might be broccoli—or flowers, Eldon thought. But what kind of flowers?

"I can't tell if it's a rose!" Shelly wailed.

"Doesn't matter!" said Pugh. "The Space Brothers are coming!"

"I don't care, you old fool! Are you my Great-Uncle Ogden?"

"I'm flesh and blood an' here an' now . . . and the Space Brothers are coming at the Blessing of the Boats," said Pugh. "Huey knows the last days are coming. I saw the fire in his eyes!"

Shelly turned to Eldon, but he already had the keys to his Citroën in his hand. "I'm going fishing."

15

Eldon stood in the picnic area at the foot of Allen Slope, taking stock of his superstitions.

His fishing rod leaned against his Citroën, which had borne him here despite the damaged fender. His creel and hip waders lay on the ground. Around his neck were binoculars. His hat lay on the Citroën's roof.

Eldon adjusted the binoculars, shouldered his creel, and threw the waders over his other shoulder. Then he set his hat on his head, careful not to snag his flesh on the fishhooks. He picked up his rod and started up the hill, following the path that he and Frank had taken in their Bigfoot foray.

His itinerary was simple: Climb the hill, investigate the cabin once more, press on to the creek and do a little fishing for sea-run cutthroat trout—while working his way down the creek to the borders of the Patterson ranch.

He figured he would reach the ranch in late afternoon. He would hide among the forest's lengthening shadows and peer down on the dope growers through his binoculars. "Just fishing" was the perfect excuse for being in the area. Besides, there was no sense in wasting a trip up the creek. Just as there was no correct time for news to happen, Eldon believed there was no correct time to go fishing. Fish were always biting somewhere in the world.

And he needed to practice his cast.

He had not touched his rod since the morning on the lawn. Since then, Eldon had identified Tumpat's corpse, come face to face with the murderous Dougie in the woods, gotten stoned, and published the tox reports scoop. He had not yet nailed Shelly, but that would come in time. He was on to the biggest story of his career. Missing the red cup hung in his mind, however. How could he confront Huey Bellows if he did not know how to cast?

He continued up the hill. At the electrical tower, he found

and set aside another broken insulator for Frank. He would pick it up on the way back. If I come back, he thought uneasily. He headed into the forest, down the leafy tunnel toward the cabin.

The police had come this way searching after Dougie. They had trampled the ferns. Rain and footprints had obliterated many of the "Bigfoot tracks" in the path. At the cabin, a few tattered streamers of yellow CRIME SCENE tape fluttered; Eldon knew that it had been searched. He set his rod and waders against the wall and pushed the door ajar, letting forest light fall inside. There were many new footprints in the dust, but otherwise the interior was as he remembered it. The window shutter swung ajar. Chips of green glass glinted in the corner.

There seemed to be no place in the cabin to hide a parcel of opium. Wait—the fireplace. The chimney. Eldon thrust an arm up the flue. There was a stone lip up there—and something resting on it within easy reach! Eldon closed his fingers around the object. It was gritty, angular. He withdrew a sooty lump of burned wood.

Good thing Shelly wasn't here to see me do that, Eldon thought.

He pitched the cinder away, turning once more to the green glass. He wrinkled his nose at the aging turd as he bent and picked up a shard. He held the sliver up to the window's light. It was like the fragment he had taken on his first visit. He had that one in his coat pocket. He took it out, held the shards up side by side. Both were green, sharp-edged, faintly convex. Did they somehow fit together? But into what?

Eldon turned to leave and noticed two large, sharp "Bigfoot tracks" pressed into the dust of the floor by the turd.

Those weren't here the first time, Eldon thought. There were no "Bigfoot tracks" in the cabin. I'd have noticed them when I first picked up the glass. Someone made them after the cops left.

His skin crawled. He backed out the door and grabbed his fly rod for a weapon. The forest was silent around him. Eldon almost barreled back up the path to the safety of the open hillside; but the thought of flight reminded him that Dougie had run deeper into the forest.

Toward the Patterson ranch.

That's why they haven't found Dougie, Eldon thought. He's hiding on the ranch. But that would mean there's no dope war—

Where the news is, you go, Eldon told himself, pressing deeper into the woods—and the trout are running up there.

Shortly, he heard water's rush and came to the creek. It was a feeder stream of the great Wahpepah River that ran into the sea a few miles above Nekaemas Bay. The creek was swollen with rain, a turbid cascade zigzagging through the forest along a shadowed cut. The sun seldom reached here. Spruce and Douglas fir were shading towers; the creek's banks were soft with moss and thick with ferns. The creek slowed into eddies and pools at the twists of its channel. Eldon stood on the bank and smiled. Cutthroat lurked in those deep pools.

He sat on a rock and removed his hat. For cuts, a bright streamer fly was the thing. A Spruce or a Bucktail Coachman. Or the Zaddack. It had worked well for summer steelhead on the Rogue River; it should work as well here in autumn for cuts.

Eldon attached the feathery fluorescent red and green thing to the leader on his line. He was reluctant to begin. He rationalized that he did not want to risk the fly, which incorporated the vivid hackles of a nearly extinct species of Indian jungle cock. Possessing the green feathers had become illegal. They were getting harder and harder to find, stashed in cigar boxes in the back rooms of out-of-the-way tackle shops, costing the world—

Eldon set aside his rod. He removed his shoes and tugged on his thick woolen socks and then his waders, counting the steps in the same way as he had sometimes forced himself to start writing when he was a fledgling reporter.

He stepped carefully into the creek, feeling his way with his toes as the water swirled around his calves. It was bracing even through the rubber waders, and he enjoyed its cold salvation. With no direct sun, there was little chance that he would cast a shadow and scare away the fish. Nevertheless, he moved quietly out into the water, planted his feet, and picked a target for his first cast.

A dozen yards upstream was a likely deep green pool. Above was a little waterfall, white water churning over rocks as the stream dropped to Eldon's elevation. The wind fortunately was at his back as he faced upstream.

Eldon raised his rod upright, stripping line from the reel with his left hand. He whipped the rod back. The line ran out behind him. He flicked the rod forward. The fly sailed over the water at the end of its leader and slapped into the moving water near the pool. Damn! Eldon thought. I really have lost my touch.

He let the weighted line sink toward the bottom and counted slowly from one. As he reached fifteen, the line stopped. Pretty deep water up there, ten or twelve feet, Eldon decided. I ought to have some luck—once I put the fly where the fish are.

He cast again and overshot the pool. Again he counted to fifteen, letting the current carry the line through the pool, and began his retrieve. He realized he was thinly filmed with sweat despite the cool air. This was the one thing at which he knew he could be graceful. He did some deep breathing before taking his next shot.

Something flashed in the eddy. Trout.

Eldon cast without thinking. The line hummed out and the bright fly splashed down on target. He counted, letting the Zaddack twist and descend like a sinking insect. He reached fifteen, paused, began his retrieve. C'mon, you mother. . . .

Nothing. It's like this drug story, he thought. I'm fishing in dark waters, but I know the fish are there.

He cast again and again struck off target. He retrieved and cast once more. This time he overshot the pool completely, his line briefly snagging on a boulder in the rapids.

"It's all in the timing," said a familiar voice. "You're hammering it."

Eldon's guts went slushy. He looked upstream. Huey Bellows stood on the bank above the rapids, wearing wading pants that were like green rubber overalls. Bellows was armed with the most formidable weapon possible—a fly rod.

"You're hammering," Huey repeated, and stepped carefully into the water. "It should be more like uncoiling a punch."

"Don't scare the fish," Eldon said. Coincidence could not have brought Huey to this place.

"I'll be careful," Huey said. "I want some bluebacks, too. I knew you'd pick a good spot."

"So you followed me."

Bellows squinted into the wind and shrugged. "You sounded like a bear crashin' through the woods. You oughta learn to move quietly."

"You do know how to do that," Eldon said.

"Nam," Bellows said and began stripping his line. "'What

Charlie hears, Charlie kills.' Looks like we've finally got around to our fishin' trip." Huey turned away and cast upstream.

Eldon watched with a sinking heart. Bellows had massive arms, yet he moved delicately. He seemed to place his fly on the wind, which carried it gently through the air to its target.

Smoothly, Huey began his retrieve. His rod whipped into a graceful bend. A strike. Huey played the fish artfully. Soon he reeled in a cutthroat.

"Nice cast," said Eldon. "Is that the fly I gave you?"

"Naw, I keep that one right here in my hat. Wouldn't risk it for anything."

"Which way did you come? Not up from the road."

"My place is over there." Huey waved vaguely downstream as he stuffed the fish into his creel. "I had to get outta the house for a while. I'm workin' pretty hard and I had to take a break, so I came fishin'." Huey cast and retrieved. "A big stained-glass project."

"That lamp you were making?"

"Naw, this is lots better: a stained-glass window."

"Like for a church?"

Bellows laughed. "It oughta be. It's big. You'd have to see it. It's a dream window."

"Got any green glass in it?"

"What's this thing you got about green glass?"

There's really nowhere to run, Eldon thought. Not in these waders. "There was green glass around Nguyen Xuan's body, Huey. Green glass at the cabin up the way. Green glass in the lucky charm you made for Truong's wife."

Huey peered at Eldon. "I truly don't know what you're talking about. But you standin' there, thinkin' what you seem like you're thinkin' takes a lot of hair. Or a lot of stupidity. You think I'd have anything to do with horrible things like that? And be as nice to you as I've been?"

"What am I supposed to think, with what I've got to go on . . . bits and pieces and a lot of doubletalk from Pugh today?"

"Pugh told you about the Space Brothers, I suppose? Haw!"

"He says they're coming at the Blessing of the Boats. And that you know something about it."

Without warning, Huey cast directly at Eldon, who jerked reflexively as the fly splashed into the water before him.

"Don't let that hook snag ya," Huey said.

Eldon watched Huey's line drift toward him, feeling his ears heat—the feather-light fly could not possibly hurt him. He felt the sort of anger that he had buried so many years ago after Billy Vogel had punched him out; that he had buried after Bernice had cast him off; that he had supressed on his lawn, trying for the red cup. This time he would stand his ground. "What kind of fly is that, Huey?"

"Green Baron. Tied it m'self." Huey flicked his line and the fly rose to the creek's surface, bright green.

"That's nothing to my Zaddack." Eldon cast in Huey's direction. The wind was still in his favor, though his aim was off. The Zaddack plunked down close enough to the big man to return Huey's challenge.

Bellows reeled in his own line and cast again, a mischievous glitter in his little eyes, and plunked his fly so close to Eldon that his leader grazed the reporter's left knee. "I know about the Thai stick," Eldon said.

Huey's jaw dropped. "What? How?"

"Read today's paper."

"I haven't. Did Art tell—?"

"I'm going downstream to check out the Patterson ranch. Want to come?"

"Stay away from there, Eldon." Huey looked worried.

"Tell me why."

"I can't. Art'ud kill me. But you've got to stay away."

Eldon was about to cast at Huey but on some last-moment whim, he cast instead into the pool; his rod quivered with the shock of a strike and bent as the cutthroat broke water. Eldon laughed as the light caught its shine. Some men fished because they hated their wives; some fished because they had too much money. Eldon fished because of the light. He played out line and worked the reel, tiring the fish until he hauled it in flopping—a creditable trout, if small.

"Mine's bigger," Huey remarked. But a bit of the fight had gone out of him.

"Just warming up." Eldon wet his hands and released the trout. Had the cast been a fluke? "I'm piecing it together and it's a hell of a story. The ranch is a dope farm. That's what the killings were all about."

Bellows gave a baboon laugh. "You aren't goin' near there. You're stayin' right here with me." Without warning, Bellows cast straight at Eldon's face.

The leader grazed Eldon's cheek and shot past into the water behind him. Eldon cast back at Huey. Eldon's cast was high—a gust of wind carried the Zaddack over Huey's head. Huey brushed the line from his shoulder. "Reel 'er in."

They faced one another, fly rods raised.

"What about the Blessing of the Boats?" Eldon demanded. "You aren't running around with that old fool Pugh without good reason."

"You'll have to lick me 'fore I'll tell," Huey said, "and I'm the one who's got the lucky fly."

He cast at Eldon. The cast sailed high, the leader passing over Eldon's head and the line floating down onto his jungle hat before blowing away. "Damn wind," Huey said and peered intently at Eldon, as if to fix him with a hypnotic stare.

It's my hat, Eldon thought. He's trying to hook my lucky hat.

Eldon stripped his line. No way was Huey going to capture his hat. The fly he had given Bellows gleamed in Huey's baseball cap, not much farther away than the red cup had been. He attempted to triangulate, using the fly and Huey's ears—which stuck out from under the baseball cap—to aim his cast; but the fly wavered in and out of focus.

Huey was making short casts in the air to dry the Green Baron and lengthen line before delivering what Eldon knew would be the deciding stroke. Huey's rod flicked backward; his line ran out straight back in slow motion. The Green Baron whirled at Eldon. Eldon twisted his torso to let Huey's cast sail past.

He thought suddenly of the Zen cast and continued the motion—threw his arms wide and let the Zaddack take flight, rolling his gaze across the white sky as his line ran out behind him. He rebounded, bringing his body and his rod back into upright position. His wrist swiveled like a gyroscope. The Zaddack whirled forward—and Eldon knew he had lost. His cast was too high.

The fly tossed crazily as Eldon's line snaked into a pale *S;* but the wind was with him. A gust caught the Zaddack and threw it at Huey. The fly arced down and hooked the front of Huey's baseball cap. Eldon popped the cap from Huey's head with a flick of his wrist. The big man yelped and grabbed after it in vain as it wobbled away through the air at the end of Eldon's line.

Eldon swiftly reeled in the hat.

Bellows sloshed from the creek and threw himself down on the bank. "You win. I never saw a cast like that. You'd have done all right in Nam."

"Yeah, right." Eldon climbed from the stream and set his rod down to examine the fly he had recaptured from Huey. It was merely a common wooly gray and brown job used for trout in northern California. It all depended on what you made of things.

Eldon extracted the fly from Huey's cap and snagged it in his jungle hat before tossing the baseball cap back.

"You're gonna keep my lucky fly?" Huey said, appalled.

"Why not? I caught it. You got it from me to begin with. Now talk."

"I gotta appeal to your common sense. To your civic decency. Don't go near the ranch. You'll ruin everything."

"Ruin what? Flying saucers coming down to get Pugh?"

Huey rubbed his eyes and sighed. "Don't I wish. That old man's half the problem. You can't tell anyone about this, Eldon. This is off the record."

"I'm not sitting on this."

"You got to! The drop's goin' down."

"You mean the growers are shipping out their harvest?"

"What harvest? They're not *growin'* dope, they're *smugglin'* dope. Dope's comin' in, not goin' out."

Eldon stared at the rushing creek, feeling the wind slowly leave his lungs and elation build in his heart. Finally, he remembered to breathe. "The tox reports. Thai stick. VHF. I understand now."

"A shipment's comin' in soon . . . a damn big one," Huey said. "I think the sheriff's layin' for the smugglers. A few months back, just after the time the ranch was sold, Art asked me to sniff around among the Vietnamese . . . about drug deals.

"Art was interested in the ranch, though he wouldn't say much more. I soon learned that Nguyen Xuan was involved . . . dealin', of course, though I don't know exactly how. That was reason enough to get more curious."

"You wanted to skunk Xuan. For what he did to Theresa."

"Sure. But I really had to find out more, to protect the Vietnamese. They know something slimy's goin' on and they're scared. When you and Shelly happened along, I thought, What the hell, I'll let them do some of my work for me, read about it in the newspaper on the johnny."

"Thanks a heap."

"Well, you wanted a story!" Huey beamed. "There's something exciting about big headlines!"

"Why was Marie Payne murdered? What about Dougie?"

"Can't say. I didn't know those people, and Art doesn't confide in me that far."

"Tell me more about this big drop."

"I've got that figured," Huey said. "Pugh's been dancin' around like a hopped-up medicine man for the last couple of days, goin' on about the Space Brothers and Bigfoot and that crap. He watches that ranch like a hawk because he thinks the UFOs will come from that direction. I put two and two together and figured out when the main drop's got to go down."

"When?"

"During the Blessing of the Boats, when the coast guard cutter and the helicopters are in the pageant on the bay. The dope's gotta be landed then."

"'They're all busy polishing their guns,'" Eldon murmured, thinking gleefully of what Marsha had remarked about her visit to the coast guard station.

"Beg pardon?"

"I'll bet the smugglers are going to run into a big federal surprise," Eldon said. "You might've told me more at the crab feed, you know."

"I didn't have it completely figured out then," Huey said. "And what could I say in front of Truong? He's a civilian. Stay away from the ranch. People sneakin' around up there will make those dopers suspicious—could scare 'em off. And they might shoot first."

"I want that story," Eldon said.

"You'll get it," Huey said solemnly. "I had a dream."

"You saw the dope smuggling operation in a dream?"

"Well, not exactly. God showed me his hand again. He was holdin' a fly rod. I thought that was kind of unusual . . . until now. I just realized that he had a rod just like yours. . . ." Huey paused uneasily. He seemed about to confess something but shook his head fiercely. "This story's gonna be told, but I had to test you first."

Huey shook his head once more. "Pugh could ruin everything. He could get killed."

"He's stuck in town right now without a truck."

"Thank God! You've got to keep him away. Promise you'll stay away, too; it's just for a couple of days."

"There's a price," Eldon said.

Huey's eyes narrowed. "A price?"

"I'm coming to your place the night of the drop," Eldon said. "It's close enough to the Patterson ranch. I'll bide my time until the bust goes down. The *South Coast Sun* will be there to get the scoop."

16

Eldon found Shelly at the docks later in the afternoon, photographing a big motorboat festooned with garishly painted toilets. It was one of the "crazy boats"—vessels homemade or imaginatively customized— that traditionally lent the Blessing of the Boats an unholy aura.

Eldon pulled Shelly down the pier, past workmen hammering together a reviewing stand that projected over the water. "Where's Pugh?"

"Repairing his truck."

"He wasn't in the parking lot . . . just his truck, next to your van. Let's hope that radiator stays broken. It'll save his life. Want to go on a drug raid?"

"What? You bet! When?"

Eldon savored her eager expression. This bird soon would be in hand. "The Patterson place is a dope smuggling depot," he said. "A big haul comes in tomorrow night by boat."

"That explains the Thai stick. That's what Huey and Great-Uncle . . . I mean Pugh . . . must have been up in arms about."

"Right. Huey gave me the lowdown today. I met him fishing. We had a nice chat. The cops are going to raid the ranch."

"Great! So that's why Art wouldn't—"

"Wouldn't what? Have you been talking to Art?"

"—wouldn't help you," Shelly finished, with a shake of her head. "With Pugh's help, we can get right down onto that ranch. He knows all the trails, remember? We'll get close-ups! Wow!"

"We can't let Pugh know," Eldon said. "He thinks the smugglers are flying-saucer people. You and I will lay low at Huey's place tomorrow night and wait for the cops to raid."

"We might miss something!"

"Such as getting killed. We'll be close enough when the action starts."

Shelly pointed out over the water. "The coast guard cutter is missing."

Eldon followed her gaze. They were not far from where the circus had pitched its tents, not far from the switchyard where Horton had swung. Vessels that would join the festival flotilla were gathering in the late-afternoon light—fishing boats, pleasure craft, tugs, and barges. Tomorrow, the bay would swarm with vessels.

"Yeah," Eldon said. "I wish we could get aboard, or aboard a helicopter that was going to swoop down."

"No, we've got to be on the ground to get good pictures."

They started for the *Sun* office. Shelly said, "I've got a better idea . . . Pugh's UFO observation tower. We can look right down onto the ranch."

"Surely you can't take photos from there at night."

"Not at night. I'd be trying to shoot action at long range in low light. But with binoculars, maybe we could *see*. We'd be that much closer when the action starts."

"Well, maybe you're right," Eldon said. "But we've got to keep Pugh in town."

"But it's his tower."

"We can't have him up there doing UFO chants while we're waiting for the raid."

"We trespass, you mean."

"It's for his own good," Eldon said. "Pugh wants to charge down onto that ranch and greet the flying saucers. He could get offed. Ruin the delivery. Spoil our story."

Shelly's gray eyes sparked. "You don't care about Pugh!"

"I care about business."

"He still could be my great-uncle. I looked at that tattoo carefully after you ran off with your fishing pole—"

"It's a fly rod. Never say 'fishing pole.'"

"And that tattooed flower could be a rose, Eldon Larkin. It could damn well be a rose." Shelly's cheeks reddened and her nostrils flared; Eldon was enthralled. "I think that tattoo tells the story of Great-Uncle Ogden's life," Shelly said. "He's been adding to it all these years. Do you know there's a *burning house* worked into the design? Just like in the movie."

"There's probably a Dewey campaign button, too."

"Uncle Ogden disappeared years before Dewey. But there's a face in the foliage that looks like Herbert Hoo—"

"If Pugh is your great-uncle, it's all the more reason to keep him out of danger. He's waited for the Space Brothers for years. What's he going to do when he finds out they're just a bunch of drug smugglers?"

"Why . . . he'll keep on waiting, I guess."

"Like Christians for Judgment Day." Eldon liked the simile. He had waited long enough for his own break. Now he would get his reward. The scoop might bring him to the attention of a big-city paper—and it would give dinner with Shelly an exciting celebratory cast, with all that it could lead to.

And I'll get at least fifty bucks from the wire service, Eldon thought. I could repair the car.

As if to mock his thought, hectic banging drifted toward them from the direction of the *South Coast Sun*.

"Pugh must be back at work on his truck," Eldon said.

"You're right about not telling him," Shelly said. "We can't put him in danger. Even if he's not my great-uncle, he's . . . a civilian."

"I wouldn't let a story get in the way of what's right."

"You're not so tough," Shelly said. "Why did you and your wife split up?"

"I don't know. A lot got left unsaid in that relationship. And I guess I should've said half of it."

"I wish all men were as sensitive as you, Eldon. You are concerned about Pugh, and that proves it. I'm not embarrassing you, am I?"

"No, no!" A bounce entered Eldon's step. A sudden glare of afternoon sun cut through the clouds.

"Oh, this is so good," Shelly said, skipping to keep pace. "Wait. I'm supposed to shoot the Blessing of the Boats. I can't miss the raid. Could Marsha shoot the ceremony?"

"Don't tell Marsha anything," Eldon said. "You shoot the Blessing as planned and we'll take off; it'll still be early. I'll brief Fiske and . . . oh, no!"

The parking lot was now in view. There, Pugh industriously pounded the crumpled rear fender of Eldon's Citroën with a small sledge. Jimbo Fiske looked on.

"Poundin' out the dents, since they bothered ya so," Pugh explained as Eldon charged into the parking lot. "Matter of honor."

"You've made it worse than ever! Give me that!" Eldon grabbed for the rusty sledge, but Pugh held it away.

Fiske puffed his pipe. "This old fella's a heck of a feature story, Eldon. He practically knows Bigfoot on a first-name basis. I see your rod's in the backseat. Catch any fish?"

Eldon got the sledge away from Pugh and threw it down. "I've got to talk to you, Jimbo. Shit! Look at my car!"

The fender was clumped like a gray metal fungus around the wheel. "Those edges will rip the tire to pieces," Eldon said.

But Shelly's sympathy was all for Pugh. "You'll never get your truck fixed today. I've got a couch in my apartment; I'll put you up there until you get your truck repaired."

"I can't hang around," Pugh said. "The Space Brothers are comin'. I've gotta be there to meet 'em. I'll hitch back to Muskrat if I gotta."

"Meet them after you've had a hot meal and a night's sleep," Shelly said.

"I'll sleep in m'pickup."

"It could rain," said Shelly. "Sleep in my van, then." Shelly stepped to the Ship of Love and threw open the side door.

Pugh wheezed. "Knew of a whorehouse looked like that in New Orleans once—" He crept forward, fascinated. "You got m'poster on the ceiling."

"Uncle Ogden was one of the greats," Shelly said.

"Proud ta see it there." Pugh drew himself up as he had when he had read out his UFO advertisement the previous day. His jaw set and his eyes brightened.

"Can you remember anything about those days?" Shelly asked.

Pugh slowly climbed into the van. He settled into the red cushions like a prince taking his ease, gaze fixed on the ceiling. "Them was good days."

"The silent-movie days?"

"Naw, New Orleans!" Pugh slapped his knee and made noises like a kettle. Then his new dignity reasserted itself. "The last good days. Before it all went wrong. Sound came in and that bastard Roosevelt started squawkin' at me. Radio was bad enough—"

"You *are* Great-Uncle Odgen!"

"I tell ya, I'm Pugh. Whatever I been don't matter." Pugh's

wrinkled eyelids came down and he smiled. "The Space Brothers'll hitch onta m'spaceship after I show 'em God in the bottom of the can. That's m'ticket." Pugh's eyes popped open and rolled. "People with their know-it-all . . . bah! Don't mean doodly when ya know where God is. Right in the bottom of th' Prince Albert can. The more cans you've got, the more God you got."

Eldon snorted. "Jimbo . . . we've got a story to talk about."

"You sure do," Pugh said. "The Space Brothers are comin' and Bigfoot's not far behind. I've got the inside skinny on that sightin' of him north of the bay."

"It fits the pattern of earlier Sasquatch incidents," Fiske said gravely. "Bigfoot was seen up there one night in 1969. A guy pulled over to the side of the road in his Volkswagen to get some sleep. Woke up about three in the morning with the bug rockin' back and forth. It was pitch dark, and all he could see outside the window was a hairy stomach—"

"I don't mean that damn Bigfoot hoax, I mean the drugs," Eldon whispered. He pulled Fiske aside and briefed him. ". . . so that's our plan for covering the raid."

"No Bigfoot, eh? Well, this is nearly as good. You think Bellows is telling you straight?"

"No reason why not. It fits what we know."

"Confirm it with the cops. Ask to go in with the deputies."

"Can't. I'd compromise Huey. But he wouldn't shuck me; I've licked him, man to man."

"What?"

"I bested him fly-fishing. Captured his soul. Got it right here in my hat."

"You sure you haven't been smoking some of that Thai weed?"

"You've got to keep Pugh here in town," Eldon said. "He doesn't realize what's going on. He could run down there looking for flying saucers and get shot. Promise him a load of tinfoil or something."

"We'll set up a cot for him in the pressroom," Fiske said. "Can't have someone shooting a valuable Bigfoot resource like him."

"I really appreciate your backing on this, Jimbo."

"I'm not paying overtime; you two will take comp time. And I still want that Boy Scout feature."

"Sure. I'll even write a feature on Pugh."

"When this is over. You've got a lot to do." Fiske puffed his pipe, gazing absently toward the bay. "'Port Jerome Opium Wars Lead to Discovery of Bigfoot.' *That* would be good copy."

The pirate galley hove into Nekaemas Bay late the next afternoon. The skull and crossbones leered on her billowing sail. The skull's grin was bloody in the beginning of sundown. Grimy tars sweated at the oars under the cat's lash. An eye-patched ruffian brandished a cutlass in the galley's bow as she approached the crowded waterfront. The galley belonged to the Nekaemas Bay Buccaneers, a service club of hale fellows, well-met in infamous rituals of public humiliation and much beer. In their ranks were judges, businessmen, and other social pillars who now and again thrust aside respectability for the buccaneer life. The Buccaneers were a fixture of Pioneer Days. Their galley always led the waterborne procession at the Blessing of the Boats.

The creature in the bow had a cruel hook in place of one hand. A moonshine jug swung from the hook by its ring. The pirate raised the jug in salute and swilled. The crowd on shore roared approval with beer bottles held high. Some danced to rock music that blared from a jury-rigged sound system.

"Goddamn childish bullshit." Eldon scowled at the crowd. Twice as many people had turned out for the Blessing as for the crab-eating contest. They had gotten twice as drunk, awaiting the ceremony—unaccountably delayed by the absence of the coast guard cutter and helicopters, an absence upon which no one seemed to ponder.

A Vietnamese woman danced alone. She seemed vaguely familiar as Eldon watched her fluid movements and the play of sunlight on her black hair. She was trim, square-faced, not particularly pretty, but Eldon was struck by her self-possession. These Asian women know what they're about, he thought. It dawned on him that getting to know the refugees would open whole new erotic vistas for him in Port Jerome. Why hadn't he thought of it before?

He checked the settings on his camera. He would shoot a picture and introduce himself, use it as an excuse to get the woman's name. The music ended. The woman stopped dancing. Seeing her face in repose, Eldon realized that it was Theresa, Huey's wife.

Oh, hell. Eldon strolled over. "Hi, Theresa. Remember me?"

"You're Shelly's friend Eldon. My husband said to tell you if I saw you that he's 'rarin' to go.'"

"Huey's not with you?"

"He's at the house. He told me to come to the festival . . . and to stay here. I'm staying with Shelly overnight." Her words were matter-of-fact, but there was an uneasy undertone in her voice. "He didn't tell me what was going on. Shelly says not to worry."

"Don't. You'll get it all in tomorrow's paper."

"I don't want Huey involved in something dangerous. Those days are behind us."

"He's doing us a favor," Eldon said. "But he's not taking any risks. So relax and enjoy this gilding of the uncouth lily of South Coast culture."

"Poor Eldon, what a grump." It was Shelly, camera in hand, her coat bunchy with extra rolls of film.

Eldon forced a smile. Perversely, he was in a sour mood. These festivities could not compare with the news bonanza promised tonight; he could barely restrain his impatience. And with a memorable scoop almost in his grasp, he worried that he would somehow blunder.

If I hadn't failed with Bernice, I wouldn't be here, he thought. I'd be in Japan or Brussels—somewhere interesting. Instead, I got left out in the rain in the Oregon woods.

Left out—that was it. He was like a character in Céline. He could never be a part of this and didn't want to be. Yet it made him envious to see people who were part of something, even if it was a drunken festival or the Nekaemas Bay Buccaneers.

A distant constellation of flashing pink lights caught his eye as it skimmed the treetops in the dusky sky across the bay. A Coastie helicopter, Eldon thought, squinting. It's heading north for the drug raid.

Meanwhile, a dwarf wearing a papier-mâché pig's head danced a hornpipe aboard the pirate galley as boats gathered astern and the reviewing stand began to fill.

"That's Ambrose McFee," Eldon said. "He's a Buccaneer."

"I just hope your mood improves," Shelly said. "Where's Pugh?"

"Right over there by the reviewing stand, with Jimbo's hand securely on his shoulder."

"Good. I'm going to start taking pictures so we can clear out of here."

Eldon watched Shelly make her way through the crowd toward the reviewing stand. On the rickety-looking platform stood the potbellied county commissioners and other dumpy officials and their dumpy wives. Conrad DeVere, resplendent with merit badges, guarded the American flag. The officials had enjoyed a few beers during the afternoon's delay. With them was the tall Catholic monsignor in surplice and purple biretta who would bestow the Blessing of the Boats. Monsignor Stonum conversed, his pleasant long face creased in a paternal smile. Eldon craned his neck to see to whom the priest was talking. Sure enough, it was Marsha, fawning outrageously.

Maybe she'll get a plenary indulgence, Eldon thought. He returned his attention to the crowd. There was Paavo the Finn, sprung from jail at last. He towered unsteadily over the heads of his fellow denizens, glaring around the big bandage on his nose. Eldon saw with amusement that Paavo was still stalked by Cap'n Jasper, although the old tar kept his distance in the crowd. Close to the reviewing stand were Fiske and Pugh. Eldon could see the editor's lips moving incessantly around the stem of his pipe. Pugh's attention was across the bay as the distant pink lights seemed to loop and hover before disappearing to the north. Pugh gave an excited little jerk. Fiske's hand clamped tighter on Pugh's shoulder and Pugh subsided.

Shown the cot set up for him in the pressroom, Pugh had become submissive, nodding wisely as if at some private insight. He had listened, nodding, ever since to Fiske's interminable Sasquatch recollections. Pugh had nodded and shuffled off to get a rebuilt radiator for his truck. Jimbo had followed, lips never still, pipe smoldering, hand clamped to Pugh's shoulder. Pugh had asked for a sandwich. Jimbo had escorted him to Pop's, still gripping Pugh's clavicle and talking. Had Fiske spent the night reminiscing to Pugh in the shadow of the offset press? In Pugh, Fiske had the truly captive audience he craved. In Fiske, Pugh had a guardian angel.

Eldon's gaze wandered on. Not far from the Siamese twins of Fiske and Pugh, waning sunlight fell on the colossal globe of the circus fat lady. The dolorous face of ringmaster Cyrus Peake was a nearby moon. They still haven't made it out of town, Eldon thought. Their axle's still broken—which is the story of this place. All the crazy flotsam has gathered at the edge of the water to receive grace.

On the reviewing stand, Monsignor Stonum warmed up, blessing the crowd as he orated prayers that Eldon could not hear; the sound system had failed. Pugh jumped in Fiske's grasp as the priest traced quick crosses in the air. Half-automatically, half in affectation, Eldon crossed himself. Nearby, a woman with ratted hair moaned in devotion, pressing a frosted beer bottle to her forehead. The tawdry sight saddened Eldon. They were all so unaware.

Tomorrow's headlines will wake them up, he thought.

A solemn hush fell as Monsignor Stonum splashed holy water at the crowd. Then came a yell: "Way ta go, Padre! . . . Now on with the show!"

The crowd cheered. Someone set off a string of firecrackers. The Blessing of the Boats began.

The galley's oarsmen strained. The vessel glided forward. Monsignor Stonum raised his hand in blessing. He would bless each small craft as it passed the reviewing stand and throw benediction across the water at the larger boats, calling down the grace of God on the vessels that were sources of livelihood and pleasure on the South Coast.

The crazy boats were no respecters of man or God, however. One cut in among the larger craft, motor roaring, racing to be first past the reviewing stand while the Almighty's favor was being served out piping hot. The crazy boat was a motorized inflatable raft, daubed with polka dots and full of drunks in clown suits. The crowd went wild. The show had begun while there was enough daylight to enjoy it. A motorboat weaved in the raft's wake; a cowboy stood behind its windshield, whirling a lasso around his head.

The two boats cut across the galley's bow. The Buccaneer oarsmen braked to keep from running them down. Magically, the water boiled with other crazy boats, more fantastic and less agile. There were barrels driven by paddle wheels; bathtubs towed by kayaks. A toilet pitched off the side of the commode-decorated motorboat. A junker catamaran dodged the splash, fouled an oar of the Buccaneers' galley, and came apart, dumping its tipsy crew into the bay. The pirates slowed to pick up survivors.

Firecrackers popped. Empty beer bottles splashed into the water. The boats came on. Aboard the galley, the pirate with the hook and cutlass pursued the hornpiping pig. Ambrose scampered over oarsmen and swung monkeylike from the rigging.

The galley's oars swept upright as the vessel neared the reviewing stand. The crew took on a naval dignity as Monsignor Stonum bestowed the blessing. Then they lowered oars and resumed their stroke, correcting course to avoid the reviewing stand.

Collision was averted by a hair's breadth. As the galley brushed past the reviewing stand, the dancing pig jumped ship. Ambrose sprang from the ship's rail onto that of the reviewing stand, saving his balance with a pirouette that won the admiration of the crowd. The reviewing stand creaked. Ambrose doffed his papier-mâché pig's head and bowed, beaming while Marsha looked disgusted.

Out in the crowd, Paavo the Finn roared, "YOU! I RECOGNIZE YOU! IT WAS YOU WITH MY WIFE!" Paavo's arm came up like a ram, pointing straight at Ambrose, and he charged.

McFee froze on the railing, eyes enormous. His mouth worked for a second before reflexes honed in countless bars took over. The little man sprang down and ran. Paavo thundered toward the pier. Eldon knew that in moments the dwarfish lecher's torso, plucked of limbs and genitals, would be flung into the bay by the Finn.

Ambrose bounded off the reviewing stand and broke away down the pier. He reached the shoreline and jumped into the crowd. Paavo swerved toward him. A rangy form dropped to its hands and knees in Ambrose's path—Cap'n Jasper, up to old tricks. Ambrose vaulted Jasper. Paavo was just behind. Jasper's ribs caught the Finn at the knees. Paavo somersaulted into the fat lady. She tripped over a pile of two-by-fours. The beams rolled beneath her plunging feet and she tumbled down the slope like a runaway planet. She plowed into one of the reviewing stand's timbers that was sunk in the wet earth of the shore.

The structure shuddered; a crossbeam dropped free. The reviewing stand creaked. The politicians and their wives started for the pier. They never made it. The timbers groaned under the sudden shift of their weight, and the reviewing stand slid into the water like a massive Tinkertoy set. Mayor, commissioners, wives,

Eagle Scout with American banner, tall priest, and fawning reporter joined the crazy boats in Nekaemas Bay.

Pandemonium. On shore, drunks staggered through a cloud of dust. Eldon could see heads like bobbing pumpkins in the water. The mayor clung to a floating beam. Marsha Cox sloshed ashore, wailing. She looked like a half-drowned rat. Conrad DeVere had his arm under Monsignor Stonum's chin and was swimming for shore, leaving the American flag spread across the water like a gaudy sheet.

Eldon held his camera high with both hands, shooting over the heads of the milling throng.

Shelly yelled to him from the pier. "Quick . . . up here! We can shoot down on 'em as they pull those people out of the water."

Eldon clambered onto the pier as fire sirens cut the air.

Theresa was there. So was Fiske, puffing his pipe and happily surveying the melee. One trouser leg was soaked. "Good copy, dee-de-dee! I was a little too close when she went. Isn't Marsha a sight?"

"I got a good one of the stand collapsing," Shelly said.

"Good, I'll need inside art," Fiske said. "This would be front-page stuff if it wasn't for that raid."

"You just wait 'til tonight, boss!" Shelly hopped with glee. "We're in such a great business!"

"Get a shot of that Boy Scout saving the preacher," Fiske said.

Shelly stopped hopping. "Where's Pugh?"

"Pugh? I had my hand right on his shoulder when the stand went . . ."

"He's gone!" Shelly yelled.

"Musta lost my grip when I stepped in the water," Fiske said. "He said those lights across the bay were UFOs, and I said that's a lot of nonsense, they're helicopters—"

"He's on his way to the ranch," said Shelly. "He's gonna get killed. Uncle Odgen!" She was off through the crowd like a shot, Theresa rushing after.

Eldon turned to follow them.

Fiske snagged his arm. "I need rescue pictures."

"Let Marsha earn her keep."

"Gimme your camera. I'll shoot the art m'self. Used to be a fair shooter in my day—"

Eldon thrust his camera into Fiske's hands and ran. A fire truck pulled into his path. He got around the truck and dodged a trio of diminutive figures—a Vietnamese man, woman, and little boy. The boy sat astride his father's shoulders, observing with solemn wonder the goings-on in this, his impossible new country.

Eldon fought his way through the milling people and ran for the newspaper office. Pugh's truck was gone. The Ship of Love was rolling out of the parking lot, Theresa's car right behind. "Wait!" Eldon screamed—in vain. The two vehicles sped north on the highway, toward the bridge and Muskrat.

Gasping for breath, Eldon reached his Citroën. Christ! The rear wheel! He got the truck open, fumbled for the tire iron, lost precious minutes prying the crushed fender away from the tire. He dropped the tire iron and leaped into the car. "C'mon, you bastard, start!" He stomped the gas pedal and twisted the key. There was a sound like gnashing metal teeth.

"Please," Eldon said. "Just one more time. Don't let me lose this story. Don't let me lose this girl." He turned the key. The engine caught with a bang. Eldon burned rubber across the parking lot and sped toward Muskrat and the Patterson ranch.

17

The sun had nearly set by the time Eldon reached Muskrat. In the deepening darkness, the ill-marked country lanes were indistinguishable from one another among the trees. Think it through, Eldon told himself. If you find Pugh, you find Shelly. Where would they go?

Not to Huey's. There was nothing to take Pugh there. To the Patterson ranch? For sure—but not straight up to the gate. Even Pugh was not crazy enough to invite a bullet; he had been alive too long. No, Pugh would creep onto the ranch along one of his secret trails. Eldon could never hope to follow.

Neither can Shelly or Theresa if they aren't right on his tail, he thought. That leaves Pugh's place. The flying-saucer tower. He hunted along the highway, searching for the sandy turnoff that he and Shelly had taken the day that they had first gone to Pugh's scruffy homestead. The wind boomed off the sea, skating down over the dunes and blowing a faint spray of sand and the smell of impending rain through the open car window. The forest seemed terrible, no longer sheltering. Shaggy branches reached down like menacing hands.

Eldon slowed lest he run off the road. A constant rubbing sound from the left rear tire didn't help his state of mind.

He gripped the wheel. The turnoff was somewhere along here.

There—that was it. He eased the car slowly up the narrow lane, turning off his headlights and driving with parking lights so as not to attract attention. The lane's turn and slope seemed familiar. He was enveloped by the forest. He remembered with a chill that the gate to the Patterson place was on the way to Pugh's. But when, after several minutes, he had not reached the gate, he knew he had taken the wrong road.

Raindrops tapped the leaves. Lights glowed through the trees. Eldon headed down a graveled turnoff, toward the lights. He came to the back of a modest frame house. The lights of other houses showed beyond. Eldon slowed the Citroën to a crawl and switched his headlights back on. Staring silently at him from the house's vegetable garden was a round-faced Vietnamese girl, no more than six. She looked at him with eyes that were like gemstones in the lights.

"Hi," Eldon called softly from the car as the rain picked up. "Where's your mom and dad?"

The child thrust her thumb into her mouth and scurried around the corner of the house. Eldon drove down the gravel street and around the corner. He hit the brake. What he saw there dazed him for a moment.

Had it not been for the ferns and the shadowy Douglas fir, he might have fallen into Huey Bellows' past—for the street was filled with Vietnamese.

It was lined with weathered frame houses—an old encampment thrown up years before to house the families of logging crews and later abandoned. Nekaemas County's new Vietnamese citizens had brought life back to the forest street. They hurried up and down, illuminated by porch lights and Coleman lanterns, turning up parka hoods against the rain. Singsong Vietnamese music played through an open window where a wok sizzled; Eldon's mouth watered at the rich smell of Asian cooking. A group stood talking on a nearby porch. They stopped abruptly and turned to look at Eldon's car.

Eldon halted and climbed out. "Say, there, I need some directions."

No one spoke.

Eldon repeated the sentence in French. The people stared uneasily. In English, he asked, "Where can I find Truong Van Vinh?"

Suddenly, tension was as pungent as the odor of cooking. An old woman grabbed the little girl who had first seen Eldon and pulled her indoors.

"Where is Truong Van Vinh?" Eldon said. A man on the porch shook his head as the Vietnamese music wailed on. Eldon walked on down the street, pulled at another man's sleeve. "Truong Van Vinh. Where does he live?"

"Sorry," the man said hastily.

A woman swung down the street toward him, carrying crates slung from a yoke across her shoulders. She wore an American denim jacket and a conical Oriental hat for protection against the rain.

"I'm looking for Truong Van Vinh," Eldon said to the woman.

The woman kept moving.

Eldon started to try French; that idea led to another. "Tran Minh."

The woman halted, looked Eldon over, narrow-eyed. She gave a sly grin and jabbed a finger in the direction from which she had come, then disappeared into the shadows as the rain came down full force.

The street emptied and doors slammed. Porch lights became bright pools of light in the torrent. Eldon hurried down the street, sliding on the wet crunching gravel, groping for a piece of napkin he remembered in his coat pocket—Tran Minh's address, given him by Stephanie Hosfelder in the bar.

Eldon got under some eaves and read the scrap of paper. No house number, just a rural post-office box number. Lines of old country mailboxes stood along the street. Vietnamese names were painted over faded American names on some of the boxes. Many contained identical bright pieces of junk mail—America had taken the boat people to its bosom, all right.

Eldon pulled out his penlight and squinted at the box numbers. He read one bank of mailboxes, then crossed to the next. Here was the number he wanted—the mailbox was painted with a gold and red South Vietnamese flag.

Tran Minh's house was a little larger than the others. Perhaps it had once belonged to a logging foreman. There was a sagging picket fence and a gate that creaked as Eldon pushed it open. A face peeked briefly around a window curtain at the sound of the gate. Eldon had the impression that the face was Caucasian, not Vietnamese.

Eldon stepped onto the porch. The door opened as he was about to knock. Tran Minh looked out at him, gold front teeth glinting. "Yah?"

"You know me, Tran Minh. Eldon Larkin of the *Sun*."

"No buy. My En'lish no good."

"Alors, nous parlerons en français."

Tran Minh stared at Eldon. *"Oui, Monsieur Larkin. C'est plus convenable."*

"Speaking French *is* convenient," Eldon agreed. "It seems to

aid your memory. I knew that we should speak it when we met
again."

"You have tracked us down."

Us? Eldon wondered whether he had heard the word correctly. *Nous*—us. Yes, he had. "I have no time to waste, monsieur. I require information. Lives may be at stake."

"Lives!" Tran Minh shuddered. "Three are dead already." He
leaned against the door. "What do you want of me?"

"I want directions to the house of old Pugh. And I must use
your telephone, monsieur. The police will be here in a few minutes. I must call my editor. It is better if you cooperate."

It was the sheerest improvisation. I'm a rude bastard when I
speak French, Eldon thought. I could pass for a Parisian. Just so
I get to his phone.

"You know everything, then," Tran Minh said. "He is here.
Come in."

Tran Minh stepped away from the door and opened it wide,
beckoning Eldon inside. Eldon stood stock-still, staring past Tran
Minh at the haggard figure sitting in the living room.

Dougie the killer stared back at him, goggle-eyed.

An electric spark snapped in Eldon's stomach as he stood
rooted to the porch. Then Dougie groaned and crumpled in his
chair, face in his hands.

Eldon stared at the grubby knuckles, the grime-caked nails.

Dougie peered over his hands in terror. "What're you talkin'?
What's that mean?"

The fear in Dougie's voice drew Eldon through the door, like
a dog to meat. It was as if he finally had Billy Vogel, and everyone in his life like Billy, in his clutches at last. "It means you've
had it, you murdering bastard," Eldon said in English. "Come
after me in a gorilla mask, will you?"

"And now you've come for me! I'm sorry." Dougie's eyes were
red-rimmed and scared. Tears brimmed over the raw lower lids.
"Oh, you are the meanest son of a bitch in the whole valley."

"Yes, I am," Eldon said slowly, to hide his astonishment.

Here was the creature who had thrust a file through Marie
Payne's blue eye; who had cut his own accomplice's throat; who
had tried to kill Eldon, too. Now he was ragged, his hair matted.
He was begging Eldon's forgiveness.

"You and your partner came after me at the cabin," Dougie

said. He pointed to a crumpled copy of the *Sun* next to the chair. "I know I'm done; you put my picture in the paper. I should've given up then."

Dougie gave a choked, exhausted little laugh, and Eldon realized what the killer must be seeing—not merely Eldon Larkin but *the reporter*. A hard-bitten, semimythical character out of old movies and half-remembered comic books, who righted wrongs and fearlessly exposed corruption. He was the scourge of villains and the prince of headlines, pursuing his quarry to the bitter end through the rainy north woods.

"Do you give up now?" Eldon asked.

Dougie nodded, extending his hands for the cuffs.

"First, you'll answer some questions." Eldon glanced at Tran Minh. He was outnumbered; he had to keep up a bold front. *"Où est le téléphone?"*

"In the kitchen," Tran Minh said.

"Bring it here."

"It is hung on the wall."

Eldon glanced around. He didn't dare leave the room. The call would have to wait. "I don't like people offing my sources," he said to Dougie in English. "Somebody kills your source, you're supposed to do something about it."

"I was ordered to do it," Dougie said, not recognizing the steal from Sam Spade.

"By who?"

"Christ, I can't tell. He'll kill me!" Dougie grimaced and shook his head as if trying to control a compulsion to blurt out all he knew. "She told us the opium days were through. She said we'd get what Nguyen Xuan got if we didn't back off." He stopped and looked quizzically at Eldon.

"Go on," Eldon said.

"Uh . . . you aren't writing this down?"

"I'll remember."

"What she didn't know was that I already had my orders," Dougie said. "She had to go."

"Why?"

"She thought I was still just an opium bagman. That I was still small-time. Tumpat grabbed her hair and I rammed the file in. Her eye just popped. I never killed anybody before. It was so easy—"

Dougie twisted over the chair's arm and retched. Eldon shuddered, watching the thug's dry heaves. Only thin yellow bile dripped onto the copy of the *Sun*. Dougie's stomach was all but empty after days of hiding in the woods.

"And then you killed Tumpat for the opium," Eldon said.

Dougie nodded and wiped his mouth, breathing hard. "We knew we had to split. We took the opium with us for a stake. But Tumpat had killed a guy before, in Borneo or somewhere. He kept talking about how easy it'd been. How easy it was to kill that redhead whore. How easy it was to kill anybody, man. Then I knew he was gonna kill me."

"You killed Tumpat instead, out on the log float."

"Yeah. I took the opium and hid out at the cabin because of the dragnet. When you came after me, I knew I had to fence the stuff before I split. I came to Tran Minh."

"And that green glass," Eldon said. "What was that for?"

Dougie only squinted and shook his head in puzzlement.

"So where'd you hide after you left the cabin?" Eldon asked.

"You don' tell!" Tran Minh said.

"Where, Dougie?" Eldon demanded. "It was on the ranch, wasn't it? With Chadwick."

Dougie's weary eyes met Eldon's almost worshipfully, like a dog acknowledging a stronger creature. He began to speak, but Tran Minh broke in harshly: "No! You go! Now!"

Dougie's gaze shifted to Tran. Eldon realized that it was Tran Minh, not he, who held power over Dougie. Dougie started to push himself up out of the chair and stopped, listening; there were footsteps outside. "God—"

Eldon turned and looked through the still-open door. Outside, the Vietnamese were gathering. They came quietly out of the darkness, stepped onto the porch or stood in the rain—men, women, children. The whole refugee community. Eldon turned back to Dougie. There were Vietnamese faces at windows behind the killer. Men pushed to the front of the crowd outside on the porch, entered the house.

Dougie gurgled, face white, his hands going slack as rubber, and he dropped back into the chair. "Don't let them—"

"Be quiet," a bespectacled Vietnamese man told him with gentle contempt. "You don't matter."

"That's right," said another. He jabbed a finger at Tran Minh.

"And you matter even less. This shame has been upon us long enough. Nguyen Xuan is dead, others are dead. We cannot have men like this one in our community. Or men like you. Truong Van Vinh is right; it makes us no better than outlaws. You have failed."

Tran Minh retorted in Vietnamese. The man with glasses shook his head and replied in English, "Your day is done."

"You are my coun'rymen—" Tran began.

"This is a new country. You cannot protect us anymore. And we do not want you to."

Tran Minh stood blinking. It was as if an internal spring animating him had snapped.

"We want you to leave us," the man with glasses said. "Find your new life elsewhere." He turned to Dougie. "You go right now. We won't bother to call the police. Don't ever come back here."

Hopelessness filled Dougie's eyes, and the intoxication of exhaustion. "I'm in deeper than I ever expected," he said.

He stood slowly, as if testing the strength of the floor, and moved hesitantly toward the door. No one moved to stop him. Dougie shuffled out the front door and did not close it behind him. He shambled down the porch steps in a sore-footed scurry, looking around as if expecting blows. The crowd parted in disdain as Dougie lurched into the darkness and the rain.

Eldon started after the apparition. "*Vous le cachiez,*" he said to Tran Minh. "You have been hiding him."

"No," said Tran Minh. "He came here only tonight."

"*Où ira-t-il?*" Eldon said. "Where will he go?"

The man with glasses answered, in English: "Into the forest, like the animal that he is. Let the forest have him. Or the police."

"Where is Truong Van Vinh?" Eldon demanded.

"He went to help a friend. He told us to say no more."

Eldon went into the kitchen and grabbed the telephone. He was about to dial the police but the stubborn thought that he wanted to walk in on the raid made him dial the *Sun* newsroom instead. Busy signal. Eldon swore; but of course the lines were tied up—the ludicrous disaster at the pier, compounded by the night's sports calls.

He hung up and addressed Tran Minh in French. "Did you tell Dougie to kill Marie Payne and Nguyen Xuan?"

"No," Tran Minh said. "For your answers, you must go see Pugh."

"Pugh is out of his mind."

"Nevertheless, he has your answers."

"Monsieur, I think that *you* have many of the answers."

Tran Minh only shook his head, crossed to the chair, and began gathering up the newspaper on which Dougie had vomited. On a shelf above the stove was a statuette of the Blessed Virgin Mary, a plaster doll dressed in blue and white robes, with a miniature gilt crown and a halo of wavy golden rays. Tran gazed on the icon.

"It is different here," he said at last, addressing everyone. "In Vietnam, we were the captains and the kings; the judges and the landlords and the priests. I was an officer. Here, it is very different. We are fishermen and woodcutters. I deal in stolen goods. Anyone can be anything. I could be a cowboy. Or Tarzan." Tran looked at the slimy newspaper and stuffed it into the stove. *"Maintenant, nous sommes plus authentiques."*

"'Here we are more real,'" Eldon repeated.

"Yes." Tran looked around him. "And so now I cannot protect any longer what I have been protecting."

One of the men in the room snorted scornfully.

"I know all about the ranch and about Chadwick," Eldon said. "But what was Dougie to you?"

"An errand boy. A go-between between the ranch and myself."

"What do you do for Chadwick?"

"I supply certain goods. He did not wish to be conspicuous about supplies. He paid me, of course . . . and there is a certain amount of protection for my people. I am . . . I was . . . somewhat their leader."

"And we were somewhat your serfs," the man with glasses said in a hard tone.

"Perhaps Nguyen Xuan was killed because he got above his station?" Eldon asked.

"I had nothing to do with that," Tran said. "That fool tried to blackmail Chadwick."

"And so Marie Payne killed him."

"She was a partner in the smuggling operation; that much was plain. A man in my position pieces things together, monsieur. Marie Payne knew this coast. It was she who selected the Patterson ranch for the smugglers. I was not sorry to learn of her death."

"Why was she killed?"

"You met the woman? And you need to ask?" Tran flashed his gold front teeth. "She tried to play Xuan and Chadwick against one another."

"To gain what?"

"Affirmation of her nature, perhaps. And blackmail money. She was very foolish."

"Dougie killed her on Chadwick's orders."

"No doubt. Dougie is not the sort of man who thinks for himself. But I can think for myself, Monsieur Larkin. I want no more of this. My countrymen are right. That is why I am being frank with you."

"Murder is a little out of your line, eh?"

"Murder has always been out of my line," Tran Minh said.

"More lives may be at stake now," Eldon said. "Which way to Pugh's?"

"Go straight ahead down the gravel road," Tran Minh said. "It connects with another and loops back to run past Pugh's house." He shook his head. "Dealing in stolen property does not pay very well in Port Jerome. I sought a higher caliber of client than Dougie. I wanted better than this. And I only wanted to help my countrymen."

"You only wanted money," the bespectacled man said. "Truong Van Vinh was right."

"Where is Truong?" Eldon asked.

"Not here," said the bespectacled man.

"Where?"

"Stay here," the man with glasses said. "Don't risk yourself."

"Ah, but I have to get the story," Eldon said. "I'll come back later, and you can tell me yours."

Eldon looked at Tran Minh, but the gap between him and Tran was too great to bridge with more words, in any language. He went out into the rain. There was no time to telephone the *Sun* now.

*   *   *

The road narrowed. Ferns reached through the car's open window. Drops of water splashed Eldon's face. He thought he saw the top of Pugh's tower ahead among the trees, through the drizzle. Here was the bend in the road, the rutted driveway. He dropped the Citroën into first gear and started up the drive.

The car scraped bottom as he topped the hill and steered down into the glade. The Frankenstein house was dark save for a dim light burning within the geodesic dome. Pugh's tower stood in the gloom. He steered around piles of junk to the back of the house. There was the Ship of Love, side door open; empty. There was no sign of Theresa's car. Eldon parked and peered up at the UFO tower.

"Shelly? Pugh? Hello?" No answer.

Maybe they're in the dome, he thought.

Eldon thrust his notebook into his belt at the small of his back, picked the tire iron off the front seat, and started for the house. There was no moon. The shadowy rubbish mounds had the aura of menace. He blundered into a pile of PVC pipe that clattered across the ground. Eldon stifled a curse and used the beam of his penlight to make his way onto the porch. Silence from the house. He forced the back door and moved into the hall. He sensed no presence—a good thing, for it was impossible to move quietly; he kept stumbling over trash. In the darkness, the house seemed bigger than he remembered. It seemed to open out, like the *Orient Star* below decks. He reached the cluttered living room and searched for a light. An unshaded lamp was bolted to the wall. The lamp worked.

In the radiance from the puny bulb, the room looked like the setting of a bad dream. The litter piles cast humped shadows onto the walls. The Prince Albert can was no longer atop the television set, but the glass Japanese fishing floats still dangled in their net, blue and green globes. . . .

Recognition hit with a jolt. Eldon pulled one of the green globes free of the net and brought it near the lamp. The float was a little one, not larger than a billiard ball. He took a shard of green glass from his pocket and held it against the float. They matched exactly, color and curvature.

Eldon whistled softly. Pugh must've given Nguyen Xuan one of these, he thought. Xuan must've been up here laying pipe.

And Xuan had it in his pocket when Horton the elephant did his thing.

The reporter rolled the float in his fingers. They haven't made these in years, he thought, recalling a beachcombing feature he had written the summer before. Floats that wash up on the beaches these days are plastic. Pugh must be old as God; old enough to be Ogden O. Sherwood.

Was the green glass float some secret token? Eldon felt a queasy fear and glanced hastily around. The silence emboldened him. If Billy Vogel were here now I'd pull his lungs out, he thought, and climbed the stairs to the dome.

A Coleman lantern illuminated Pugh's spaceship hangar. No one was there.

The tinfoil spaceship was complete. It gave off a crinkly gleam in the lantern's hard glare as Eldon circled the finned base. The ship reared askew like a child's rainy-day project, patchworked, absurdly oversized. Yet the fanciful rocket had an awkward grace. Weeks of careful work were represented here. The crinkled foil had been painstakingly smoothed and molded onto the chicken-wire frame, the irregular sheets joined with crimped overlapping folds.

"Orville, it'll never fly," Eldon said wryly.

He shivered in a sudden cool breeze from above and peered upward. Beyond the ship's wheeled nose was blackness. A section of the geodesic dome had been removed, opening the hangar to the night sky. The wagon tongue near the spaceship's nose hung out through the hole, waiting for a passing flying saucer to "hitch on and pull."

Eldon shook his head and flashed the Coleman lantern around the big room. Nothing but stray scraps of tinfoil and other odds and ends. You'd think he'd load some provisions if he was about to take a trip into space, Eldon thought; but I suppose a trip to heaven is first class all the way.

He went back downstairs with the lantern and took a last quick look around. He had to talk to Fiske. But a quick search showed that perhaps the only thing Pugh's junk collection lacked was a telephone.

I'll lie low here, Eldon thought, and get down to Patterson's gate when I hear the police sirens. With any luck, I'll meet up with Shelly in the raid. I hope she's all right. I've got to have a photographer. I gave my damn camera to Fiske.

He realized he couldn't tell which was more important to him, Shelly or the story. He had been in the woods so long that he couldn't tell the difference anymore.

Maybe that's what makes a good reporter, he thought, heading for the back door: when you don't have anything else in your life that's important; when good copy's all there is.

Eldon stepped from the porch, holding the lantern high. As he passed by the Ship of Love, he reached out to close the side door—and froze in shock at what he saw inside the van in the lantern's harsh light.

Shelly's camera bag rested neatly on the passenger's bucket seat.

The coldest shudder Eldon had ever experienced surged through him, his skin rising in goose bumps that felt like marbles. Shelly would never take off into the woods after a story without her camera.

He almost dropped the lantern and rushed back into the shadows around the house. Get hold of yourself, Eldon thought. If they were still around, they'd have nailed you by now. He played the lantern within the van. No sign of struggle. No key in the ignition. No blood.

Shelly probably was alive, then. A hostage? His mind raced. The smugglers must have Shelly—why else would she have abandoned her camera? Probably they had Pugh, as well.

He had to call the cops—and Fiske. Where was the nearest phone? Huey's house. He reached into the van and pulled Shelly's camera bag to him. This story was getting bigger by the minute.

He switched off the Coleman lantern and set the camera bag on the front seat of his Citroën. Then he slipped the key into the ignition and turned it. The starter spun with a groan. "Calm," Eldon said. "Calm." On the third try, the engine caught and he got under way. He eased along the driveway and up the hill. The motor lugged as he made the crest and nearly died as he went over. Eldon hit the gas hard. The car bottomed out and then bounded forward. There was a terrible rasping from the damaged wheel well. The engine died. Eldon twisted the key. The car rolled downhill, the rear tire rasping. The engine revived at the bottom of the hill. He maneuvered through the turn and down the tunnellike lane. As he approached the Patterson ranch, the engine died again.

"Our Father who art in heaven"—*I'll never make another pass at Shelly,* Eldon told God as he rolled abreast of the Patterson gate. *I'll always treat women with respect. I'll tell everyone about You.*

Piety and momentum carried him past the deadly gate. A Hail Mary and a couple of Glory Be's revived the engine once more. Then there was a sudden vicious shredding noise, and Eldon knew that the tire had gone. He veered off the dark road and into the gloom of the forest. The Citroën hit the underbrush with a crunch and jerked to a stop.

Eldon dropped over sideways in the seat and lay listening, heart pounding. There were only the sounds of the forest and the hushed wind off the sea. Eldon eased the door open and quietly slid from the car, pulling the camera bag with him. He eased the door shut and hurried down the road, keeping to the shadows and glancing back to see whether the car was visible. He didn't think so. *Thank you, God.*

How far was Huey's house? Could he find it in the dark?

After some minutes, he heard the dim pulse of rock music in the distance. Eldon moved toward the sound, automatically stepping in time with the beat and feeling suddenly chilly as the sweat on his body dried in the night air. It was going to be all right, dammit. He still had his notebook, a camera, and his lucky hat.

He recognized the tune well before he reached Bellows's mailbox—the Rolling Stones' "Satisfaction." It was coming from Huey's house, repeating over and over, as if on a tape loop. Eldon hurried down the lane.

The house blazed with light. The Rolling Stones thundered. He made for the porch door.

Something huge slammed into his back. A forearm like an iron bar clamped across Eldon's windpipe, blocking his desperate shout. Steel flashed before his eyes—a wicked double-edged military knife gripped in a dark anthropoid fist.

18

Eldon clawed at the massive arm blocking his windpipe, thrashing with all his might. His eyes started from his head. His limbs were made of lead. He was flying. His back slammed the ground and his attacker, silhouetted in the light from the house, jumped astride his chest. The knife point pricked his throat.

"Eldon!" The attacker was Huey Bellows.

"Hahh . . ."

"Boy, am I glad to see you," Huey said. "What were you doin', sneakin' up on me in the dark like that? You sure gave me a scare."

Gave *you* a scare? Eldon tried to say; but all that came out was "Hahh." He pushed feebly at Bellows. "Haoff."

"What?"

". . . *off* . . ."

"Oh! Sorry!" Huey jumped off Eldon's chest and helped him sit up. "Just sit and get your breath. I should've known it'd be you. But I didn't think you'd walk."

"My car crapped out up the road." Eldon rubbed his throat, momentarily beyond resentment or fear. He saw without wonder that Huey was oddly dressed—dark clothes, boots, and a floppy military fatigue hat like Eldon's. Bellows's collar was turned up and his hands and face were streaked with some dark substance.

"Let's get you up," Bellows said. "You'll live. Come in the house."

He pulled Eldon up, got the camera bag, and steered him onto the porch. They entered Bellows's workshop, full of grinders, soldering irons, and silica dust. The half-completed lamp shade stood on its work stand. A big rectangular frame covered by a canvas leaned against the far wall. Eldon, blinking in the bright light, saw that Huey wore army jungle fatigues and that the streaks on his face were olive green camouflage paint.

Bellows turned a knob mounted near the work table; the Rolling Stones faded. "I've wired the whole place for sound."

"What's this Green Berets getup?" Eldon said.

"Green Beret, no way. I was a redleg. Artillery recon. You said you wanted to get onto the ranch when the raid went down. I'm going to take ya in."

"We've got to call the cops," Eldon said. "Shelly's gone. I think the smugglers have her. And Pugh, too. He made a break during the Blessing of the Boats. He took off in his truck heading this way, and Shelly tore off after him. I found both their vehicles at Pugh's place and no sign of either of them." Eldon lifted the camera bag. "This is Shelly's; I found it in the van. She'd never leave it behind."

"No more'n a soldier'd leave his weapon," Huey said with a quick nod of agreement. "Christ! Don't this raise the stakes!" He pulled Eldon into the living room.

Truong Van Vinh rose to greet them.

The Vietnamese wore black and green tiger-striped fatigues and jungle boots, and his face was streaked like Huey's with olive green paint. The uniform was tailored to Truong's small frame and creased knife-sharp. Parachute badges, Vietnamese and American, were embroidered over his shirt pockets. Truong wore a beret with a gold wreath pierced with a flaming arrow.

Oh, no, Eldon thought.

Truong smiled. "Eldon Larkin. As expected."

"Can I have some water?"

Huey thrust a plastic military canteen into Eldon's hand. As he drank, Eldon noticed a knife strapped to Truong's boot. He stared at the knife until Huey spoke.

"You may have to use that pigsticker tonight, Truong; Eldon says the druggies have got his girlfriend."

"Did you serve in Vietnam, Mr. Larkin?" Truong asked. "No? We'll make a war correspondent of you tonight."

"I just about became a casualty in the driveway," Eldon said.

"Hee, hee," Bellows said. "Shoulda heard yourself squawk."

"Come on, Huey, where's the phone?" Eldon said.

"Haven't had one for years," Huey said. "I hate the damn things. They were always ringin' off the hook in the artillery control center in Nam. I couldn't get any sleep. Worse, I couldn't get away from the war. Siddown, Eldon."

Bewildered, Eldon dropped onto the sofa as Truong unfolded a white survey map and spread it out.

"We're here," Huey said in a voice belying his fearsome appearance; he sounded like a conspiratorial boy. "Here's the Patterson farmhouse. We can slip in along the base of the dunes here without being seen."

"There's a clear path along the beach," Truong said.

"Damn it, they'll be landin' the dope on the beach," Huey said without rancor. "We don't want to run into them. And we don't want to get caught in a cross fire when the cops move in.

"They've . . . got . . . Shelly," Eldon said. "And maybe Pugh." He gripped Huey's sleeve. "We've got . . . to tell . . . the police!"

Huey nodded happily. "What do you think about goin' in to save her, instead?"

Dainty prickles danced across Eldon's skin as he stared at the war-painted lout. He became aware of the living room's decor. A framed set of military ribbons and insignia hung on one wall. A print of army helicopters was tacked on another. UH-1's, Eldon thought. Also known as Hueys.

On the ends of the mantel were miniature U.S. and South Vietnamese flags, hanging from little brass flagpoles mounted on tooled brass bases. Next to each flag was a chromed 30mm shell. In the center of the mantel was the framed photograph of a young soldier: Huey Bellows—slimmer, neater, beardless features unravaged by war. But the same little eyes that now regarded Eldon gleamed in the photo beneath the service cap's leather visor, like those of a mad squirrel.

"You're out of your mind," Eldon said.

"No, I'm not, Eldon. Because I've *been* outta my mind, and I know what it feels like. This isn't it." Huey's gaze went to his picture. "I didn't tell you all of my dream yesterday. There was more, but I didn't tell you for fear of changin' it."

"Changing what?"

"Why, tonight's events." Huey put a green-striped hand on Eldon's knee. "I dreamed about our patrol tonight. In the dream, I saw a safe way onto the ranch. God pointed the way after he started fishin' with your rod."

"I've never heard from God in my life," Eldon said. "Let's call the cops."

"The cops move in, and they've got a hostage situation on their hands and a ship offshore with millions in pot aboard; that's dynamite, Eldon. The little lady'll never get out alive. But we can pull her outta there and avoid all those problems."

"You two got dressed up like this because God told you to save Shelly?"

"Naw, we were gonna take you onto the ranch anyway . . . kind of a surprise. You've gotta be there tonight, Eldon. That's what seein' your fishing rod in the dream means."

"How're you going to save Shelly?"

"While they're busy landin' the dope," Huey said. "Truong and me have the skills. And the best weapon there is." He tapped his head. "Between our ears."

"Truong," Eldon said. "What about you?"

"Huey is my friend," Truong said. "I will help him. Do you know the things this man has done for us in this country?"

"Didn't he tell you about respect for law and order?"

"When Huey told me of the raid tonight, I realized I must risk something in order to nurture what I have here," Truong said. "They could as easily have taken my wife and children as your photographer. After tonight, these outlaws will learn that we Vietnamese will no longer be victims. And the Vietnamese will learn that they need no longer fear Tran Minh."

"They don't fear Tran anymore," Eldon said. "I just came from there. They've run him off."

Truong grinned. "So they have acted, at last. I can do no less now; a man helps his friends."

Eldon goggled. A few years in Port Jerome had turned Truong into a raving macho coastal dweller, complete with Vietnam flashbacks. Was it caused by some quality in the air? Another few rainy winters and this architect-turned-woodcutter would be armwrestling Paavo the Finn at the bar in the Dead Man's Hand.

Eldon looked into Truong's hard gaze. And he'll be winning, too, he thought.

Huey pressed in. "You a real reporter or not? Do you want this story or don't you?"

Eldon peered around the living room, noting more military memorabilia—an ashtray from the Army Artillery and Missile School at Fort Sill, Oklahoma; a stained-glass lamp shade set with enameled military crests. He wondered how Theresa, or any woman, could put up with it. "Where's Theresa, Huey?"

Huey blinked once, hard, as if he suddenly had dropped down to earth. "At the festival—"

"No," Eldon said. "She chased after Shelly. But she didn't go to Pugh's. I thought she came here."

"She shoulda been back by now," Huey said, suddenly worried.

"Dammit," Eldon said, "if you had a phone, we could call and see if she's still there!"

"Be calm," Truong said. "What could possibly have happened?"

"Where is she?" Huey said. "She'd have come right back—" He stopped.

"What is it?" Eldon said.

"What if she went to the cove—"

"You mean you didn't tell her that—"

". . . and ran into some of those bastards out there?" Huey finished. "This wasn't in the dream!"

He sprang for the door, Eldon and Truong following.

It was a short frantic jog through the woods to the turnoff to Smuggler's Cove. Huey led the way. Eldon expected the big man to crash through the woods like a tank, but Huey moved as lightly as Truong, who scampered behind him. At the turnout at the base of the dunes, they found Theresa's car, parked and dark. Eldon's penlight showed footprints going up the dune face.

They scrambled up the sand slope, keeping low, and hurried to the shelter of the pines on the cliff. They lay on their bellies and peered down into the cove.

"What do you think. . . ?" Eldon began.

"Silence," Truong said.

They lay silently. Eldon listened to the drumming of his heart, feeling the pine needles press his chest and the dampness of the sand under his body.

"One man," Truong whispered at last. "With a shaded flashlight. A lookout."

Eldon scanned the beach below. In the interval, his eyes had adjusted to the darkness. Something like a big faded firefly was moving down on the beach. In *his* cove.

"Smuggler," Huey said. "God, what if—"

"This tears it," Eldon said. "We've got to call the police."

"They've got my woman," Huey said. "We're gonna get us a prisoner."

Huey and Truong began whispering. Eldon stared at them in the dark. Truong slipped off on his belly. "Wait here," Huey ordered.

The big man disappeared. Eldon waited, heart drumming. The thought crept up on him: This is *good copy*.

He tried to disregard the blotchy phantoms that his eyes threw up on the screen of night and to follow the faint glow moving around the beach.

Had the light disappeared? Eldon listened but heard only the sound of breakers in the cove.

Suddenly, Huey slid in beside him. Eldon jerked in fear. "We've got our prisoner," Huey said. "Let's go."

"Where's Theresa?"

"We're gonna ask him." Huey let go a big breath. "Truong wanted to get him off the beach first. He's right. I'd have killed him then and there if I'd thought he wasn't going to talk."

There was a crunching in the vegetation. A figure appeared, gasping with fright, pushed by a smaller figure that Eldon knew was Truong. "Down the path, you," Truong said.

Eldon and Huey stood up. The taller figure whimpered in fear when it saw them and said, "Oh, shit."

"I've frisked him," Truong said. "He's not armed. Now, back to the car."

They shambled across the dunes. Truong kept a grip on the prisoner's bunchy sweater and prodded him with the point of his knife. They reached Theresa's car. Huey grabbed the man by the throat and slammed him against the vehicle. *"Where's my wife? What'd you do with her?"*

"Leggo!"

"Where is the woman who was driving this car?" Truong said.

"Help! I know my rights!" The captive sounded very young.

Eldon flashed his penlight into the man's eyes. "You've got a big problem, asshole; we're not cops." He had always wanted to use that line. "Now answer the man."

Truong held his knife in the penlight's beam. The captive made a sound like a deflating tire. Huey's hand clamped down again. Eldon studied the prisoner's contorting features. He was in his twenties, well groomed, smooth-faced. His sweater was something from a stylish outdoor store. He had the porcine good looks of a fraternity kid.

"Give him some air to talk," Truong said to Huey.

Huey let up.

"*Tên yí?*" Truong snapped. "What is your name?"

"Rod Austin."

"Where is the woman?"

The young man's teeth chattered. "They took her up the beach. To the ranch house."

"Is she okay?" Eldon demanded, before Huey could resume his special brand of questioning.

"Yeah. Yeah. We couldn't let her snoop, y'know. Not since we caught the other one."

"Another woman?" Eldon said. "Shaggy black hair?"

"Yeah. That's right. We caught her in the woods. Ow . . . no! She's okay, too, I swear!"

"What about the old man?" Eldon said.

"No old man. Agh. . . !"

"What are you going to do with them?" Truong said.

The kid began to cry. "We just took them to the house. Judas Priest, I told Chad we were in over our heads."

"Larry Chadwick, eh?" Eldon said. The captive nodded, wretched and eager, squinting into the penlight's glare. Eldon contrived a chuckle. "We know all about your operation, kid. You *are* in over your head."

"Please don't kill me!"

"Enough," said Truong. "When is the delivery?"

"Two-thirty this morning!"

"That's when they land the drugs from the ship?" Eldon asked.

"Yes, yes."

"How many men do you have?" asked Truong.

"Seventeen! Counting me!"

"How many guns? What kind?"

"No guns!"

"I don't believe you," Huey said, and cuffed the youth's jaw. "You're gonna die."

"*We don't have guns! Please!*"

Huey stepped back in disgust. "He's peed himself."

The prisoner slid down the side of the car and wept in the sand. Eldon remembered his own terror aboard the *Orient Star* and a nervous chuckle escaped his throat. *He* had not peed himself. And now he had one of Dougie's buddies in his thrall.

That puzzled him. What was a fresh-faced kid like this doing in cahoots with a punk like Dougie?

"Please, please." The captive wept. "Chad said nobody'd get hurt, he said it'd be easy money. I want the money for school . . ."

"What'll we do with him, Huey?" Eldon asked.

"Stash him," Huey said. He pulled something from his pocket. Eldon heard masking tape being stripped back. He turned the penlight downward and saw that Huey held a set of keys that had been taped together so that they would not jingle.

Huey opened the car's trunk. "Get in. If anything happens to my wife, pray that I never come back to let you out."

Sobbing, the young man crept into the trunk. Huey slammed the trunk lid and straightened, seeming to rear against invisible cables that bound him in the darkness, as if he were King Kong or Sampson lashed by the wrists between pillars. He looked like a swaying mountain.

Eldon wet his lips. "We've got to tell Art Nola."

"Art doesn't have your luck!" Huey touched the brim of Eldon's jungle hat, caressing the cloth as if it were a butterfly's wing. "Your luck's right here . . . in the fishing fly you won from me. It's not just a news story tonight, Eldon. The stakes are sky-high now, and you've got to help us win the game."

Eldon's jaw muscles twitched as he realized what Huey was proposing. "Luck's no good against seventeen men. You're crazy if you don't think they have guns. They've killed three people already."

"*Some* of them don't have guns. The kid believed it."

"What the hell's the difference?"

"That's right. Who needs a gun? You strangle 'em with wire. You've got to learn to improvise." Eldon's gut turned over as Huey continued: "Millions in drugs have to be landed and moved out fast. That means very few guards on the girls."

Huey took a few deep breaths and went on. "We scout the situation. If we can't deal with them . . . okay, okay, we pull out and get the cops. Otherwise, Theresa and Shelly will be caught in a cross fire." Huey paused, breathing hard. He forced out the final words: "And I'm not gonna let them kill my wife."

"It might work," Truong said. "But I will do the scouting. You two must stay here."

"Like hell," Huey said.

"They have your wife," Truong said. "You can't be expected to act reasonably. Eldon is an amateur. Huey, you know this work is not a game."

"That's right," Eldon said. "While you go in, Huey and I can go get the fuzz."

"No way," Huey said.

"One man has less chance of being seen or captured," said Truong. "We must have information before we can know what to do."

"They have Theresa!" Huey said.

Eldon felt the emotional tug-of-war between the two men, realizing that the vanquished Republic of South Vietnam, embodied in Truong Van Vinh, was the cable binding Huey Bellows. Next, they'll swap lodge handshakes, Eldon thought.

"Truong, you can case the joint and get back scot-free if any one can," Huey said at last. "Once you've got the lay of it, we go in."

"I'll start now," Truong said. "Meet me back at your house." He removed his beret, unpinned the wreath, and handed the insignia to Bellows. "Nothing must shine."

"I'll keep it for you," Huey said.

"Thank you, *em*." Truong was gone.

"This is a South Vietnamese ranger badge," Huey said.

"A ranger? He's an architect," Eldon said.

"War makes us into other things. Damn, I love those people. I love that man. *Em* means brother. We're not going to let him down."

"Where's the closest house with a phone?"

"We don't need a phone. We got our keen eyes and silent feet." Huey's hand clamped Eldon's arm. It might have been the grasp of Bigfoot. "You think I'm gonna let that little man hang his hide out there while I loaf in the rear area? Let Truong risk his neck just to get some info for the cops? Let them save my wife while I hide out?"

"This is a job for the police. We're not playing war."

"No, we ain't," Huey said. "I played enough games in Nam. Whorehouses, beer busts, crack-ups. Patrols that went nowhere and fought nothing and no one. Wasting time with that black marketeer Tran. You weren't there, so you can't understand it. So here it is: *I let those people down*."

But I do understand, Eldon thought as the trees seemed to rise around him in the night like the pillars of a cathedral. All my life, I never felt welcome in church.

Eldon was filled with remorse. Remorse for what? For not doing well. For not standing his ground aboard the *Orient Star*.

Or anywhere, he thought. Run now and run for the rest of your life. Run now and admit you've pissed away five years playing a game, the same way you did your marriage. And . . . this is *good copy*.

There it was, in all its savory obscenity. Which is why I'm not going to do it, Eldon thought. I'll ditch this loon in the dark and go for help. "You've got me there, Huey. I want the story."

"I know ya do. I respect ya for wantin' something. Nothing stops reporter Eldon Larkin. Into the car."

Huey drove them back to his house. On the way through the kitchen and into the living room, Huey hung the car key on a nail. Eldon eyed the nail. When Truong returned and they started out again for the ranch, he would double back and take off in the car, prisoner and all.

"We've got to get you ready," Huey said. "We can't waste time." He took a stick of camouflage paint and began striping Eldon's face. "Your pants are dark enough but your jacket's too light-colored. Put on this fatigue blouse."

The shirt was of jungle cut—baggy, thigh-length, with huge slanted breast pockets and capacious pockets on the skirt. It bore camouflaged U.S. Army insignia, black-stitched on the faded green cloth, including the name tag BELLOWS. It pulled easily over Eldon's jacket. The sleeves hung over his hands.

Huey grinned. "With that hat of yours, you'd pass for a trooper, in low light, anyway. Hair's kinda long, but then, there weren't any barbershops in the boonies. Twist your belt over so the buckle won't shine."

Huey cut lengths of brown twine from a ball on the table. These he tied around Eldon's baggy sleeves at biceps and fore-arms. "So the cloth won't snag bushes," he said quietly. "I did all this hundreds of times before going on patrol. I still remember how to do it. I sure wish you walked quieter."

"I was a Boy Scout," Eldon said.

"Stick with me but don't climb up my ass," Huey said. "Move careful and take your time. Watch where you put your feet . . . solid ground, not brush. Don't look over the top of things; squat down and look around 'em. The idea is not to make a silhouette. Blend into the background. They don't know we're comin' and that's in our favor."

"Not the way the Cong always knew, eh?"

Huey shook his head. "Those poor bastards were just as lost as we were. One time, we laid ambush along a jungle trail. Laid there half the night. It was so dark, I couldn't see my weapon. Ants crawlin' on me. Sweated like a pig. And then we heard the VC comin' down the track . . . ten or a dozen of 'em, chatterin', smokin', clangin' their cookin' pots. You'd think it was New Year's. They thought they owned the night."

"What did you do?"

"Blew 'em away, whaddya think?"

Eldon imagined the gun flashes as Huey continued: "I started to get scared after that one. I saw how cheap life holds people. You know the rest, my last patrol and how God later saved me. But I let the Vietnamese down when I cracked up. I ran out on 'em. I've got to square that."

"Oh, I don't know."

"I had greater plans than this, Eldon. Seems to me a war intervened. I had a choice: Take my bugeye Sprite across the mountains into the East and see what there was to see and get my ass drafted, or enlist and see Stephen Crane's combat."

Give me a break! Eldon thought. But the urge to laugh was overcome with wonder that Bellows had once owned a Sprite and had read *The Red Badge of Courage*. "Which did you do?"

"Enlisted. And I screwed up. That was followed by years of craziness and despair." Huey handed Eldon a sheathed military knife like his own. "But finally Theresa came into my life. Now I'm gonna win Theresa back. She's one Vietnamese I'm not letting down." Huey folded his hand over Eldon's and the knife. "I saw in the dream that you've got to help me. How, I don't know. You've got to come along."

Huey's little eyes glistened. Embarrassed, Eldon said, "I hope you didn't break the camera."

"When I jumped you? Better check it."

Eldon opened the bag. Shelly carried a light, neat Nikon FM. He tested the cocking mechanism and shutter, switched the built-in light meter on and off, examined the array of lenses, selected the 28mm lens and snapped it into place. "We're in luck. Everything's all right. There's plenty of film. And the strobe is charged."

"I don't want that flash accidentally going off."

"If it does, you won't be around to order souvenir prints."

Huey laughed nervously and sat flexing his hands. "Come look at my dream window while we wait."

Eldon grabbed the camera bag and followed Huey back into the workshop. Huey stepped to the tall shrouded rectangle leaning against the wall and tore the canvas away.

It was a stained-glass window a yard wide and six feet high. Eldon could not make out the design. There seemed to be human figures in the glass, but the window was dark and dull against the wall, with no light behind it. Huey slid the heavy window in front of a brace of pole-mounted studio spots and snapped them on. "Whaddaya think?"

Now the design blazed. Eldon stared. The window was pornographic.

A youthful Huey Bellows gaped upward from the embrace of a Vietnamese whore, his rosy glass ass thrusting into the center of the window's design. Tran Minh, a lesser figure, reeled back naked, dick swinging, arms thrown up in supplication, trollops and trampled banners beneath his feet. Huey and Tran gazed agog at the descending figure of God Almighty, who was dressed in farmer's overalls, his milky glass beard streaming. Helicopters whirled around God's head. His great kindly hand reached down toward Huey.

"God wore Can't-Bust-'Em's?" Eldon said. "I thought you only saw his hand."

"Well, yeah, but I had a definite impression of God's body, like through a steamy glass shower door. He was naked. I added the overalls because God was too big hung, y'know? It'd have overwhelmed the design. I added the helicopter angels, too. But the rest is as true to life as I could make it."

"Amazing." Eldon went forward. The detail was rich. A miniature jungle battle was being fought in a luminous green border of marijuana plants. Eldon tapped the window. It thumped flatly, with no reverberation. The glass pieces were fixed solidly in the lead channels. "Sound work."

"It took me two years. I only finished it recently. I know what it means now." Huey wiped his palms on his thighs. "Let's wait outside, let our eyes adjust to the dark."

Outside, as they passed the car, Eldon rapped on the trunk. The man inside hammered frantically in reply.

"What did that guy say his name was?" Huey asked.

"He said Rod Austin."

"What kinda name's that!"

"Uh, English?"

"No, what kinda *name* is that? That's no kinda name for a dope smuggler. For a dirty kidnapper. His name should be Sluggo or something."

"Right." You'll be out of there shortly, Austin, Eldon thought. I'll interview you while Art puts you in cuffs. And then we'll get a straitjacket for Huey.

Bellows squatted in the shadows. He took out his map. "Gimme your penlight." Huey pulled something from his pocket and slipped it over the flashlight before snapping it on. "An old sock. Keeps the light dim so they can't spot you. And it saves your night vision," Huey said as he played the diffused beam over the map. "Here we are. Here's the road and here's the ranch."

"Where's Pugh's place?"

"Here. This is the highway. Muskrat's up here."

"I can about tell how Pugh and Shelly worked down onto the Patterson property."

"Sure. Those 'secret trails' of Pugh's would follow the terrain."

"Where *is* Pugh? That worries me."

"He'll have to look out for his own self. We've got enough worries."

"I didn't see any cops on the road. No police cars."

"Likely they'll come from the north, above Muskrat."

"Yeah."

"I pretty much know the lay of things; I was on the ranch a couple of times to fish, when old man Patterson still owned it," Huey said. "We stay in the trees, working north along the foot of the dunes. Pretty soon, we'll come to a rise . . . see it on the map here? Don't walk over it; lay down flat and crawl. The farmhouse is sure t'be lit up. We'll find our way. Now . . . you know how to look at things in the dark?"

"How?"

"The edges of your retinas are more sensitive in low light. More cones or rods there; I forget which. So don't look straight at things. Look to one side, and you'll see them clear enough."

"That's like investigative reporting."

"You're gonna get a hell of a story tonight, Eldon."

It all started to make a crazy kind of sense to Eldon as they sat waiting. Here they crouched in military regalia, ready to go against the enemy. A prisoner in the car trunk. Eldon made sure his notebook was secure in one of his capacious pockets.

He grinned in the darkness. If only Shelly could see him now! Well, maybe she soon would, at that. His throat tightened and he thought about fear. He'd stick to his original plan. The map had showed him the way to safety—keep the ocean on the left to head north.

There was a movement in the brush and Truong slid in beside them.

"Is Theresa all right?" Huey demanded. "What did you see? Can we get to 'em?"

"Both of them are all right," Truong said.

"Oh, thank God!"

"It is better than we could have hoped," Truong said. "All activity is centered on the barn. Men going in and out. Theresa and Shelly are being held in a bedroom on the first floor of the farmhouse. The bedroom window looks away from the barn. There is a single guard, a man sitting in the room with them."

"Is he armed?"

"I saw no weapon."

"Others in the house?"

"Three men very busy with a radio in the front room. It would be nothing to slip in through a window, knock on the bedroom door—"

"—and take out their guard when he answers the door!" Huey chortled and smacked his fist into his palm. "And then climb out the window and be outta there, *di di mau!* Oh, that's how an operation *should* go down!"

Eldon felt his temples tighten, the way they sometimes did

when Fiske was belaboring a particularly abstruse point of editing. He licked his front teeth. He wanted to say "Nothing doing," but his mouth refused to shape the words.

"Show me the map," Truong said. "We go along the dunes here, to this rise. Stay behind the rise and regroup in this stand of trees behind the house and go down to get the women."

"How far from the trees to the house?"

"Say, two hundred meters. Another two hundred from the house to the barn, where the action is. Eldon can stay in the trees and cover our rear."

"But he'll miss the action."

"It's okay," Eldon said. "Probably I shouldn't get too close."

"If we don't come out, you go for help," Huey said. "But if this can be done, I've got to do it."

"We will do it together," Truong said.

"My brother," Huey said.

And then the smugglers will have a couple more hostages, Eldon thought. And if they haven't decided what to do with two roaming women, they'll sure have some ideas once they've grabbed a couple of guys in camouflage paint and military fatigues. They'll kill all of them.

"Let's move out," Huey said. "Truong's the point. Eldon in the middle. I'll bring up the rear."

I'm in it now, Eldon thought, the way Huey was in it in Vietnam. But they'll never catch me. I'm the one who's coming back to tell the story.

Truong rose and walked into the darkness. Eldon shouldered the camera bag and followed.

19

"We keep about five meters apart," Huey said softly. "If you get confused, Eldon, give a little whistle."

"Okay."

"And keep that lucky hat on tight. Hee-hee! Gonna love readin' about myself on the johnny!"

Eldon did not reply. The mantle of a reporter's invulnerability settled upon him. There was something charmed in being the storyteller. Frank had talked about it on the hillside; Dougie had acted it out in Tran's house—it was what people made of you. The biggest story of the year was about to break. One way or another, he would be on the spot, with notebook and camera.

The cops and the coast guard will swarm over this place like ants, he thought. It won't matter whether Huey and Truong pull off this Green Berets stuff or not. I just hope the cops hit fast enough that nobody has a chance to get hurt.

The little patrol worked its way along the edge of the dunes, moving in shadow through the scrub grass that shored up the mountain range of sand. Eldon listened to the unseen ocean and to his own breathing and the soft footfalls of his companions. He gripped the camera bag tightly. This was what being in enemy country was like.

Sure glad I've never had the honor, he thought wryly.

Truong stopped, raised a hand. Huey placed a hand on Eldon's shoulder and pressed down. Eldon crouched.

"We're doin' fine so far," Huey whispered. "Oh, Theresa, I'm comin'."

Truong slipped back to them. "The rise is just ahead. Now we crawl."

Eldon fell into the sand and squirmed forward, awkwardly dragging the camera bag. At last, he pushed it ahead of him. That was better.

"Keep your ass down," Huey whispered, "or you'll get it shot off."

Eldon's hands grew clammy. They crawled up the rise and looked down onto the Patterson ranch. The ranch house and the barn beyond blazed with light. Eldon could hear the revving of big engines. A pair of long-haul freight vans stood ready to be loaded. The drop was on, all right.

"The place is lit up like a Christmas tree," Eldon said. "We can't get anywhere near the house."

"Sure we can," Huey said cheerfully. "Look at the terrain and the lay of the shadows. And everybody's lookin' the other way."

"Move to the right," Truong said. "Into the wood line. Then down toward the house."

They slipped back behind the rise and hurried along in a crouch. Eldon tried to swivel his gaze everywhere. He felt better once they were in the trees. It was now or never. "I gotta take a crap."

"Keep a tight asshole," Huey said.

"I gotta take a leak."

"Which is it?"

"Both, both."

"Well, go take care of it. We gotta have your full attention."

Eldon scuttled into the trees with the camera bag. His bladder truly was calling to him. He could give Huey and Truong proper sound effects to allay any suspicions. He went about ten yards into the foliage, stopped and unzipped. The night air was cold on the head of his penis. He stood there awaiting results, looking fearfully around. He felt as if he were standing at a urinal in a crowded rest room, with the eyes of a line of anxious men upon his shoulders. In such circumstances, he would fix his gaze on the urinal valve and read the incised lettering on the stainless steel head, ROYAL QUIET-FLUSH II—SLOAN VALVE CO. USA, wondering what had become of QUIET-FLUSH I. Usually that did the trick. But now there was no valve to read.

Huey's whisper came through the trees: *"Eldon, come on."*

"I'm coming. Hang on."

Eldon's bladder released. He aimed the disappointing trickle onto some leaves so that Huey and Truong would be reassured by the patter of water. He looked through the trees toward the farmhouse and barn. Something was rolling out of the barn, too low-slung to be a truck. Its headlights flashed on and it moved in the direction of the beach, a pale gray oblong shape with big wheels.

One of those old navy amphibs, Eldon thought. A "duck"—
that's how they'll get the dope off the ship. But it can't be two-
thirty. They've started early. Something's wrong.

He glanced at the sky. Clouds brooded in the darkness over
the ocean. They're trying to get the stuff landed before the storm
hits, he thought. I've got to get moving.

Eldon pulled the camera from the bag and mounted the strobe
as the trickle of urine stopped. He was much too far away to take
a picture, of course, but he should be ready no matter what. The
strobe gave its faint bumblebee whine as Eldon shook off, zipped
up, and quickly moved away through the trees, putting the ocean
on his left. The northward path would take him deeper onto the
ranch, but there was no helping that—Huey and Truong blocked
a return south. He'd work parallel to the farmhouse, cut right,
climb the ranch fence, and be back out on the road. With any
luck, he would come out close to where he had abandoned his car
and then could head back to Huey's.

He picked up his pace, jogging clumsily over the rough
ground, clutching Shelly's camera as the bag bounced and swung
from his shoulder. The wind brought the snort of engines—another duck pulling out of the barn. A distant pink light flitted in
the trees, far off to his right. Was it a coast guard helicopter,
about to attack from across the road?

Distracted, Eldon barely heard the low animal growl. Then
the watchdog that had confronted Huey Bellows exploded from
the darkness in full barking fury.

Eldon yelled and jumped sideways into the trees. The dog
lunged and overshot, whirled after him. Eldon hit the camera
trigger, firing the strobe directly into the dog's eyes. The dog
yelped in dismay. Eldon swung the camera bag over his head like
a flail and brought it down on the dog's head with a crunch and a
tinkle of glass. The animal cried and staggered. Eldon fled into
the forest.

He crashed through the underbrush, heedless of his noise. It
was like plunging down a dark funnel. The Nikon swung around
his neck. The dog barked furiously behind.

He cut farther right and found himself running up a wooded
hill. The dog bounded after, snarling but wary. Eldon stumbled.
He grabbed a stout fallen branch and turned with a vicious swipe.
The dog snapped at the club but danced back. Eldon hurried

crabwise up the hill, club raised. At the top, he slammed into a low wire fence that vibrated like a string instrument. The wires burned as he struck them. The dog was ten yards away. Eldon threw the club at the dog and turned to vault the fence.

He got one foot onto the lower strand of wire and screamed in surprise as he grabbed the upper wire. The fence was electrified! It was charged with low-grade current designed to hem in live-stock—and discourage human trespassers. The dog charged. Eldon threw a leg over the wire and the current bit his crotch. With a rising whoop, Eldon somersaulted over the fence. He heard something tear and landed hard on his back on the other side of the barrier.

He scrambled up in panic. The growling dog trotted up and down behind the electrified fence, a flap of Eldon's pants dangling from its jaws. Eldon clutched his burning groin and stumbled into the forest.

Oh God, had he lost them on the fence? Were his balls sizzling on the wire like unspeakable giblets? Where was the road? Eldon wailed in terror, clutching his crotch with one hand as he pushed away foliage with the other.

His feet slapped asphalt. The road! He stood gasping on the pathway to safety, half-doubled over, and groped down the front of his pants with hands still tingling from electric shock. His testicles were still attached! They had not been burned off! His life had not changed. . . . Cool wind caressed his buttocks. The dog had ripped the seat of his trousers. However, he did not seem to be bleeding. He had lost Shelly's camera bag but her Nikon was still around his neck. The tiny red spark of the strobe unit's indicator light showed that the unit was charged and ready. His notebook was in his pocket. And best of all, his lucky hat remained securely on his head.

He was relieved but too desperate to feel elation. He did not recall this hill. He must be north of where he had left his Citroën, well past the ranch gate—too far up the road to reach Huey's house quickly. He forced his leaden feet into motion, northward. The police would be in that direction.

Above the treetops was the distant pink blur of running lights. Eldon's terror reasserted itself as the lights disappeared. He would miss the story! And having a rescued Shelly see him covering it.

North, Eldon told himself, and stumbled up the road, rubbing his groin.

"*Hold it!*"

Flashlights blinded him. Eldon stood stupidly in the glare, hand still down his pants.

"Quit beating off and *get 'em up!*" The menacing scream destroyed any hope that this was the law. Men rushed him from the darkness, tore the camera away, and threw him hard on his face to the pavement. Eldon retched. They manhandled him to a standing position and dragged him to the fence.

"What were you doing trespassing?" someone demanded.

"I'm lost. My car broke down. I wanted to get to your ranch house to telephone for help. But your damn dog chased me."

"So you climbed an electrified fence, huh?" The man gave Eldon a shove. "Why didn't you use the gate?"

"I'm lost!"

"Lost in the middle of the night with a camera around your neck?"

"I take pictures of birds. I didn't want to leave it in the car."

"Oh, man!" someone else said. "First those women and now him. Our cover's blown. We gotta split."

"No way," the first speaker said. "We take him to the house, same as the others. And nobody's finking out."

There was a tense silence. They all seemed so young. Eldon thought of the youth locked in the trunk of Huey's car as they pried open the stock fence with branches and shoved him through. Someone on the other side grabbed his collar and jerked. "Take it easy, dammit!" Eldon blurted.

"These red-necks are tough bastards," another youth said.

Eldon tried to think as they surrounded him and marched him down the hillside. There were six of them, he decided, counting out of the corners of his eyes. The prisoner in Huey's truck made seven. Three that Truong had seen tending the radio in the house made ten. Another one guarding Shelly and Theresa—eleven. The remaining six to pilot the ducks and bring the dope ashore in the amphibs. A well-manned operation. Lousy odds, any way you looked at it. However, they apparently hadn't encountered Huey and Truong—and didn't know about the police raid. There might be a chance of rescue.

A better chance of being caught in the cross fire, Eldon thought bitterly. Where the hell are the police?

He clamped his hands atop his head as he walked, gingerly took them away as the fly hooks in his hat pricked his palms. The hat had brought him such grand luck so far!

"I don't like this at all, man," one of his captors said. "This was all supposed to go smooth, man. Slide into town during the red-neck festival, do the unloading and head back home. Get rich and drink a little beer in the bargain. Simplicity itself."

"Quiet! Little red-necks have big ears."

"Aw, he's a big fat red-neck; he doesn't know anything. His buns are hangin' out of his pants. Old dog gave you a run for your money, huh? Shit, it's raining again."

"Move ass," the leader said. "No way we can postpone the drop."

Someone poked Eldon. "How d'you stand all this rain?"

"I wear a hat, to keep from melting."

"Ha, ha, that's good! Did you go to that crab-eating contest? I never saw anything like it. There sure are a lot of fat women around here. Tough luck for you. But we're just passing through. It's back to the big city and wine, women, and song—"

"Hey, will you be cool?" the first speaker said.

The other gave an excited laugh. "Okay, okay. Don't worry, man, we'll let you go . . . after a while." There was frantic barking, up the hill. "What's that dog at now? More red-necks up the hill?"

They grabbed Eldon's arms and quickened the pace. Suddenly, a low shape hurtled down the hillside with terrified animal yelping. Flashlights snapped on. It was the watchdog, in full flight.

One of the smugglers shined his flashlight up the hill as the dog streaked past: "Someone's up there!"

More lights flashed on. Raindrops drifted through the sweeping beams. Eldon craned his neck. He thought he saw a man standing in the trees. He looked to one side as Huey had said. No, it was too big to be a man—

"You're spooked," the leader said. "It's a shadow. See?"

"Then what scared the dog?"

"Sasquatch, maybe!"

That brought nervous snickers. Eldon's skin crawled. He tried to look back as his captors shoved him along. They crunched into a last copse of trees. The farmhouse lights glowed ahead, through the drizzle. Eldon looked away to preserve his night vision. Not quickly enough; blotches swam before his eyes. He squeezed his eyes shut, opened them hopelessly. The world looked like a dark, rained-on watercolor.

And then Eldon nearly cried out. A face floated in the bushes like a dream visage. Shaped at once like a bear's head and a man's, shaggy, too large to be human. There were no details. Eldon looked to one side. A finger seemed to raise itself to lips in the sign for silence—too long a finger and too thick. The disembodied face floated toward him through the afterimage of the house.

The group reached the bushes and crunched through. No one was there.

Eldon looked wildly around. Were Huey and Truong still at the fence line, waiting for him? Were they about to burst from the darkness waving knives? Or would they come silently, like the face he had imagined in the woods, and garrote the smugglers with wire?

His teeth chattered. To calm himself, he focused on the farmhouse. Here was danger as terrible, as final as that he had faced aboard the *Orient Star*. Suddenly he felt composed. Fascinated, even. He was nearing the heart of the mystery.

He glimpsed activity at the barn as he mounted the slippery porch steps. In the porch light he saw that he indeed had been captured by children; one looked as if he could barely shave. They all seemed to be in their early twenties. They opened the door and shoved him into the living room. A man at the radio sprang up as Eldon stood blinking in the light.

"What's this?" the man snapped.

"Another snooper, Chad."

"Shit." Chad pronounced the word precisely, his voice turning cold. The sound of it was like a black stone blade sliding between Eldon's ribs, for he had seen the man before.

The chiseled features, the flesh tanned as though by lamps, the blow-dried blond hair, the expensive pullover sweater with the properly placed alligator—Larry Chadwick was immutable. He was just as he had been when he had raised his cocktail glass in the Timber Topper, at Stephanie Hosfelder's side.

"Shit," Chad repeated, studying Eldon.

Eldon realized that Chad was not swearing but describing him. Chad's mouth was a precision cutting machine, Eldon thought, full of capped teeth like a rack of fine china. In the darkness of the bar, Eldon had been unable to see Chad's eyes. He looked into them now. They were purest lapis lazuli, and no more alive than stones.

"He claims he's lost," one of the kids said. "But we caught him climbing the fence."

"Frisk him," Chad said.

"We did."

"Do it again," Chad said with authority.

Hastily, they patted Eldon down. This time, they found his notebook and handed it to Chad. Chad ruffled the pages, glanced at the scribbling inside, and tossed the notebook on the table. "Anything else?"

"He had a camera." The Nikon was handed up from the rear of the group.

"What were you going to do?" said Chad. "Keep it as a souvenir?"

"We came as quick as we could, Chad. What now?"

"Get down to the barn," Chad said. "The ducks are away. We need every hand unloading so we can clear out fast."

"And him?"

"He goes in with the others." Chad picked up an automatic pistol that lay next to the radio and lined the weapon up with Eldon's midsection.

Chad studied Eldon as his minions shuffled out the door.

"You're no cop," Chad said, "wandering around in the woods with your ass hanging out of your pants. And you're not one of the neighbors. The question is, what are you?"

"I'm a bird-watcher. I live in Regret."

"Name?"

"Eldon Larkin."

"What's that on your face?"

"Grease. I had trouble with my car." Inspiration drove Eldon's tongue. "My wife and I were bird-watching. We had trouble with the car and she went down to the beach while I worked on it. It got dark and I couldn't find her. Then your hands jumped me. They didn't have any right to do that."

"What's your wife look like?"

"She's Vietnamese—"

"What's her name?"

"Theresa."

"So I guess Huey Bellows got divorced."

Eldon felt the floor falling away. Without thinking to ask permission, he pulled up a straight-backed chair and sat down.

"That notebook," Chad said, with a sudden awful smile. "I place your name now. Eldon Larkin . . . you wrote those newspaper stories. You were in the bar the other night. Come for one more story, eh? Who squealed?"

Eldon shrugged. "Nobody. I just put the pieces together."

Chad's face had the imperial cast that Eldon had seen in the bar. "Who squealed? *I want to know*."

Eldon shrugged again, without control. He felt the same terror he had felt when he was cornered in the bowels of the *Orient Star*—but now there was nowhere to run. "A piece here and a piece there," he got out. "That's how it's done. You shouldn't have put your name down for the radio license."

"I had to leave my signature," Chad said. "I calculated everything. Except that you'd find it." Abruptly, his expression was feral. He shouted, "I'm on my way *up*, damn you! I will not become shit on the bottom of anyone's shoe. This caper will fix me for life; it will put me high above all the crap . . . and I *will not be dragged back down!* Not by shit like you!"

Eldon said nothing.

Chad relaxed. His eyes were still dead. It was as if he had decided to become angry and now to become calm. "Hey, Ahmed!" he called. "Bring 'em out here!"

A door opened in the hall. In a moment, Shelly and Theresa straggled into the living room, shooed by none other than Stephanie's bridegroom, Ahmed, in dungarees now and armed with a nightstick. The women were bedraggled but appeared unharmed.

"Hell, now they've caught Eldon, too," Shelly said. "What's that stuff on your face?"

"You don't look your best, either," Eldon said, smiling to hide his shame.

Shelly glowered. But Theresa took Eldon's measure with glittering eyes. After the Thai pirates, this probably doesn't seem any worse than a flat tire, Eldon thought.

"So you see we've got your two snooping chicks," Chad said. "Your final story's not gonna get written."

Eldon was speechless for a moment. Then he said, "What are you going to do with us?"

Chad gazed from Eldon to Shelly to Theresa and back again. Eldon imagined the brain behind the stony eyes pondering the new data, weighing alternatives, measuring the odds. Rain tapped the window. Suddenly, there was a frantic rapping at the glass. Chad pivoted like a gyroscope, bringing the pistol up with an animal grace. Eldon had time to snap his gaze along the pistol's barrel to the pale blotch of a human face beyond the rain-smeared glass. The gun made a great flat slap, which for an instant blurred his vision and numbed his cheeks. Shelly's scream cut through the sudden ringing in Eldon's ears. He saw that the window and the face were gone and rain was coming in.

Chad sprang against the wall next to the window. Ahmed ran out the door with ready club. There was silence. Then Ahmed called from outside: "You got 'im good, man!"

"Up!" said Chad. "Everyone outside. I want you to see."

They stumbled through the door ahead of Chad and down the porch. Ahmed stood over a man lying facedown in the mud. In the light from the shattered window, Eldon saw that the victim wore a white T-shirt, and he knew it could not be Huey or Truong.

"Turn him over," Chad told Eldon.

Eldon knelt and pulled. The man was heavy as a sack of sand. At last, he got the man over. It was Dougie, features ruined by the bullet and streaming blood. Dougie's mouth worked. Sound came out like a far-off radio. Eldon could not understand what Dougie was saying. "Hello! Hello!" Eldon shouted, as if his words could part the scarlet curtain and pull Dougie back from death.

Dougie gagged and groped at his gory jaw. Eldon gripped Dougie's hand and bent close. "Hello!"

Urgent noise came from the smashed face—blurred, distorted speech, a kind of gagging sound. *"Big . . . foot!"* Dougie said: Eldon was certain of it. "The woods!" Dougie said. Then the voice ceased.

Eldon let the corpse drop. He saw with a shudder, in the window's light, a human tooth sticking flat to his bloody palm.

"Shit, man, that could've been one of us," Ahmed said.

"I saw exactly who it was," Chad said. "He was too stupid to just get lost, like I told him to. Instead, he got his picture in the paper. These three snoops are going to wind up just like this squealer here."

Not if I get you first, Eldon thought. The thought's clarity startled him; he felt no anger. It was written across his mind in letters of ice. He knew as surely as he knew his own name that he would kill Chad if he could.

"The boys may not go for that," Ahmed said nervously.

"What they don't see never bothers them, that's their motto," Chad said. "Bunch of pissant college punks. They're in this for the money; they can damn well earn their share."

"So how do we get rid of 'em?"

"The same way we'll get rid of this dead shithead," Chad said. "I've already thought of everything. Now back inside, you three. Walk backward, nice and easy."

Chad backed them into the house, through the living room smelling of cordite and into the bedroom. He locked them inside.

Eldon looked around for a weapon. There was only a double bed, a tatty lamp, a couple of chairs—not the sort of place where he wanted to spend his last hours. The window was slightly open; Eldon went there at once, only to see Ahmed on guard outside. Damn it, where were the police?

"He didn't want to risk being in here with three of us," Shelly said, breathing hard. "I think they only have the one gun. That's a plus."

"No, it's eight or nine shots," Eldon said. "Did they get Pugh?"

"How did you know?"

"I've been to Pugh's house . . . and then some."

"Pugh drove there and took off down one of his trails, laughing and yelling like a maniac. I chased him; I didn't even stop for my camera. He ditched me. The smugglers must've heard the yelling, because they showed up and grabbed me. They brought me here . . . and that's when I found out they had Theresa, too."

"I lost your camera bag in the woods," Eldon said disconsolately. "I clubbed the watchdog with it."

"I hope you got him good," Shelly said. "At least you saved the camera."

"Yeah, I brought it right to you."

Theresa was staring at the partly opened window. "Shelly," she said, "step over by the window with Eldon. Let yourselves be seen."

"Why?"

"To block the view into the room."

Shelly stepped next to Eldon. Theresa seized the bedspread's corner and threw the hanging edge aside.

Truong Van Vinh slid from beneath the bed.

20

Prickly numbness twined up Eldon's legs like vines. No—he must not faint! Snorting air through his nose, Eldon sat heavily on the bed.

Truong squatted and held a finger to his lips for silence. "We go out the window," he said, mouthing the words. "One at a time."

"Where the hell did you come from?" Eldon whispered.

"Through the window, after they took the women out of the room. Now get ready. Huey will deal with the guard."

Eldon's mind whirled. He was going to live! He twisted and peered out the window, watching Ahmed pace back and forth outside, huddled in a parka against the rain. Then the guard passed the window and did not return.

Eldon caught his breath and listened over the drumming of his heart; but there was only the rising rain, static from the radio in the living room, and Chadwick's voice, muffled through the bedroom door, calling to his ship.

Truong stepped to the window and lifted the frame. It moved upward and stuck. Truong paused, lifted. The window rasped. Truong stopped. Carefully, Truong inched the frame upward. Eldon swallowed. Shelly shifted her weight. Theresa watched silently.

Truong pushed the window wide. "You first," he mouthed to Eldon. "Step quiet."

Eldon lurched too quickly off the bed, skidded on the bedspread that Theresa had thrown aside, and hit the floor with a slam.

They froze. The radio buzzed in the living room. Nothing else. "Come on!" Truong whispered. "Out! *Di di mau!*"

Eldon scrambled to the window. He thrust one leg through, straddling the wet sill and groping with his foot until he planted it on a crate that Truong had pushed against the house. The cold wind fanned his exposed buttocks as he slid out backward, gripping each side of the window. His other leg was still hooked over the sill when he felt a light tap on his shoulder.

Eldon glanced back, expecting to see Huey's whiskered face, and stared straight into a pistol muzzle.

"Your ass is out a mile," Chad said.

It's true, Eldon thought. A pistol barrel really does look like a subway tunnel from this end.

"Just freeze, in there," Chad said loudly, "or Fatso's done for. I *thought* you kids got a little quiet. Especially after I heard that thump. So I came around to check. Now back inside, slowly."

Chad chuckled as Eldon almost lost his grasp on the window frame. Truong helped him climb back in.

Chad stepped onto the box with pistol ready. "Back off. Hands way up." He swung smoothly in through the window and looked Truong over. "I guess you polished off Ahmed, but that's no loss . . . one less witness."

The smuggler stood for a moment, reflecting. Then: "Gonna have to act. You're all going on an ocean voyage."

Eldon imagined the ocean's cold waters closing about him. The four of them would be shot off the stern of the dope ship once the ship was far at sea. Eventually, he might drift bloated into Smuggler's Cove and wash up on the beach. Jimbo would put what was left of him on the front page of the *Sun*.

"You're not going to do a damn thing to us," Shelly said coldly.

Chad waved the gun at Truong. "I suppose he's a paperboy."

"Anything happens to us and the whole story about you goes into print," Shelly said. "Nguyen Xuan and the elephant, Marie Payne, the Santa Barbara address, the dummy corporation, the drop for cargo in Eugene, the escape route to Canada, your L.A. backers, all of it. We've connected it all. It's set in type. It'll be published tomorrow unless we get back and spike it."

Eldon was puzzled. Eugene? Canada? Los Angeles backers? She's making it up, Eldon thought, praying against reason for the success of Shelly's bluff.

"Just you remember," Shelly said, "missing reporters bring more reporters."

"Aw, I wanted to hear about high journalistic principles, like in that *President's Men* movie," Chad said. "I guess there's no higher principle than your skin, huh?"

Shelly was silent.

Eldon measured the distance between himself and Chad with his eyes, noted Truong doing the same. Theresa, too. And Shelly. Four sets of eyes seeking a way to cover the distance before it could be spanned by a bullet.

"Forget it," Chad told them. "There's no way. We might as well head down to the boats." He tossed Eldon a key. "Unlock the bedroom door." When Eldon had done so, Chad commanded, "Hands on your heads. Follow me one at a time into the hall."

Chad backed into the doorway. Huey Bellows stepped from the hall's shadows and dealt him a tremendous rabbit punch. The pistol sailed from Chadwick's grasp and landed on the bed. Eldon grabbed it. Truong and Huey landed on Chadwick. Eldon aimed the pistol at Chad's face.

"Haw, commando classic!" Huey said. "Theresa, thank God you're safe!" He blew his wife a kiss. "After I cold-cocked the guard, I saw Son of Satan here come out with the gun. So I dropped back and circled around." Huey grinned like a wild man with raw meat. "You've got to pick your plays. We're rollin' now! Cookin' with steam! Eldon, you're my man forever for what you did out there."

"You risked your life for us," Truong said, "leading them away from our position like that."

"You did *what*, Eldon?" Shelly asked. *"Right on!"*

"It was close, I tell you!" Truong said. "One of them came right up behind us. Big as an ape. But never mind that now; this one is coming around."

Eldon's neck prickled as Chadwick's eyes popped open. The eyes were cold no longer. They were cauldrons of hate. There was not a trace of fear—only the imperious glitter. Eldon was seized with the idea that Chad had faked unconsciousness, was plotting how best to move the chess pieces and sweep the board. He felt a visceral impulse to pull the trigger and extinguish the evil brain.

Huey jerked Chad to his knees. "Truong, keep watch from the front room, make sure nobody walks in on us."

"Wait!" Shelly yelped. "The Coasties are here!"

Eldon looked out the window. A pink glow drifted in the distant woodline, though the beat of an engine was covered by the sound of the rain. "It's the helicopter I saw in the woods."

"I saw it, too," Huey said with a smile. "Those angelic lights took me back to Nam. God's trolled me here like a hooked fish, all the way from that first whorehouse vision. Hey, what's that face—?"

Huey gaped at something outside. Eldon looked through the window again and thought he saw a face at the edge of the illumination cast by the lights in the house: The face, he thought, that had floated before him in the woods.

Chadwick broke from Huey's grip and lunged straight into Eldon. Eldon felt the pistol wrenched from his hand as he slammed into the wall. Chadwick straight-armed Shelly and dived through the window. Huey was after Chadwick with a shout. There was the flat report of a shot and Huey dropped, thigh spouting blood.

Theresa slapped her hands on the severed artery and bore down. Blood sprayed as if from a broken hose as Huey writhed. Truong whipped off his belt to make a tourniquet as another bullet shattered the window.

Eldon didn't think about it. He sprang through the bedroom door, ran through the living room and down the wet porch steps, skidding in gravel as he rounded the corner of the house. In the glow of the house lights, he saw Chad running up the slope. Eldon jumped over Dougie's body and pursued as Shelly burst from the house with her camera, yelling, "I'm going to get this shot!"

By God, so you will, Eldon thought, picking up speed as rain splattered his face.

As he ran, he saw everything in a curious slow-motion panorama. Ahead, Chad drifted toward the forest's sepulchral darkness. Overhead was the storm-white sky. In the corner of Eldon's eye was the distant seashore and the lights of the ducks as they landed their illicit cargo. The machines seemed to float through the dark surf, pivoting and wheeling, sailing in high arcs.

Chad turned, backpedaling. The pistol flashed brightly. The shot went wild. Eldon closed in. He burned with the spiteful fixed intention not to let this quarry escape. Chad was every Billy Vogel, every thug in a gorilla mask, every nasty red-neck, every person who had wounded or scorned him. Eldon had been running since Berkeley, but he was no longer in retreat; he was looping back toward home.

Chad halted and and raised the pistol. Eldon threw himself down, skidding flat in the mud as a bullet buzzed overhead. He had not heard the report. He scrambled up and churned his way up the hillside as Chad fled. The gap between them was widening.

Then Eldon saw the pink glow of the helicopter's lights through the trees ahead of them. Eldon heard no motor but the lights were like fire. Chadwick veered and ran into the trees—and burst back out, fleeing downslope toward Eldon as the helicopter lights swung off abruptly and were gone.

Eldon tackled Chadwick. They fell heavily and rolled down the slope in the rain, fighting for the gun. Chad yelled incoherently. Eldon grabbed after the pistol, got hold of Chad's wrist and bit down on the arm. Chad slammed his palm into Eldon's face and pushed. Eldon twisted his face away. Chad clamped hands onto Eldon's head and screamed as he came away with Eldon's jungle hat and a palm full of fishhooks.

The pistol hit the ground. It seemed to Eldon as if he had his entire life in which to pick it up. Chad lunged after the weapon in slow motion, Eldon's hat still hanging from his hand. His mouth was open as he screamed. Eldon knew that the contest was over and that he had won. He scooped up the gun as casually as if he had plucked it off a table and let his arm uncoil, pointing the automatic straight at Chadwick, finger curling around the trigger. It was the purest moment of Eldon's life. He knew that if he had to, he would pull the trigger and, knowing that he could, knew that he would not.

The pistol's muzzle smacked Chad's forehead. The smuggler jerked up short, gasping. Shelly caught up with them and shot a flash picture; in the strobe's sharp flare, Eldon saw blood trickling from the little circular punch mark the pistol muzzle had made in Chad's forehead.

"My hat stops bullets," Eldon said.

Chad kept glancing into the forest as he plucked at the jungle hat hooked to his palm. The eerie wail of sirens drifted up the hill.

"What a shot!" Shelly said. "Front page! Wire service all the way! This is going national! The police are here, Eldon!"

Eldon jerked his hat free of Chad's hand and slapped it on his own head. "Walk."

"There's something *big* in the trees!" Chad said, eyes huge.

"I don't care if it was Santa Claus," Eldon said. "Now march."

Eldon and Chad shuffled down the hill as Shelly ran toward the ranch house. Presently, Eldon saw the flash of her strobe there. The rain began abating, and the scene below was laid out clearly. Patrol cars clustered like white metal fireflies around the house. Their lights threw dazzling blue and red beams and their radios made a din. An ambulance rolled up and its doors opened. As Eldon and Chad reached the house, Huey Bellows was rushed out on a stretcher, leg wrapped in compresses. A medic held high an IV bag connected to Huey's arm; but the big man was conscious and clutching his wife's hand and very much alive.

Eldon looked around as the ambulance pulled away. Ahmed staggered past under guard, groaning and rubbing the back of his head. Truong Van Vinh talked with a state trooper beside Dougie's tarp-shrouded body. Men wearing windbreakers marked DRUG ENFORCEMENT ADMINISTRATION shouted instructions. A line of frightened smugglers, in wet suits or rain gear, were marched past by coastguardsmen armed with M16's. The smugglers flinched and covered their faces at Shelly's flash. They won't be so young when they get out of jail, Eldon thought with pleasure.

"Eldon!" Shelly rushed up. "You were *terrific*! Hold it right there! Chadwick, get your hands away from your face, you bastard!"

Eldon straightened proudly as the strobe's flash stroked him with its glow. He was glad he wore his lucky hat. He felt rakish, *macho*. Shelly was his and the night was young.

"Who wants this one?" Eldon called. "I've got the ringleader here."

Uniformed sheriff's deputies recognized Eldon, took the pistol, and handcuffed Chadwick and led him away.

"Amazing . . . a man almost kills you and then just walks out of your life," Eldon said.

"He wanted to kill us all," Shelly said in an awed tone. "Eldon, you're the bravest man I know."

"Well, I don't know about *that*," Eldon said. He held his arms wide. "Come here."

Shelly gave Eldon a brisk sisterly hug. "My hero." She pecked his cheek. "I don't even mind that you lost my camera equipment. It's insured."

Eldon tried to gather her in closer.

Shelly broke away: "Art!"

Art Nola strode through the melee, long raincoat flapping, loosened necktie blowing in the sea breeze. Shelly threw herself into the detective's arms. Art caught her and whirled her in an embrace and they kissed.

My ass is hanging out of my pants, Eldon thought.

He tugged his long military shirt down as he stumped wearily over to the embracing pair. Art let go of Shelly and thrust out a hand: "Looks like you did some good work tonight, Eldon. Hey, are you all right?"

Eldon looked down at himself. "That's not my blood."

Nola looked uncomfortable. "I didn't mean for you to go through this. I owe you an explanation."

Eldon let Nola pump his hand as he peered closer in the pulsing glare of the emergency lights. It was the necktie he'd noticed in Shelly's van, all right. "Yes . . . an explanation."

"I leaked information to you to put pressure on the smugglers," Art said. "The feds were hot to make the strike, but the smugglers were preoccupied with their little civil war. I thought a close-to-the-nerve newspaper story might scare 'em into making their move. You were just the man."

"What did you leak?" Eldon asked. "Oh . . . the tox reports you gave Shelly."

Art nodded. "I think the story you wrote finally got the bad guys off the dime."

"You didn't tell me what you were doing!" Shelly said.

"You didn't ask; you just snatched up those tox reports," Art said fondly. "You didn't need to know."

"We nearly got killed!" Shelly said.

"I know . . . and I'm truly sorry," Art said, hugging Shelly once more. "I never imagined you'd come charging out here into the line of fire."

From the way Shelly looked at Art, Eldon knew that Nola was forgiven. That stuff about the L.A. backers and all was true, Eldon thought. Art told her. Jesus, she's sleeping with a source. "You should've told me." He was addressing Shelly, but Art said, "You'd never have agreed to 'plant' a story."

"You should've told me," Eldon repeated.

"About us?" Shelly said. "You're such a hard-nose. Would you have understood?" She wept a little. "Huey Bellows got shot, trying to help Theresa and me."

"I owe him one," Art said.

"He's braver than you thought," Eldon said.

"Amen," Art said. "Well . . . I guess you'd like your scoop. Come on."

Art led them toward the barn, where floodlights burned. "Your scoop is twelve tons of Thai stick, the largest drug bust in the state's history. Most of it's ashore; some of it is still on the ship that the coast guard cutter intercepted at the three-mile limit. That cargo's worth eighteen or nineteen million dollars on the street."

Eldon reached for his notebook, but it was back at the house. He still had his pen. He scrawled the figures on his hand. "How'd you find out about it?"

"Fishing," Art said.

"Say again?"

"They attracted attention to themselves by closing off Patterson's fishing hole," Art said. "They ran people off with dogs. People got disgruntled, started reporting suspicious activities. We've had our eye on them ever since."

A low-flying coast guard helicopter cut overhead, headlights glaring whitely. It was a big roaring Sikorsky HH-52A in coast guard white and red that buffeted them with its prop wash as it passed. That's not what was in the woods, Eldon thought.

"We lit 'em with 'night sun' lamps on the Coastie choppers," Art said as the helicopter receded. "They looked like a covey of quail, dispersing in all directions."

"Yeah, a chopper knocked Chadwick for a loop up on the hill, or I'd never have caught him," Eldon said.

Art shook his head. "We didn't have a chopper up on the hill. They were all down at the beach or out with the cutter."

"I saw pink lights."

"The lights are white."

Something big in the trees, Eldon thought, and shivered. He started to argue, but Art gestured expansively toward the barn, as if he were personally responsible for the scene illuminated under the generator-powered lights.

It reminded Eldon a little of the fateful day at the circus when Horton had crushed Nguyen Xuan and Shelly had bounced into his life—and into Art's. Fatigue-clad police with M16's, their features tinted by flashing prowl-car lights, fairly danced with elation around a ragged pyramid of big cubical aluminum cans higher than a man. Deputies tossed more of the silvery containers down from a parked duck.

"Have a closer look," Nola said and grabbed a can that had been pried open. It was packed with hand-size bundles of Thai stick.

Eldon removed a packet. The dried marijuana, bound with twine, was rough and slightly sticky to the touch. Bits of dark leaf crumbled in his fingers as he inhaled the rich ropelike aroma. If Shelly and I had had some of this good stuff in her van, things would've been different, he thought.

"We called in U.S. Customs and the DEA, staked this place out by land, sea, and air," Art explained as Shelly moved off and began shooting pictures. "After we'd established what was going on, we plotted the raid. The smugglers brought their equipment in at night; they made trial runs to see if they were being watched. We just let 'em practice; you should've seen how those ducks looked when they went out through the surf with their lights on! When they came back in, there were times they were riding up on the waves vertically. It looked as if they were flying. It was fabulous."

"Those were Pugh's UFOs," Eldon said.

"UFOs?"

"A crazy old coot who lives up the way kept telling us about UFOs landing on the ranch. Looks as if he was telling straight, after all. He led Shelly onto the ranch tonight . . . and now he's nowhere to be found."

"Maybe we better start looking for a stiff."

"Go easy on that talk."

"Hey, guys," Shelly called from the side of the barn, "come look at this."

She stood near a cache of small red metal cans that glittered dully. Eldon looked, blinked, looked again. "Prince Albert tobacco cans."

"Just right for street sales," Art said. He popped the lid from a can to display a packet of Thai stick within. "They apparently planned a bit of repackaging."

Eldon spied something gleaming on the ground. A green glass fishing float about the size of a golf ball. He picked it up and rolled it in his fingers. "He's been here. Pugh."

"The old man?"

"Everywhere he goes, Prince Albert tobacco cans turn up. And green glass. I found some of these fishing floats in his house tonight. Pugh and Shelly started out for the ranch from there, down a secret trail."

"Let's find that trail," Art said.

Truong Van Vinh still had the map he and Huey had used to plan their patrol onto the Patterson ranch. Studying it, the former ranger pointed out likely lines for trails in the wooded terrain. Sure enough, searching with flashlights, they found a path leading into the woods not far from the barn.

Eldon, Shelly, Nola, and Truong picked their way along the path, armed with flashlights. It was difficult to follow in the darkness. Shelly flashed her light around nervously, calling first for Pugh and then for Uncle Ogden.

"We've got to find him," she said. "He could be lying out here hurt or—"

"Is this the way you came?" asked Art.

"I can't tell. It was dark and I was scared. But I don't think the smugglers caught him."

"You didn't hear any shots or anything?"

"No shots," Shelly said. "No."

"Hey!" called Truong, who had taken the lead. "Look at this!"

They hurried up the path to Truong's light. The Vietnamese stood in a clearing that had been created long ago by logging. Old stumps rose like vine-covered plateaus in the darkness that now seemed to be touched with the first hint of approaching dawn. In the center of the clearing, against one of the stumps, was the latest in what had been a night of incredible sights.

"It's a shrine," Truong said.

Their lights shone on a tinfoil dome a couple of feet tall, open at the front and decorated with dead light bulbs and bits of colorful junk, a messy pile of scrap that glistened from the recent rain. In the shrine's center, a green glass fishing float and a small plastic rocket swung from threads. The miniature planet and miniature spaceship seemed to orbit a Prince Albert tobacco can.

"The green glass was just a religious trinket," Eldon said. "No wonder it didn't make any sense to me." He shook his head in wonder.

There was something in the tobacco can. Eldon picked up the can and pulled out a religious card bearing a picture of Jesus and a piece of damp paper.

When the angels and chariots of fire lighten this earth, all false creeds will be exposed. The Lord's chariots come to render his anger against those that hide behind his name. Ye may entertain angels unawares. The Star Days are upon us.

"There are more Prince Albert cans over here," Truong said. "A big pile."

Eldon turned his beam. "They're new. I'll bet the old man was slipping down to the barn and pilfering from the smugglers' stash of cans." He shook his head. "A dope syndicate next door, Dougie loose in the woods, and what does Pugh do? He builds a tinfoil spaceship to attract attention to it all."

"What could the old fool have been thinking?" Truong said.

"He's *not* a fool," Shelly said. "How'd he evade the smugglers? How'd he get away from the dog? And where *is* he?" She raised her voice and called: "Pugh! Uncle Ogden!"

The tracks led up the hillside, along an obscure trail. They followed the trail, struggling through brush and slipping on ferns. At last, and sure enough, the winding track led them to Pugh's house.

Shelly broke into a trot, still calling Pugh's name. The men followed her. They reached the house and went inside, but the house was just as Eldon had seen it earlier. No one was there.

On a hunch, Eldon made his way through the living room and climbed the stairs to the dome. The old man sitting in his spaceship in the wake of Oregon's biggest dope raid would make a pretty good sidebar, he thought.

Dawn's light was flooding into the hangar through the opened dome. In the steely glow, Eldon saw that the tinfoil spaceship was gone.

No, he decided, I will not try to figure this out. He went slowly back down the stairs. "He's not up there, either."

"He must be lying in the woods somewhere!" Shelly cried.

"There's no need to assume the worst," Eldon said. "None at all."

Shelly bit her lip. "I suppose you're right. Christ, what a night it's been. I'm not cut out for this kind of work."

"What d'you mean?" Eldon said. "You're a great shooter. You eat it up."

"It eats me," Shelly said. "It's like the first day I was here, when I almost got sick when you brought me ice cream. The adrenaline carries me, and afterward I'm wrecked. I don't want to do this kind of work."

"That's a pretty quick decision," Art said.

"I decide things pretty fast," Shelly said. "I don't want to go to every murder and dope raid in Nekaemas County, hunt for lost people, always making sure I'm on the outside looking in . . . I want to be with you, Art."

Art looked startled but pleased. He started nodding, a bit like a puppet.

Boy, have you got your work cut out for you, Eldon thought.

"I'm not strong like Eldon," Shelly went on. "And I know what he's been thinking, and he's right . . . about having an affair with a source."

Eldon stood silently, wondering whether to reveal what he had discovered upstairs. She'll find out for herself soon enough, he thought.

"Oh, Eldon, look at you!" Shelly said with a laugh. "You've given up so much for this story . . . you've risked your life, you've almost lost your teeth, you've put up with me, and you've even lost your car."

"I got the scoop. The Citroën wasn't worth a damn anyway."

Shelly stepped up to Eldon and pressed something metallic into his hand. He saw that it was a car key.

"The van's yours, Eldon. I won't be needing it, and I want you to have it because you saved my life. I can't think of anyone who'll treat it better."

Eldon found himself closing his hand over the key. "Thanks. I'll treat it better than the Citroën, that's for sure. You're still invited to dinner." He paused. "Bring Art."

The least you could do was be gallant, Eldon thought as he left the house and limped back down the hill. He made his way along Pugh's secret trail, picking his way carefully through the rain-soaked foliage to the clearing with the tinfoil shrine. He gave the little scrap temple a tired salute as he passed and began composing his lead:

Nekaemas County sheriff's deputies and federal drug agents seized twelve tons of high-grade marijuana north of Port Jerome in a night raid that marked the biggest seizure of drugs in Oregon history. . . .

He wondered whether he should tell Jimbo about the missing spaceship or the face in the trees—that he had been aided in capturing Chadwick by Bigfoot and a flying saucer. He wondered whether he should eat steak and eggs this morning. He wondered whether he would ever get laid. He felt so weary; he might have survived a shipwreck or completed one leg of some vast journey. He longed for the feel of rain on his face.

Eldon emerged from the trees and crossed to the barn. It seemed like a very long way. Now the morning sun had risen and shone brightly behind him, the sky was blue, the air sharp and clear and bracing. He reached the mountain of silver cans. Waving to the deputies, he climbed slowly to the top of twelve tons of contraband marijuana. A few of the deputies laughed and applauded.

Standing up here feels almost as good as smoking it, Eldon decided as he reached the summit and faced the sea.